PRAISE FOR DEAN KOONTZ

#1 *New York Times* Bestseller

"America's most popular suspense novelist."

—*Rolling Stone*

"Koontz has always had near-Dickensian powers of description and an ability to yank us from one page to the next that few novelists can match."

—*Los Angeles Times*

"Tumbling, hallucinogenic prose."

—*New York Times Book Review*

"Dean Koontz is not just a master of our darkest dreams but also a literary juggler."

—*The Times* (**London**)

"Dean Koontz writes page-turners, middle-of-the-night-sneak-up-behind-you suspense thrillers. He touches our hearts and tingles our spines."

—*Washington Post Book World*

"Koontz has a knack for making the bizarre and uncanny seem as commonplace as a sunrise. Bottom line: the Dean of Suspense."

—*People* **magazine**

"Positively twitching with suspense. Another sure-fire hit from a thriller master."

—*Booklist* (**starred review**)

THE
FOREST
OF LOST
SOULS

THE FOREST OF LOST SOULS

A NOVEL

DEAN KOONTZ

THOMAS & MERCER

Text copyright © 2024 by The Koontz Living Trust
All rights reserved.

Published by Thomas & Mercer, Seattle

www.apub.com

Amazon, the Amazon logo, and Thomas & Mercer are trademarks of Amazon.com, Inc., or its affiliates.

ISBN-13: 9781662500510 (hardcover)
ISBN-13: 9781662517785 (paperback)
ISBN-13: 9781662500503 (digital)

Cover design by James Iacobelli
Interior illustrations by Edward Bettison
Cover images: © Mark Fearon / ArcAngel; © Northern Owl, © Tanarot1992 / Shutterstock; © Folio Images /Offset

Printed in the United States of America

This book is for Jessica Tribble Wells, Gracie Doyle, and the entire lovely team at Thomas & Mercer, who have made this phase of my journey by far the most pleasant and inspiring since I first sat down at a keyboard so many years ago.

What starts out here [in the US] as a mass movement ends up as a racket, a cult, or a corporation.

—Eric Hoffer, 1967

ONE

THE PAST
IN THE PRESENT

1

HARBINGER

The white mountain lion, an albino female, is rarely seen in this county, though she seems to roam only here. The astonished few who have caught a glimpse of her remember the place, the day, the hour, and the circumstances as vividly and indelibly as they recall any event in their lives. Like others of her species that are of a more common coloration, she mostly sleeps by day and stalks the world in darkness. Whether she appears pale and fluid in a shadowy forest, striding through a meadow at dusk, prowling a ridgeline in little more than starlight, or crossing a highway at night, her eyes like yellow lanterns, she is beautiful and terrifying, a majestic three-hundred-pound predator that inspires awe and terror in the same instant, a kind of sacred love.

She has been seen in a moonlit cemetery, gliding like a spirit among the headstones. She has lazed on the steps of a church in the first radiance of the hidden sun before it rose above the mountains. She has been observed drinking at dusk from the water in the deep lakelet that formed in what was long ago a stone quarry. These sightings and certain others have led some to attribute to her a dire prognostic power. They claim she's an omen of death because a groundskeeper died of a heart attack a day later in that cemetery, because the minister of the church perished in a rectory fire soon after the lion's dawn visit, and because two children drowned in the quarry pool less than twenty-four hours after the big cat drank from it. Those who give credence to this superstition call her Azrael, after the angel of death. Of course, people die with regularity whether Azrael appears or not. Perhaps the only death she will truly foretell is her own, when her twenty years are behind her and she retreats to some place deep in the forest, there to lie on the couch of her own everlasting sleep.

2

THE WATCHER IN THE WOODS

For three days, a watcher takes up various positions among the trees. Because he moves only within purple shadows as the traveling sun elongates them, he apparently believes he can't be seen. When he startles a flock of birds roosting overhead, he must assume their sudden, noisy eruption into flight means nothing to the woman whom he's observing. Judging by the frequency with which his binoculars reflect sunlight and reveal his position, Vida decides that the watcher is not experienced at surveillance. When he indulges in marijuana, he seems to think she cannot smell it when she's sitting on her porch, at a distance of perhaps forty yards. However, her senses have not been dulled by the riotous mélange of odors common to places that are said to be more civilized than this rustic realm.

Although city-born, she's been gone from that place for twenty-three years. The metropolis is a memory so faded that it seems to have been no more than a dream.

She has long been of the land. She's been formed by the truths of the wilderness, by the wonder and the myths that nature inspires, by hard experience, by love and loss, by the prophecy of a traveling seer in a white robe and yellow sneakers.

The watcher among the trees does not worry her. The forest is hers not just by day but also by night, when the moon is her lamp whether it has risen or not. She knows most of the paths, and when she does not know the way, the children of the forest will lead her where she needs to go, in safety. Sooner or later, the watcher will come to her with a confidence that he will learn is misplaced.

3

SHE

In Vida's dreams, the forest goes on forever. If in reality it has limits, it is nonetheless so vast that a full and happy life can be lived within its columned chambers and in the open meadows that it encircles. Among the inhabitants of the forest are mountain lions and bears, which are to be feared, although they are less dangerous than some human beings. As for wolves, she fears them not at all.

Her five-room home is of native stone and timbers, with a slate roof. It was built seventy years earlier under the supervision of her uncle Ogden. The house stands in the foothills and backs up to the woods. The front porch faces a meadow fifty yards in diameter. Great mountains loom on three sides; on the fourth, the descending phalanxes of trees are little thinned by the valley where, at the moment, a still mist lies like a frozen river.

Throughout the residence, the floors are red-brown waxed concrete. Walls paneled in golden pine have been shellacked to a soft gloss. Although the bedroom is small, it is large enough. The eat-in kitchen is a generous space, likewise the bathroom and the library with its hundreds of books. Her workshop, where she cuts gemstones *en cabochon* and polishes them to perfection, is slightly larger than the room in which she sleeps.

The property lies remote, beyond the service of all public utilities. Propane provides gas for cooking and fuels a generator.

A deep well issues a sparkling flow as pure as the headwaters of Eden.

Uncle Ogden didn't want a phone. After he died at the age of eighty-five, ten years ago, Vida installed a satellite dish on the roof and, through it, obtained cell service. She hasn't made more than ten calls a year since then, mostly to arrange appointments with a doctor and dentist in the nearest town, which is more than nineteen miles away.

Although homeschooled, she's never used a computer other than the one in her phone. What she knows of social media appalls her. She has no need to stream anything. A turntable linked to quality speakers summons music from her uncle's collection of vinyl records. Otherwise, her entertainment needs are provided by books and nature.

Should she wish to assess the current condition of the world beyond these woods, she has a radio. She rarely turns it on. Because she has lived her life in pleasant seclusion, she has never been subjected to the tide of misinformation and fearmongering that seems to be the news as the authorities shape it; therefore, she recognizes agitprop for what it is.

This Monday morning in May, as she prepares breakfast, she listens to Arthur Rubinstein's recording, with the Guarneri Quartet, of the Brahms Quintet for Piano and Strings in F Minor, opus 34. As always, this music moves her, though not to tears as it did in her youth. She is now twenty-eight.

Somehow, the music evokes from the humble kitchen a grand sense of place. The morning light shimmering in polished pine cabinetry; the black-and-white two-inch ceramic tiles that check-erboard the countertops; the O'Keefe and Merritt six-burner three-oven stove from 1949; the Philco refrigerator of similar vintage: Everything speaks of dependability, of an age when proud manufacturers could not have conceived of a policy of planned obsolescence, when often the consumer was knowledgeable enough to repair most appliances. The kitchen is a timeless space in a world where time erodes all else.

Having learned much from her uncle, Vida has, since his death, replaced the compressor, condenser fan, and evaporator fan in the refrigerator, and has maintained all the systems on the property.

After eating breakfast and washing the dishes, she threads a supple leather holster onto her belt and inserts a can of bear spray in it. She has firearms but never carries them on her placer-mining expeditions.

Burdened with only a cooler that contains flexible cold packs and two bottles of water and a protein bar, she leaves by the front door and engages both deadbolts. The back door is likewise secured.

The metal casement windows feature pairs of twelve-inch panes with a sturdy center post. Even if the glass is broken out, neither pane is wide enough to admit anyone above the age of five.

There is a basement where she stores canned goods and freeze-dried food in vacuum drums. The lower realm has no window or exterior door; the only entrance is from inside the residence.

Behind and to the north of the house stands a smaller building of stone. It contains a backhoe, a riding lawn mower, a workbench, an extensive collection of tools, the generator, and racks of spare propane tanks.

Included is a stall for her midnight-blue 1950 Ford F-1 pickup. Thirty-two years ago, her uncle added rack-and-pinion steering and replaced the engine. The vehicle is a workhorse and a beauty.

The placer mine lies two miles from here, but no road leads to it. She walks there and back two or three times a month.

This is the first time she has left the house since the man in the forest has put her under surveillance. Whatever his intentions, he is unlikely to follow her, for to do so would be taking a greater risk of being exposed.

She enters the forest by a deer trail at the west end of the meadow and turns to look past the house, across the field to the forest in the east. The sun is behind him, so his binoculars don't reveal his position, but she can almost feel him out there, perhaps much as an exorcist might feel the presence of a demon hiding bone-deep in the body of the possessed.

This is largely an evergreen wilderness, pines and firs, but it includes communities of deciduous trees that have begun to leaf out with the coming of spring. The undergrowth is mostly western sword ferns, snowy wood rush, maidenhair spleenwort, and ribbon grass.

A maze of deer trails winds through the rising foothills and ravines, offering novice hikers a false sense of direction while providing myriad paths to nowhere and a variety of deaths. Of the few nature lovers who venture into this primeval vastness, fewer still are unwise enough to do so without preparation and provisions.

Vida knows the terrain as well as she knows the rooms of her house. The beaten paths lie in sun-dappled shadow, but unique rock formations and a tree disfigured by a lightning strike, as well as other landmarks, allow her to proceed almost at a run, too fast for the unknown man to follow her even if he is of a mind to do so.

4

THE EARTH PROVIDES

Here where the trees relent, sun and shade contest throughout the day, and false Solomon's seal flourishes knee-high. Early sprays of white flowers, like clustered kernels of freshly popped corn, are bursting through densely layered light-green leaves. Vida negotiates this barrier at the point where she's always passed through before, tramping on only those plants that she crushed previously.

Beyond lies the six-foot-high bank that defined the river's edge when, decades earlier, the watercourse had been wider in this section than it is now. She descends a weedy incline to a bare alluvial field that varies between eighteen and twenty-two feet in width and extends three hundred yards. Along the far flank of this gently sloped expanse of sediment, tangerine-scented sweet flag brandishes tall, swordlike leaves in the breeze, and the land steps down to a new riverbank beyond which cold, rushing currents speak in a double tongue of spirited splashing and sinister susurration.

Like her uncle before her, Vida works the alluvial field as a placer mine. Rain and wind ceaselessly smooth away evidence of this labor so that it is necessary to mark the point where she stopped on her most recent expedition. This she has done with a two-foot-long circus-tent spike that, at the end of the day, she always pounds into the soft soil near the slope of the new riverbank.

The spike also serves as a belaying pin to which is tethered a canvas bag that contains waist-high wading boots, a folded length of heavy-gauge plastic sheeting, a mattock, a spade, a spare spike, a mallet, a seining pan, and a pair of work gloves. The bag is buried under a few inches of soil, so that it won't draw the attention of anyone passing this way. She retrieves it.

For ten years, since her uncle's death, Vida has labored in this remote field alone, without encountering another soul. Chances are small that anyone will find and steal her humble tools. Given the hard work required to exploit the deposits here, it's even less likely that anyone who discovers her at this task will want to stake a claim to part of the placer mine. However, because her uncle Ogden took precautions, so does Vida.

She locates a width of the current riverbank that is free of sweet flag. One side of the heavy-gauge plastic sheeting has been treated with a silicon spray to make it especially slippery. She unfurls it down the slope to the land near the water's edge, the lubricated side up. The corners at the top of this chute feature brass eyelets; using the mallet, she inserts the two spikes and pounds them deep into the earth to secure the plastic.

A very long time ago, the river had been not only wider here but also slower moving, because the gradient diminished to such an extent that the rushing water came almost to a stop, forming a small lake that appears to have been about fifty yards wide and three hundred yards long. The land dropped again beyond that point, and the flow gained momentum, hastening away. During the centuries that this condition existed, the quieted water dropped what sediment it carried out of the mountains before rushing onward, thus creating the field from which her uncle earned his living for decades.

Maybe a century or two ago, something changed the river's course, perhaps a seismic event, and the eastern side of the lake suffered a collapse. The water followed this sudden new declivity, draining the elevated portion of the lake, which Vida now exploits.

Many gemstones are hard, dense, impervious to the wear that Nature imposes on everything else. Released by weathering, they can be carried great distances by water and concentrated in riverbeds or deltas or the floors of oceans, in what are called "placer mines."

The alluvial soil is soft. For the most part, the spade is sufficient to the task, but once in a while she needs the mattock. She conveys shovelfuls of dirt to the silicon-treated plastic chute, until several cubic feet have mounded below, on the flat shelf at the edge of the river. Even on a cool day like this, the work raises a sweat, and she needs the bottled water that she brought with her.

The treasure she seeks is more often found in the first eight inches of soil, though the entirety of the dig must be panned, just in case. Neither she nor her uncle has scooped deeper than three feet, usually only two. Very likely, valuable stones can be found farther down, but to seek them, she needs noisy machinery and a long sluice box capable of handling an enormous quantity of soil, all of which would call unwanted attention to her operation.

This is federal land. Although Vida is committing no ecological damage and although the government will never exploit this placer mine, the bureaucracy, given the opportunity, will come down on her as though she's the greatest despoiler of Earth in the history of the planet, if only because they have nothing better with which to occupy their time. To escape their fury, she must remain a simple scavenger of gems, with limited ambition.

Now she takes off her gloves, puts on her hip boots, picks up the sluice pan, which has a fine-wire bottom, and descends to the river. She kneels in the shallows, next to the mound of soil that slid down the chute. She fills the pan with dirt. She lowers it into the cold current, gently shaking it, letting the river lap over the rim. The water dissolves the soil and carries it through the wire; nothing is left except two worthless gravelstones and a twist of fossilized root.

She repeats this process until the mound of soil is gone, and then she climbs the bank to feed more cubic feet into the chute. At the four-hour mark, she pauses to eat an energy bar. After finishing the confection of nuts and chocolate and berries and protein powder, after washing it down with bottled water, she continues the task at hand for another three hours.

As she labors, her mind drifts neither to the man in the woods, who will no doubt still be watching her house when she returns, nor to any calculation of the value of the gemstones she finds, but to *Moby-Dick*, which she has recently begun to read for the first time. She is just past the middle of the book, and the calm, good-humored Stubb has harpooned, chased, and killed a whale with no more evident doubt about his actions than he might show while smoking a pipeful and quaffing a mug of ale. The casual cruelty of those, like Stubb, who believe they are engaged in virtuous business for the benefit of everyone leads her inevitably to dwell upon the ten months that she and José Nochelobo had been lovers, before his caring nature had been the end of him at the hands of someone like Stubb.

Next to her uncle and her father, José was the best man she's ever known. Others as good no doubt exist, but she lacks evidence.

5

GOODBYE AND HELLO

When Vida is not yet five years old, Uncle Ogden comes for her in Los Angeles. Her father, Louis, a twenty-seven-year-old police officer, has been killed in the line of duty. She's never known her mother, who died in childbirth. Theirs is a family that has thinned out generation by generation, and no one is left to take her but her sole uncle, who is in fact her great-uncle, brother to her mother's mother.

Ogden is seventy-one, tall and fit. But for his snow-white hair and seamed face, he looks as though he might be the star of that old movie, *To Kill a Mockingbird*. His impressive vitality, direct stare, patient manner, and tendency to speak directly and succinctly, using silence as if it were itself a word, intimidates the child-welfare bureaucrats who would prefer to deny him custody if only to confirm their power. However, in his will, Vida's father leaves everything to Ogden and strongly expresses that his daughter should be awarded to her great-uncle. No one can claim that Ogden is motivated to take custody of the child because of the wealth that comes with her. Once the mortgage and other debts are paid, her inheritance totals just sixteen thousand dollars. A hearing is conducted, during which the old man's determination to do what Louis asked of him convinces the judge and the masters of the system that he will exhaust them with his persistence if they don't relent on their desire to consign the girl to a torturous series of foster homes.

Although Ogden could have driven her to his mountain home in two days, he makes a four-day journey of it in the Ford F-1 pickup, showing Vida the wonders of nature en route and providing her with simple but charming pleasures that are new to her. A petting zoo. A church carnival where he throws baseballs at tenpins and wins a teddy bear. Her first experience of snow and first snowball fight.

Our memories from early childhood are far from indelible; they fade until, by our late teens, if not before, they are like yellowed photographs from a previous century. However, though Vida remembers little about her heroic father and nothing about the house where she lived with him, her memories of that journey from Los Angeles remain vivid more than twenty years after the fact.

By the time Uncle Ogden brings her home, she knows that she is safe and that he will never fail her.

The house in the forest is out of a fairy tale. Many weeks pass before it seems more real than magical. As the years go by, the place holds for her—and always will—a quiet enchantment.

In preparation for Vida's arrival, her uncle has added a second armchair and lamp to the library. Under the window stands a twin bed with a cream-colored chenille spread, and folded across the foot of it is a beautifully patterned Pendleton blanket in soft blues and grays and rich red. For years to come, on many an evening, they sit in this room while he reads to her. When she is older, each of them settles down with a different book in a shared, comfortable quiet. Through thirteen years of primeval nights, as owls make their queries and wolves celebrate the moon, she sleeps here; sometimes lulled by the rataplan of rain on the roof, sometimes by a soughing wind that ferries snow across the mountains, she sleeps; in quiet weather and in storms, she sleeps encompassed by the amazing people who live within the pages of the books that are shelved on every wall of the room. When she dreams of those storied souls, she feels watched over by the kindest of them, and she does not fear those who are unkind because this is her uncle's house into which the wicked dare not venture out of their chapters.

If Vida's first view of her new home charmed her (as very much it had), and if the library-bedroom delighted her (of which there was no doubt), her uncle's workroom intrigued her no less than might the quarters of a venerable magician and seer. The arcane tools and devices on his workbench—a dop, a lapidary's magnifying glass, a tumbler-polisher, a variety of grinders, a small lathe with a diamond blade—are mysterious, but the contents of the shallow drawers in his product cabinet are what most inspire wonder.

Some of the drawers are lined with black velvet, others with white, and all are divided into compartments. The gemstones—sorted by variety, size, and color—are displayed against whichever velvet best presents them. Perhaps two-thirds are small, but others are large enough to be cut for centerpiece stones in pendants, brooches, and rings. The sapphires come in several colors—shades of green, yellow, blue, and red. There are gems of other kinds—topaz, garnet, amethyst, and chrysoberyl.

The stones in a natural state are dull compared to those that have been cut and polished, but all of them dazzle young Vida. At first, she thinks her uncle must be rich. She will learn that placer mining of gemstones such as these, including their preparation for sale to makers of jewelry and decorative items, can reliably provide a middle-class living and allow for the accumulation of savings by a freelance prospector like Ogden, for as long as the deposit lasts; however, his only chance of getting rich is to unearth a few megagems of splendid brilliance and without unfortunate inclusions, which is unlikely to happen. Meanwhile, there is the hard work of panning the placer mine and long hours in the workshop.

The first night that she sleeps in her new home, in spite of the delight she has taken in this place, she weeps for her lost father, who is trapped in her dreams and can never know the joys of this new life of hers. Once, she comes awake to find that a reading lamp is switched on and turned low. Her uncle sits in an armchair, watching her. Maybe he *is* some kind of magician and seer, for he knows what misery sleep has brought her. He has a soothing voice that rumbles on the low notes when he says, "It's all right, child. He's safe now, and he knows that you are, too." When she slips once more into slumber, her dad is there to say goodbye. He walks away into the faceted light of a gem, which shines brighter with him in it. At least for that night, she weeps no more in her dreams.

6

THE BOX

This is a house where two lives have been lived so well, with such love and in such a spirit of peace, that Vida is never overcome by loneliness here. Her lost uncle exists not merely in her mind but also seems alive in every room, in memories like vivid apparitions.

Even when, as now, she is away at the placer mine, the house feels occupied. If a burglar forced entry under the impression that the residence was deserted, he might halt a step past the threshold, become convinced that he was wrong, and retreat without risking an encounter.

This is not to say that the house is haunted, for it is not. To this point, only Ogden has died within these walls, peacefully in his sleep. As much as he loved this world, he lived in anticipation of another, and he was not of a mind to cling to this place either because of melancholy longing or fear.

Nevertheless, rich years of love, laughter, compassion, and kindness can imbue a home with a strange aura of life all its own, a resonant echo that speaks not to the ear but to the heart. There are special places and objects to which those who have a sensitive spirit might be drawn.

Sealed in bright-yellow giftwrap foil and never opened, the box has been stored on a high shelf in the bedroom closet since shortly before Vida turned twenty-eight, where it has been for many months. Now and then, she takes it down to wonder about its contents. She resists opening the package because a still, small voice tells her that wanting to know isn't good enough. She must wait till she feels an urgent *need* to know, for then the contents will mean more to her. Even when that voice is perplexing, she has learned to heed it.

The box, the closet, the house await her return.

7

THE FIRST GRAVE

In the late afternoon, when Vida returns from the placer mine, the breeze is coming from the east, and on it she can smell a faint trace of marijuana smoke. The sun is balanced on the highest peaks of the western mountains, its light slanting across the meadow at the ideal angle to paint the lenses of the binoculars orange, but she doesn't bother surveying the eastern tree line for the sentinel.

He will not watch forever. When he's done watching, he will pay her a visit for whatever purpose. Only then will she disrupt her day to take the time needed to deal with him.

She doesn't go directly to the house, but first follows the memorial path.

Although she has a riding lawn mower, she never cuts all of this expansive grassland. As needed, she crops it in a radius of thirty feet around the house, shears a pathway to the center of the meadow, and mows an eight-foot-wide clearing around the headstone that bears her uncle's name.

This is a county that still allows burial on private property under certain circumstances and for a consideration. She had dug the grave with her uncle's backhoe, which he had used to excavate a new septic tank two years before Vida came to live here and which he had taught her to operate when she was sixteen, so she might be able to prepare his resting place when the time came. The funeral home transported the casket to the site and lowered it into the grave.

In addition to the name, the only other thing incised in the gray granite is a line of verse that he chose: I SAID TO MY SOUL, BE STILL, AND LET THE DARK COME UPON YOU.

From a pocket of her jacket, she produces a small drawstring bag of the softest cotton, which contains what she panned from the placer mine today. "It was a nice haul, Uncle. When I was done, I raked the dig, filled it in, and smoothed it over so it isn't a wound in the earth. Just as you taught me. A doe came to visit with her fawn. The little one was all legs and curiosity, but the mother kept it at a distance. I was surprised to see a buck, its growing antlers velvety. I hope it was the father of the fawn. It's nice to think it might've bonded with the doe for the long haul rather than for one season. Anyway, I'll work the stones to your standards. I haven't lost a customer in the past ten years. Some of them swear you must still be alive and on the job. Well, in a way, you are."

On this Monday in May, as the sun slips from sight, the western mountains are crowned with carnelian red. The darkling eastern sky is sapphire blue and diamonded.

8

THE DANGER OF SEEING AND BEING

The second armchair, with footstool, remains in the library, as does the bed on which Vida slept for thirteen years. She reads in the chair and sometimes takes an afternoon nap on the narrow bed, surrounded by the palisades of books.

At night, she sleeps in the bedroom that her uncle occupied. She has made it over to her taste, which is pretty much his taste, but more so. A colorful Pendleton blanket, stretched across a frame, hangs on a wall. A Navajo rug warms her bare feet when the waxed-concrete floor is cold. A painted *trastero* contains all the jeans and shirts she needs, plus her two dresses.

Before retreating to the bathroom to shower, she steps to the bedroom window and pulls aside the panels of the white, translucent curtain that's lightly embroidered with butterflies in white thread and has a yellow-ribbon hem. She removes the bug screen and props it against the wall and cranks the casement panes out to their full extension. Although a little evening air will freshen the room, she opens the window because, intuitively, she expects Lupo to visit.

The hot shower soothes the muscles she strained at the placer mine. As she rinses the shampoo out of her hair, she is turning one of today's stones over and over in her mind's eye, a butterscotch-yellow chrysoberyl twice the size of her thumb. Even in its rough form, she sees what she believes might be an exceptional example of chatoyancy, which is also called "cat's-eye effect." If she cuts it properly, maintaining as much weight in carats as possible, it will have considerable value. More important: It will have great beauty.

She recalls a conversation with her uncle two years before he died, when she was sixteen. He was plainspoken, but there were occasions when he sought words that might define—although not explain—something ineffable.

On a Sunday in that late July, having washed and dried and put away the dinner dishes, they sit in rocking chairs on the front porch, enjoying coffee spiked with Baileys. While the sun lays a golden haze across the meadow, butterflies dance weary-winged above the grass, seeking rest from the day, as shadows spill eastward.

"Now I'm almost eighty-four, I no longer mind saying things that might make me seem foolish."

"You're the farthest thing from foolish, Uncle."

"Being human, I'm the nearest thing to it, the very thing itself. I've at last made peace with that fact."

"So then, what foolish thing do you want to tell me?"

"It started when you were ten or eleven. Since then, you turn up more and better gemstones than I do, on every expedition."

"I'm sure that's not right."

"But it is."

"Whether it is or not, I don't see why it makes you foolish."

"That's only the setup for what you'll think is silly when I say it. You're drawn to beauty as surely as hummingbirds are drawn to nectar."

"Who isn't drawn to beauty? Everyone is."

"No. You aren't drawn like others are. You see beauty where others never can. You see it with something other than your eyes."

"Now we're deep in the silly zone. Do I see it with my nose?"

"At the placer deposit, with nothing to see but sediment, you always choose the more rewarding square meter to dig."

"I still say it isn't always."

"It is always, sweetheart. Always, always. Often, when you've found remarkable stones within six or eight inches of the surface, you dig no deeper, when anyone else would."

"I think the word for that is 'lazy.'"

"No. You move to another square meter and continue to work. During the past year, without telling you, I've several times gone the next day and dug deeper where you stopped. I've never found a stone. Somehow, you knew there was nothing more to be found."

"Oh, Uncle Ogden, really, I'm no psychic gemstone diviner."

"I didn't say you were psychic. Nothing as pulp fiction as that. You're something else there's no word for. At least, no word I know. It's not just the gemstones. It's also other things, like the wildflowers."

"What wildflowers?"

"Any wildflowers. When the meadow's full of them, you rush about with your clippers, snipping this and that with no apparent calculation—and every bloom in the bouquet is perfect."

"Really now, that's Nature's work, not mine."

He says, "I've gone out to pick a bunch of my own, with great care, but when I compare my bouquet to yours, it's pathetic. The colors are less rich. Some petals are spotted or missing."

"Well, see, you're my honorary papa. So you want to believe I'm special."

"Have you looked at yourself in the mirror, sweetheart? You're special whether you think you are or not."

Emphatically, if not sharply, she says, "Not! I'm not special. I'm just me. All right? So let's just shut up about it."

After a silence he says, "Are you okay?"

She can't at once respond. She sips her coffee and finds it difficult to swallow. When she says, "I didn't mean to snap at you," her voice breaks, and she doesn't like that.

He says, "No big deal. You didn't draw blood. If that's what you intended, we'll get out my files later and sharpen your teeth."

It's difficult to be angry with this sweet man. In fact, she isn't. She's been shaken by a long-unresolved grief and by the sudden recognition of a misgiving that has grown from it.

In time, when she's sure that she's in control of her emotions, she continues. "Everyone said my mom was special, bright and funny, so pretty, but I never knew her. My dad was a hero, but he was with me such a short time. What I have left of him is . . . fading. Fading. It doesn't pay to be special in this world, Uncle. In fact, it's dangerous. I just want our quiet life. Our work, the meadow, the forest—and you."

"Then I'll live another eighty-four years."

"Good," she says.

Days later, when her uncle continues this conversation, Vida discovers his purpose hasn't been just to encourage her with loving praise, but also to warn her that a girl with special qualities should live fully, yet with caution in this world of envy, bestial desire, and cruel deceit. The misgiving she's felt since she was orphaned isn't irrational; Ogden shares it, and it's common sense.

She has been keeping a diary since she was ten. In addition to much else, she records in it these conversations with her uncle as accurately as she is able.

❦

By the time Vida has finished showering, dried her hair, and dressed, Lupo has not arrived. She cranks the casement window shut and covers the panes with the embroidered curtain.

In the library, she makes a selection from the collection of vinyl recordings and puts the platter on the turntable. Speakers in all rooms give forth Beethoven's Piano Concerto no. 4 in G Major, opus 58; Glenn Gould on piano is backed by the Baltimore Symphony Orchestra.

Above the turntable hangs a pencil portrait of her uncle as a young man, rendered in marvelous detail. In the lower right-hand corner, instead of the artist's signature, there's a small, stylized image of a deer, specifically a fawn. Although Vida has lived with it all these years, sometimes when she looks at it, she thinks about what she found on the back of the portrait, after Ogden's death, and she is moved by the memory.

Before beginning to prepare dinner, she cranks open a kitchen window. No curtain hangs here, and the pleated shade is raised.

If Lupo fails to come this evening, she won't worry about him. He lives in two worlds with consummate grace, and sometimes she is half convinced that he's immortal.

9

LYING IN THE DARK

After clearing the table, Vida sits in the library to read *Moby-Dick*. In the comfort of the ship, having killed a leviathan, Stubb eats a slab of the flesh by the light of a whale-oil lamp. Meanwhile outside, frenzied sharks attack the carcass and are in turn attacked by harpooners. The whale is hoisted for the salvage of its blubber, while its rotting head, which is one-third of its length, hangs over the side of the ship until its valuable contents can be hauled out by the bucketful. These events are so vividly portrayed that the author's horror—inspired by the arrogance, avarice, and cruelty of human beings—can be endured only for thirty pages in one sitting. Vida doesn't enjoy the novel, but it offers a warning alike to the one that her uncle delivered. To compensate for the darkness of the prose, she plays Mozart's Clarinet Concerto, K. 622, for the golden light of its ecstatic sound.

Before going to bed, she cranks shut the window in the kitchen and puts down the pleated shade. Lupo never comes while she sleeps.

Perhaps her intuitive expectation of a visitor was inspired not by him but by the watcher in the woods.

Lying in the dark, head pillowed, she ends her day by speaking the same words with which she has ended every day for years. "My life passes like a shadow. Yet a little while, and all will be consummated."

She falls asleep as the last word issues through her lips.

10

NATURE'S BOUNTY

Tuesday morning, Vida rises in a bright spirit of expectation and preparation. This is a fine day for preliminary gem evaluation and for seeking the bounty of field and forest. In summer, there will be blackberries and wild strawberries and many varieties of mushrooms. Here in the spring, she is limited to a mushroom hunt.

After breakfast, she spends an hour in her workshop, using a loupe to examine the gemstones found the previous day. Of eighteen sapphires, fifteen are in shades of green or yellow, so small that they allow minimal or no cutting. They are best used to enhance decorative items or for inexpensive multistring necklaces called rivières; she has a client who buys them by the pound. The remaining three are blue and promising, in need of study prior to being cut.

After she puts all the sapphires in the tumbler-polisher, the pleasant silence of the room gives way to the equally comforting hum and slosh and muffled rattling from the small machine.

In addition to the sizable butterscotch-yellow stone, there are three smaller chrysoberyls that might be called canary yellow. In rough form, they give her no reason to expect they contain either the oriented inclusions that will produce a cat's-eye effect or the angled fibers of an asterism that will result in a highly desirable star cabochon. She puts them aside for further consideration.

When she sets out on the mushroom hunt, she takes the can of bear spray in her belt holster, though not in expectation of a bear.

She never carries a gun of any kind, for there is nothing in this world that she can imagine shooting. Her uncle owned a rifle, a shotgun, and a pistol. He insisted that she learn to use all those weapons, and out of respect for him, she took instruction. Since his death, they have been in their latched cases, stored on a high shelf above the food supply, in the cellar. She takes the guns down only rarely and always because of the good memories of Ogden that they evoke.

She makes no effort to survey the eastern woods in which the watcher has thus far remained. Until he reveals himself, her interest in him is for the most part exhausted.

She crosses the meadow to the northern flank of the forest and enters the trees. The low *bruu-ooo* of rock doves gives way to the humming whistle of their wings as flocks take off at her approach, effortlessly threading their way through the maze of boughs and branches, through layered shadows and intrusions of sunlight.

The grassy clearing she seeks is half a mile from her house and smaller than her meadow, but the treasure here can't be found nearer home. *Morchella conica* are common in spring and among the tastiest of mushrooms. She visits here every few days during the season to harvest the best specimens, which mature with surprising quickness. They're best when not yet fully grown.

These mushrooms have tall light-brown caps with intersecting vertical and lateral ridges. She cuts them at the base of the stem and puts them in brown paper bags that she buys by the boxful for this purpose; there are edible mushrooms of other varieties to be gathered in the summer and early fall.

In 1953, a year after Ogden came home from the Korean War, he was, among other things, taught about mushrooms by a Native American friend, a Cheyenne, who gathered fungi with gratitude to Nature. Personally rather than because of any tribal custom, the same friend declined to violate the earth to rob it of its jewelry, but guided Ogden to the placer mine and thus gave him his future.

As Vida works, a hawk glides in its gyre. Abruptly it plunges to the meadow, ten yards from her. The prey—perhaps a field mouse—lives long enough to issue a miserable squeal as it is torn from the land and perishes in the ascent. Like Vida, the hawk is on the hunt, and though she pities the mouse, she makes no case against the bird.

At home once more, with three bags full, she cleans the morels and sets aside a portion to have with dinner. The remainder she submerges in a special vinegar flavored with a subtle herb bouquet; she seals them in three mason jars to be stored in the cellar.

After a light lunch of salad and chicken breast, as she puts away the washed dishes and utensils, she hears an approaching vehicle. Visitors are rare; these days, she never invites anyone.

Whatever is about to unfold, it won't involve sudden violence. If that were the watcher's intention, she wouldn't have been subjected to three days of observation before this moment.

11

HE KNOWS NOT WHO SHE IS

When Vida steps onto the front porch, a vintage Pontiac Trans Am—from the late 1980s—comes to a stop, having raised a thick plume of dust to wither in its wake. The elephantine pulse of the idling engine dies, and the subsequent quiet, though only what it had been, seems funereal. The driver steps out and closes the door. Exiting the car, he holds his cowboy hat in hand, but he pauses to set it on his head just so before he approaches.

Vida has seen countless such hats, but she can't say if this is by Stetson or Resistol or some minor maker, because she doesn't care about such things. Judging by the precision with which her visitor places his hat and adjusts it, and considering the way he carries himself with a subtle swagger, she judges him to be a vain and calculating individual, possibly a narcissist.

If she were a gambler, she would bet a hundred dollars to a dime that this is the watcher in the woods, at last come forth to advance whatever scheme he's taken so much time to develop.

Thirtysomething, tall, lean but muscular, he's wearing brown leather boots, tailored khakis, and a tan shirt. A department patch on the right sleeve and a badge with nameplate where a shirt pocket otherwise would be do not surprise Vida. Not much does.

He halts at the foot of the porch steps. "Ma'am, I'm Deputy Nash Deacon, with the county sheriff. I've a need to talk with you."

He's neither handsome nor unattractive, plain enough that only his mother or his wife would recognize him under any circumstances, if he has a wife. He has no memorable feature other than his brown-black eyes, in which she sees a rapacity perhaps akin to what the field mouse saw if it met the gaze of the predator that snatched it from the meadow as Vida had been gathering mushrooms.

"That's a most unusual patrol car," she says.

"My own wheels. I'm a deputy, but I'm not here as a deputy."

"The uniform seems to say otherwise."

"I just got off duty, didn't take time to change."

"Do you have more ID than what you're wearing?"

He climbs one step, flips open an ID wallet, and holds it out to her. As far as she can tell, it's the real thing, with a photo. Also real is the light fragrance of marijuana.

"What's this about?" she asks.

"It's best if we sit a spell and chat."

"Last I heard, I can have an attorney present when I talk to an officer of the law."

"Like I said, ma'am, I'm not here in that capacity. And I'd rather not be."

"You'd rather not be. Yet that's how you introduced yourself."

He is quick to take offense at her restive response to his informal assertion of authority, but he's professional enough to bite back his exasperation. "Sorry if I got off on the wrong foot."

She needs to hear him out and learn his game as much as he needs to say his piece, so she moves back from the steps.

Although her beloved uncle has been gone for ten years, she keeps two rockers on the porch, with a small table between them.

Deacon is only the second person to sit in Ogden's chair in a decade. This is more a violation than a desecration, but Vida finds that she is clenching her teeth.

They sit in silence for the better part of a minute, staring out at the meadow where, just above the blades of grass, midges ceaselessly agitate. From her uncle, Vida has learned to use silence as a tool for encouraging others to think about what they just said or to give them the opportunity to retract some error that they shouldn't have put into words. The deputy uses silence, instead, as if it were a vise with which to squeeze his companion into a state of discomfort.

When that doesn't work with Vida, Deacon is first to speak. "How many acres is this spread?"

"Never thought of it as a 'spread.' It was my uncle's retreat, and now it's mine."

"Eighty acres."

"If you knew, why ask?"

"For the most part surrounded by federal land. It's a lonely place by any measure."

"Not lonely," she corrects. "It's peaceful."

"People wonder why a young woman such as you would hide herself away like this."

"Am I hiding? I seem not to be hiding from you. What people would they be who wonder such things?"

"Townspeople."

"They're twenty miles away. I go into town just once a month. And they're obsessed with me? How desperate are they for gossip?"

Relaxing in her rocker, Vida begins to arc it slowly back and forth, but Deacon remains rigid in his chair. "They understand a man like him, Ogden, being the way he was. But you—"

"A man like him?" she interrupts. "What is it they think they understand about him?"

She's staring at Deacon now, and he knows it. He shifts his attention from the meadow to her. "Korea. The war. How he came back changed—stressed out and antisocial."

"My uncle was kind and personable and more sociable than most people. He didn't suffer from post-traumatic stress disorder."

"If you say so. I'm glad to hear it."

"My uncle also didn't suffer fools easily. The way he saw it, there are too many of them out there, all hell-bent on making other people as unhappy as they are. Too many and more every year."

The deputy attempts reconciliation. "Don't forget my line of work. I know all that too well."

"If you say so," she replies. "I'm glad to hear it. By my uncle's service, he earned some peace and happiness. He found it here. That's all."

Deacon's silence now seems to have a new purpose, as if he's casting around in his mind for a fresh approach that will assuage the offense she has taken and alleviate the ill will he has brought upon himself.

He's incapable of that, and thus he resorts to an authoritarian tone and an implied threat. "We both know why I'm here."

She smiles because the last thing he expects is for her to smile. "If you're not here on official business, may I call you Nash? Good. Nash, you apparently mistake me for a mind reader or a criminal mastermind with great powers of deception. I'm glad *you* know why you're here, but I'm really clueless."

A moment earlier he had unsuccessfully sought a way to appease her. Now he reacts perversely to her smile and the concession she has made by using his first name. His god is power, and he doesn't have the grace to mediate a more agreeable relationship than the one that he established when he arrived in the thunderous, supercharged Pontiac Trans Am and declared his need to talk with her. Previously cool and officious, his tone is now icy when he repeats, "We both know why I'm here," as if blunt repetition identifies his statement as a dogma of the Church of Nash, which may not be challenged.

Vida waits without speaking.

She had waited for years until José Nochelobo came into her life and became her love, her lover, waited without knowing what his name would be or what he'd look like, but bided time with patience, certain that innocents and repenters receive the happiness that is the promise in the warp and weft of this woven world. Nearly a year ago, when José was taken from her after only ten months together, her grief was profound, but it didn't destroy her. Hope is armor against despair, and as her uncle taught her, patience is a polish that keeps that armor bright. We can't know the ultimate why of anything, although if we train ourselves to read the intricate fabric that time weaves, we see a pattern certain to console and inspire.

And so, since José Nochelobo's death, Vida has waited patiently for all the good that is promised to come next, as she waits now in her rocking chair for Deputy Deacon to say something more.

Aiming a glare at her that is meant to be a blow, which lands with no more force than a shadow, he says, "Belden Bead."

With puzzlement, she says, "Belt and bead?"

His hands have moved from the arms of his chair to his thighs, where they are now white-knuckled fists. "It took me a while to see what must've happened and a while longer to find evidence of it, but I know what I know, and *you* know what I know, and there's no chance of you escaping the consequences." He looks toward the part of the meadow that is second in significance only to the spot where Uncle Ogden is buried. "Would've been quite a job if you didn't have that backhoe."

"Belt and bead," she says more to herself than to him, as if trying to make sense of those three words.

Deacon gets to his feet, opens his fists, and blots one hand against his shirt before realizing a perspiration stain will reveal his anxiety. He isn't as sure of himself as he pretends to be.

"Belden Bead was my cousin," he says, his voice flat, emotion pressed from it perhaps to compensate for the sweaty palm and to convince her that he's all business, that he'll succeed at what he intends. "Belden and I were born the same month, same year. We grew up together, each other's best friend. I became an officer of the law, and he became what he became, but we never drifted apart. We remained close in our way. I protected Belden, and he made my life easier whenever he could." Deacon crosses the porch to the steps, descends to the yard, turns, and looks up at her where she stands at the railing. "I want what I want, and I want this to be as smooth as glass between us. I came today to let you know the consequences. You think about your situation until you fully understand there's just one path forward for you. I'll give you some time. I came off mean today. I won't be that way once we've settled on the terms of our arrangement. You'll find me agreeable enough. You'll be happy with me—and if you aren't, it'll be only because you don't want to be."

He proceeds to the Trans Am and opens the door and takes off his cowboy hat and spins it onto the passenger seat.

Before Deacon gets into the car, Vida says, "What do you want from me?"

"Look in a mirror. You've got what I need, and you need what I can give you, now that you've been alone the better part of a year."

"Say it plain—what you want."

"Submission," he says.

She watches him drive away, until the Trans Am is out of sight, until the plume of dust settles in his wake and the air is clear.

12

DISTANT CRIES

She spends the rest of Tuesday afternoon in her workshop, where the tumbler-polisher continues to prepare the sapphires, which she checks on from time to time.

The large chrysoberyl is rough and requires cobbing, a light hammering to knock away brittle material. This done, she moves to the trim saw. The six-inch circular blade, cooled by running water, rotates at four thousand surface feet per minute. The risk to her fingers—the stone is handheld—is the greater hazard, though she wears a welder's shield to protect her eyes. She needs to begin by giving the chrysoberyl a flat bottom, for the cat's-eye effect is best achieved by shaping the stone *en cabochon*. Close attention as well as much patience are required, and she is at the job for some time. In her current circumstances, the work is a blessing, because such concentration is required that her encounter with Deputy Deacon recedes so far to the back of her mind that it might have been an unpleasantness experienced years earlier.

When the bottom of the chrysoberyl is rough-sawn flat, it needs to be subjected to grinding, first with coarse silicon carbide and then with finer abrasives. Grinding will be followed by sanding. When the sanding is done, the bottom of the cabochon will receive a preliminary polish before she shapes the remainder of the stone. She might finish the process by late Friday afternoon.

With the stone sawn flat, she has accomplished enough for the day. She turns off the light and goes to the kitchen to prepare dinner—buttered fettuccini with peas, dusted with Parmesan. She prefers the delicious *Morchella conica* cut and raw atop the pasta.

Before attending to dinner, she raises the pleated shade, removes the screen, and cranks open the window beside the back door. The sky is so red that the pale grass of the meadow appears to be afire, and the forest is as black as char.

Perhaps she hears them calling in the far distance, though she might be imagining the sound. They howl to warn others from poaching game on their territory, to call the pack together after a hunt, to mourn the loss of one of their own, as well as for other reasons, and every cry that issues from them is of a different character. At times they howl for the sheer pleasure of being together, and though this is a sweet sound, people who are not trained to distinguish one cry from another are nonetheless chilled by it. Wolves were once eradicated from this region; now they have a home here again, though their lives are hard and their numbers small. Their voices are a kind of music to Vida, and she doesn't fear them. They don't attack people. They kill only to eat. They don't kill for pleasure and then leave the prey to rot. They never kill their own kind. Vida listens, and the tepid breeze, infused with the scents of field and forest, carries the sounds of birds going to their roosts and toads waking to the promise of an approaching moon. If the wolf cries were not imaginary, they have quieted.

13

LIFE PASSES LIKE A SHADOW

Eleven months earlier, on the Saturday afternoon in late June when José Nochelobo dies, the sky is the gray of saturation and so low that the peaks of the western mountains seem to ascend forever into the clouds, as if they provide a path between this world and the mystery that is the next.

The town of Kettleton rolls across and down the foothills, providing an illusion of slow but perpetual movement, although in fact it is a community of inertia, little changed over the decades. Its buildings are refreshed and repurposed on occasion, but they are rarely torn down and replaced.

At twelve thousand, the population is static. Most promising young people leave after high school and return only to visit their families. An almost equal number of newcomers trickle in, escaping the crime in the mismanaged cities or fleeing high-tax states, at least for a while charmed by the prospect of quiet small-town life and the majesty of the mountains.

North of Kettleton, below the soaring peaks and above the foothills, lies what county maps call the Grand Plateau. There, on more than three thousand acres of level and almost treeless land, a company named New World Technology seeks final approval to build a project that promises to bring desirable jobs to Kettleton.

Throughout the county, the project inspires more detractors than supporters. Mayor Harlan Cotter—in conjunction with county officials, leaders of community organizations, and three pastors—has arranged a public forum for the afternoon to provide a civil atmosphere in which all viewpoints can be aired and misinformation can be dispelled in a respectful yet authoritative manner.

Because the number of residents expected to attend exceeds the capacity of any indoor venue in town, the block in front of the courthouse is closed to traffic for the event. A collapsible platform—erected every Halloween, Independence Day, and Christmas Week to elevate prize judges and local dignitaries above the parades they review—has been removed from storage and assembled.

The crowd is even greater than what was anticipated, filling the street, encircling the elevated dais, and lining up in tiers on the courthouse steps behind the speakers. The day is warm but not sweltering. A storm might break before all interested parties have had their say. Although more than half those present believe their community and their lives will be negatively impacted if the project on the Grand Plateau is approved, and although somewhat fewer than half disagree with that position, their anxiety has not progressed to anger. Kettleton is no Eden; evil has its outposts in this county, but thus far the people haven't deeply divided themselves into angry factions based on such shallow differences as class and race and sex and politics. No one expects—and few would openly condone—an act of violence on this occasion.

The four speakers are scheduled to alternate, pro and con the project, although the event is not structured as a formal debate. When each has had his or her fifteen minutes, the audience will be invited to present questions until all have been satisfied or a sudden rainstorm forecloses further discussion.

José Nochelobo, thirty-four at the time, is the third speaker. He's a former history teacher and now, for two years, the youngest principal in the history of Kettleton High School. Both as a teacher and an administrator, he's also served as the coach of the school's winning football team. Three months previously, although unarmed, he overpowered a school shooter, a drug-addled boy named Tom Kyte; two students were wounded, but because of José's quick, selfless action, none died. He's well liked, almost universally admired, the closest thing Kettleton has—or has ever had—to a local celebrity, though with grace and self-deprecating humor, he turns aside all praise.

He has good looks without vanity, strength without insolence, courage without ferocity, and Vida is in love with him. He wants to marry her, and she wants to be married. However, she has hesitated. After more than two decades during which she has lived largely as a recluse, she doubts that she has the refinement and poise to be the wife of a man who, as principal and coach and mensch to all, is at the center of the town's social life. José assures her that she has the wisdom, grace, and personality to win over everyone, as she has so totally enchanted him. On this day, when she sees him with the others on the stage, waiting his turn at the microphone, he seems like the suitor from a fairy tale, not a prince but princely, and she decides that she's been a fool for not at once accepting his proposal. She wants to marry him as soon as possible.

To avoid being a distraction when José steps forward to accept the mic and make his presentation, Vida hasn't taken a position close to the stage, but stands toward the back of the crowd. José is no rabble-rouser, is not given to the deceptions and distortions of politicians. He walks the edge of the stage, relaxed, never raising his voice. He's been speaking only three minutes when it's evident that the audience finds his case surprising but compelling.

The five teenage boys, students at one of the county's two other high schools, carry two bottles of water each, not to slake their thirst but to incite a moment of turmoil. From one end of the closed block or the other, the loud air horn of a truck blares with such volume that José stops speaking. In the crowd, heads turn in search of the disturbance. Just then, as one, the teenagers pelt José Nochelobo with ten bottles, then bolt through the thousand or more people who are gathered in the street, disappearing before anyone quite realizes what has occurred.

Battered about the chest and head, José is startled. He loses his balance. The speakers' platform is a mere seven feet above the pavement. The portable steps, which have been rolled against the stage and locked in place, feature metal treads and handrails. He stumbles and drops to his knees and pitches off the stage, headfirst down the stairs, unable to arrest his fall.

From her position, Vida isn't able to see what has happened to him. However, judging by the reactions of the other speakers and by the cries from those at the front of the crowd, she's afraid that José might have suffered a serious injury even in that short plunge. As the truck horn falls silent, she tries to press forward. The shock of the incident seems to have congealed the multitudes into one creature with thousands of incoordinate limbs that resist her passage.

As at any large public event, EMTs are present to respond to any emergency. By the time Vida reaches the stage, José has been transferred into an ambulance. A siren shrills.

Kettleton Memorial is eight blocks away. Her pickup is parked behind the library, in the opposite direction from the hospital. The streets will be clogged with traffic if the milling crowd disperses. In the clutches of anguish-anxiety-dread, Vida doesn't fully realize she's set out on foot, running on a sidewalk, until the courthouse is a full block behind her.

Time and distance are distorted as in a nightmare. Eight small-town blocks seem to stretch into eight miles. Although she's young and fit, with the stamina to endure a marathon, she feels as though she's run so far that she'll collapse in breathless exhaustion, for her heartbeat is accelerated by both effort and foreboding.

When she arrives at the hospital and hurries under the roof of the portico at the emergency room entrance, no ambulance is present, and she realizes that she hasn't heard a siren for several blocks.

Pneumatic doors whisk out of her way. An auburn-haired and freckled woman with emerald eyes sits behind the reception desk.

Vida says, "My fiancé," even though she has not accepted José's proposal, says it because it's an incantation to ward off evil, a petition and prayer. "José Nochelobo, my fiancé, something happened at the courthouse."

The receptionist is compassionate and gracious, but kindness can pierce with a unique pain when it conveys news that cannot be endured. "Oh, dear girl," she says as she rises from her chair. "Oh, God, honey, I'm so sorry. Here, come here, sit down." But Vida does not want to sit down, and though she can read the message that those emerald eyes convey as surely as she can read the inclusions in a gemstone, she says, "I need to be with him, he'll be okay if I'm with him, take me to him." But she can't be taken to him because he is not here. The receptionist holds her, and although Vida doesn't want to be held because of what being held in these circumstances must mean, she nevertheless finds herself holding fast to the woman much as a shipwrecked sailor holds fast to whatever debris will keep him afloat. José's neck was broken, and he died either at the site of the incident or in transit. He's been taken to the coroner, who will perform an autopsy, and that is it, that is all, that is the end. That is the official story.

14

THE COMFORT OF THE MOON

The January night when Vida's police-officer father dies, the moon is not where it should be in the sky.

From early childhood, Vida has been fascinated by the moon in its eight phases, though she delights most of all in its fullness. She has dreams in which she lives in a castle in a lunar crater. Other dreams are ornamented with scores of luminous moons the size of baseballs that hang in the air in her humble home, as weightless as Earth's ancient satellite floating in space; they rotate away from her, this mistress of the moon, to grant her unobstructed passage as she moves room to room. Sometimes she wades through a dream river, reaching down to pull small moons out of the water as if they were fish. There is a dream of a meadow where, while sheep graze and wolves watch without violent intention, the mother who died in childbirth reaches up to pull down the moon, which fits her hand as if its great size and far position have been an illusion, and Mother throws the moon to Vida, and Vida throws it back to her mother, and with each exchange of that sphere, the two of them grow closer, until they are in each other's arms.

The night that Vida becomes an orphan, the next-door neighbor, Mrs. Valenski, as sweet and wrinkled as a raisin, is babysitting until Father comes home from a tour of duty ending at midnight.

At 10:07, according to the bedside clock, Vida is awakened when a hand smooths her hair off her brow. She startles up from her pillow, but she is alone. As she swings her legs out of bed and sits on the edge of the mattress, she hears her father speak her name five times, his voice softer with each repetition. Although usually deep in darkness at this hour, the bedroom is in part revealed by soft, silver light, and the remaining shadows are not black but midnight blue—or so she will remember them in years to come—for the moon is huge and framed within her window. That uncurtained pane faces due north, and never before has the moon been captured in it.

Vida knows she's awake, even though the moment is infused with the strangeness of a dream. She gets out of bed and steps to the window and gazes at the immense moon that seems to be plunging from its orbit, at the world washed in its eerie radiance. Although she knows she should be afraid, she isn't. She curls up in the big chair and draws around her a knitted afghan that's draped across the arm. She feels safe in the glow of the misplaced moon, and soon she falls asleep again.

Shortly after midnight, she is awakened by Mrs. Valenski, who enters the room in a yellow fan of hallway light, talking to God, asking the Lord for help, her voice quaking with emotion. The old woman sees the bed empty and Vida rising out of sleep by the window. The chair is large enough for woman and child. Mrs. Valenski slides into it and enfolds the girl in her arms. The full moon is now in another quarter of the sky where it belongs, invisible from this north window. The moon is gone, and so is Vida's father.

15

A WHITE FEDORA

Although eleven months have passed since José Nochelobo died, the visit by Deputy Nash Deacon is connected to that tragedy. Vida is not surprised by this. Since that horrific afternoon in front of the courthouse, *everything* that happens in her life is intimately related to that cruel event. The consequences of José's death arrive in little ripples and big waves, and she expects a long time will pass before the last of them washes over her, allowing something good and clean to come her way. Life always eventually offers us a lamp to press back the darkness humanity brought into it so very long ago, a lamp if we are able to see it and seize it; so said her uncle, who had seined her from the sediment of the city.

As the last light of day fades beyond the open kitchen window, she enjoys Parmesan-dusted fettuccini and peas in butter sauce, with a mound of the morels that are among the tastiest of all mushrooms.

In her current mood, Mozart's G Minor Symphony no. 40 is the ideal accompaniment to dinner. She wonders what Lupo thinks of the music if he is nearby in the night and contemplating a visit.

After dinner, she retreats to the library. She wants no more of *Moby-Dick* right now. She returns it to the shelves, perhaps forever, and takes down Emily Brontë's *Wuthering Heights*, which she's read twice, though she has no illusions that the character of Heathcliff can prepare her for the likes of Nash Deacon. She understands the deputy and is well prepared for him.

During chapter 13, she falls asleep in the armchair and dreams of Lupo. She is in Kettleton, where fog has invaded like a portent of a sea that will rise here following a cataclysmic change in the contours of the planet's crust. But for the pale candescence of a full moon, which the fog veils but also transmits faintly into every street and dismal alley, no light burns in the town. All is quiet, as if the residents have been washed away from here and to a mass grave in some terrible abyss. She wants desperately to be in the warmth and safety of her stone house, but the layout of the town isn't as she remembers, and in fact this Kettleton is an inconstant maze that's being continuously reconfigured. She almost cries out for her uncle to help her, to guide her, but she is stricken by the idea that if he answers her and appears, this will prove that she is as dead as he is and can never escape this place. Instead, she hears herself whisper, *"Lupo."* Before she can repeat his name at greater volume, he manifests out of the fog, his lantern eyes aglow with the warmest light she has ever seen.

Wuthering Heights slips off her lap and falls to the floor of the library as she wakes and sits forward in the armchair. He's nearby. She knows, without knowing how she knows, that he's nearby.

She steps into the kitchen, where she has left the window open, but Lupo is not there. She waits. She speaks his name. Still he does not appear.

When he visits, he seems to seek only companionship. He likes to listen to her voice. He will submit to her touch. Sometimes he accepts food, but not always. There have been nights when he sleeps at the foot of her bed for a while, though he's always gone in the morning, as if he was never there.

He seems to know when she is lonely and is aware of those rare moments when anxiety afflicts her, as it does now. Some would say that she anthropomorphizes his behavior, attributing to him human emotions and intentions that he doesn't possess. Those are people who see only the surface of the infinite layers of our laminated reality.

In the hallway, convinced that Lupo waits on the porch, Vida hesitates with her hand on the knob of the front door. If he's out there, she has a special and timely task for him.

She turns to the closet to the left of the door and plucks the white fedora off the shelf above the rod on which her coats hang. She had found it after the fact, when she'd disposed of everything else. She should have thrown it out or burned it. However, there's nothing about the hat that obviously connects it to Belden Bead; it's stylish, yes, in his signature way, but it's not the only one of its kind in the world. No doubt there's DNA on it—loose hairs, sweat, skin oils—that might be damning in a courtroom. Until now, Vida has thought she kept it as a kind of totem, a symbol of her triumph, here to remind her, in times of anxiety, that she is brave and competent in a crisis. Now she wonders if she kept it because she had an unconscious, prescient recognition that a time would come when she would need it as she needs it now. Experience has taught her signs and portents are to be taken seriously.

When she opens the front door, Lupo is on the porch.

16

BLACKBERRIES

She first sees Lupo the previous September, almost three months after José Nochelobo's death.

Because grief is blacker when she's inactive, Vida stays busy to dull the claws of anguish that lacerate her, exhausting herself by day's end in order that she can sleep. On this fateful afternoon, she hikes much farther than she needs to go, to the most distant place where she knows that wild blackberries might be found. She carries a picnic cooler lined with brown paper.

She reaches a ridge where the trees thin out. Past the crest, the land slopes in a long meadow where wild grass has been cropped by bighorn sheep. In the past, she stood here to watch them grazing, either rams or ewes, never males and females at the same time, for they live apart except when they mate in November and December.

They are always alert for bears, wolves, coyotes, and mountain lions. They shy away from people. At the sight of Ogden, they had always galloped, nimble and sure-footed, off the pasture and up a nearby rocky escarpment where few if any predators could follow.

At the moment, no sheep are present because ten wolves have claimed the meadow. Vida has never seen a pack this large before. Six appear to be newborns from the spring, still young enough to stalk one another and tumble about in games that serve as practice for the hunts they will one day join. In fact, sometime in winter, fully grown, some will split off to go exploring and form a pack or packs of their own.

The scent and sight of Vida bring their focus to her, but they study her for less than a minute before they return to their leisure or their play. Had she been Ogden or perhaps anyone else, they would have casually retreated from open ground and into the trees, with an air of prudence rather than fear.

The most interesting individual in the pack is obviously its leader, whom she decides on the spot to name Lupo. He is big, more than two feet tall at the withers, surely five and a half feet from point of shoulder to point of butt. He must weigh a hundred eighty pounds or more. She knows he is the leader because he holds his head higher than the others do, and his tail is straight up whenever he observes her.

Aside from his great beauty, the most interesting thing about Lupo is that he is apparently half wolf, half German shepherd, yet occupies the highest position of respect, which makes him something of a mystery if not a miracle. The others are typical gray wolves, with coats of gray, white, black, and brown hairs. Lupo's coat has some gray, a little white, but is mostly black and wheat gold. His broad skull and wedge-shaped muzzle are of equal length, so his face is less pointed than those of the others; his ears are set higher and are more erect than his pack mates' ears.

The wild loops of fruited brambles continue for about a hundred yards along the high end of the meadow, often fully exposed but also tangled through flourishing goat's beard and fireweed and grass. In addition to large game like deer and bighorn sheep, wolves eat small mammals, birds, fish, snakes, frogs, insects—and fruit. Armed with many thorns, these berried vines defend against most creatures of the wild, and even birds harvest less because the plants do not offer a sturdy perch. Therefore, the berries are fat and ripe and plentiful.

Vida's intention is to pile the fruit on the paper lining in the cooler; instead, she removes the paper and sets it aside. Having pulled on nitrile gloves to guard against purple fingers, she fills the eight-quart cooler. As she carries the container and paper into the meadow, the wolves fall still and intently watch her.

Although she knew why she took the lining from the cooler, she is nonetheless mildly surprised when she puts the brown paper on the ground and pours the berries onto it. She returns to the vines and kneels there and watches the wolves.

Lupo is the first to approach the offering. His black nose works its many muscles. He lifts his head and stares at her. His eyes are bright with intelligence. He smells the berries again and then eats a portion of them. As if by psychic invitation from their leader, the younger wolves come forward two at a time, and after them the elders. They have no knowledge of math other than whatever sense of proportionality instinct provides them, yet each takes what seems to be a fair share, as though there is a respected pack rule against gluttony at the expense of others.

As Vida watches them, she can't easily formulate a satisfying explanation of why she has given them this bounty. Eventually she decides, *I do this for you because I am powerless to do anything for my lost parents, my uncle, or José Nochelobo.* That is true, but it is not the full truth, which will be revealed to her only in time.

17

WOLVES

Past midnight, having left both *Wuthering Heights* and the dreams of a ghost town that haunted her nap in a library armchair, Vida steps onto the front porch where Lupo is waiting. He sits at the head of the steps, alert, her friend since she fed him and his pack wild berries eight months earlier.

Although he could have leaped through the kitchen window that she left open for him, he presumes to enter the house only when she is awake. She can't explain how he knows when she's sleeping or why he respects her privacy on those occasions. The connection between them is more than the human-canine bond; it's a covenant so precious to her, of such a mysterious—even mystical—nature, she is loath to question or analyze it, out of concern that to do so would diminish the strange but comforting allegiance that has formed between them.

She had last seen him three weeks earlier, on the alluvial field, where he visited while she worked the earth for her living. As always, he came with his pack, which then numbered five. Some of the nine that once followed him evidently had gone off to form another pack, though it was likely that a couple females remained with him and were in the dens they had made, sheltering with their offspring until the newborn pups opened their eyes after two weeks and became confident of their footing in three.

Now, as ravelings of clouds seem to test the blade of the moon, Lupo's companions are nowhere to be seen, although they are surely nearby, concealed and watching. Lupo remains sitting, neither prostrating himself nor exposing his belly while the other wolves can see him. In the house, in Vida's domain, he will invite a tummy rub and a cuddle, but never in the wild.

"I am so pleased to see you," Vida says.

His tail sweeps the porch floor.

"I was dreaming of you just a minute ago. Can a dream draw you to me?"

His tail moves, but slower, and he cocks his head inquiringly.

"What do I think? I think it can. Maybe especially now, when I'm in some trouble."

Lupo's tail quiets, and he gets to his feet.

She feels not in the least foolish when she describes her situation to this creature. "There's this man, Nash Deacon. I can deal with him, but I need to know for sure what he knows."

She holds out the white fedora once worn by Belden Bead, and Lupo comes forward to sniff it.

"Can this man be found?" she asks.

Lupo meets her stare. His eyes seem to offer not only depths to be explored, but also realms other than the kingdom of wolves in which he is a prince.

"What do you think, Lupo? Can this man be found?"

After tipping his head back and flaring his nostrils to test the air, he turns and pads down the porch steps.

As the cricket chorus ceases celebration of the night, Vida follows Lupo across the area that she regularly mows and then along the path to the center of the meadow, where her uncle lies beneath a granite monument. During this part of the search, the lord of the wolves keeps his nose close to the ground, like a myopic scholar with face pressed near the faded pages of an ancient volume, the better to study an account of a lost moment in history.

Lupo circles the gravestone, head raised now, surveying the moonlit meadow. With Vida following, he moves south, eventually crosses the dirt driveway, and wades into another expanse of tall grass.

The night, which seemed mild when they had been on the porch, feels colder now—as though, by an inversion of the laws of physics, the thermonuclear stars in their infinitude have begun to chill the universe. Vida shivers as the wolf moves inexorably toward what she has asked him to find.

When Lupo stops and turns and looks up at her, the crescents of ice in his eyes are reflections of the moon.

Even after eight months, there has been no subsidence of the soil, for she had been sure to compact it well. The grass has fully recovered from the excavation.

Considering how swiftly Lupo has located this interment, Vida imagines it will be even more easily found by a cadaver dog trained to smell and seek human remains. Nash Deacon, being a sheriff's deputy, might have brought such an animal onto her property when Vida was at the alluvial field or elsewhere.

Eight months earlier, there was no enforcer of the law to whom she could turn for help or exoneration. Nor does any law now exist that serves the likes of her, other than the natural law by which she lives and by which the world is ordered and healed, if sometimes slowly, through the passage of time. Her problem is that she must live moment to moment, and her next crisis is fast approaching.

When she follows Lupo out of the unmown grass, his loyal pack of five is waiting on the unpaved driveway, their coats silvered by moonlight and their interest attested by animal eyeshine. He leads them single file toward the house, and Vida follows.

She sits in a rocking chair, and the wolves lie contentedly on the porch, with Lupo at the head of the steps, so that he can survey the meadow where crickets are in chorus again. On a few occasions, Vida has given the wolves treats other than blackberries. She has nothing to give them now, and they want only companionship. They breathe in the night and all its fragrant information. They sigh and yawn. Some snore, but they don't all sleep at the same time, because they are by nature prudent sentinels. One sleeper sometimes whimpers or even issues a cry of distress, but the others have good dreams, which they signify only by thumping their tails on the floorboards. Vida finds their contentment comforting.

When she wakes hours later, the night is gradually retreating from the blush of dawn, and the wolves are gone.

18

THE UNDERTAKER'S DAUGHTER

The previous year, one week after the July Fourth holiday and three weeks following José Nochelobo's death, Vida is sitting on the porch, reading Thomas Merton's *The Seven Storey Mountain*. Twilight is pending when the approaching growl of an engine causes her to look up from the page. A well-maintained vintage motorcycle, a Big Dog Bulldog Bagger, a touring bike with wide-swept fairing and large saddlebags, swings off the driveway and rolls to a stop on the lawn.

The biker puts down the kickstand, leaves her helmet on the Big Dog, and comes to the foot of the steps. She's twentysomething, a fresh-faced blonde with eyes the purple blue of polished fluorite. Vida has seen her before, but she can't remember when or where.

"I'm Anna Lagare. My father, Herbert, owns the funeral home. I'd have called ahead, but I don't know of any number for you."

"Hardly anyone does. Come on up."

When Anna Lagare is settled in the second rocking chair, she says, "It's beautiful here. All anyone might ever need."

"More than enough," Vida agrees. "It fills you up."

The visitor looks at the palms of her hands. They appear clean, yet she wipes the left across the right, the right across the left. She has a fey quality, as if she's been compelled to come here under a spell and waits now for her purpose to be revealed to her. After a hesitation, she says, "My dad prepared José Nochelobo's body."

"And ten years ago, he prepared my uncle's."

Anna Lagare is as direct as she is soft-spoken. "You didn't come to the viewing."

"No."

The visitor looks up from her hands. "Later, I saw you at the cemetery service when José . . . when he was lowered."

"I could deal with the casket when it was closed."

Anna hugs herself, hands hidden between her arms and torso. "People say he was so happy, how it was between the two of you."

Vida puts her book aside on the small table between chairs.

Nodding as if they have just agreed about something, Anna focuses beyond the porch, on her motorcycle. The touring bike's saddlebags must be full, because a suitcase is strapped to the back half of the saddle. "You think everything's fine, moving along nice and comfortable, then something happens and you see the truth, and you don't even recognize where you are."

"What is it you don't recognize?"

"Kettleton, for one thing. It's not the same, is it?"

"No."

"It never will be again, will it?"

"No."

"It was never before a place that was first about money. Even if I felt safe here, it's not what I want anymore. I'm leaving. I have this friend in Texas, in this town that's not small but not so big, either. She says it's more the way things used to be."

Intuition has Vida on a high wire, balanced in a stasis between steps, eager to know but afraid to anticipate what might be coming. The past and future are gathered in this moment, the past to be explained, the future to form out of that explanation.

After a silence, Anna says, "There's nothing you can do about it. Nothing that wouldn't bring hell down on you."

"Do about what?"

"If I were you, I'd want to know, even if there was nothing I could do about it. Just to get on with life, I'd want to know. And so I wouldn't trust the wrong people, wouldn't unknowingly put my affairs in the hands of the people who did it."

"Who? Who did what?"

"Just so you understand, if you think you can do anything about it, you'll be crushed."

"Tell me, Anna."

"You're nothing to them. Promise me."

To get the woman to continue, Vida says, "I promise. I've already been crushed. I don't want any more."

"So then, you know my father is also the county coroner."

"Yes."

"He performed the autopsy on José Nochelobo."

"Yes."

"Except he didn't."

Wait without thought, Vida told herself, *for you are not ready for thought.*

"The EMTs brought the body at ten minutes until five that afternoon," Anna continues, "and Dad signed for it. I was preparing to help him. I don't do autopsies, but I'm a licensed mortician. While I was getting the instruments ready, he began examining the subject, starting with the neck injury. He always talks as he works, recording what he finds. Suddenly he went quiet and covered the corpse. The deceased. I'm sorry. José. Dad covered José and said he was too important to the town, too well thought of, for us to do anything but a careful postmortem. He wanted to find the EMTs who handled the body, talk to them. Dad said it had been a long day, he was too tired to do the job justice. He wheeled José into the cold-holding room and delayed the autopsy till morning."

Vida waits. The shadows are growing longer, the air cooler, the sky a deeper blue in the east.

Anna's hands appear from under her arms and slide slowly from her shoulders to her elbows to her shoulders, up and down, up and down, as though she's cold and trying to warm herself. Her attention remains on the bike. Clearly, this woman doesn't want to be here. She is eager to hit the road. In spite of her youth, however, she seems to lack the modern mindset that would allow her to start a new life by leaving her current one as a participant in a lie.

"My father's not a medical examiner, just the coroner, but he follows the rules of evidence. I never touch the . . . the subject of an autopsy. Except to help my father turn over the person on the table. But this was José. I mean, my senior year, he was my history teacher, before he was principal. All the kids liked him. I had, you know, a bit of a crush on him. He was so young, gone so suddenly. It was shocking, and my father's behavior was odd, and *it was José*—so when I was alone, I went into the cold-holding room and pulled back the shroud."

Anna needs a moment.

Vida waits.

"I looked at his face," Anna continues. "I turned his head, like my father had turned it, and I saw what my father must have seen. The wound."

Vida repeats, "The wound." Those two words have a taste like when she has sucked on a paper cut.

"It must have been an air rifle," Anna says. "Not a pellet gun. It was a puncture wound, like from a needle."

"A hypodermic needle?"

"Yeah. The wound had self-sealed. It could easily have been overlooked, except that the impact had enough velocity to rupture capillaries, which immediately bled into surrounding tissue. There was a bruise as big as a dime, with a little dot at the center."

This news implies a conspiracy so grotesque that Vida might not believe it if the messenger were anyone other than this soft-voiced woman whose distress is evident but tightly controlled. At the same time, in the deepest turning of the nautilus that is her mind, she has suspected his death wasn't the freak accident it had seemed to be. José was charismatic, an effective organizer, a born leader, with the hard truth on his side—and therefore a threat to certain powerful individuals. "You're saying a tranquilizer dart, like they use with wild animals."

"Like that but different. If they meant to kill him, it won't have been a tranquilizer. A toxin of some kind, maybe a fast-acting nerve agent."

"Do you hear yourself?"

Anna meets Vida's eyes. "Yeah. And I scare myself. I know so little, and yet I know too much."

"If there was a hypodermic dart, does your father have it?"

"Probably not. It penetrated the muscles that surround the cervical vertebrae. José probably lost the use of his legs in a para-plegic spasm. The dart maybe came loose when he fell. Came loose, was trampled, broken, swept aside in the chaos."

"Or snatched up and pocketed by someone in the know," Vida says. "By another speaker on the stage."

"Anything is possible now," Anna says, and it seems that her fluorite eyes are growing less blue, becoming a darker purple.

No longer able to sit still, Vida thrusts up from the rocking chair. She has nowhere to go. She stands by the railing, staring toward her uncle's gravestone. "I was there. I didn't hear a shot."

"An air rifle is very quiet."

"Where was the shooter?"

"Had to be behind José. But if it was someone on the steps, others would have seen who did it."

Vida agrees. "So it was someone in the courthouse."

"It wasn't anyone from Kettleton," Anna says. "With an adapted air rifle of that kind, one shot so precisely placed—the shooter had to be a professional and one hell of a marksman."

Another thought occurs to Vida. "The shot was timed to make it appear that José lost his balance when he was hit by the bottles of water those kids threw. They were part of it. Or were used without knowing they were being used."

That realization leads to another more terrible. Before Vida can voice it, her visitor rises from the rocking chair. "Oh, God."

As darkness slowly suffuses the eastern sky, as sunset paints the waning day coral pink and gamboge gold, the white mountain lion, she whom they call Azrael, comes out of the tall grass to the south and pauses on the driveway to assess the meadow, the house, and the women on the porch.

19

NEWS OF THE DEAD

Here in this dismal July, with José not yet gone a full month, as Vida stands on her porch with Anna Lagare, she can't help but think that, if the manifestation of the albino mountain lion is an omen of death impending, the warning has come too late. José is in his grave, and no massive rock will be rolled from it, nor will a fiercely radiant celestial being announce a resurrection.

The big cat's body is sleek, her legs muscular, face flat, ears cupped alertly. Her long tail has thick fur and is heavy and serves to balance her when she's stalking, running, leaping, climbing. Her sharp, hooked claws are retracted into her soft, padded paws, but they can spring forth and gut her prey in an instant, though her kind tend to kill with one well-aimed bite of their powerful jaws. Her glossy white fur seems luminescent in the gathering twilight.

Vida's uncle taught her much about mountain lions and cats in general, that she might have the proper respect for them. She does not worship Nature itself or any creature in it, as the Egyptians, four thousand years earlier, worshipped a cat goddess among other deities. In that far place and time, when a house cat died, the family members sheared off their hair to express their grief. They usually mummified the cat, and often mummified mice to entomb with it, so that it might have food in the next life.

Vida is in such awe of the massive albino creature that she understands how people can attribute supernatural powers to such a being, especially in a time when they feel the institutions they rely on are failing them. It's human and sane to want peace and to yearn for transcendence in this world of war and insistent nihilism.

"She's just a mountain lion," Anna says. "For all the stories about her, she's just a mountain lion."

From the tone in which that statement is made, Vida concludes that Anna won't feel safe until she is on the road. In fact, she might suspect that even the sweet town in Texas might not be far enough to ensure her safety from the forces at work in Kettleton. Whether she wants to or not, she sees before her an omen.

The great beast proceeds to the center of the lawn and peers along the path toward Uncle Ogden's grave. Following a hesitation, with no further interest in this property, she continues northward, into meadow that has not been mowed. As the previously coral-and-gold sky now likens itself to a blazing furnace, as the summer-paled grass appears to burn with a fire that fails to consume it, Azrael doesn't just recede into the distance but seems to deliquesce into the twilight, a shape of white mist that evaporates into the gloom.

Vida returns to the realization that occurred to her after she concluded that the bottle-throwing kids were enlisted in the assault on José whether they knew it or not. "Did he really break his neck?"

Still looking after the vanished mountain lion, Anna says, "When I saw the puncture wound, I didn't examine him any further. The EMT who got to him first said his neck was at an impossible angle, but that's just something he said."

"Possibly something he was paid to say."

"Possibly. A heart attack wouldn't be right for a man as young as José. Nobody would believe suicide. Any accident—a fall down the cellar stairs, a house fire—would be suspicious. But if an accident occurred in front of a thousand witnesses, who would question it?"

Vida gives voice to her latest insight: "If it was murder, they needed the fall to hide the truth. If a nerve toxin killed him, they had to be sure he didn't simply drop to the stage, but took a more dramatic tumble. When the dart hit him, someone on the stage must have put a hand on his back, pretending to steady him, but shoving him toward the stairs. The dime-size bruise could be dismissed as a consequence of the fall—unless someone looked too close."

Anna continues to stare at the forest that received the lion into its boughed and ferny gloom.

"Will you be all right?" Vida asks.

"I don't like myself right now—being scared. But it would be worse to stay here and pretend things are like they always were."

"If your father didn't perform the postmortem, then he must have falsified the autopsy report."

"When I found the puncture, I went down the hall to his office. Door was closed. I heard him on the phone, arguing with someone. He sounded more afraid than angry. He kept saying Aubrey this and Aubrey that. Only man I know by that name is Aubrey Norland."

As the crimson light retreats and the sky darkles, the air is no colder, but Vida is chilled. "José's attorney."

"My father wanted Norland to forge some document showing José specified cremation. My father was part of this vicious business, but he hadn't thought what might happen. Now he began to wonder how long a nerve toxin might be detectable in the flesh of the deceased. Weeks? Months? Years? From what I heard, Aubrey Norland refused the request and assured my father that no one would exhume the body."

Anna moves to the head of the porch steps, beyond which the land—and more than the land—is fast fading into darkness. Though she has a friend and a destination in Texas, she looks lost.

"Your dad is well respected," Vida says. "On the town council. President of the local Better Business Bureau. Why would he involve himself in something as terrible as this?"

"He's made a nice living, doing what his father did before him, but he's never happy. He's distant, keeps himself to himself, so I don't really know him. But one thing I *do* know is he always wanted something more, bigger, better. Maybe he didn't even know what that was, but as the years went by, especially after Mom died, he wanted it with growing desperation. Suddenly Kettleton isn't a backwater anymore. It becomes a center of action, an ocean of money washing up around it. Some saw how they could scoop up buckets of it. This kind of money doesn't just buy cooperation. It buys souls."

Vida says, "José never accused any of them of being bought, never so much as implied it. He based his case entirely on facts."

"Yeah, but to some people, the truth is a gun to their heads."

"I'm so sorry," Vida says. "This isn't easy for you."

"Whatever else he's been," Anna says, "he was my dad. But now."

"I'm sorry," Vida says again, at a loss for words.

"I can't look at him anymore."

Anna descends the porch steps, and Vida follows her to the motorcycle. "How many people were involved in this?"

"I don't know. And you don't want to know. Just stay away from Aubrey Norland. I felt I had to warn you. In fact, stay away from town, like you did before José. Make your life here."

Vida persists. "The boys who threw the bottles weren't charged with even just a misdemeanor."

"If charges had been brought, even as juveniles, there would be a court proceeding. They couldn't risk an investigation, testimony under oath, none of that. So it had to be that this was just boys being boys, didn't mean to hurt anyone, basically good kids, sorry as hell for the prank they pulled, no reason to ruin their lives."

As Anna pulls on her helmet, Vida says, "Seems the district attorney must be one of them, maybe the sheriff."

"There's no way of knowing. It's not everyone in Kettleton. It's a small group. But no way to know who's corrupt, who isn't."

Vida persists. "At the graveside service, somebody said one of those boys is Morgan Slyke. He lives with his parents on Long Valley Road, ten or twelve miles from town. Goes to Long Valley High."

Reflected in the face shield of the helmet, the last crimson light in the sky masks this woman's face and confers on her a new and less lovely identity, as though she isn't just a mortician but instead some blood-smeared Presence that has come from the far shore of a river where gondolas carry passengers in only one direction and gondoliers like her pole their way back to this world alone.

"Yeah. And another of those boys, Damon Orbach, is the son of Perry Orbach, largest landowner in the county. Don't be stupid, Vida. Nothing you do will bring José back. With billions of dollars on the line, there's no justice except the kind that can be bought."

Vida says, "Truth can't be repressed forever. It'll come out."

"But if it does, most people will still believe what isn't true, because the truth is heavy to carry compared to the lightness of a lie." Anna reaches into a pocket of her jacket. "I don't know what this means." She withdraws a folded slip of white paper. "I considered not giving this to you. I came here only to warn you not to trust anyone. I don't want to inspire you to do anything foolish. But it was in the pocket of the shirt José was wearing that day. It was his . . . and he was yours . . . and so."

Vida unfolds the five-by-six-inch piece of notepad paper and reads the eight words, which are not in José's handwriting: " . . . two moon sun spirit below the smoking river." She looks up at her visitor, whose face is still invisible behind the reflected sunset. "What does this mean?"

Anna says, "I've asked around. Discreetly. Rings no bells for anyone. Maybe it doesn't mean anything."

"No. It means something," Vida says, for the words hearken back to some enigmatic advice she was given a long time ago.

"Maybe it would be better if you decided it doesn't."

The bloody light slides off the face shield as Anna Lagare swings aboard the motorcycle, yet still she seems to have no face. As she starts the engine, all that's visible within the helmet are two pale crescents that partly define sockets that seem eyeless.

As she drives away, a single headlight guides her along the dirt lane, across the meadow, away into a world gone wrong.

20

THE BOX AND THE ATLAS

After Anna Lagare is gone, Vida takes the yellow gift-wrapped box from the closet and holds it as she sits on the edge of the bed.

Embossed in script, the words *Happy Birthday* flow in ordered lines across the package.

It's been in her possession two weeks. Intuition tells her that it's not an ordinary gift. Now is not the time to open it. An inner voice not her own says, *Every ending is a beginning, but this is a beginning on which you're not yet prepared to embark.*

She smooths one finger along the midnight-blue ribbon to where it ravels into a bow. Some days it seems her life is *unraveling*, but she refuses to pursue that indulgent line of thought. That is not the kind of woman she wants to be or has ever been.

José hadn't fallen in love with a woman capable of wallowing in self-pity and victimhood. Dignity is a consequence of perseverance, persistence, endurance. She intends to remain the woman he loved, and avoid all temptations to become someone else.

She returns the package to the closet.

Smoking river. The collection in the library includes books of state history, a keen interest of her uncle. Among those volumes, a thick atlas contains hundreds of maps, each with an index. None of the handwritten words on the scrap of paper Anna found in José's shirt pocket is capitalized. However, "smoking river" suggests a watercourse, and "two moons" might be a small town, a campground, something. However, hours of poring through the indexes fails to reward her with a revelation or even the faintest clue.

Long ago, a woman of strange power had warned her, "Moon, sun, and smoking river. To chase the meaning of those words will put you at great risk. Be patient, and the meaning will come to you, for that is who you are. All things come to you in their time."

21

THE SUITOR

On this Wednesday eleven months following José's death, less than twenty-four hours since Nash Deacon told Vida that he expects her submission, after she's slept in the rocking chair while wolves shared the porch and has awakened to find them gone, she's too tense to continue shaping the cat's-eye chrysoberyl that she'd previously sawn flat. Such work requires focus and patience.

She isn't going to sit waiting for Deacon's return, because to do so would be a kind of submission. She doesn't intend to submit to him in any way whatsoever. He might not come today, perhaps not even tomorrow. He's Machiavellian enough to torment her by delaying. She won't waste her days in the expectation of his return, while hour by hour her nerves grow as taut as violin strings. She must stay busy.

Although she wouldn't usually return to the placer mine for two weeks, she sets out with a can of bear spray holstered on her hip and two bottles of cold water in a small cooler. The early-morning forest is full of birdsong, a tapestry of woven light and shadow.

On her approach, squirrels spring up the fissured bark of tree trunks, not to the safety of high perches, but only far enough to watch her with interest as she passes.

In this deep shade, knotted cranesbill thrives, as do Bethlehem sage and pulmonaria. Among the dark-green leaves and white flowers of wake-robin, a red fox is foraging. Alert to Vida, it follows her with grave curiosity, wending through beds of toadshade, white baneberry, and ferns, among the last of which it vanishes.

With a shovel at the alluvial field and with a seining pan at the river's edge, she passes five hours. The first three reward her with nothing other than the benefits of exercise, but in the last two hours, she pans three important gemstones that, over centuries if not millennia, have weathered out of the rock that imprisoned them. Being crystals of corundum, which is natural aluminum oxide, they are therefore sapphires, but with one difference. Gem-quality corundum crystals come in a rainbow of colors; however, when a pink sapphire contains enough chromium to make it red, it is called a ruby. In the rough, these three rubies are so large that each might, when properly cut, provide a gem in excess of ten carats.

After cleaning up the excavation and burying her gear as usual, before heading home, she hunkers at water's edge and wets each of her finds in the river and holds it in the palm of her hand to study it not merely for what can be seen, but also for what it makes her *feel.* Her uncle used to call this "Vidanalysis." At first he'd used the term teasingly, but later with wonder and respect. Even at this early stage, by some mysterious power of perception that even Vida can't explain, she nearly always intuits the potential of any rough gemstone. In addition to the finished weight in carats, three things affect the value of a gem: color, clarity, and cut. She's convinced that all three of these big beauties will prove to be rich in color and of purest clarity. She will not make an error in the cutting.

She's been given great value for her work, and she's grateful. If there are such things as signs and portents, then three large, bright rubies might be interpreted as a promise that for every dark figure who enters her life, such as Nash Deacon, light will be provided to her three times over.

When Vida arrives home and unlocks the two deadbolts and lets herself inside, she goes directly to her workroom. She places the three gemstones in a drawer where the compartments in the sorting grid are lined with white velvet.

A day of labor leaves her in need of a hot shower, but first she steps into the kitchen to get a bottle of tea from the fridge.

In the center of the dining table stands a white bowl holding a dozen red roses artfully arranged with delicate ferns, the product of a well-trained florist. Nash Deacon has been here.

22

THE FORTUNETELLER

Vida is ten years old when a raven-haired woman pays Vance Burkhardt cash in advance for three months' rent and moves into a ramshackle house that stands on his property, directly across the county road from the entrance to Ogden's eighty acres. This tenant—always in canary-yellow tennis shoes and an immaculate white robe with a hood—glides around like the ghost of someone pleased to be dead and engaged in a happy haunting. She drives a battered white Volkswagen bus on each side of which are painted the same words in elegant calligraphy: *Look with kindness on those who suffer, who struggle against difficulties, who drink unceasingly the bitterness of this life.* She pounds two tall iron stakes into the front yard and strings between them a sapphire-blue cloth banner decorated with crescent moons and silver stars, bearing seven intriguing words in coppery script: *The truth and the future revealed here.*

Three days in a row, Vida walks to the end of Ogden's private lane and sits in the grass beside the road, where yellow butterflies perform a silent aerobatic ballet. She watches as county folks visit the fortuneteller with surprising frequency.

On the fourth day, Vida crosses the highway and climbs the steps to the porch where the woman sits. "How much do you charge for the truth and the future?"

"At your age," the woman replies, "you haven't yet forgotten the truth. You don't need me to remind you of it."

That response requires some consideration before Vida knows what to ask next.

The lady is lovely. The most striking—and mysterious—thing about her is that her age can't be determined, at least not when her hood is raised. She might be twenty or nearly fifty or past sixty. She seems to be a different age at different moments, as if she has lived a life of such importance that three significant periods of her journey are represented with equal force in her countenance. That's an odd thought for a girl of ten, and Vida doesn't voice it.

Instead, she says, "Well, I didn't come to hear what truth you know. I'm sure you know a lot, and it's really interesting stuff. But what I'm wondering is how much it costs to have my future told."

The woman closes the book she's been reading, puts it on her lap, and lays both hands on it. She leans forward and smiles. "I charge whatever you value least."

This is proving more difficult than Vida expected. "You mean like . . . a penny?"

"I don't work for money, dear. Unless that's what you value least. But don't bring me what you think I want. Whatever you can agreeably do without, that casts a shadow on your happiness—bring me that. Or if it's a thing you can't carry, shed yourself of it by sharing its name, and in return I'll tell your future."

"I'll need to think about this," Vida says.

"Yes, dear, I would advise that you do."

Vida descends the porch steps and then turns to the woman. "Mr. Burkhardt told my uncle you rented this place for three months. So you'll be here tomorrow when I come back?"

"One thing does seem to suggest the other."

"Mr. Burkhardt says he doesn't know your name."

"This isn't much of a house. There's little that I could do to damage it. Mr. Burkhardt is charging twice the usual rent because I prefer to provide no ID. He puts great value in cash up front."

"Why wouldn't you tell him your name?"

"I tell no one my name. Some know it without being told. Others would be frightened to hear it or would think me quite insane if I told them."

"*Are* you insane?"

"I'll leave that for you to decide after our third encounter."

"Well, but I'll only be coming back tomorrow."

"No, dear. Twice more."

"Oh. I guess you know because you can see the future."

"Past, present, and future are one. To know the first two is to know the third."

"Well, okay," says Vida, and she finds herself on the far side of the county road, heading home.

23

SNAPSHOT

A live rattlesnake—a beheaded bird, a pile of excrement—would not have alarmed Vida more than do the roses on the kitchen table. They constitute a smug announcement of a courtship to which she'll never consent and as well declare that Deacon already has power over her that cannot be resisted.

Having entered by the front door where both deadbolts had been engaged, she goes now to the back door and confirms those two locks are likewise secure. He can't have entered through one of the narrow casement panes. Nevertheless, Vida tours the house, checking windows one by one; all are intact.

She doesn't expect to find him lurking here. He's not going to be rash and force himself on her this soon. He enjoys psychological games and believes that by such torment he can, over time, unnerve her, break her spirit, and take control of her. Judging by all the available evidence, he has practiced his techniques on other women, and he's one of those men for whom having power over his partner is perhaps more satisfying than the sex itself.

The bathroom window is louvered and small, eighteen inches wide and a foot high, offering no ingress to anyone, but she finishes her search there.

On the counter next to the sink, she keeps a convenient dental-care organizer that holds her toothbrush, a stack of paper cups, and a small bottle of mouthwash. This white ceramic piece is designed to accommodate two brushes, and for the first time since her uncle's death ten years earlier, a second one is upright in its slot.

In the sink are thick gouts of brittle green foam, spat-out toothpaste that has been there long enough to dry. Vida's brand is white, not green. She opens the mirrored medicine cabinet. The only item he's added is a tube of his toothpaste.

From the cabinet under the sink, she extracts a roll of paper towels and a can of Lysol. She washes away the green foam. As she disinfects the sink, countertop, and toilet, a warmth rises in her face exceeding what she felt while digging for gemstones.

He has not only violated her house. He has also staked a claim to territory in her mind from which he can't be easily evicted. He intends to deny her peace, to undermine her self-confidence and self-respect. He won't succeed.

After wrapping his toothpaste and brush in used paper towels, she drops them in the waste can beside the vanity. In the morning, she'll collect trash from throughout the house and make her once-a-week drive to the county dump.

She returns to the entrance to the kitchen and stands staring at the flowers on the table. She is trembling not with fear but with indignation.

She should have anticipated this. Deacon is a deputy sheriff. Police agencies have battery-powered devices that can open the best deadbolts in an emergency; there are laws defining when such lock-release guns can be used, but Deacon is not a lawman who abides by the law.

A small white envelope is fixed to a plastic stake inserted in the floral arrangement. She wants to throw it away without opening it, but if he's been foolish enough to leave a handwritten note, it's evidence that she should preserve.

Instead, the envelope contains a snapshot. It's a picture of Belden Bead, alive and grinning, he who in fact lies in the grave that she dug with the backhoe eight months earlier, that Lupo found just last night after being offered Bead's scent on the white fedora.

24

THE BIRD ASSASSIN

During the summer of the previous year, after Anna Lagare goes off to Texas on her Big Dog Bulldog motorcycle, Vida gives a lot of thought to whether or not she has a realistic chance to act against the powerful individuals who have conspired to shape the future of Kettleton to the ends that most lavishly enrich them. She's reached the conclusion that the way before her is narrow and perilous, but not hopeless. She must proceed with great caution, both to protect herself and to avoid putting anyone else in jeopardy.

At the cemetery on the day José was buried, she'd overheard one mourner telling another that one of the teenagers who'd thrown those bottles of water, Morgan Slyke, lived eleven miles out of town, on Long Valley Road. A month after Anna's revelations, Vida drives ten miles from the Kettleton city limits before beginning to check the names on mailboxes.

The Slyke family's white clapboard house with columned porch is well maintained but of no particular style, likewise the three-bay detached garage. Encircled by white ranch fencing, the property encompasses two or three acres of meadows.

Across the road from their residence, the land is undeveloped. Grassy hills roll up to a woodland of red oaks. On still higher ground, the evergreen forest commences.

At home once more, Vida consults her maps of the hiking trails that wind through the county. She discovers that a forest-service road will bring her to the first ridgeline of pines, about a hundred yards above where the red oaks surrender dominance.

Over the next two weeks, Monday through Friday, setting out just before dawn, Vida drives her 1950 Ford F-1 pickup along that unpaved lane, stretches of hardpan alternating with gravelstone. The half-hour journey begins in darkness and proceeds through feathery shadows branching off quills of early sunlight. After parking among the trees, she crosses the ridge on foot, descends through ranks of pines, and settles in the discreet shade of the oaks.

She has an excellent view of the distant Slyke residence that stands on the far side of Long Valley Road, and she pulls it close with high-power binoculars. Gradually she establishes the family's routine. On weekdays, at 7:15, a man of about forty leaves in a white Ford Explorer, heading toward Kettleton. Fifteen minutes later, a woman of a similar age, wearing what appear to be pale-green medical scrubs, leaves in a Honda, also bound for Kettleton.

The sixteen-year-old son, Morgan, is the only one left at the house until his parents come home from work. The kid doesn't have a summer job but spends the days on chores such as mowing the lawn and painting the ranch fencing. The pace at which he works suggests indolence is a strata in the bedrock of his character. Most days, he puts a beach towel on the front lawn and sunbathes in nothing but a pair of bikini briefs, sometimes also toning himself with dumbbells and wrist weights. Vida pegs him as an exhibitionist.

On both Mondays, the kid seems to be occupied with in-house chores and doesn't come out until between two and three o'clock in the afternoon. For more than an hour, Vida watches him use a .22 rifle to shoot birds in flight, mostly crows but also hawks. Little bursts of feathers spray like small, black fireworks. Wings swoon, and bodies plummet. When he is sated with killing, he scours the property for dead birds, gathering them a half dozen at a time and carrying them to the woods behind the residence, where he tosses them away among the trees, perhaps because his parents would not approve of such slaughter.

Once Vida has established the family's routine, she parks on the shoulder of Long Valley Road, a quarter mile from the Slyke house, and waits for the father to go to work. Remaining at a distance, she follows him into Kettleton, to the county power-and-water authority, where he parks in one of the spaces reserved for employees. The sign that heads his slot bears the name RANDALL SLYKE.

The next morning, she follows the mother to the offices of Dr. William Polk, who is one of the town's three dentists. Mrs. Slyke's medical scrubs suggest she's a dental assistant or a hygienist.

Vida takes a weekend to decide how to approach the boy when he's home alone. He's tall, lithe, muscular, and looks more like nineteen than sixteen. If he's an idle narcissist assailed by violent fantasies, if he kills in excess of twenty birds in a single shooting session as a means of relieving the pressure of those dark desires, he might be dangerous should she press his psycho button.

She doesn't want to harm Morgan Slyke, but Anna Lagare's visit has left Vida needing to know the truth, even if she can never act on it to obtain justice. If a conversation with the boy proves to be perilous, that's all right. She has her own strengths, and her ways. Come Monday, she will give him a chance to prove he's righteous.

25

BAR THE DOOR

With her visit to Morgan Slyke, on a Monday in August, more than nine months earlier, Vida unexpectedly became vulnerable to Belden Bead, the closest thing this rural county had to a gang boss. Now the consequence of her encounter with Bead, eight months ago, has put her under the thumb of Nash Deacon. Or so he thinks.

Red roses are a lover's gift, but the photo of Belden Bead is a rapist's threat. Deacon means to say, *I know where his body lies, and though you and I will enjoy a creepy romantic courtship because it titillates me, the outcome is already determined. When I am ready to have you, then you will submit to everything I demand.*

Using the long-neck butane match with which she lights candles for her dinner table, she sets fire to the picture of Bead, burns it in the kitchen sink, and washes the ashes down the drain.

After pouring the water out of the floral arrangement, she drops the roses into the plastic bag lining the kitchen trash can.

She goes to the cellar, where steel shelving units hold a year's worth of canned and freeze-dried food against the day when foolish politicians might precipitate a food shortage. Famines are seldom the fault of nature, nearly always the consequence of either human idiocy or a sinister intention to use starvation as a weapon.

At least for the short term, she intends to carry a handgun. Her uncle's rifle, shotgun, and pistol are in appropriate cases, atop one of these shelves. Or they were. Deacon has been in the house long enough to discover the weapons, and confiscate them.

He could return while she's showering. Or sleeping.

Installing new deadbolts will provide no security. A police lock-release gun is the ultimate passkey.

In the smaller building behind the house, where the pickup is parked and the propane-fueled generator labors, her uncle Ogden's workbench and tools await her. Because of the skills he taught her, Vida has been able to attend to everything that needs to be repaired.

Here also is an uncommon weapon, concealed behind the supply of lumber and plywood that she uses for various projects. Days after Anna Lagare's visit, Vida dreamed of the fortuneteller whom she'd met long ago. In the dream, she'd been told to acquire this thing. That nameless woman is to her an oracle, and she doesn't question such instructions. She had driven out of state to make the purchase at a shop where no ID was required. She had since practiced for hundreds of hours and had become a master marksman. At the moment, she needs only to assure herself that the weapon is still where she's hidden it, and it is. Nash Deacon has not found it.

From her supply of lumber and plywood, she selects an eight-foot-long birch two-by-four. She locks it in the pair of woodworking vises at opposite ends of the workbench. With a handheld circular saw, she cuts it into forty-two-inch lengths.

From a cabinet of many drawers that offer a variety of nails, screws, nuts, bolts, fasteners, and other small items, she selects eight two-inch screws and then four steel-strap U-shaped brackets, each of which features two holes in one of its legs. She carries all that, plus a power drill and selected drill bits, into the house.

In the kitchen, she bores four holes in the doorjamb, two on the left, two on the right. She changes the bit to convert the drill into a power screwdriver, anchors the brackets, and inserts one of the two-by-fours. With that entrance barricaded, she doesn't bother engaging the deadbolts. She repeats the process at the front door.

Whenever she's out of the house and the two-by-fours aren't in place, Deacon can enter, but he can no longer surprise her when she's at home.

At last she can take a shower and steam away the muscle pain that lingers from the labor at the placer mine, without worrying that she might be reenacting the key scene from *Psycho*.

26

THE YOUNG PSYCHOPATH AT HOME

On that Monday in the previous August, Vida parks in a lay-by and walks the last quarter of a mile to the Slyke house.

Although she takes no pride in Nature's gift, she knows men find her exceptionally attractive. She doesn't need to have attended public school to understand what fantasies preoccupy self-absorbed teenage boys like Morgan. She's wearing a white T-shirt, no bra, faded-denim cutoffs, and pale-blue sneakers with white ankle socks. With her hair tied in a ponytail, she is able to pass for a high-school senior, and she feels confident that she can conduct herself like one well enough to support her impersonation. To the best of her knowledge, the kid has never seen her before.

Vida climbs the porch steps, rings the bell, waits, and rings it again. Just as she wonders if the boy has gone out while she's been en route, the door opens.

Morgan is barefoot and shirtless, in a pair of faded jeans. His tousled hair, heavy-lidded eyes, and soft mouth suggest that he has been rung out of bed by the doorbell and isn't yet fully awake.

Imagining how a cheerleader might speak to the school's star quarterback, Vida says, "Hey, hi, I'm Connie Cooper. We moved in up the road. I thought I'd introduce myself."

He regards her with bewilderment, wiping a hand down his face as if to strip off a cobweb he walked through. "Introduce yourself?"

"Yeah, you know, 'cause we're neighbors and all. Like a mile or so up the road, but there aren't a lot of right-next-door neighbors around here. Says 'Slyke' on your mailbox. What's your first name?"

He still seems puzzled, uncertain, but the clouds lift a little when he looks her up and down in a slow, bold assessment. When his gaze returns to her eyes, he says, "Morgan Slyke."

"Cool name. My favorite breed of horse is the Morgan. I had one before we moved here. He was so beautiful. And really strong."

That is all a lie, but she hasn't come here with the intention of telling any truths.

He looks past her, toward the driveway. "Where's your wheels?"

"I walked. I walk a lot. I just got some county trail maps. Looks like great hiking territory. I like to stay in shape."

"You said your name," he remembers.

"Connie Cooper. Friends call me Ceecee." He looks as though he'll stand here all day in a state of stupefaction, so Vida tries to finesse her way inside with a come-on. "You're in great shape. Driving into town for this or that, I've seen you in the yard, seen you working out. Are you on the football team? I'll be a senior at Long Valley High this fall." She can't tell if he's dubious or just has a slow computer between his ears. When he wipes one hand down his face again, she realizes he's wasted on something—at nine o'clock in the morning. "I failed a grade," she adds, "'cause of some bad shit I got into. Can't wait to be done with the school thing."

He stands a little taller. "Teachers was done with it years ago. They don't give a shit. Now it's all about nothin' but doin' time, them and us."

"That's for sure the truth."

"Doin' time."

When he fails to invite her inside, she says, "Maybe I can say hello to your folks."

"Like introduce yourself."

"Yeah."

"Nobody home but me."

She cocks her head. "So why am I standing out here on the porch? You afraid of me, Morgan Slyke?"

He rises out of his fog enough to smile. "I think maybe I could be." He steps back. "You maybe want to come in for some breakfast, Ceecee?"

Entering the house, she says, "You cook?"

"Monday breakfast is special. Monday breakfast isn't about cookin' anything." He closes the door and heads back along the hallway.

Following him, she says, "What's Monday breakfast about?"

The kitchen decor is calculated country. The knotty-pine table has four captain's chairs with tie-on green cushions.

"Warm a chair," he says. From a cabinet he extracts two tall glasses and puts them on the table. "I celebrate with mimosas."

"What're you celebrating?"

"Monday." He opens the refrigerator. "Monday is my day of celebration." He takes a carton of orange juice from the door and brings it to the table.

"Why Monday?" she asks.

"Weekends are for makin' money. Mondays are for doin' what I make money for."

Pouring half a glass of orange juice for each of them, she says, "Where do you work weekends?"

"All around," he says as he opens an under-the-counter wine cooler and extracts a bottle of chilled champagne. "I work all around, here and there, wherever there's my kind of work to do."

"What kind of work is that?"

"The kind of work pays big but you don't break a sweat."

"How many guesses do I get?"

"How many guesses do you get?"

"To name what work you do," she says.

"I already told you what work."

"I get it. You're a man of mystery."

He likes the sound of that. "Exactly! I'm a man of mystery, Ceecee Cooper." He picks up a dish towel from beside the sink.

At the table again, he falls silent, attempting to open the champagne. The wire hood caging the cork is a simple fixture, but he struggles with it before stripping it off and throwing it aside with a snarled curse. He's in no condition to operate heavy machinery.

He pulls the cork. A large volume of thick, white foam gushes from the mouth of the bottle and down the neck into the dish towel.

Morgan grins at her. "That's the same how it looks like when *I* get off."

"You're bragging now," she says as he pours champagne.

From a bread box, he retrieves a package of cinnamon buns topped with icing and pecans. He tears it open and puts it on the table.

He sits across from her. They clink glasses and sip mimosas.

"What'll your mom and dad say about the champagne?"

"They don't say nothin' to me about my Mondays or nothin' else. They know better."

"You gotta tell me how I get a deal like that with my parents. They're always at me about something or other."

"You want to know?"

"I *need* to know."

"Two things. First, they gotta be afraid of you. So afraid they put a deadbolt on their bedroom door so they can sleep. Second, they gotta know it's not going to be forever, you're gonna get out, never come back."

"Your parents are really afraid of you?"

"They better be."

"How do you pull that off?"

"They don't make rules, I don't make trouble. It's been that way now for like three years."

As Morgan plucks a cinnamon roll from the package, Vida asks, "Weren't you afraid they'd send you somewhere to be rehabilitated?"

When he laughs, he unconsciously squeezes the roll, and some of it crumbles across the table. "See, I made up this story how my old man has been molestin' me since I was five years old, and how she knew but let him do it. Rehearsed the hell out of it, gave them a performance. I was so convincin', they're scared shitless I might walk into that stupid damn church of theirs one

Sunday and shout it out, every nasty detail, overturn their borin' lives, the reputations that matter so much to them."

When Morgan bites off half the roll and chews vigorously, Vida says, "You really despise them."

Speaking with his mouth full, he says, "Why shouldn't I?"

"Did they beat you?"

He swallows noisily. "Shit, no. Those two feebs wouldn't dare touch me. *Wouldn't dare.*"

"I mean, when you were little."

"They brought me into this sick world, didn't they? That's enough to hate them, don't you think?"

"The world is screwed."

"Six ways from Sunday. I didn't ask to be born. They humped me into this world and ruled me and churched me, tried to shape me into knee-benders like them, and what I've done to those two pussies isn't half what they deserve."

Although Vida expected to find that Morgan was a problem kid, this boy is further out there than she imagined, as if he's come to Earth from the dark side of the moon. Getting into this house might prove to be a lot easier than getting out unscathed.

"We're cool, Morgan. I know where you are, but I'm not there yet. I mean, with *my* shitty parents. I hope they take it in the neck someday, but it won't be me that does them. I just want out the door and away."

He stares at her intently as he finishes his cinnamon roll and washes it down with mimosa. The kitchen is shadowy, but his pupils are tiny, as though he's in bright light, perhaps because of the drugs with which he's begun this day of celebration. Everything must look darker to him than to her. "Want me to deal them out for you? You be somewhere with an alibi. I can ghost through it sure enough."

"Jesus," she says.

"I'm serious."

"You sound serious."

"I'm dead serious."

"That would be something."

"Wouldn't it? Wouldn't it be somethin'?"

He's flying. Whatever's got him eight miles high makes him mercurial and dangerous.

Meeting his stare, she takes quicker and shallower breaths, as though his offer excites her. "Let me think about it."

"You think about it. I'm here for you."

"No one's ever been here for me."

"That's changed. Each of us, we got what the other needs. Am I right?"

"No one's ever been more right."

"The bell rings and there you are. How's that happen?"

"I saw you in the yard. Saw you working out."

"You just ring the bell, and here you are."

Pouring more orange juice, she says, "Things happen because they're supposed to happen, how I kept seeing you in the yard."

He pours champagne. "And you liked what you saw."

"Totally," she says.

27

THE BIRDS' REVENGE

"There's colors all around you, Ceecee Cooper."

"What colors?"

"All the warm colors. Like you're so ready, you're shinin'. But you'll have to wait till later."

"Wait for what?"

"Wait to ride the rocket. I'm up so high, girl, I can't get my dick up with me. The physics of it just don't work."

"You sure are up there, but you're worth waiting for."

"You want some of what got me here?"

"What is it?"

"Weed."

"Can't be. I don't smell it."

"Yeah, 'cause I don't smoke it. Doin' dabs."

"Dabs are powerful shit," she says.

"These are special dabs, fully spiced."

"Spiced with what?"

"Maybe DMT or somethin'."

"Better not be fentanyl, you drop dead on me."

"He wouldn't do that. He'd never do that. He's not some pusher for China wants to kill American kids. He only cares about money."

"Who does?"

"Old Bead."

"Old Bead?"

"Belden Bead. I do a job for him. No one does a better job for him. I'll get you a taste of this stuff. You'll see."

Vida shakes her head. "Not now. If I take some, then when you come down from where you are, I'll be up. I want us both in the same space, you know, when we take that ride later."

He nods vigorously and claps his hands with delight. "Hey, I need some candy. Good chocolate. There's a box in the fridge."

"You stay there," she says. "I'll get it for you."

When Vida brings the candy to the table, Morgan puts a hand on her butt and slides it between her legs, pressing the crotch of her denim shorts. She endures his touch long enough to take the lid off the box, whereupon his attention is redirected to the chocolates.

She returns to her seat. "When did you start using weed?"

"Seems like always."

"You don't remember."

"Sure. I was thirteen. Old Bead saw hustle in me. Got me workin' the middle-school crowd." Morgan pops a candy into his mouth.

"Who is this Bead guy?"

Morgan sorts nervously through the variety of candies, as if deciding which one to eat next is more stress than he can handle. "Bead is gonna move me up soon. The day he moves me up, I drop out of Long Valley High, get out of this house, get myself an apartment, cool wheels. I've been savin' for the day."

"But who is he?" she presses.

"Who is who?"

"Bead."

"Old Bead."

"You keep saying."

He picks up a candy, reconsiders, puts it back, and selects another. "Bead is Bead. Everyone who knows how things really are, not just how they seem, they know Bead."

"Yeah, well, I'm new in town."

He looks up at her. "Hey. I forgot. You're fresh. You sure are fresh."

She watches while he eats the piece of candy. Then she says, "So this Bead guy."

"His daddy, Horace Bead, old Horace and Katherine, they own all kinds of shit. Belden got himself a law degree from Yale so he'd know how to get around the law. He doesn't practice. Belden Bead, he's too busy to have time for lawyerin'."

Morgan startles, knocks the candy box aside, shoves his chair back from the table, and sways to his feet. Attention fixed on the ceiling, he turns in place.

Getting up from her chair, Vida says, "What's wrong?"

"Birds," he whispers.

"Where? I don't see any."

"Birds but not birds. Like birds but with people faces. Mean faces." He seems to be overcome by awe rather than fear. *"Look at their eyes."*

"Morgan, it's the spice. In the dabs. What? Mescaline or LSD?"

Closing his eyes, covering them with his hands, the boy speaks in a voice so deadpan that, in these circumstances, it's eerie, as he might sound if they were, in fair weather, having a discussion about how best to avoid being struck by lightning the next time they were outdoors in a thunderstorm. "The best thing is to keep your eyes covered. If they can't see your eyes, they can't tear them out. You're safe if you just keep your eyes covered until they go away."

Vida has never until now been in the presence of someone spaced out and hallucinating. However, intuition tells her to respond to his delusion as if it were real rather than try to argue him out of it, offer sympathy rather than argument, mercy and comfort rather than disparagement.

"I'm here for you," she tells him. "If I can't see these things, then they can't see me. If they can't see me, they can't peck out my eyes. That's how it works."

Morgan stands there like the searcher blinding himself while other children scurry away for a game of hide-and-seek. "Maybe it works that way, maybe, but be careful."

"That's how it works," she insists. "I'm safe. What do you need, Morgan? What can I do for you?"

"If I don't lie down, it'll get worse. If I lie down long enough, they'll go away. Everything always goes away."

Leading him to a bed is not a good idea. "I'll get you to the sofa in the living room."

She snatches up the dish towel from the breakfast table. With her other hand, she grips his left forearm without pulling his hand from his eyes, and she gently leads him. The drug seems to have cast a gerontic spell over the boy; he shuffles along like an old man.

When he is lying on the sofa, she kneels on the floor beside him. "Keep your eyes closed, but take your hands away from them. I have a cloth to lay over your eyes and keep you safe. That'll be more comfortable."

"They're still here," he says. "I can hear their wings."

When Morgan moves his hands and lowers his arms to his sides, Vida places the folded dish towel across his eyes and brow.

"It's cool," he says.

"Yeah, it's still damp with champagne."

"Are you goin' now? Don't go."

"I'll stay a little while."

"Now they're talkin'. You hear them?"

"No."

"I don't like when they start whisperin', the things they say. That makes me dizzier."

"Then don't listen. Listen only to me. We'll talk together until they stop whispering."

Although he shuffled like a fragile old man as she led him to the sofa, he now seems like a small child. She holds his hand in both of hers.

In his current condition, Morgan's memory of what has occurred between them is sure to be full of holes. Vida takes a chance when she mentions the name of the boy who, according to Anna Lagare, had also thrown bottles at José Nochelobo. "So who's Damon Orbach?"

Morgan frowns. "How do you know Damon?"

"I don't. When you said Horace and Katherine Bead own all kinds of shit, you said 'just like Damon Orbach.'"

"Why would I say that?"

"How would I know, baby? You said what you said."

"Damon doesn't own nothin'. His dad, Perry, he's the big bear in the county. It might all be Damon's one day, except his old man is such a hard-ass he'll never die."

"So Damon's a friend of yours, huh?"

"We hang out. We got similar grievances. That's what Damon says. 'Similar grievances.' Man, I'm pressed."

"Impressed with what?"

"Pressed. Like a weight on me. Like you're layin' on me, but not that nice. You gotta lay on me."

"We'll do the laying later, sweetie. When you feel better. You sell dabs or something to Damon?"

"Shit, no. Old Bead would cut my nuts off."

"Why?"

"Only Bead supplies Damon and only what Bead wants him to have. He doesn't want any chance of Damon flushin' himself."

"Flushing himself?"

"Takin' an overdose. I am so heavy." He's slurring his words. "I never been so heavy."

"Are you all right, baby?"

"I'm a freakin' whale. But I'm okay. Don't you go nowhere."

"Where would I go?" she asks.

"I'm slidin' away, but I'll be back."

"I'll be here."

Below the dish towel, his mouth forms a loose smile. "I'm a man of mystery." And then he's snoring.

She lifts the cloth from his eyes and takes it to the kitchen. With paper towels, she quickly cleans off the breakfast table and tucks the two chairs under it. She returns the carton of orange juice and the box of candy to the refrigerator, the package of cinnamon rolls to the bread box. She washes the two tall glasses, puts them where Morgan found them, empties the remaining champagne down the drain, turns on the water long enough to flush away the smell, and wipes the sink dry. When she leaves, she takes with her all the used paper towels, the empty champagne bottle, the cork, and the wire hood that once restrained the cork.

Removing every proof that she's been here is not likely to induce him to believe that he hallucinated her as he did the birds with human faces. However, intuition suggests that without evidence of her visit to prod his memory, his recollection of what she looked like and what he told her will be hazy at best. Intuition has always been reliable, and not merely in the search for gemstones. Her intuition is a gift no less than it is for Lupo and the wolves that he leads through the perils of the wilds.

She walks the quarter of a mile to her pickup and returns home by way of the forest-service road rather than pass by the Slyke house again. During the drive, she mulls over what she has learned and what, if anything, she can do with the knowledge. She suspects that even if Morgan never discovers that she was Connie Cooper, he'll eventually come into her life again and with lethal intent.

28

LOVE NOTE

Now, nine months after her visit with Morgan Slyke, Vida has burned the photo of Belden Bead that Deputy Nash Deacon left to torment her. She has thrown away Deacon's gift of red roses and disposed of his toothbrush and toothpaste. Having also braced the front and back doors with two-by-fours to defeat his police lock-release device, Vida takes a hot shower.

After the shampoo rinses from her hair, as steam fogs the glass of the stall and clouds the air, she's quickly overcome by a feeling that she usually must concentrate for some time to achieve, by a perception that she is liberated from the tyranny of self. Perhaps this is not merely a feeling or perception, but a true condition; she isn't interested in analyzing the moment, only in the experience of it. She dwells neither in the past nor in the future, assailed neither by memories nor by expectations. Awareness of her body—its current aches, its potential for pleasure—recedes from her. She does not think, but is thought; she does not know, but is known. She is the rushing water and the susurrant sound of it. She is the heat of the water and the steam. She waits as patiently as she has at times waited for wolves, although in this instance she is awaiting something greater for which she has no image, waits without either hope or foreboding. When she becomes aware of her hair slick against her neck, the contours of her body as the flow of water shapes it, and the residual fragrance of soap, she has submitted again to the tyranny of self. Although she has arrived at no new comprehension of herself or of the world as she's known it, she's no longer weary.

She dresses for the evening. In the library, from her uncle's collection of vinyl recordings, she selects Mozart's Piano Concerto no. 23 in A Major, K. 488. For a minute or so, she stands very still, listening to the opening movement. No matter how often she hears this music, it inspires a soaring optimism.

In the kitchen, she goes to the refrigerator to get the bottle of iced tea that she'd wanted earlier, before she found the roses and the photo of Belden Bead and been distracted by the need to dispose of them. The previous day, she'd baked an egg-custard pie but hadn't cut it. She'd intended to have a slice for dessert this evening. The pie has been violated. Nash Deacon has not simply cut a piece; he's treated the entire pie as if she prepared it just for him, digging into it here and there, consuming what he wished, returning it to the fridge with his dirty fork. Beside the pie lies an envelope.

With Rubenstein's performance of K. 488 filling this small house, the base emotion of anger in all its gradations eludes her. She is instead filled with steely resolve and courage that are more in the spirit of the music.

She uses a spatula to scrape the remaining pie into the trash bag to which she'd consigned the roses. After washing the baking pan and the fork, drying them, and putting them away, she sits at the table with the message he left while she was at the placer mine.

The envelope isn't sealed. From it, Vida extracts a sheet of paper, which she unfolds. Apparently, he wrote it on his computer, but he won't have saved the document. To a court, it proves

DEAN KOONTZ

neither intent nor the writer's identity. He has invited himself to dinner.

> Dear One,
> I am so looking forward to a home-cooked
> dinner tomorrow evening at six o'clock. I
> have no special requests when it comes to
> the menu. I'm sure whatever you prepare
> will be as perfect as you are. I ask only
> that, of your two dresses, you wear the
> white one. Our mutual friend, rest his
> soul, once saw you in the black dress
> and said you were ravishing, but the
> white one is more in harmony with this
> happy occasion. Love and kisses.

She had worn the black dress to the cemetery when José Nochelobo was interred. She doubted that Belden Bead—"our mutual friend"—had been at the service.

Using the butane match, she burns the letter and envelope in the sink and washes the ashes down the drain.

She ties shut the plastic bag containing the roses and the egg-custard pie and carries it to the trash can in the back building, for conveyance to the county dump on her weekly visit.

On this eventful Wednesday, perhaps forty minutes of light remains before the white shoals of high clouds will be alchemized into bright coral reefs and then washed into night. Returning to the house, she pauses to watch a golden eagle—identifiable by a seven-foot wingspan, feather patterns, and golden nape—as the bird glides effortlessly above the meadow, a beautiful and graceful presence even as it is a terror to every creature that it hunts.

In the house once more, Vida inserts the two-by-four in the brackets flanking the back door. She replays Mozart's K. 488.

She opens a bottle of cabernet and pours a glass. Fills a pot with water and puts it on the cooktop to bring it to a boil. Opens a package of fettuccini. Takes a container of homemade Bolognese sauce from the freezer and puts it in the countertop microwave to thaw. She lights two candles in cut-glass cups.

As the water is heating and the Bolognese is growing soft, she sits at the table, sipping her wine and listening to the music and thinking about Nash Deacon.

Tomorrow evening should be interesting.

29

WHAT SHE VALUES LEAST

The shades have been drawn over the windows. Reflected light from the sole candle quivers on the ceiling, as if a trembling spirit hovers above ten-year-old Vida and the robed mystic.

With legs as massive as bedposts and a slab top, the kitchen table has most recently been painted pea-soup green, but a Joseph's coat of colors is revealed through the many nicks and scratches, testifying to previous incarnations.

Vance Burkhardt rents the run-down house fully furnished. Though many of his tenants are on the dole or engaged in enterprises condemned by the law, as well as being users of addictive substances that don't come cheap, they never steal the furniture because it has little value and is too heavy to be moved easily. Mr. Burkhardt says he chose each item at various country auctions based on just three requirements: that it be ugly, be badly scarred or poorly repaired, and be too heavy to inspire his indolent tenants to steal it.

Vida assumes that the house is often dirty and smelly, but the current tenant, the nameless woman, appears to have scrubbed into every corner. Nothing is tacky to the touch, and the air is sweet.

With her hood draped behind her and raven-black hair framing her ageless face, the woman opens the opaque plastic bag that Vida gave her. The paperback book slides out onto the table.

"A book is what you value least?" the seer asks.

"Not all books. I love books. But not that one."

"What is wrong with this one?"

"It's full of meanness and anger, and it wants me to believe things that aren't true."

"You always recognize truths for what they are and lies for what they're not?"

"Who doesn't?" Vida asks.

"Legions," says the seer.

"Well, but will you take this as payment?"

"I always accept whatever currency seekers bring to me. By their payment I know them entirely. Once I know them, I can tell them what they have come to hear, although they might be surprised to hear it. In this case, however, in order to know you, to fully know you, I must read the book to consider your assessment of the author's intent."

Disappointed, Vida says, "How long will that take—a week, two weeks?"

"I'm not a slow reader, dear. Return at nine tomorrow morning. Now, as a reward for your patience, I will tell you something you don't know."

Vida sits up straighter in her chair. "Something to come?"

"No. Something of the past that prevented something that might have come to pass. You know that the man who shot your father five years ago was hit by your father's return fire. Both died. No one told you that the man your father shot did bad things to little girls. They felt you were too young to understand. What your father didn't know—couldn't know—is that if the man he killed had lived, one of the girls that monster would have later assaulted was you. Your father died not only for all the children who would have been victims—he died as well for you, whom he loved with all his heart."

Shaking with emotion, with sorrow and fear and wonder, and with confusion, Vida pushes her chair back from the table and gets to her feet. "How? How can you know?"

"Past, present, and future are one. To know what's coming is to know what has been. It's important that you know what your father's sacrifice prevented, as you will see on your next visit."

Vida turns from the table and finds herself on the far side of the county road, on the dirt lane leading home.

30

THE SERPENT'S COURTSHIP

Thursday morning, the day after Nash Deacon left his toothbrush and roses and a photo of Belden Bead, Vida removes the two-by-fours that brace the front and back doors. She undoes the four steel-strap brackets and drops them in a Ziploc bag with the eight screws. She fills the holes. Tomorrow, she'll sand the fill and shellac it to match the wood. On further consideration, she has decided that barricades aren't the way to deal with him.

At eleven o'clock, when she departs on a task that will give her an option she hopes not to use, she locks the deadbolts against all intruders other than the deputy who calls himself her suitor.

She has a busy day.

As six o'clock approaches, the kitchen table is set for dinner. No flowers. No candles. No tablecloth. Two plain white plates on the red Formica. Beside each plate is a paper napkin on which lies only a dinner knife, no fork or spoon.

He wants to mock and diminish her, as well as unnerve her, with a charade of romance. If she understands Nash Deacon—and she does—he'll bring a bottle of wine. Beside the plates, she has placed not glass stemware, but instead disposable plastic picnic cups.

Her two dresses remain on hangers. She wears hiking shoes, a pair of roomy Levi's that are comfortable when she works the placer mine, and an untucked plaid-flannel shirt.

A few minutes before six o'clock, the mountain quiet is broken by the rumble of the Pontiac Trans Am's powerful engine. It draws nearer, so near that the sound vibrates the kitchen window glass. A sudden silence lasts until a car door slams shut.

She has left the front door open. She will not go forward to greet him.

He hesitates on the porch. Then the door closes behind him and footfalls sound in the hall. Whatever he imagines she did to Belden Bead, Deacon seems unafraid of her. Of course he has disarmed her.

When he appears in the open archway, he's wearing dressier boots than before, pressed jeans instead of uniform khakis, a blue-and-black-checkered shirt, and a different cowboy hat than the one he wore previously, black and of a better quality. He's carrying a bottle of wine in one hand and a small gift-wrapped box in the other.

He's had time to think about the role he wants to play, and he is more relaxed than on his first visit. When he sees how she is dressed, he grins broadly and shakes his head. "You're a piece of work, sweet thing. This is just about what I expected."

Vida says nothing.

Entering the kitchen, he surveys the table setting and shakes his head again. He puts down the wine—her favorite cabernet— and the little gift box. He takes off his hat and drops it on one of the spare chairs.

"Most men," he says, "comin' around for a dinner date, they would be mighty offended by the implied insult of all this here."

"And if they were smart, they'd leave."

"Most would, I suspect. But I'm a different breed from them. I always have enjoyed women who present a challenge."

"This isn't a date," she says.

"You're mistaken there, sweet thing. I'm sure you remember how I paid my respects the other day and stated my intentions as would any honorable man."

As Deacon opens the correct cabinet and takes two wine-glasses from a shelf, Vida says, "This is a business meeting."

"Oh, darlin', that makes you sound like a whore. You do have the equipment to be a high-priced item. But if that's what you were, I wouldn't be here. I never paid for it, and I never will."

"The business to be discussed is what will make you go away."

"I'm not goin' nowhere, girl. You're honey, and I'm the bear. There's but one way that story unfolds."

"I can hurt you bad. Don't think I can't or I won't."

As he puts the glasses on the table, he says, "A bear can take a hundred stings, two hundred, and he just sits there eatin' honey. He knows every pleasure worth havin' comes with a bit of pain."

She bluntly defines him. "Rapist."

"There's not another woman alive who would say so. Those ladies who've been with yours truly will tell you how they were gentled, charmed, and satisfied."

She keeps the table between them as he retrieves a lever-action corkscrew from a drawer. He's as familiar with the house as if he's been living here for some time.

"Keep an open mind," he says. "Get to know me. I've got my admirable qualities. You'll come around. I know you will."

"You think I murdered Belden Bead. So then why won't I kill you?"

Laughing softly, he peels the foil capsule from the cork. "You don't scare me, darlin'. I figure Belden was being Belden, and you acted in self-defense. You don't have true murder in you."

"If it was self-defense, why did I dig that damn big hole and put him in it?"

"Well now, that's sure to be part of our dinner conversation. I'm most interested in hearin' your story."

He removes the cork and inhales the aroma from the ullage. He pours a small sample, swirls it, smiling at Vida over the rim of the glass. He tastes the cabernet, is satisfied, and pours two servings.

"You'll be drinking alone," she says.

He slides her glass across the table, a wafer of light wobbling on the surface of the wine, and places it beside her plate. "Let's sit and enjoy for a while before havin' dinner."

When he settles in his chair and sips his cabernet, she stands with her back to the sink, watching him.

"There was this lovely woman," he says, staring into his wine as if it is a memory pool. "Not as lovely inside as out. She was somethin' of a snob and very proud—a shallow person, I regret to say—but she was physically a stunner. This terrible thing happened. The thumb and index finger on her right hand were cut off." He looks up at Vida. "Hey, darlin', I'm sorry. What the heck am I thinkin'? It's a good story, an instructive little parable, but not dinner conversation."

Vida says nothing.

"Well, all right then, if you're curious. By the end, it's actually an inspirin' story. Hopeful. This lady, she thought she was perfect. And she truly was a perfect beauty. But when she lost those fingers, she was devastated, so depressed. Her face and body were unmarked, as special as before, but she felt disfigured. Her image of herself collapsed. That pride I mentioned was gone. She wasn't smug no more, or snarky. But when she discovered she was still wanted, still very much prized, when she realized there are caring men in this world who can judge a woman by the complete package and overlook a bit of ugliness here or there, she was deeply grateful that she didn't lose more fingers or even an entire hand, and her gratitude made her passionate. She gave her all, as long as she was wanted."

Tormenting Vida like this gives him pleasure. The trick is to indulge him in his psychological games while she deftly plays one of her own. If she denies him too adamantly, with withering scorn, he will resort to violence with which she might not be able to deal successfully. On the other hand, if she yields too quickly, he'll suspect that her submission is a ruse to encourage him to let down his guard. Intuition tells her that he expects to take a while to break her and looks forward to inflicting a series of fractures to her self-respect and spirit. To maneuver Deacon into a position of vulnerability, she must ever so slowly bend to his intimidation until he's confident that she'll eventually capitulate with just enough resistance to make his conquest exciting.

"If I've got to listen to this shit," she says, "I'll need that cabernet." She sits across the table from him and picks up the wine he poured.

He smiles and raises his glass in a toast. "To Belden Bead. He'd be amazed to learn he's become a matchmaker."

"The only thing he's become is dead."

"Hush now. I won't accept your confession."

"Wasn't a confession, merely a fact."

"Last thing I want is you in prison instead of under me."

"Won't be either one."

"Only other option you got is me dead."

She raises her glass. "Here's to that."

"What're you—five feet four, five? Hundred ten pounds?"

"I don't own a scale."

"I bench-press three times your weight."

"Stress like that could give you a heart attack."

"Pressin' *you* might give me a heart attack, how good you look. I'll take the risk."

"Is that talk your idea of how to romance a lady?"

"You start actin' like a lady, I'll change my talk."

She takes one, two, three sips of wine because she knows how he'll interpret that. "Are you married?"

"I once was, fourteen years ago."

"She come to her senses?"

"She up and died on me."

"I'm guessin' not cancer."

"Why couldn't it have been?"

"The way you said it."

"How'd I say it?"

"Like, 'Hey, shit happens.'"

"Which it does more days than not."

"She fall down the stairs?"

"You amuse me."

"Not my intention."

"This drug addict, Lyle Sussman, broke in the house when Tanya was alone. Raped her, beat her to death with a hammer, stole a little money."

"You ever catch him?"

"The next day."

"Good police work."

"Home security camera gave us a clear picture."

"He get himself shot resisting arrest?"

"We found him in the woods, where he lived in a tent. By then he'd taken his own life."

"Hung himself from a tree limb? Threw himself off a cliff? Set himself on fire?"

"Coroner said it was likely an overdose."

"'Likely.' Not as specific as you'd expect from a coroner."

"Sussman was a homeless addict with a long rap sheet of petty theft, no known family. Just your essential nobody. There was heroin at the scene, a syringe, a little cookin' kit. Not a case where the law requires toxicology."

She resorts to her wine again and then says, "So you didn't tell him there was a security camera at your house."

He drinks some wine and puts the glass down and leans forward with his muscular arms on the table. "You do really tickle me."

"How much did Sussman want paid to rape and kill her?"

"A hundred up front, then four hundred plus ten decks of heroin when it was done. You're so smart, maybe you want to guess the true cost?"

"Once you knew Tanya was dead, you went to Sussman's tent. You probably didn't even take the four hundred with you. And only one packet of heroin."

Pouring more wine for himself, Deacon says, "He wasn't goin' to need ten decks."

"You watched him cook the heroin and inject it."

"He was so happy that I was pleased."

Vida says, "You must've gotten the heroin from Belden Bead."

"My cousin was the go-to man in this county. He gave it to me free, an expression of family solidarity."

"Either he or you doctored the packet with something to be sure it would kill Sussman."

Pushing the wine bottle toward her, Deacon says, "Digitoxin."

"So he had a massive heart attack within a few minutes."

"Almost immediately, chokin' on his vomit. Darlin', it's like you were there. You really are somethin'."

"All it cost you was a hundred dollars."

"Not even. Before leavin' that tent, I took back the seventy-six bucks he hadn't spent."

"Frugal of you."

"Waste not, want not. So slidin' Tanya out of my life cost me twenty-four bucks. Then of course there were the funeral expenses, though I saved a pretty penny by goin' for cremation and a little urn rather than embalmin' and a casket."

Pouring more wine that she doesn't intend to drink, Vida allows the bottle to rattle once against the glass. She doesn't overplay it by faking an extended tremor.

"Why did you want so bad to be rid of Tanya?"

"You wouldn't ask if you'd known her."

"But I didn't know her."

"She wasn't the sparklin' conversationalist that you are. She wouldn't stop talkin' about babies."

"She wanted a baby?"

He softly drums the fingers of both hands on the table, making a sound like the rataplan of rain on a roof. "Wouldn't shut up about it. I wasn't bangin' the bitch to make babies. I was bangin' her to bang her. We had different ideas about the purpose of marriage."

"Ever consider divorce?"

"Not after she betrayed me."

"She betrayed you?"

"She went off the birth control and got herself knocked up."

"But the baby was yours?" Vida asks.

Deacon's hands go still. His expression is a disquieting mix of astonishment and keen vexation. "Tanya didn't need more than what I gave her. Of course the baby was mine. You want to cut to the chase and do it now, see what I've got for you? You get it from me, you'll never want it from anyone else."

The impression of self-restraint that he projects might be less absolute than it has seemed. Deacon enjoys toying with Vida and is perhaps content to do so for a few days before forcing himself on her. However, a cat that appears to take deep and abiding pleasure in tormenting a mouse can suddenly bare its fangs and surrender to the prey drive that is the essence of its nature. There is a risk that he will make a move on her before she can lead him to the resolution she has devised.

To mollify him, she says, "It was just the word you used—'betrayed.' I misunderstood."

His stare is fierce, a wordless command to submit or face the consequences, but Vida senses that it would be unwise to look away too soon.

"You know what your problem is, darlin'?"

"I guess you'll tell me."

"That damn library of yours. You're so bookified, you overthink everythin'. A man just plainly speaks his heart, and you *analyze* his words, analyze a whole different meanin' into what he says. How many books you read in your twenty-eight years?"

"Hundreds, I guess."

"Shit, girl, that isn't livin'. That's just *readin' about livin'*. Don't go analyzin' me. Just listen to what I really say."

"All right."

"Is that askin' too much?"

"No."

"Books make snobs out of people, make them proud when they hadn't ought to be, when they don't really have nothin' to be proud about. You understand me?"

"Yes."

"I've seen people so bookified and arrogant, the only thing that might save them from themselves is if someone poked their eyes out and blinded them from ever readin' again."

He drinks a little wine, and she looks away from him.

After a mutual silence, she says, "The lovely woman who lost a thumb and finger—did she come before or after Tanya?"

"After," he says without hesitation. "Committin' to the wrong woman was the biggest mistake I ever made. I won't make it twice."

Vida is surprised to find herself taking a sip of the second serving of wine, which she had intended not to drink. She puts the glass down.

When she looks at Deacon, he sees something in her eyes that elicits a smile from him. "Scares you a little, how much I've told you about things I've done."

"Doesn't scare me," she lies. "But it does surprise me."

"You think I told you enough to hang myself if you go tell the sheriff and get his suspicions up, and so now I'm out on a limb as far as you are with what you did to Belden Bead."

"Not at all. You wouldn't have told me if it put you out on a limb."

"Exactly right. You're as smart as you are good to look at. A girl with a brain as hot as yours, how much hotter must you be down between your legs, where it really counts? If you want, you go into Kettleton tomorrow and have a chat with the sheriff. It won't bother me at all, darlin'."

She waits.

He takes pleasure in making her wait. He swirls the wine in his glass and savors its bouquet. He sluices it back and forth through his teeth as if it's mouthwash, swallows, and sighs.

"When I came here the day before yesterday, there was this thing I neglected to tell you. That was my last day as a deputy. Sheriff Montrose retired with a heart condition. The city council appointed me interim sheriff until the election next year. I'll win another four years because the powers that be will see to it that I run unopposed. You understand what this means?"

Her mind quickens through the ramifications of what he has just revealed. "You can contrive to have someone discover Belden Bead's grave on my property. Kettleton isn't really Kettleton anymore. It's a small-town version of Gotham City, but there's no Batman to clean it up. Nothing you've told me can be proven, and no one will believe you'd have bared your soul to me. Somehow you'll seize my property. I won't have money for a good attorney. The public defender assigned to me will work hard to ensure that I'm convicted—if I don't first commit suicide in jail."

His plain face takes on a powerful character it didn't have before, his features transformed by savage delight. Although he isn't handsome, he suddenly has a fearsome charisma. "Damn it all, girl, you don't belong on the farm team your uncle trained you into. You're quick enough to earn a place with us winners in the major leagues. You see how it can be for you?"

Her hand has closed again around the wineglass, but she doesn't lift it from the table. "No way I want it to be."

He says, "You sleep on the situation tonight. In the mornin', you admit you screwed up, how you treated me here this evenin'. I come back tomorrow, we have us a nice dinner date, and we see how we fit together. You're gonna like how we fit together. What I can make you feel is somethin' you never felt before or imagined you could. When we become a team, we can have whatever the hell we want, what with all the money comin' into this county. Darlin', strange as it might sound, what you're gonna find in submission is freedom. You marry me, then with you comes the holy glow of José Nochelobo, which is somethin' I know how to use. And you get a real life, not a life in books. All the rules your uncle trammeled you with will wither away like spider silk. You'll be more powerful than you ever thought possible, everyone eager to please you. You'll dream new dreams—and make them come true. There's nothin' you can want you can't have."

Except love, she thinks, *and true freedom and the peace that comes with virtue.*

She says, "You make it sound inevitable."

"I'm only givin' you a chance to realize your potential."

Indicating the house with a sweep of her hand, she says, "This has been my life."

"This has been your prison. If you choose to have a *real* life, it can begin tomorrow at dinner."

He leans back in the chair, both his face and posture conveying confidence that the proposal he has made—the threat of brutal rape and violent death contrasted with the promise of a life of pleasure and transcendence—will result in the submission that he requires. Submission without resentment. Transcendence through the eager embrace of nihilism. Like all his kind, he believes everyone is by nature irredeemably corrupt from birth. He's certain that, if she admits to her corruption, she'll awaken and become a reflection of him. He has traveled so long in darkness that he can't even imagine that a path of light exists.

"Now, let's finish this good wine with whatever dinner you've prepared for us. I'm sure it'll be amusin'."

With the revelation that he's the sheriff and that all those who hated José Nochelobo for speaking the truth are Deacon's allies, this evening has proceeded along none of the paths Vida envisioned. More than ever, her fate depends on how she conducts herself, on maintaining a perfect deception, though every moment provides her with a chance to make a mortal error.

He has to believe, without suspicion, that she's bending slowly to his intimidation. She needs Nash Deacon to return the following day with the conviction that she is afraid of what could happen to her but is at the same time tempted—although not yet seduced—by the future of power and excess he offers her. Before he leaves this evening, there are things she needs to know to shape her strategy, to evoke in him the state of mind that will make him vulnerable.

Before rising to put dinner on the table, she swallows some of her wine, swallows more, and then drains the glass.

His expression suggests that he infers from this what she wants him to infer.

"I can open another bottle when we need it," she says as she gets up from her chair.

She's stone-cold sober and expects to remain that way. However, if the cabernet sauvignon dulls her senses, there is no risk that he will take advantage and assault her. Rape will be his last resort. He wants her to descend into helplessness and give herself to him tomorrow, whereupon she'll have surrendered her dignity and traded her self-respect for survival on his terms. He's fool enough to believe that she could do such a thing.

31

DOG COLLAR

As Vida attends to dinner, Nash Deacon rises from his chair and moves around the table to pour a third serving of wine for her. He could have reached her glass while sitting down, but he means to loom over her and brush against her as he undertakes this task.

He seems even taller and more formidable than when he first entered the kitchen. As her options for resistance have decreased, she feels as if she has been diminished physically.

"Now you put out the meal you first intended, darlin', whatever you meant to go with paper napkins and plastic cups, before you knew about my new exalted status, before our little come-to-Jesus meetin' when you got a truer sense of the situation. Don't fancy it up to please me. I want to see where your mind was at when I arrived."

After Deacon returns to his chair and freshens his wine, Vida sets out a dish containing a full stick of Danish Creamery butter, and with it a box of saltines. Then she sits across the table from him once more.

He's smiling, genuinely amused. "No water for the cups?"

"No. They were for wine in case you brought any. But then you knew where to find the glasses."

He opens the box of saltines and extracts a sleeve of crackers. "Did you think I'd be angry?"

"I thought you'd get the point."

"The point bein'?"

"This won't be easy for you."

"Now you know I'm sheriff, what do you think?"

"This won't be easy for you," she repeats.

"What's worth havin' is never easy."

He takes six crackers and slides the open sleeve across the table to her.

"I'm not a rude guest. If my hostess wants to serve me nothin' but sour lemons, I'll eat them, rind and all."

He spreads butter on two crackers and makes a sandwich of them.

He eats it in two bites.

"Good butter. So what about you?" he asks.

"What about me?"

"Are you angry?"

"Hell yes."

Buttering two more crackers, he says, "As angry as when I first came through the door?"

That is a question to which the answer must be calculated if she's to lead him where she wants him to go. After a hesitation, she lies. "I guess not. I should be even angrier, but then I . . ."

"Then you what, darlin'?"

"Then I think—what's the point?"

"Is that bitter resignation or just practical adjustment to changed circumstances?"

She dwells on the question in silence. Then: "Both."

"So maybe this will be easier for me than you first thought."

"No."

"No?"

She says nothing.

After consuming the second pair of crackers, he takes a little wine and says, "Eat somethin', darlin'."

Because a man like him believes that women are always driven by emotion rather than reason and that under stress they will always prove weak, he expects her response to be puerile. What she says must support his perception that she's sliding into submission whether she realizes it or not. She says, "This is stupid. Why're you doing this? I don't want to do this anymore."

"Don't be childish, darlin'. Poutin' doesn't become you. You had your reason for layin' out this feast, and I have my reason to enjoy it. You need to finish what you started and eat your dinner like a good girl."

He butters two more crackers, presses them together, reaches across the table, and puts them on her plate.

As Deacon fishes more saltines from the sleeve and makes a third sandwich for himself, Vida says, "Belden Bead has been under my meadow for eight months. Why are you just now after me about it?"

"Like I do when I'm off duty in my Trans Am, Belden drove a car made before GPS, a '70 Plymouth Superbird Hemi, so no authorities could ever track where he went. When he disappeared, car and all, some thought he got wind of a Drug Enforcement Agency operation comin' down on him, so he skipped to Mexico, left the Superbird there, and flew out to where he kept his offshore money. It didn't make good sense he'd do that, but then no other explanation made any sense at all. Eat your buttered crackers, darlin'."

"I'm not hungry."

"Eat them anyway."

He devours his third pair of saltines before continuing.

"Three weeks before Belden visited you, you went to see Morgan Slyke, callin' yourself Ceecee Cooper, but the boy didn't realize who you really were. The kid is totally wasted that day, passes out, and when he wakes up, he can't remember what he might have told you, though he recalls talkin' about Belden. The kid is worried sick. He right away goes lookin' for Connie Cooper, these new neighbors, but seems they don't exist. Now he's panicked. Takes him more than two weeks before he dares tell his buddy, Damon Orbach. The description of this Cooper girl doesn't ring any bell with Damon, who never met you. Without tellin' Morgan, Damon goes straight to Belden, who supplies him with spiced dabs and other shit. Damon means to get special treatment by sellin' out Morgan. The description of this Connie is so vivid, down to your dimples, that Belden, who thought you were the hottest thing he'd ever seen, realizes you could pass for eighteen. He doesn't tell Damon that Ceecee is you. Belden's alarmed you're pokin' into what happened to Nochelobo. Apparently, without tellin' anyone, he came to see you eight months ago—and he's been missin' ever since."

As Deacon talks, he butters two more saltines and drops this second sandwich on her plate beside the first.

Playing to his expectations, she says, "I don't want it."

"I know you don't, sweet thing. But if you won't eat your nice little sandwiches, I'll feed them to you. I won't mind doin' it, if you want. You need to keep your strength up for our next date."

She engages in a brief staring contest but then picks up a pair of buttered crackers. She loathes him and can't conceal it; however, his narcissism allows him to interpret loathing as fear and continue to believe that she can be made to submit to him and like it.

"Belden's parents, Horace and Kathie Bead, are county royalty," Deacon continues, "upstandin' citizens. They can't breach the wall between the family's legit and dark-side businesses. So they bring in a man named Galen Vector to run Belden's operation until they hear from their son, which they never do. The new boss is on the job for seven months before Damon Orbach rats out Morgan Slyke yet again, tellin' Vector how Morgan, flyin' high, told some girl about Bead payin' them to prank José Nochelobo with water bottles and how a few weeks later Bead disappears. Galen comes to me. I hear a description of this Connie Cooper, I know she can't be anyone but you. Those eyes that are as much green as blue, and all the other qualities that are put together so damn well in you. Even if Morgan Slyke hadn't been high that day, he might've spilled his guts to you hopin' you'd let him plant some seed. So I came sniffin' around, eventually brought a good cadaver dog, found what I found, started runnin' surveillance on you all by myself. And here we are, fallin' in love in spite of I'm sixteen years older, our first date drawin' to a successful close, finishin' our wine before we kiss good night, dinner tomorrow already set, and more than dinner. Now, darlin', be a good girl like I know you can be and eat the crackers I was so sweet to butter for you, and tell me what went down between you and Belden."

Calculatedly, Vida eats the first pair of crackers with slow and exaggerated chewing, as might a mulish child who knows she has lost a contest of wills and wants to delay acknowledging the fact. She lingers over her wine before consuming the second saltine sandwich almost as slowly as she did the first.

If amusement lies behind his venomous smile, it's the amusement of a cobra. His eyes bring to mind Poe's raven, for they have *all the seeming of a demon's that is dreaming.*

He says, "You mock me, so I'm supposed to think you're a rebel and not scared in the least. Ah, missy, you're such an innocent. All you just accomplished was make cracker eatin' more arousin' than any porn film. Now tell me about Belden—my dear departed cousin, who is so much missed."

Vida grimaces and closes her eyes and massages her temples with her fingertips. "Tomorrow."

"What about tomorrow."

"I'll tell you all of it when you return tomorrow."

"The night is young, darlin'."

"I drank too much wine too fast, on too little food. I have a vicious headache. I'm nauseous. I'm . . . just . . . very, very tired and confused. You came here with big news that changes things, so many things, you being the sheriff. I've got to think. Think it through. Right now I can't. I can't think clearly right now."

He is silent for a minute or so, and then he says, "Before I leave, you unwrap what I brought you."

As he slides the gift across the table, she opens her eyes. The small shiny-blue box is tied with red ribbon shaped into a lavish bow.

"I saw your hobby room," he says, "whatever craft thing it is you're doin' there with all those colorful stones. You'll look good in this. You'll look just right."

She slips the ribbon off the box and removes the lid. The item is wrapped in folds of pale-blue tissue paper. It spills into the palm of her left hand. The flexible silver-mesh necklace is an inch and a half wide. A polished black bead of what might be sphalerite is inset in the center of the woven silver. The piece is designed to fit snugly around the neck. A jeweler would call it a "choker." Others might refer to it as a "dog collar."

The necklace is lovely, but she will neither say so nor thank him for it. Such a premature surrender will sharpen his suspicion.

He gets up and comes around the table.

She rises to her feet, not sure what to expect, ready to put up a fierce struggle if it comes to that.

When he says, "I'll put it on for you," she considers throwing it on the floor, considers politely declining the gift, considers saying she'll wear it tomorrow evening. However, intuition tells her to say nothing and allow him to put the necklace on her. She will resist if he tries to give her that good-night kiss he promised.

As he takes the choker from her hand, she doesn't look at him. He stands behind her, gently pulls the mesh tight, and fixes it in place with the clasp. He doesn't press himself against her, although he kisses the nape of her neck.

She startles at the kiss, but then he turns from her and steps away.

He retrieves his cowboy hat from the chair on which he left it. He looks at her, his expression as smug as she could have wished it would be. He believes the dog collar already has an invisible leash attached to it. Her head is partly bowed. She lifts her chin in defiance, but she presses her lips together as though biting back words that might anger him—conflicting responses that he is likely to read as evidence she's come halfway toward the submission he desires.

"Clear your mind, girl, and think things through like you need to. I'm a patient man, though it would be purely stupid not to put an excellent dinner on the table tomorrow. Wear that white dress of yours. With high heels." He places his hat on his head, adjusts it, slides his pinched thumb and forefinger around the brim as though to say, *Good evening, ma'am.* He steps out of the kitchen, leaves the house, and closes the front door behind him.

Vida remains where he left her until the engine noise of the Trans Am recedes into silence.

Reaching behind her neck with both hands, she releases the clasp. She puts the dog collar on the table.

She knows what she has to do, and she knows what peril lies before her. Even if she's fortunate, even if she's able to dispose of Nash Deacon—who will come after her next?

32

THE VENERABLE BEAD

Eight months earlier, when Damon Orbach tells Belden Bead about the hot girl who came to the Slyke house under a false name, how she conned the drugged-out Morgan and drained him of certain knowledge as if she'd opened a petcock in his head, Bead reacts with all the caution, discretion, wisdom, and manners that might be expected of the son of one of the county's most powerful families. Shaped and refined by the scholars and philosophers of Yale, he is an attorney who employs his knowledge of the law to avoid arrest and prosecution for acts that the great unwashed consider criminal but which are, in his more cultured view, merely the efficient servicing of the needs of those people who yearn for calm in a turbulent world. Or who are desperate for some stimulation to save them from the sea of boredom in which they are drowning. Or just want to exercise their God-given right to get wasted as often as they can afford. So after a week of scheming, wearing a white fedora, white pin-striped Givenchy suit with a brightly patterned shirt, dressy brown-and-white loafers, a Rolex watch, and two rings on each hand, he arrives in his black 1970 Plymouth Superbird Hemi. He parks in the yard and lays on the car horn for longer than a minute, waits, then pounds the Klaxon for perhaps half a minute more.

When Vida doesn't make an appearance, Bead exits the muscle car with a manila envelope in one hand and stands at the foot of the porch steps and calls her name several times. In an imperious voice, producing almost as many decibels as the car horn, he declares that he knows she's at home, that she knows who the hell he is, that they have an issue to discuss, an accommodation to reach, and that he needs to get back to town for a dinner engagement.

Since her conversation with Morgan Slyke, Vida has cautiously researched the great Bead. She knows what car he drives. Among other things, she knows he usually travels in the scowling company of two muscle-bound gunmen named Hanes and Rudy, whom some locals refer to as Jane and Judy, although never within their hearing. This time, Bead appears to have come alone, which might support his contention that his purpose is to negotiate with her rather than terminate her. In spite of his flamboyant attire, he is said to manage his empire from behind layered curtains of deniability, as prudently as befits the godfather of mountain crime. But it is rumored that, at times of intolerable frustration, he takes the chains off his Mr. Hyde and becomes a horror.

When at last Vida steps onto the front porch, she's wearing a roomy gray sweatshirt and jeans tucked into cowboy boots, something of a contrast to Bead in his finery. "What do you want?"

"Peace," he says.

"Then why did you start a war?"

His eyebrows seem to rise halfway to his hairline. "Terrence Boschvark and his company started the war, bombed us simple country folk with megatons of money. There's no defense. I'm just determined to get my share instead of becoming a battlefield casualty."

"And you'll do anything to get that share."

"Oh, I can think of things I wouldn't do. I'm not as greedy as others I can name. Now, we can stand here talking at each other from different altitudes until we're hoarse. Or if you'll extend a little Kettleton County kindness, invite me to a rocking chair, sit with me long enough to hear me out, much misery can be avoided by everyone."

"I can't be bought."

"I don't want to buy anyone. I'm here to explain, persuade."

"And if I'm not persuadable?"

"You've nothing to fear from me. What should scare the bejesus out of you is a four-hundred-billion-dollar corporation still guided by its self-adoring idealistic founder, with a mission statement so noble and poetic it makes stonehearted hedge-fund managers weep. An entity like that, run by a man like Terrence Boschvark, can grind a thousand Vidas to dust and get away with it. I am a messenger, not a hatchet man. If you'll listen to what I've come to say and if you're wise, you'll accept what I propose and get on with your life here, as your uncle got on with life after he put *his* war behind him."

Considering that Belden Bead arrived with much horn blowing and that he's dressed as if he thinks a new disco era is at hand, Vida finds it hard to believe he's just a well-meaning messenger or negotiator. Nevertheless, her investigation into José Nochelobo's death has hardly begun; she has much to learn, and it's possible that she will learn something true and useful even from a man as deceitful as Bead.

She invites him onto the porch and directs him to the chair she usually occupies. On this occasion, she finds it more advantageous to be positioned to the right of him rather than to his left.

After hanging his fedora on the finial that caps one of the stiles supporting the headrail of the chair, he sits with the nine-by-twelve envelope on his lap. He shoots one cuff of his rainbow-hued shirt and then the other, displaying an inch of fabric past each coat sleeve. He adjusts his collar and smooths his wheat-colored hair with both hands.

He is a good-looking man, with eyes the blue of robin eggs and as clear as if he just stepped out of Eden into this broken world, where he's not yet seen wickedness. His face is open and smooth, but his mouth is soft and suggestive of decadence.

Bead says, "Terrence Boschvark isn't an idealist. He's one of those messianic freaks who go down in the history books for all the wrong reasons. You understand?"

"Nothing," Vida replies, "is more dangerous than a man who has no humility, who sees himself as a savior but lacks mercy and pity, lacks any quality of the divine, let alone divinity itself."

"Then you know what'll happen to you if you try to thwart him."

"Maybe I don't care what he did."

"Oh, you care. You're the kind who can't not care."

"Did he direct you to enlist those boys to pelt José with bottles of water?"

"You have to understand my situation."

"Willing accomplice?"

"I am not a man with scruples, but I am a survivor. Boschvark has saturated this county with private investigators. He knows all the power players, who has done what, by what levers all of us can be controlled. The man has a thousand ways short of violence—major financial tools, political connections—to persuade or destroy those who are straight arrows. When it comes to the rest of us, he has the state attorney general in his pocket, also several key figures in the Department of Justice in Washington. If he says 'sic him,' then I'm done. Happily, he prefers to use me, and I have no choice but to be used."

"So you enlisted those five boys."

"The point was to humiliate Nochelobo, not to kill him."

"Humiliate him? You think that makes sense?"

"No one could know he'd fall down those steps just wrong enough to break his neck."

"He didn't break his neck," she says.

"Read the autopsy."

"Herbert Lagare falsified the cause of death."

Bead regards her with a credible approximation of amazement. "Good old Herb Lagare? Chamber-of-Commerce Bible-study United-Way Herb?"

With his steady stare, mouth agape in what seems to be genuine incomprehension, jewel-ringed hands relaxed on the large envelope, he's a convincing picture of disbelief.

She says, "You really don't know about the air rifle?"

"Air rifle? What air rifle?"

Deception can't change the color of a deceiver's eyes. However, as her uncle told her twelve years earlier, she sees with something other than ordinary vision. With the same nameless sense by which she knows where gemstones are and aren't to be found in the placer mine, she knows that Belden Bead is lying and is oh-so-quietly alarmed.

She says, "It fired a hypodermic dart loaded with what must have been a potent neurotoxin. That's what killed José. There had to've been a highly skilled shooter at a courthouse window. The dart staggered José, and the rest was choreographed so he was tumbled down the steps, making the report of a broken neck credible."

"Wait, wait, wait—get real. That's tinfoil-hat stuff. Who would think up a crazy trick like that, take such a risk?"

"You just told me Boschvark is messianic, capable of anything."

"But he's subtle, cold, not hotheaded. He wouldn't sanction such a public hit in front of so many potential witnesses. Someone has lied to you, sold you coal and called it gold."

"It *had* to be in public. José was so charismatic that he was turning the voters against the plan. If he had an accident in a lonely place, everyone would have been suspicious."

"Look, I understand you loved the guy, and I don't mean to diminish him in any way, but Nochelobo wasn't *that* charismatic. Boschvark wasn't concerned about him."

"I know what happened," she insists.

He shakes his head and sighs. "You can't comprehend how a man like Terrence Boschvark operates. He'd never risk order-ing someone to harm you physically. He can easily deal with his enemies without violence. Here's what I mean, his style, how he works. Listen and learn. You inherited this land from your uncle. You think he owned it. Maybe he did. But Boschvark is able to work through bureaucrats in half a dozen agencies to build a case that your land has been poisoned by something you've been doing here. Or the Native American nation that once owned it was never paid properly. Or an endangered species lives here and nowhere else."

"I'll fight for my land."

"If you can get an attorney, in the end you'll discover he was paid by Boschvark to betray you, but you won't be able to prove it. And forget about poisoned soil and all that. The assault on you will be more profound. You'll be evicted within thirty days, without compensation. Then where will you go? Your heart is here."

"Evicted? There's no mortgage. No overdue taxes."

"In here I have your fate." Bead pats the manila envelope, and the gesture conveys the same vanity with which he smoothed his hair earlier. He gets erotic pleasure from being in league with those who can crush anyone they choose. He is aroused and his desire sated by violence, whether it is the kind that leaves his target physically broken and bloodied or with a mortally wounded spirit. "Boschvark doesn't even know about this. I've learned a thing or two from him, and I've put this together myself. He doesn't know you've been running your little investigation. I don't want him to know because whatever you got from Morgan Slyke, one of my boys, will reflect badly on me. I don't want Boschvark distrusting me. In this envelope are copies of documents that were recently printed on paper milled seven decades ago, bearing the correct signatures and seals of that time. The originals, superb forgeries, prove your uncle never bought this property from a previous owner, that it was county-owned land when he moved onto it, that he illegally homesteaded these eighty acres by paying a bribe to the Kettleton County assessor, who was then also the tax collector, a man named Gregory Gattigan."

Vida conceals her anger. She senses that everything now depends on Bead believing that she's beginning to realize he and Boschvark comprise a force as irresistible as an avalanche. In a voice bled of all conviction, she says, "No one's going to buy what you're selling."

"I also have here a copy of a notarized statement from Bethany Gattigan Dirks, daughter of Gregory Gattigan. Bethany swears under penalty of perjury that her father, with only one month to

THE FOREST OF LOST SOULS

live, confessed to her that he altered the historic county land maps to remove eighty acres from public holdings and place them on the tax rolls under the ownership of your uncle Ogden."

Bead takes such sadistic delight in Vida's torment that the decadence previously suggested only by the softness of his mouth is evident in his lacerating stare, in his cruel smile. The tip of his tongue licks the curve of his mouth, revealing a satyromania that alerts her to a danger greater than the forged documents present.

"Now," he continues, "don't think poorly of Mrs. Dirks. She's seventy-six, a pitiful widow. For too long, she's lived on a skimpy Social Security check and the little she makes from seamstress work. She regrets that all she had to sell was her integrity, but it was worth a pretty penny to me."

Vida says nothing. She wants him to think that her silence is the silence of one who knows she is defeated but can't bear to admit as much. He must not think she might in any way strike out at him.

"All the documents, plus a letter requesting an interview with you, are in this envelope from the current assessor."

She can see that the envelope bears her address and a postage-meter tape dated three days earlier.

He offers the envelope to her, but she doesn't accept it, so he places it on the small table between the rocking chairs.

"If you assure me that you'll stop playing Nancy Drew," Bead continues, "and if you, at my direction, produce a short handwritten letter signed by you, no one will evict you."

"A letter saying what?"

"It'll be dated the day before the tragedy. To José Nochelobo. A very angry letter. While he was at work, you let yourself in his place with your key. You'd baked his favorite cake to leave as a surprise. You saw a few things that needed to be tidied up, and while you were attending to that, you stumbled upon his collection of child pornography."

"You son of a bitch."

"You know my mother. So in the letter you break up with him. You can't tolerate such perversity. You urge him to get counseling."

"He didn't have child pornography."

"The sheriff has locked away the collection."

"Then either you or Boschvark's people, someone at New World Technology, planted it the day José was murdered."

"Your letter, with your prints and DNA on it, added to that box of filth, will lend credibility to the evidence of his sick mind."

"No."

"That's not an option."

"It's my only option. No."

"Here's what you should consider while you think about it."

"I don't need to think about it. I won't do it."

"Before you give me your final decision, understand that the sheriff has told no one about that collection. None of us wants to destroy Mr. Nochelobo's reputation unless it's absolutely necessary. Unfortunately, he was so persuasive that even now, after his death, people rally around his crusade as a memorial to him. We hope their passion fades. If it does, there'll be no need to reveal his sexual attraction to children. In time, as the New World Technology project advances, his nasty collection and your letter will be destroyed. We won't make it public out of meanness alone. It's only insurance."

"You're disgusting, all of you."

Bead consults his Rolex. "I have that dinner engagement."

"Then go choke on something."

"If you won't write that letter, Vida, you *will* be evicted. Where will you go? How will you get the money that the endless litigation will require?"

She says nothing.

"If you won't write the letter, Sheriff Montrose will feel a moral obligation to reveal the collection of kiddie porn and launch an investigation to learn if José, as a teacher, might have forced himself on any minors. I guarantee a few will come forward."

He could have presented the copies of the forged property documents in a folder. There is no reason to deliver them in an assessor's envelope with dated postage-meter tape, as though she received it in the mail. Unless . . . Unless, once she has written the letter, after he has overpowered her—*maybe with chloroform,* an inner voice suggests—raped her while she's unconscious, and staged her suicide, he can then scatter the envelope and its contents beside her corpse, to establish why she took her life. In the new Kettleton, there will be no investigation or autopsy.

With a note of desperation meant to convince him that the fight has gone out of her, she says, "I want to stay here. Have to stay."

"Then back off."

"And if I do, I'll really be allowed to stay here?"

"I don't have any use for this shitty place. No one does. Just keep yourself to yourself. Stay out of the way of the money train."

"But do you promise? You swear?"

"I promise. I swear," he lies.

She remembers the lascivious intent he revealed when he licked his lips. She sees sick desire in his stare, those eyes the cold, pale blue of Namibian smithsonite. His soul is harder than any gemstone.

She should have armed herself with her uncle's pistol. She hadn't imagined that Bead would be so reckless as to move directly to violence. She thought he'd come to level a warning at her and give her a few days to acquiesce. If that was his intention when he arrived, he has since decided on a different, more brutal resolution to the problem she presents.

"Come on, Vida. You've got nothing to gain by refusing, and everything to lose. Let's write that letter and get on with our day. I don't want to keep my dinner companions waiting."

There are no dinner companions. His deceit is palpable.

The prospect of allowing him into her house is intolerable. Her options will be limited when he crosses the threshold.

She gets to her feet and approaches the front door and halts. "The envelope. The documents."

When Bead reaches down and plucks the envelope from the table, Vida hikes up her sweatshirt from her right hip and draws the can of bear spray from the holster attached to her belt, the only defensive weapon she'd thought necessary.

Whatever Bead sees from the corner of his eye, it's enough to make him drop the envelope, reach under his coat, and pull a pistol from his shoulder rig. As he turns toward her, the expanding cloud of repellent is still dense when it bursts against his face, oiling him with an instant sheen. Tears flood his eyes, severely blurring his vision. His pupils will have instantly swelled wide, letting in a blinding farrago of amorphous shapes of light. She gives him the full seven-second charge, so that though he turns his face away, he remains in the cloud of capsaicin. Then she throws the can aside. Even as Bead is retching, he's gasping for breath, like a two-headed beast in conflict with itself. He can't find fresh air, feels as if he's suffocating. His ears should be ringing as loud as a siren, further disorienting him.

He opens fire. He can't see her. She'd be dead if he could discern even the vague shape of her. But he fires a round and then another, trusting to luck and proximity, a power freak suddenly powerless, frightened and furious. The hard crack of each shot is reverberant and hollow, as though Bead and Vida are kenneled by the porch, the cacophony of bestial combat trapped and ricocheting along metaled walls.

The cloud of repellent expands past Bead and beyond the porch, but though its diffusion is propelled by highly pressurized gas, the peppery particulate appears to disperse sluggishly. It seems to Vida that both she and her assailant are moving in slow motion, as though the watch spring of the universe has unwound, time itself running out. She holds her breath as she steps into the third shot, which tunnels through the air maybe a foot wide of her. Violence is by its nature swift, but in this moment of mortal danger, she picks up a rocking chair and rams her assailant with it as if moving through some viscous fluid. Like a deep-sea diver laboring under miles of water, he staggers backward into the porch balustrade, reflexively firing the gun once more.

That shot sets right the universe, and time surges full speed. As Bead falls, he seems to fling the pistol away as if shocked by it. The weapon clatters across the porch floor, and Vida quickens after it, breath held and eyes squinted to slits.

Gun in hand, she turns to Belden Bead, where he sits on the porch floor with his back against the railing balusters, eyes still pools of tears but his breathing no longer labored, as though some source of mercy has granted him surcease from the effects of bear spray. In his fall, he has shot himself in his left leg, his thigh. Judging by the blood spreading through the fabric of his suit pants and across the planking, she figures the bullet severed the femoral artery. He is bleeding out fast, and he knows it.

If his recognition of his fate should humble him, it does not, and neither does imminent death wring from him a plea for help. He doesn't damn her, as she might expect, but contents himself with calling her names that deny her personhood, that reduce her to an inanimate sex toy, a tool for masturbation. In sprays of jalapeño spittle, various obscene words for one female anatomical feature spew from him repetitively, with increasing ferocity, as if this is not a man insulting her, but instead a demonic parasite that resides in Bead and hates her because it will be evicted from this world when its host dies.

Vida stands over him, watching him die, offering Bead no aid, no pity. If something possesses him, it does so at his invitation, and if nothing has possessed him, he is a self-made monster, the spiritual brother of the man who killed her father, conspirator in the death of José Nochelobo, one of the legions who lust for power and draw across the world a darkness that denies the light by which the universe was conceived.

He falls silent, and his eyes widen, and for a moment Vida thinks he has died. Suspended over the abyss by a gossamer filament of life, he speaks in a raw, thin, quavering voice colored by what might be wonder or even awe. "Who are you? What are you? Where did it come from, the moon, so big behind you?"

Twilight has not yet arrived. The moon has not yet risen.

Belden Bead breathes out the last of his life.

She can't report what's happened. They will distort the facts into proof of murder. For her, Kettleton offers no law or justice.

33

THE SECOND GRAVE

Having foregone embalming and the attention of a mortuary's makeup artist, rolled for a few revolutions in a drop cloth secured with duct tape, his pistol and small squeeze bottle of chloroform wrapped with him, Belden Bead, crime lord of the mountains, lies on the porch, waiting for burial without honors. Wisely, he had brought no cell phone that, by its GPS pings archived in the cloud, could have proved he'd come here. Now the meadow and the forested uplands stand testament to the truth that those who lust and live for power contribute nothing useful to the world other than the nutrients that their decomposition will add to the soil.

After hosing away the blood and letting the planking dry to see what stains may still need to be addressed, Vida sits for a while on the porch steps, thinking through the actions she'll take. She must be sure to see through the surface of the situation, understand all the possibilities that could take root beneath it.

She senses truth in Bead's insistence that the murder of José was a deviation from the protocols by which Terrence Boschvark labors for his billions. The great man has so many minions in the ruling class and bureaucracy that he can accomplish his ends with only rare resort to physical violence. However, if he had arranged José's assassination, Boschvark had indeed placed himself in such jeopardy that he wouldn't take half measures with Vida. If he thought she had discovered the truth or was even just searching for it, he would deal with her no less violently than he dealt with José. When such hard measures are taken, men like him don't follow them with half measures. Boschvark wouldn't go to the bother of manufacturing evidence that Ogden bribed the assessor to alter the county land maps, so that Vida could be evicted.

Therefore, it's almost certain that Bead—alarmed by Vida's investigation, without approval from Boschvark—concocted the threat to destroy José's reputation with a trove of child pornography. Bead alone schemed to manipulate Vida into writing the letter he wanted. Bead, not Boschvark, crafted the text of the letter so that, if she had written what he dictated, authorities could view it as something she meant to give to José but never had the chance to deliver before his death. If the letter was found with the envelope of documents from the assessor's office, the assumption would be made that the discovery of the kiddie porn had left her in shame and despair, after which the prospect of eviction was all she needed to conclude life was no longer worth living.

Consequently, this was Bead's scheme, as he claimed, and he most likely hasn't told anyone that he was coming here. He must have an accomplice in the assessor's office, someone who had no choice but to do his bidding for whatever reason, someone willing to attest to the authenticity of the forged documents if it comes to that but who is unlikely to know that Bead meant to deliver them in person and then murder her. No one knows where Bead is—or can know where he's gone when he vanishes.

If anyone other than Bead has learned of her visit to Morgan Slyke, that person might suspect she's somehow involved in Bead's disappearance. However, if she seems to back away from further investigation of José's death, no one will have reason to pursue her. Knowing Bead, they might intuit what he attempted and to what end his intentions led him, but the sheriff isn't likely to arrive with a brace of deputies and commence digging for the Plymouth Superbird Hemi, because that will literally be opening a very big can of worms.

Night has come. The moon has risen above the cold and barren granite peaks of the mountains. A few isolate clouds, shaped into arctic masses, drift across the sky, reflecting the lunar light as might icebergs on a northern sea. Great horned owls, vigilant for prey, are *hoo-hoodoo*ing one another, now and then taking wing to chase down earthbound creatures with devastating effect, in this world of the perpetual hunt.

Finished analyzing the situation, Vida ties a rope to the wrapped cadaver and drags it off the porch, down the steps, to the nearby Plymouth in which Bead arrived. With effort, she wrestles the grave-readied bundle onto the back seat.

From the multipurpose building behind the house, she retrieves the John Deere backhoe with which Uncle Ogden had, among other things, excavated the cavity for the massive septic tank that he had constructed and with which, fifteen years later, Vida had dug her uncle's grave. The backhoe features a roof rack of lights, and it's a workhorse, but the job ahead of her is formidable. Ideally, the finished hole at the southern end of the meadow will be three feet wider, a foot longer, and three feet deeper than the car. She'll have to construct it with a ramp leading down to that space in which the vehicle will rest.

The ruckus of the backhoe engine rackets across the grassland and through the trees, but there are no neighbors near enough to be disturbed. And those who choose to live in this remote territory are as incurious as they expect others to be.

With the aid of quarts of black coffee, several big chocolate-chip cookies that she had baked the previous day, and mint-flavored antacid tablets, Vida finishes the first phase of the job shortly past four o'clock in the morning, after eight hours of unrelenting effort. With the moon far into its descent, she drives the Plymouth and its profoundly silent passenger down the ramp and into the hole. She parks closer to the right flank of the pit than to the left, so that she is able to open the driver's door wide enough to slip out of the car.

Although she's exhausted, she returns to the backhoe. She fills the space around the car and begins to cover it.

An hour after sunrise, with songbirds gracing the day and hawks taking up the hunt that the nocturnal raptors have forsaken until dusk, the Plymouth is concealed under six or eight inches of soil. The situation is not ideal, but Vida can do no more until she has gotten some rest.

Later, fortified by five hours of sleep and a hearty breakfast eaten past noon, she returns to her work. Even after the Plymouth lies three feet below the meadow and she's driven over it uncounted times to compact the fill, a big mound of excavated earth remains. Over the next few days, she will distribute it across the southern end of the meadow, although some will have to be kept at the site to be added to the grave as the loose soil naturally settles and forms into a telltale declivity. Eventually, she'll gather ripened grass and strip it and scatter its seeds across the bare earth.

She garages the backhoe for the day. A hot shower is bliss.

On slices of whole wheat—two slathered with mustard, the other two with mayonnaise—she builds a pair of sandwiches from cold roast beef, Havarti cheese, shredded lettuce, tomato, and sliced gherkins. With a bottle of good cabernet, she takes dinner in a rocking chair on the porch.

Vida has finished one sandwich when the breeze gently tumbles the white fedora across the yard.

Belden Bead has been dead twenty-four hours. Casketed in the Plymouth. The windows had broken out to admit cascades of earth as the soil had been compacted. The crime boss of Kettleton County is beyond any possibility of being reunited with his hat.

Before attending to her second sandwich, Vida hurries into the yard to retrieve the fedora, lest it might be carried aloft and spun away. Not a single drop of blood mars it. Although the hat has been blown hither and yon during the night and through the following day, it looks as white and properly blocked as it had been when she'd first seen Bead wearing it.

Experience has cultured in her a belief in signs and omens. The fedora is a humble object. If Belden Bead hadn't perished by his own misdirected violence in his attempt to kill her, the hat might even have a comical quality. Nevertheless, it is invested with portentous meaning by virtue of its pristine condition and Nature's use of wind and night to conceal it from her until this moment.

Vida stands in the yard, turning the hat in her hands, deciding what she should do with it. Millennia earlier, when hunters ventured into the wilds with bows and arrows, when they killed a deer or a pheasant, they not only brought the meat to their tables, but also made a coat from the deer's hide or used the bird's feathers to enhance a garment. Nature is honored by the full and wise use of what it provides.

With sudden conviction, Vida puts on the hat. A perfect fit.

One day it might be useful. Just a hunch.

She returns to the porch, to her chair, to her second sandwich. The cabernet held by the stemware is a deeper red than the sky. Soon after darkfall, when an early moon rises, its spectral light traces the beveled edges in the cut-crystal bowl of the wineglass, transforming those patterns into hieroglyphs awaiting translation.

Turning the glass in her hand, Vida remembers the raven-haired woman in the ramshackle house, eighteen years earlier, and the sign in the yard decorated with crescent moons and stars. *The truth and the future revealed here.*

34

WHAT THE SEER SEES

The pea-soup-green table is speckled with other colors where the surface has been chipped or scratched to reveal the past in the present. As before, the paper blinds are closed over the windows, though on this occasion the nameless seer has lit three candles in glass cups, when previously only one was provided. Subtly shimmering luminous circles overlap one another on the table; reflected on the ceiling, their light dances with greater sprightliness, forming a pattern suggesting a mystery in need of a solution.

The book—payment for the seer, which Vida brought the previous day—lies before the woman. A soft draft stirs the candle flames, and fingers of light smooth across the paperback, as if a ghostly presence can read it by touch without opening it.

Facing ten-year-old Vida across the table, the seer says, "You were right when you said this book is mean and angry, that it wants you to believe things that aren't true."

"But," says the girl, "you wanted what I valued least. I'm not sure what else I could pay you with."

"Oh, this is ample payment, child. Not this evil little book. The payment is your ability to perceive the anger and the lies that the story promotes. I am well rewarded to see that in you."

Puzzled, Vida says, "I'm not sure I understand."

"One day you will. You might have an old soul, but you are still very young."

"So then . . . will you tell my future?"

"If you're sure you want to hear it."

"That's why I came the first time. That's why I've come back twice. So do you use a crystal ball, cards, tea leaves?"

"No, child, I need none of that. Your future will be full of strife and struggle, loss and grief, doubt and fear, and pain."

Vida is silent, waiting. At last, she says, "That sucks."

After a Mona Lisa smile comes and goes, the seer says, "Your future will be full of peace and comfort, love and joy, hope and fortitude, solace and delight."

After another silence, Vida says, "Which is it?"

"Which is what?"

"Well, gee, that sounds like two different futures for two different people."

"They are one and the same future, dear. All those things will be yours to experience."

"Okay, but . . ."

"But what?"

"I mean . . ."

"You mean?"

"I thought there'd be . . . details. Like—what strife? What joy? What loss? What love?"

The paperback is gone. Vida hasn't seen the woman take the payment. Indeed, the seer's hands have remained below the table. It's as if the book has been washed away by the rippling waves of candlelight.

"It's not for me," the seer says, "to paint your future in fine detail. It's yours to paint. If I revealed it, then you would have no life to live, only a role to play, a script to follow."

This seems to be a nice lady, and Vida is loath to suggest that she is either a fraud or just plain silly. She can only say, "Well, I guess I see why you don't take money for this."

The enigmatic smile comes again, widens, and is accompanied by a soft laugh. Her hands appear and fold together on the table. "Do you know what a myth is, Vida?"

"Sure. An old, old story about something that never happened even though people once thought it did, or pretended to think so."

"You're a smart girl."

"I read a lot. My uncle and me, we don't do TV."

"Myths are more than stories. They're also lessons. Longer ago even than history knows, when our species was young, we acted far more on emotion than on reason. It's still a dangerous tendency of our kind, of human beings, but back then we were even more childlike than now. We weren't ready for higher knowledge. We wouldn't have understood if directly instructed. Do you follow me?"

"Sort of, I guess. All right."

"And so," the seer continues, "myths were inspired, initially to instill in people the idea that this life has meaning, and over time to help that idea strengthen into a conviction. This took many centuries, but there was no reason to be in a hurry because time as humans perceive it is an illusion."

Although she's a girl who is interested in many strange things, Vida is overcome by a mild frustration. She curls her toes in her shoes, shifts in her chair, and sighs. "Then why do clocks work?"

"Past, present, and future exist all at once, but that's too much for humankind to handle, too confusing. We need them to flow one into the other in an orderly fashion. So we perceive time as we need to perceive it to cope. Or the perception of time is a crutch we've been given, whichever you prefer to believe. And so—clocks."

"Maybe I'll understand when I'm like a hundred," Vida says.

"Long before then, dear. Myths, as I was saying, were lessons by which we learned how to think about the world we can see and the world we can't. For countless centuries, it wasn't the truth of the myths that mattered, but the new ways of thinking that they subtly taught us. Over millennia, myths evolved to lead us ever so slowly to a deeper understanding of the world and our place in it, the reason for our being, slow enough for us to handle it all."

"Like taking baby steps."

"Exactly. We took baby steps as a species until eventually we arrived at the revelations, the truths, on which our civilization is built. But all the myths that instructed us are still relevant, in part because they made us what we are, and in part because we still need stories to teach us how to live, as we keep forgetting."

"This is making me dizzy."

"Not at all. You aren't a dizzy girl."

"So that's all the future you're going to tell me?"

The seer opens her clasped hands, revealing a white flower with thick, waxy petals. The bloom is so large that it couldn't have been concealed in the small hands of the seer. The bloom is three times the size of the largest blossom from a magnolia tree, and the petals are thicker, as if it is carved from ivory.

Vida says, "Where did *that* come from?"

"Where all things come from. It is the amaranth. The undying flower of myth."

The woman passes it across the table. Vida shakily receives it.

The flower is so beautiful, so radiant in the low light, that Vida feels a special responsibility not to damage it.

"We are," the seer says, "made of all the myths that brought us through millennia to the truth, but there is one in particular that you will shape your life around."

Sensing that the amaranth up lights her face in a way that the candles never could, Vida says, "What myth is that?"

"You'll know in time. You'll be a champion of the natural world and all its beauty, the guardian of wild things, for you'll neither wish to dominate nature nor confuse it with what is truly sacred."

"I don't know what that means."

"You will. One day. Be brave."

That word sort of scares Vida. "I'm not brave."

"You are the essence of bravery, child."

"Why do I need to be?"

"Because all things will come to you, good and bad. The bad is yours to cure by action, the good to enjoy and share. Remember these words, girl, these words that will be of especially great importance one day—*moon, sun, and smoking river.* To chase the meaning of those words will put you at intolerable risk. Be patient, and the meaning will eventually come to you when you need it, for that is who you are. All things come to you in their time."

"I don't understand."

"You will."

The seer waves a hand across the three glass cups. The candles are extinguished as one, and the room falls into a darkness that is little relieved by the wan daylight passing through the mottled window shades.

Vida rises from her chair, turns from the table, and finds herself in warm morning light, on the far side of the county road, walking home on the dirt lane, the long stem of the amaranth tucked behind her right ear.

This time, unlike on the two previous occasions, she realizes more clearly and urgently that she has transitioned here from the kitchen in the ramshackle house as if by magic or in a trance. She halts and starts to turn back—thinks, *Don't!*—and then hurries along the colonnades of trees, under the vault of their branches, eager to get home and show her uncle the amaranth.

Climbing the porch steps, she reaches for the flower tucked behind her ear. It is not there.

Frantic to find what she has lost, she retraces her steps across the yard and all the way to the end of the long unpaved driveway, but she is unable to retrieve even one waxy petal. She stops at the county road and stares at the house where the seer waits with fortunes untold and strange truths to impart.

Although, for the time being, young Vida is more mystified than enlightened, she understands that the amaranth was for her and her alone to see, that she should hold the image of it forever in her mind and take courage from what it promises.

35

SUBMISSION

Friday evening, twenty-four hours after Nash Deacon first came to dinner at his own invitation, the kitchen is more welcoming for their second "date." The table is draped with beige linen trimmed in lace. Vida does not have—or desire—expensive things; however, when her uncle was alive, he gave her items that he thought a girl should have, to add charm to holidays and special occasions, including four place settings of fine china. The white plates have narrow gold rims, as do the saucers and coffee cups. The cut-crystal stemware was also a gift from Uncle Ogden. She has purchased roses for the centerpiece, although they are white rather than red. The napkins match the table-cloth. There are no paper towels or plastic cups.

As instructed by Deacon, Vida is wearing her white dress, though with sneakers rather than the high heels that he specified. Full compliance in every detail would lead him to suspect that her submission is too sudden, too complete—therefore insincere. The snugness of the silver-mesh choker is a constant reminder of the psychological leash he intends to attach to her, a reminder that encourages her to do what must be done as soon as circumstances allow and without misstep or misgiving.

Remember what he is. He paid a junkie to rape his wife and beat her to death with a hammer. Then he arranged the killer's death with a doctored overdose. The wife's murder is in the public records, though not the truth of it.

When she hears the Trans Am approaching through the eastern woods with a growl like a monster in some Scandinavian legend, Vida puts a loaf of home-baked sourdough on a cutting board and sets the board on the table. She pours cabernet, an inch more for her than for him. She places the glasses according to where she and Deacon sat the previous night.

As before, she has left the front door open. As before, he closes it behind him when he comes inside.

Stepping into the kitchen, the sheriff surveys the table. His smile is alike to that of a man who, having whipped a dog yesterday, is pleased to see the creature shrink from him today.

Vida offers no smile of her own and strikes no appealing pose, but faces him with the sullen expression of one who resents that she must put herself on display.

He takes off his hat and fans himself with it. "Young lady, I swear, if this was the dead of winter, you'd have no need of a furnace or a fireplace, what with the heat you put off yourself. That dress becomes you like I knew it would."

She crosses her arms. "I don't have to make nice. I don't have to like this."

"I understand how this is a moment that sticks in your craw. For sure, darlin', you don't have to like it. But later, when that dress isn't between us anymore, you'll like it well enough."

He puts the hat on the chair to the right of the one in which he'll sit. He's dressed much as he was the previous evening, but he's added a lightweight sport coat.

She says, "You wanted to know about Belden Bead. Sit down with your wine, and I'll tell you what happened to the bastard."

"So you don't have time for small talk? How my day was, how yours was, whether we saw a good movie lately?"

"Whatever you get from me, you don't get small talk. You don't get to humiliate me by making me play girlfriend."

His soft laugh is knowing and self-satisfied. "Honey, if I want to humiliate you, I got more interestin' ways than that. Sadly, you continue to underestimate me when you think you won't eventually be into this relationship and havin' fun. You just need to get over not doin' this by choice—and you will."

"What does that make me, then?"

"What does what make you?"

"Doing it not by choice but doing it anyway."

"Practical," he says. "It makes you practical."

"It makes me what I could never be."

"You'll be surprised what you can be."

"Not as low as you."

"You'll find yourself lower, darlin'. And likin' it. So tell me about Belden Bead. What befell the poor man?"

"First I've got to set the soup to simmer." She turns to the pot on the stove and picks up a ladle and stirs long enough for Deacon to do what she believes and hopes he'll do.

She sets aside the ladle, puts the lid on the pot so that it's canted to let the steam escape, faces him again, and sees he's done it. He's in his chair where she wanted him, but his wineglass is the one she meant for herself, the fuller of the two. Deacon distrusts her enough to switch the stemware and wait to see what happens.

She settles in her chair and picks up the glass meant for him and drinks from it without hesitation. She takes more than a sip, a lavish swallow.

Part of her strategy is to lead him to believe she's drinking to excess in order to numb herself for the ordeal of going to bed with him. He'll think she's drinking on an empty stomach; however, less than an hour before he arrived, she ate a substantial meal of steak and eggs, high protein that will digest slowly and somewhat delay the wine's effect. While she tells him about Bead and endures his questions, she should be able to consume two generous servings of cabernet faster than is wise without losing her edge—maybe three or four glasses if she can pull off another trick that she's set up.

She asks him to slice off a heel of the uncut loaf of sourdough and pass it to her. He watches as she butters the bread and takes a bite and swallows and drinks more wine. Then he butters a slice for himself. He drinks more judiciously than she does as she recounts the threat Bead made to have her evicted, describes why she began to suspect he intended to kill her, and comes at last to the bear spray and the gunfire and the backhoe.

Through all of that, she has poured a second glass from the bottle on the table and nearly finished it, while Deacon has drunk little more than half of his first serving.

His eyes, previously a sooty shade of brown, look almost black and as deep as wells. "So you're sayin' it was an accidental death?"

Vida shakes her head. "He shot himself when he meant to shoot me. That's not accidental. That's stupid."

"You have more of that bear spray?"

"Got to have it. There's always bears."

"Just so you know, I'm quicker and smarter than Belden."

She watches him swirl the wine in his glass.

He says, "You dug a mighty big hole for the man."

"Wasn't for the man. It was for the car. A man as small as he was hardly needed a hole at all."

"You could've dug no hole, called the sheriff instead."

"Sheriff Montrose sold himself to Boschvark even before you got the top job and started sucking on the New World Technology nipple."

Deacon is amused or pretends to be. "That won't work."

"What won't?"

"Offendin' me until you turn me off. All you do is turn me on more. I don't take offense."

"Because you have no shame."

"There you go. Plus I believe in payback. You stick it to me, later I'll enjoy dealin' out the payback."

She resorts to her wine and then says, "If I'd called Sheriff Montrose, I'd be rotting with Bead in his car, under the meadow. He'd have put me under."

"That's probably true. But then what you did brought you to me. Like destiny."

"Destiny is a clean thing. This is dirtier. This would be fate if it was anything. How hard was it to drive all the honest cops out of the department?"

"It's taken a determined effort."

He finally sips more wine.

She says, "What kind of man has no shame?"

"The kind who knows what he wants and always gets it. You'll come to appreciate that, darlin'. When you admit you belong to me, you'll feel safe, because no one dares damage what's mine."

"You can't own a person."

"Well now, I already own you, girl. You just don't want to know it yet."

As if the intensity of his stare disturbs her, she looks away and then quickly meets his eyes again to assert that she doesn't fear him, but looks away once more.

"Got to finish the soup." She knocks against the table as she gets up from her chair. She carries the nearly empty wineglass to the cooktop, rattles it against the counter as she puts it down.

"The bread is good," Deacon says. "You made it yourself?"

At the stove, taking the lid off the pot, she says, "I don't like store-bought bread."

"It's got a nice crust. The egg-custard pie you had in the fridge on Wednesday—that was homemade, too."

"Yeah." She picks up a bowl of egg whites prepared earlier and drops the contents into the pot.

"What soup are you makin'?"

"Lentil with bacon and chopped hard-boiled-egg whites."

"I like the smell. The soup's and yours both."

Picking up a half-empty wine bottle from the counter and pouring, she says, "Finished with a few ounces of Napa's finest."

"Main course in the oven smells grand."

"Pork tenderloin with roasted potatoes."

"You're a twofer, darlin'. Kitchen to bedroom, you got what it takes to fill me and drain me."

He's pushing her to gauge whether her resentment and bitterness are to any extent giving way to resignation or perhaps even to the spiritless apathy that a victim can retreat into when there is no hope of escaping some horror. There is risk in being either too obstinate or too compliant. She must seem to be in retreat from hope but not yet on the brink of imminent surrender—indignant enough to want to insult him, but fearful enough to be concerned that she might goad him into assaulting her.

Emptying the bottle brings the wine in her glass nearly to the brim. "Well, Sheriff, filling you might take an hour, but I suspect draining you won't take a minute."

This time, Deacon doesn't say whether he finds her response amusing, offensive, or both. "You just gave yourself two glasses of wine in one. You chug that, you'll have had four. Don't get sloppy."

The cabernet she poured from the now empty wine bottle beside the cooktop is actually grape juice. Rather than risk affecting a slur that might be unconvincing, she adopts a sullen impudence, which is likely to seem childish to him and to comport with his belief that women are lesser creatures in thrall to their emotions. "Maybe the best way I get through this is unconscious."

"It's how I like it now and then," he says. "Especially makes sense the first time. No need to hear what silly shit you might say, won't have to keep tellin' you to shut up. I can concentrate better on the basic merchandise, all its qualities. Plus when you wake up, it'll be different enough to seem like we had our first time twice in one night. Just don't get sloppy. You puke before you pass out, I'll make you eat it when you wake up."

He's an abomination. Hatred isn't a strong-enough word for the feeling he evokes. She represses any evidence of her abhorrence in favor of appearing weakened by fear and grieving for the loss of freedom that is inevitable if he moves in with her. She holds her wineglass in both hands to bring it shakily to her mouth, and she lets it chatter against her teeth before drinking. She won't go so far as to pretend dread by letting a trickle spill down her chin; she's certain she'll need a white dress for one future occasion or another, and she doesn't want to have to buy a new one.

"Come sit down."

"I'm good here."

"Come sit and be yourself with me."

"Who am I being already if not myself?"

"You're playin' a cold fish."

"I am what I am."

"Which isn't that."

"You'll see."

"Come sit down. Tell me about your day."

"The soup is almost done."

"It's simmerin'. It won't burn."

"I don't want . . ."

"I know what you don't want. What you think you don't want. What you pretend you don't want. Come sit down."

"I mean, I don't want this to go wrong. The dinner. I don't want you to be upset."

"You don't want me to be upset."

"Yes."

"That's new for you, darlin'."

"I mean angry. I don't want you to be angry. I'm trying with this dinner. I really am. I'm trying to . . . come to terms with what's happened, what is. It isn't easy."

"It can be easy."

"Well, it isn't."

He samples his wine. "What do you imagine I'm like when I'm very angry?"

"I don't know."

"You must have some thoughts on the subject."

"Yeah, but I don't *want* to think about it." She drinks her faux cabernet.

"I was never angry with Tanya, my wife, just frustrated by the endless naggin' about a baby. I don't get very angry, darlin'. I just get done what needs done."

She sets her wineglass on the counter. "I'll serve the soup. You want to hear about my day, then I'll tell you about it when we sit down to the soup."

Two deep bowls stand on the counter, one nestled in the other. While Deacon watches her, she sets them side by side and ladles soup from the pot until both bowls are full. She takes his bowl to the table and then brings her own and sits.

"Your wine," he says, because she left it by the cooktop.

"I'm dizzy. A little queasy."

"What did I tell you?"

"I know."

"I don't ever want to see you pour it down like that again."

"Two glasses are my limit. I never have more. Until now."

"I hope that's true. From now on, it'll be true. I'll see to that. Eat some soup. It'll help."

She picks up her spoon but only stares at the soup.

"Is this a sayin' grace house?" he asks.

"Mostly."

"Just eat. You say, 'Thank you, Nash,' and just eat."

Vida doesn't thank him, but she eats.

After he watches her for a minute or so, he attends to his soup, having seen the bowls filled from the same pot. "This is delicious, girl. Got some bite to it."

"A touch of jalapeño," she says, which she added to explain why his tongue and throat would burn from just the second spoonful.

He says, "So much flavor."

"Seven different herbs plus the bacon," she says, which she employed not merely to enhance the flavor of the lentils, but also to mask the faint taste of the key ingredient in the event that he should be sensitive to it.

"I could take a second bowl of this."

"There's plenty."

"It's good sopped up with bread."

"Don't forget there's pork tenderloin for after."

"I have big appetites, darlin'. You'll learn how big."

In about three minutes, his table manners less than refined, Nash Deacon has eaten most of his soup. His voracity is desirable in this case, for symptoms of monkshood poisoning can become extreme in as little as two minutes and never take longer than ten to manifest.

She says, "You ever heard of a place called the Smoking River?"

"Not around here."

"The words 'two moon, sun spirit' mean anything to you?"

His spoon clatters into the bowl and he sits up straight, eyes shocked wide, though he's not reacting to her question. The heat he attributed to the jalapeños has abruptly progressed to a numbness of tongue, throat, and face. When he says, "What is what you did this," he is not only incoherent but also slurs his words. His vision will have suddenly blurred. The skin over most of his body is tingling.

As Vida gets to her feet, Deacon thrusts up and knocks over his chair and falls to the floor.

She circles the table, plucks the inch-thick breadboard out from under what remains of the loaf, and stands over the sheriff as he gropes under his sport coat as if he's come to serve papers but has forgotten in which pocket he carries an eviction notice. She assumes that he has a pistol in a shoulder rig or a belt scabbard, and it's the latter. As Deacon fumbles the weapon from the holster, Vida chops hard at his wrist with the edge of the breadboard. He drops the pistol. She throws aside the board and snatches up the gun, determined that this will not be a near thing, as was the encounter with Belden Bead.

Slick with sweat, Deacon's face is pale clay, molded and carved by rage that is less an expression than a revelation of the deformed mind his plain features can no longer mask. She turns from him as he vomits, and she walks out of the kitchen.

36

THE THIRD GRAVE

In the library, Vida puts Mozart's piano concerto K. 488 on the turntable and sets the volume slightly higher than usual, using the glorious music to mask the noise of Deacon thrashing and gasping in the kitchen. The sheriff is a tall, muscular man capable of making a lot of noise in his death throes.

Western monkshood, also called "wolfsbane," has a toxicity equal to that of any lethal plant. The roots and leaves are especially poisonous. That morning, she had gathered it from the upland meadow where, on Tuesday, she had filled bags with her favorite mushroom, *Morchella conica*. Nature provides weaponry as readily as sustenance.

Aconitine and aconine are the poisons in monkshood. Because those substances can be absorbed through the skin with lethal effect, Vida wore nitrile gloves and a face shield while crushing and then steeping the plants. Filtered through muslin, the resultant clear liquid would have provided swift justice to Sheriff Deacon. However, to increase potency, Vida had boiled and reduced the brew to a thin syrup, concentrating the unwholesome chemicals.

A fully satisfying reaction to monkshood can take from just ten minutes to a few hours. It has been Vida's intention to ensure her unwanted suitor will succumb in a timely manner, both as a matter of mercy and in the interest of getting on with the work ahead of her.

The deep, white bowls had been stacked one atop the other, and the bottom bowl had contained an inch of the reduction. Even if the sheriff had come to the cooktop as she had separated the bowls, he probably wouldn't have noticed the puddle of clear liquid in one of them before Vida ladled lentils into it. Besides, his suspicions were allayed when she'd drunk the wine he'd switched with hers, and there was nothing alarming about being served soup out of the same pot from which she took hers.

His vision will cloud and grow dim. Creeping paralysis of the respiratory system, declining blood pressure, and a faltering pulse will leave him weak. As his body temperature falls, he will feel as if his veins carry ice water rather than blood, and he will begin to shudder uncontrollably. Paralysis of the heart muscle will be the ultimate cause of death.

Eighteen years earlier, the seer with raven hair said, *You'll be a champion of the natural world and all its beauty.* If indeed that's what Vida is becoming, it seems that she will be required to do hard things. Perhaps that should be no surprise. Nature herself is as hard as she is beautiful, red of tooth and claw.

Vida waits fifteen minutes before returning to the kitchen. Nash Deacon is dead—and something of a mess.

She rolls him facedown and with some effort pulls off his sport coat to search its pockets.

On that afternoon eight months ago, intending murder, Belden Bead hadn't carried his phone, for its transponder could produce evidence putting him at the scene of the crime. Nash Deacon has not been quite that circumspect, although the phone Vida retrieves from an interior pocket of his coat is evidently not the one connected to him by a telecom account, but instead a cheap disposable for special occasions. He surely didn't purchase it with a credit card or from any vendor who might know him. Therefore, no one will be tracking its signal to search for Sheriff Deacon when he goes missing. She will nevertheless smash the phone with a hammer before burying it with the lawless lawman.

She rolls up the corpse in a drop cloth and seals that shroud with duct tape. She cleans up what mess remains.

The sky darkles from blue to purple to black, and the stars are born again as they have been every night for billions of years, and the moon rises as it has risen for somewhat fewer billions of years, and for the second night in eight months, the insistent growl of the backhoe carries across the meadow and fades into the sound-baffling forest.

During the hours of labor, as Vida operates the machine from the elevated driver's seat, mosquitoes forage through the darkness for blood, but not one lands on her exposed skin; in all her years, none of their kind has bitten her. Neither do night moths flutter about her, nor do the day flies annoy her. She has never been stung by a bee or nipped by a spider. There comes a moment when a ghostly presence appears beyond the certain identification that the lights of the backhoe might have provided, a pale and fluid form low to the ground, like a humbled spirit that must crawl the territory it is condemned to haunt. Vida believes this is Azrael, the albino cougar that appeared in a bolder fashion on the day when Anna Lagare, the mortician's daughter, came to visit. If the big cat is here as an omen of a death to come, it doesn't linger to impress Vida with its dire message, and she fears neither Azrael nor what its apparition is said to foretell. She watches it deliquesce into the dark, and she continues digging a grave for the man and his Trans Am. Later, when she's in the pit, hoisting soil out with the long, jointed arm of the backhoe, she considers the placer mine, where over centuries Nature has deposited beauty and treasure. In this hastily stocked placer mine of Vida's creation, nothing lovely or of value waits to be found, but if eighteen years ago the seer was right about her purpose and destiny, this too is an essential work of Nature.

37

MY HEART IS READY

The meadow earth is soft, and the first strata of rock lies deeper than the grave of the man and his machine needs to be. Vida is motivated to work without rest until Deacon and everything of his, including his hat and the silver-mesh dog collar, is under compacted soil. Something more explicit than the intuition that previously served her well, some power of perception for which she has no name, warns her that the perils she's put behind her will be greatly exceeded by the threats that are still to come. She intends to be ready for them.

The cosmology influenced by modern physics might contend that the past and present and future exist simultaneously and eternally, that all time is unredeemable, leading to only one possible end. However, if that is true, she's no less obliged to make choices, take risks, stand for what she believes in, endure the consequences. To do otherwise would be to concede the world to those who distill ever more potent evil in the chambers of their hearts.

She showers as night wanes, falls into bed at first light, and dreams of gemstones scattered among skeletons.

At eleven o'clock Saturday morning, after five hours of deep sleep, she eats a breakfast of lentil soup, pork tenderloin, and roast potatoes. She uses her everyday dishes rather than the fine china that she reserves for special occasions.

She retreats to the library to finish *Wuthering Heights*, which she'd begun on Tuesday, after Nash Deacon's first visit during which he revealed that he sought her submission. The perception of looming danger remains strong, but she needs a respite from the expectation of violence, a relief that only a Brontë can provide. After all, the river does not race and swell over its banks *in anticipation* of the storm, and trees don't char on Monday *in consideration* of a forest fire on Tuesday. She has no need to panic.

With an hour of daylight remaining, having finished the novel, Vida walks down the unpaved lane and crosses the county highway to the house where the nameless seer in yellow tennis shoes and a white robe had given her the amaranth nearly two decades earlier.

Vance Burkhardt, who rented to that mysterious woman, has been dead twelve years. His estate sold the property to a congregation of forty Christians who had been conducting Sunday morning services in a VFW lodge rented by the hour. The decaying house was repaired by volunteer labor. A five-hundred-square-foot addition expanded the living room and provided an altar. The house served as rectory and place of worship for ten years, until the minister experienced a moral panic and conversion to a political puritanism that subverted all doctrines, reimagined the nature of sin, and defined as evil those behaviors that for most of human history had been thought virtuous. A third of the communicants were awakened by the preacher to this new belief system. A schism developed. On a rainy Sunday, one of the newly enlightened parishioners came to church with a pistol and killed four of the old-school worshippers before being shot to death himself. The congregation dissolved. Mortgage payments ceased to be made. The minister became the manager of a Starbucks coffeehouse. The property reverted to the bank. The bank could find no buyer and ceded the parcel to the county in lieu of unpaid taxes.

The front door hangs open on two of three hinges, which are so corroded they don't work. Those windows that are not broken out have been etched by blown grit, crusted by snail trails, and peppered with fly excrement that in concert form colorless images capable of inspiring such angst and despair that they might excite in an artist a furious commitment to the renewal of the abstract-expressionism movement. The light of the westering sun has a drowned quality, as if the house is underwater. As she walks through the place, deep shadows gather everywhere and sometimes seem to crawl as if they are not mere shadows.

The kitchen cabinets of the remodeled rectory must have had some value, for they have been stripped out with the appliances. The painted table, on which the seer set her candles, is long gone with the chairs. The room is an empty shell. In addition to a loose windowpane that stutters under the influence of a breeze, the only sounds are those made by whatever small creatures live behind the wallboard and, from time to time, announce themselves with brief, frenzied scuttling.

She breathes a dust that is surely constituted in part of dry rot and mold spores and desiccated insects, but she smells the hot wax of the seer's candles and the faint attar of roses that she had assumed came not from the candles but from a subtle perfume worn by the enigmatic woman.

Eighteen years earlier, in this humble place, Vida's journey took a turn she didn't understand at the time. She still doesn't fully understand, but she knows it was the right turn to have taken, no matter where it leads.

"My life passes like a shadow," she says. "Yet a little while, and all will be consummated."

She walks home in the dark.

The moon is not risen, though it will rise.

The owls are silent, but soon they will call to one another. That night, her uncle Ogden visits Vida in her sleep. He speaks not a word. Perhaps the dead are able to talk only in those dreams that are nothing more than dreams. To guard the secrets of the world to come after this world, maybe the dead are forbidden to speak to the living when the dream is also a door through which a lost uncle can visit a beloved niece in need of guidance. In the dream, Vida is restlessly walking the rooms of her house, dressed for hiking, when her uncle appears. She follows him into the night meadow, into the forest. The phosphorescent glow of the moon, as if emanating from the trees rather than from the heavens, lights the winding paths trodden by generations of deer. She can hear no sound but a faint moaning like the wind, but there is no wind; only she and her uncle move, and otherwise a profound stillness lies over all things. Ogden leads her three miles, to a ravine where a small plane crashed four years earlier. The bodies of the pilot and passenger were bagged and borne by litter to a barren ridge, where they were loaded into a search-and-rescue helicopter. Disassembling the battered double-prop and carrying it out of the wilderness is a task too difficult and dangerous to be undertaken. Vida wades through bristling brush to a ragged hole in the fuselage. The interior is as black as ilmenite crystals until she leans through the gaping wound in the plane, whereupon the soft, effluent, moonlike light that seems to issue from the trees now radiates as well from the interior surfaces of the aircraft. She studies what she is shown, and she knows what use it will have for her. By one of those transitions so fluid as to remind a dreamer that she's dreaming, Vida is trailing her uncle along the fractured table rock of a bare ridge. To the right of the ridge lies an abyss, a void without light, and from there issues the faint moaning like the wind in this windless night—a beseeching sound, a lamentation. To her uncle and to the void, she hears herself say, "My heart is ready."

She wakes and sits up in bed, in darkness that she has never feared. Although she knows not what is coming, she repeats the words she spoke in the dream, without vaunt or bravado, with humility and a daunting sense of her chances of success: "My heart is ready."

38

WHAT HE VALUES LEAST

Sam Crockett is a boy of many enthusiasms, each embraced as fully as any other. The mysteries of ancient Egypt, who built the pyramids and how. The myths of the ancient Greeks and Romans. UFOs, life on other worlds, what waits to be discovered on the dark side of the moon. The United States Marines, their history and triumphs and sacrifices, this battle and that, the details of their dress uniforms, their courage and sense of honor. Trains, their lore and history, the *Irish Mail*, the *Orient Express*, the *Night Ferry* from London to Paris, the *California Zephyr*. Psychics, clairvoyants, mediums, and fortunetellers.

The year that Sam is thirteen, the woman in a white robe and yellow sneakers sets up shop in an old house rented from Vance Burkhardt. In calligraphy on both sides of her VW van are these words: LOOK WITH KINDNESS ON THOSE WHO SUFFER, WHO STRUGGLE AGAINST DIFFICULTIES, WHO DRINK UNCEASINGLY THE BITTERNESS OF THIS LIFE. A sign in the yard promises that the seer will reveal the truth and the future.

That is an irresistible offer to many in the county, not least of all to Sam, especially because he is enduring the most difficult year of his young life. Of those whom he knows to have visited the fortuneteller, few will discuss what she told them. Those who do make revelations all claim to have received predictions of good health, of unexpected money soon to come into their hands, of love on the way, of wrongs done to them that will be set right; however, they appear unsettled, are unable to make eye contact, and seem to be lying. If they are disturbed by what the seer actually told them, Sam should not want to subject himself to whatever the cards or the soggy tea leaves tell her. But the price is so right. They say the woman takes no money, asking only that you bring her the thing that you value least. Sam knows what that is. No brooding is required.

Besides, he wants to be a Marine when he grows up, and no one with the thinnest thread of cowardice sewn through him can hope to be a Marine. Courage is required no less than honor. He need not be fearless; fearlessness is foolish. However, every fear must be faced down, chained, and kept in check. If the seer has something godawful to tell him, he'll just have to hear it, consider it, and then get on with life.

The rental property in which the woman has set up shop is eight miles from the house where Sam lives with his mother, Pauline, but that distance is no obstacle. He has his bicycle, and school is out.

He arrives as a man and woman drive away in a Buick sedan. They look grim.

The fortuneteller, who stands on the porch to watch them leave, is somewhat of a surprise to Sam. Although he knows about the robe and the canary-yellow sneakers, he imagined that she must be witchy or maybe sinister like the Romany crystal-gazers in those old movies about werewolves and the like. Instead, she has a pleasant face; something about the way she looks, something that he can't define, encourages him to trust her and feel safe in her company.

She welcomes him into the old house and conducts him to the shadowy kitchen, where he sits across from her at a painted table. The window blinds are drawn shut. Candles glimmer in three small, red glasses. The room should be spooky. Instead, it feels mysterious but unthreatening, the way places are in adventure stories set in exotic lands, like a hidden room in an abandoned palace or a chamber in a castle tower where a wizard casts and conjures on behalf of the righteous king.

"What have you brought me, Sam?"

"How could you know my name?"

"How could I not?"

"So wow. You really have power."

"No power. I want none. But I see."

He thinks about that, wondering how much she sees, how deeply. Having come here to ask about the future, specifically his mother's future, he only now considers that the banner staked in the yard, the blue cloth with silver moons and stars, promises not only that this woman will reveal the future but also the truth. She knows his name. How much more about him will she come to know as they proceed? There are a few things about himself that he would rather she not see, faults that he must conquer if he's ever to become a Marine. Perhaps the true cost of her revelations isn't the thing he values least but also the full truth of himself in embarrassing detail.

"Yes," she says, though he has asked no question.

His heartbeat accelerates. Being committed to going into battle and putting your life at risk is only one kind of courage. Another and necessary kind of courage, which he has come to understand by reading adventure novels, is to know yourself for what you really are, accept what that is, and correct those habits and attitudes that need to be corrected. You can't be a hero if you run away from either the enemy or the truth of yourself. Now he understands what he hasn't quite appreciated before: The second kind of courage is harder than the first.

"Exactly," says the seer.

His hand shakes as he shuttles the large manila envelope across the table, past the triangulated candles.

When she opens it, twenty-six snapshots slide out and spill across the many layers of color in the scarred and chipped table-top. "These are of your father."

"Yeah. I don't want them. They're the thing I value least. That's what they say you want."

"Why don't you value them?"

"You're a seer. You know already."

"To receive what you came here for, you must hear yourself say why you would throw these away."

Sam affects a deadpan voice. He dares not allow himself anger, for that will give rise to other feelings he can't control. He is determined to be strong, self-controlled. "He left us. Seven months ago. He wanted her more than he wanted my mother."

"And more than he wanted you."

"It's my mother I'm worried about. He went out of state with that . . . that woman. Another state where it's not easy for Mom to make him do what's right. He's got money, not just what he took from the bank without telling her, but he won't send her a dime. She took a second job to keep from losing the house. She cries at night in her room."

Sam stops speaking, stares at the candle flames. He has allowed resentment to enter his voice, which could lead to stronger emotions that will undo him. The seer sees, and she waits to be told what she already knows. In time, Sam says, "He never calls. She emails him. He answered just one, said he's never coming back. She kept hoping, but now she's finally going for a divorce. I never want to see those photos again, his face."

"What about your father himself?"

"What about him?"

"Do you value him?"

"What's to value? He's a creep. He wasn't who he seemed to be. He pretended to be someone he wasn't."

"Do you love him?"

"No. Hell no." He considers the hardness in his voice. "I don't hate him, either. There's nothing to hate. He's a big nothing. He's empty. It's almost scary how empty he is. No, not almost. It's scary how empty he was. I don't want to feel anything about him. I won't give him that. Don't say I have to love him no matter what."

"You don't, Sam. Nor do you have to respect him."

"Yeah, well I don't."

"But you must honor him."

"Honor him? What's to honor?"

"He's your father."

"He's got no honor himself."

"That's on him. Let it not be true of you. You don't need to respect him, but you must not disrespect him. Never seek to harm him. Never allow hatred in your heart. By dishonoring him, you would dishonor yourself. Pity him and leave him to his own destruction. That's already your intuitive reaction, and it's the right one."

She slides one photo back to Sam, a shot of him with his dad in front of a Christmas tree, the year he got his bicycle. "I'll take the rest as payment, Sam. But you keep that one all your life, to remind yourself not to dishonor him as he dishonored you and your mother."

He stares at the photo. "Keeping it feels weird."

"But does it also feel right?"

"No. It feels . . . I don't know."

"Those are my terms," she says. "I keep the rest, but you keep that one. Now what did you come here to ask me?"

There must be a draft that Sam doesn't feel, for the flames in the votive cups swell and lick above the ruby rims. Shaped on the wall, their light undulates like spirits swaying to music in some sphere beyond his hearing.

He has come to a sudden recognition that knowing the future can be a burden too heavy to be carried, a cause for despair. He winnows through the many questions he has conceived and finds only one that seems safe to ask. "My mother's depressed, so beaten down by what my father's done. Will she . . . will my mother ever be happy again?"

"In time, yes. Your mother is stronger than you think."

That is good to know. The seer's answer brings Sam much relief. He could ask how long his mom will be sad before she's happy again, how long her rediscovered happiness will last, whether he will make her proud and be part of the reason for her happiness. However, each question opens the door to dark knowledge. No one is happy all the time and forever. He doesn't want to hear that his mother will be happy for five years and then be struck down by disease or violence before she's forty.

"What else?" the seer asks.

"Maybe that's enough. Knowing she'll be happy."

"What about you?"

"There's a lot of stuff I'm better off not knowing."

"True. But maybe there's a question or two worth risking."

He watches the three figures of light pulsing on the wall, looks down at the photo of him with his father, and meets the woman's eyes again. "Will I be like him?"

"Your father?"

"Yeah."

"Like him in what way?"

"Will I betray people?"

"No. Not you. Never."

"Will I . . . be happy?"

"Your life will be full of good cheer and delight until there comes a valley of great suffering and sorrow. But if you do not despair, then beyond that valley will be new heights of happiness greater than anything you had experienced before. There will be dogs and one even better than dogs."

He doesn't know what to make of that prediction, what he should feel, whether he can feel anything other than dread in anticipation of that "great suffering and sorrow."

As other questions come to mind and seem urgent, Sam rises from his chair, with the photo in hand. "I better go."

"I am glad you came, Sam Crockett."

"Me too. I guess."

At the threshold to the hallway, he looks back at her.

Whatever draft caused the fire to dance high on the wicks has withered away. The candle flames are contained within the red-glass cups.

The kitchen has grown darker, but the woman has not, as though shadows are enjoined from diminishing her presence.

Outside, Sam puts the photo of his father in his shirt pocket. After he has cycled halfway home, he stops along the side of the road and extracts the snapshot to look at it again. He considers tearing it up and throwing it to the wind.

He didn't promise the seer to keep it. Not directly. Yet in a way, leaving that house with it was a promise. Breaking an implied promise is a kind of betrayal. He returns the picture to his pocket.

He doesn't go directly home. He doesn't have the heart for home just yet. He cycles, cycles, and the afternoon wanes, and the summer light distills toward a brandy hue.

His mother is back from work by now. Soon she's going to start worrying about him. Whether he has the heart for it or not, he has to go home.

Leaving his bike in the backyard, he stands staring at the house. Then climbs the porch steps. He hears music. She hasn't played music in seven months. It's that Paul Simon album she has so long enjoyed. "Graceland" is playing when he steps through the back door into the kitchen.

His mother is spooning a mixture of sliced fresh peaches and raisins into a pie shell. The kitchen smells wonderful. She used to love cooking. But for a long time, they have been eating takeout, pizza, sandwiches.

She looks up and smiles. "Where've you been, Sammy? I was just wondering if I should be worried."

Because he doesn't trust himself to speak, he goes to her and puts his arms around her as she sets aside the ladle.

Hugging him, she says, "What is it, sweetheart?"

He cannot speak. He holds fast to her.

Smoothing his hair with one hand, she says, "Everything's going to be all right."

Sam finds his voice. "I know."

"I mean it. We're going to be fine."

"I know."

"For a while," she says, "I didn't think so. But then today, something changed."

"What? What changed?"

"I don't know really. A feeling. Suddenly it felt like none of it mattered so much anymore. I just knew we'll be okay. We have each other, and we'll be okay. I've been frozen in worry, like encased in ice, and the worry just melted. We'll get through this."

He says, "I know we will. And we'll be happy."

"Of course we will. Why wouldn't we be happy?"

"No reason," he says.

Good cheer and delight . . . until there comes a valley of great suffering and sorrow . . . then new heights of happiness . . . dogs and one even better than dogs.

"No reason at all," he says, and he puts out of his mind the predictions he paid for with the photographs of his father.

TWO

THE HUNT

39

PREPARATIONS

Whoever comes next to kill Vida is not going to arrive on this fair Sunday. She has enough time to make preparations.

Nash Deacon had his experience of monkshood soup early Friday evening and was interred with his Trans Am before dawn Saturday. As sheriff, he is expected to be available to his office in the event of a crisis, but in this case he surely ignored that obligation. He would not have wanted anyone to know where he intended to spend his weekend or to what wicked purpose. Although arrogant and confident, he nevertheless considered that Vida, having dealt with Belden Bead before him, might be not merely obstinate but restive, incapable of the submission he demanded. The advantage of his size might ensure he could over-power and rape her, but he couldn't know that being brutally raped would break her spirit. Although he'd confiscated her guns, she might wound him or, failing that, might publicly accuse him of rape. If he couldn't break her, he wouldn't hesitate to kill her and use his power as sheriff to thwart an investigation or frame an innocent for the crime. He'd brought a disposable phone instead of the one at which his dispatcher could reach him, so whether or not to communicate with his underlings remained his choice. Even if Deacon expected to force her to submit as soon as Friday evening, he would have allowed himself the entire weekend to use, humiliate, and further psychologically shred her. No one is likely to be concerned about him until he fails to show up for work on Monday.

Even then, they won't know where to start looking for him. But in a day or two, Damon Orbach—the only son of the county's largest landowner, teenage druggie, and best friend of Morgan Slyke—might see a connection between the disappearances of the new sheriff and Belden Bead. He might remember the phantom Connie Cooper about whom he'd told Bead, and he might share his suspicion with whoever is his current supplier of dabs and other drugs. If not Damon, then Morgan Slyke, who's out of school and working for Galen Vector, will think of Connie. Or someone of whom she's unaware could know something damning. She assumes she has a few days to prepare for whatever's coming, but it's best to get it done today, before nightfall.

She makes a demanding trip into the forest, bearing the weapon and ammunition she'd bought in an adjacent state eight months ago and had hidden behind her supply of lumber and plywood. She brings as well one thing she is loath to be without if she cannot return—the drawing of her uncle that has hung in the library. She removes it from the frame, rolls it, and inserts it in a cardboard tube after stripping from the tube what Christmas wrapping paper remained on it. She travels three miles to the damaged twin-engine airplane. From what she'd read about the crash when it happened, she does not expect the vessel to be grounded at the end of a debris trail, as in the dream. It's wedged in a pair of immense pines, twelve feet above the ground. Its speed had diminished when it shredded the uppermost branches of other evergreens. As it angled toward the massive and interlaced pines, it lacked sufficient velocity either to shatter through them or be fully deconstructed by the impact. Smaller branches were shorn away, but the larger limbs held fast to trunks and snared the aircraft. The tail assembly is mangled. Both wings are bent and broken but still attached to the fuselage. The nose wheel remains with its fairing, although the wing wheels are gone. Even as the tragic essence of the scene inspires pity, it's such a compelling juxtaposition of thriving nature and failed technology that it seems as if it might be an installation by an artist.

No one seeing her in other circumstances would imagine she has the strength to haul forty pounds on her back, up steep slopes, across such distances, while also attending to demanding tasks at the plane, seldom resting more than two or three minutes at a time.

To most people, she appears to be nothing more than arm candy. She is often dismissed as being as shallow as the Hollywood beauties who lay claim to intellectual substance by embracing causes about which they know nothing more than what image consultants tell them. Vida makes no effort to win over those who make that judgment. Life is too short to spend any of it justifying herself to people who shape their opinions of others on first impressions and biases.

Often in her isolate and quiet life, she has paused to consider how fortunate she has been to be profoundly known and appreciated by at least two people. Her uncle saw the true and deepest Vida on his first encounter with her and always loved her for who she was in all her complexity of mind and heart. José likewise knew her soul; she believes he would have wished to marry her even if she had been plain of face and form. Although charismatic, he wasn't classically handsome. Indeed, his round, pleasant face was like those of many comical sidekicks in numerous movies.

But anyone wise enough to see past his appearance knew that intelligence, kindness, and compassion made him special. If Vida never knows another person the equal of those men, she's known more love than many ever do in this often loveless world. She'll be eternally grateful for the love she's received and given, regardless of what is to come.

By five o'clock, she returns to her house, having made all the necessary preparations on the mountain. Never before has she taken guidance from a dream, but what strikes other people as bizarre or inadvisable makes sense to her. The world is strange beyond knowing, and life is a journey through wonders, toward mystery.

Following the death of Belden Bead, these past eight months have been frustrating because she's dared not investigate José's death aggressively. She's had to be content with subtle inquiries, roundabout research, and theorizing from the barest facts, lest she raise suspicions among those who have the power to issue warrants and dig up what she has buried.

During that time, she's known the moment would come when events beyond her ability to imagine would suddenly accelerate her along a path leading to justice for José Nochelobo and perhaps ensuring the success of the cause for which he died at the hand of an assassin. The late Nash Deacon is the agent of that acceleration. Vida faces the future with new excitement. But she suspects that she'll unlock the truth and spare Kettleton from the intentions of Boschvark and his associates only at the cost of her life. She has seen signs and omens, more than just the wraithlike passage of Azrael while she dug the pit for Deacon and his car.

She prepares a simple dinner of fresh fruits, cheeses, jams, and bread of her own making.

She fills the house with music. Beethoven's Piano Concerto no. 2 in B-Flat Major, by Glenn Gould and the New York Philharmonic.

Soon, a vivid image arises in her mind's eye—herself sprawled dead in a forest glade where blue wildflowers nod in a breeze.

Sometimes, great music excites her mind not only to an intense enchantment with the beauty of this world but also to a spiritual yearning for the mysterious and even greater beauty of some world beyond life. And sometimes stress conjures macabre images of no importance or meaning. This blue-flower death tableau seems not to arise from either the beauty of music or the bane of stress. This feels like a vision of inescapable fate.

Whether that is true or not, the thick fig jam on French bread is exquisite with the Gruyère, the sliced apple crisp is sweet and well married with the gouda, and everything else on the table is to her liking. She will resist death with all her might, but what will be will be. And what will be cannot be allowed to detract from what is, from the beauty of the music or the flavor of the food, because all she has is the moment; all anyone ever has is the moment, and moments, each in succession, are precious.

40

THE RIGHT HAND OF EVIL

Regis Duroc-Jersey is always affronted and angry when he has to meet with Galen Vector, the unsavory operator who has been installed in Belden Bead's position by Horace and Katherine Bead following their son's sudden disappearance eight months earlier. Vector's management of illegal drug sales, human trafficking, loan-sharking, massive fraud perpetrated against the state disability fund, and murder for hire cannot be faulted for inefficiency. The man knows what he's doing. However, his affectation of sunglasses at all times, even at night, his pencil-line mustache, and a broad gap between his upper incisors for which he has sought no periodontal fix render him too absurd to be even a rural crime boss. He has a fondness for plaid slacks and brightly colored polo shirts, and on the rare occasion when he wears a suit, it's a cheap off-the-rack garment accompanied not by a proper necktie but by a bolo with a turquoise clasp. His degree is in money laundering or something, acquired from a state university with fewer ennobling traditions than any McDonald's franchise. Galen Vector is manifestly *not* of Regis's class, and Regis feels diminished every time he meets with the man. Regis Duroc-Jersey III is New World Technology's junior vice president of community relations and Terrence Boschvark's right-hand man, facilitator for the Kettleton project, an important position for which he has been schooled by

Montessori, Pencey Prep, Harvard, and a family whose expectations are so high that Regis has suffered nosebleeds most of his life.

On this occasion, he and Vector, each having disabled the GPS in his SUV, arrive at the abandoned sawmill an hour after nightfall, Regis by way of the compacted-gravelstone lane that once served the enterprise, the crime boss by a forest-service road. As always, they park at opposite ends of the long-decaying mill.

Regis steps out of his company Lexus and locks it and stands listening to the wilderness. He is at least a mile from the nearest residence, six miles from town.

Affronted and angry, he is also deeply uneasy. The moon has not yet risen, and starlight fails to define either the buildings or the surrounding forest that lump together in a glob of imminent threat. The primeval darkness disturbs him less than the silence that seems as perfect as in the vacuum between the stars. This hush suggests the forest is a dead realm, but of course it teems with life even at night, perhaps especially at night. Therefore, the uncanny quiet feels conspiratorial, as if legions of sharp-toothed predators know he has arrived, wish to deceive him into thinking they don't exist, and will pounce on him the moment he lets his guard down.

City-born and city-shaped, Regis isn't just out of his element in Kettleton County; he's deeply *offended* by the place. Instead of manicured parks and botanical gardens, there are meadows that have never been mowed and unkempt forests. Animals of infinite variety shit wherever they want, and no one ventures into the woods or fields to pick up the crap in plastic bags for proper disposal. Instead of a Starbucks, there are establishments like the hole-in-the-wall called Java Joe's that also sells doughnuts and muffins with no respect for those who have problems with gluten. The only restaurant in town offering duck is Hazel's Homestyle, where the menu trumpets "Quacker a la Orange"; instead of tablecloths, paper placemats feature a grotesque cartoon of Hazel in an apron and chef's hat.

The people are the worst of it. Because they can grow their own food and hunt game for their meat and fix anything that breaks down, they think they know what life is about. However, they would have no idea how to conduct themselves in a private jet or how to get a good table in New York's finest restaurant. They are stubborn people who don't know what's good for them, and most of them refuse to learn. They need to be put through a rigorous reeducation process to better program their minds, but because most of them are gun fanatics, that is not currently a viable resolution to the problem they pose.

Even when Regis Duroc-Jersey isn't in an infuriating backwater like Kettleton County, he suffers constant anxiety. Because he is so perfectly put together and conscious of appearances, no one suspects his inner life is in turmoil. He lives with the constant fear that he'll be a failure, that he might *already* be a failure. He is thirty years old and has not yet either founded a business grossing at least half a billion dollars per annum or become the CEO of a multibillion-dollar company. He makes a salary of nine hundred thousand dollars a year, with a long list of benefits, has four million of investments and six million in stock options, but *he's thirty years old*. In a mere five years, he will potentially be seen as over the hill by the cruel standards of Silicon Valley or by the criteria of whatever pitiless engine of change comes after Silicon Valley. If by then he fails to accumulate at least three hundred million, he will be deemed out of sync with the times, old, elderly, an embarrassment to anyone seen with him. *He has to gain momentum sooner than yesterday!* America is being reshaped from democracy to oligarchy. Regis absolutely must be one of those oligarchs giving the orders, because he has spent his life taking orders, and he's sick to death of it.

He switches on his flashlight and carves his way through the night and then through the age-skewed shadow-draped architecture of the sawmill that is being gradually deconstructed by gravity and the weather. Although the night is windless, a draft weaves among the massive posts that support the roof beams, softly rattling loose sheet metal somewhere. The littered concrete floor is puddled with foul-smelling water and no doubt copious quantities of rat urine. On his way to a previous meeting here, Regis once saw a rat as big as a dog. Although Vector, who hadn't seen it, insisted it must have been a possum, Regis remains convinced it was a fifty-pound rat and that the moldering sawmill is a mutant womb gestating numerous monsters in preparation for some looming Armageddon.

Outside again, at the north end of the main building, he finds Galen Vector waiting for him on the plank-floored bridge spanning the river that tumbles from its origin high in the mountains. When the mill was in operation, water was diverted to the sorting chutes that carried logs of different sizes to the saws most appropriate for them. With no moonlight to silver its whorls and ripples, the rushing water slithers like an oil-black snake, infinite in length, either issuing from or returning to a pit at the core of the world.

Vector splays two fingers across the lens of his flashlight to dim it, and Regis does likewise as he approaches the rendezvous point, but enough light exists to reveal that the crime boss wears plaid pants with what appear to be snakeskin cowboy boots. As usual, dark glasses screen Vector's eyes. Regis realizes he doesn't know what color those eyes are or if they have any color at all.

The center of the bridge on this remote and abandoned property is the mutually preferred venue when Vector and Regis must meet, to ensure that no evidence is produced regarding the nexus where the interests of the Bead criminal enterprise, crooked politicians, and Terrence Boschvark meet. If Vector or Regis were ever followed by an agent with audio gear featuring a powerful directional microphone—or if one meant to betray the other by recording a conversation—the roar of water as it quickens into rapids under the span would foil the plot. They face each other— much too close for Regis's taste—and speak as softly as possible while still being able to hear each other.

"Something has happened to Nash Deacon," Regis reveals. "He might even be dead. If he is, we know where. We need your people to investigate—and urgently."

41

THE BOX

After dinner, Vida takes the box from the shelf in the bedroom closet. Because she has handled the package with great care over the past eleven months, the yellow paper and blue ribbon look pristine.

A free end of ribbon from the bow passes through a paper-punch hole in one corner of a four-inch-square white envelope, securing it with a knot. On the envelope is her name in José's neat handwriting. The envelope is sealed. She hasn't opened it because it might have a message revealing the nature of the gift. She means to read the card only when the time has come to open the box.

This birthday gift, which José had intended to give her, was passed along by his brother, Reyes, who had flown in from Miami to attend the funeral, clean out José's house, and settle the estate.

Now, as on other occasions, Vida sits on the edge of her bed with the box on her lap. As before, an inner voice that's neither hers nor José's warns, *Every ending is a beginning, but this is a beginning on which you're not yet prepared to embark.*

If she's to be killed in the days ahead, whether in a forest clearing graced with blue wildflowers or elsewhere, she doesn't want to die without knowing what gift her lover, her fiancé, intended to give her. However, she's aware that life is a layered tapestry, with recondite meaning below the surface. Mundane and mystical threads are equally strong and essential to the integrity of the fabric. If she opens the package, she won't be felled by a curse for violating some occult proscription against doing so; the hidden dimensions of life aren't as portrayed in pulp fiction, neither irrational nor realms of unrelenting menace. But if she ignores her intuition and opens the box, perhaps what lies within might set in motion a chain of cause and effect that will put her in greater danger than she would be otherwise. Her intuition, her ability to see what others can't and know what others don't, has served her well, and she is not fool enough to fail to keep faith with it.

She returns the box to the high shelf and tucks it into a corner, concealing it with a spare pillow and a folded afghan, so that an intruder, in her absence, will not see the bright giftwrap and be tempted to open the package.

This has been a long, busy day, and she is weary. She's early to bed because she must rise at first light. Rise and be ready for those who drink the wine of violence.

The dream of her uncle and the crashed airplane represented more than a prediction; it had been a warning of an inescapable threat. Someone will come for her either tomorrow or the day after tomorrow. Her only ally will be the wilderness, nature and all its creatures, which Vida has been told she's chosen to protect. Chosen by destiny. Which means the shaper of nature, of all things within the universe and outside it. Perhaps the seer at that painted table in that old house was insane. After all, does it not beggar belief to claim that such a solemn responsibility would be conferred upon a girl who works a placer mine and spends so much time learning humble skills like carpentry, backhoe operation, locating wild blackberries, and differentiating between edible and poisonous mushrooms? On the other hand, it is true that no creature of the wild has harmed her, that foxes often attend her progress through woods and meadows, that deer frequently visit her for hours as she seins the spaded earth for gemstones. And wolves are her friends.

As Vida rests her head upon her pillow and draws up the covers, she puts all doubt and worry behind her when she recalls something the seer said. *Although the world is a place of wonders, Vida, what can be seen of it is the least part, and what can't be seen is the magnificent why and how of the world. Happiness and peace require patient waiting for the sight that at the moment can't be seen.*

And so she sleeps.

42

THE BATS TAKE FLIGHT

Strangely, to Regis Duroc-Jersey, the rapids roaring under the bridge sound less like rushing water than like a fierce fire in a blast furnace where ore is being smelted into iron. Sometimes he is certain that he hears screaming within that ceaseless detonation. He attributes this to exhaustion. Striving to profit handsomely from the slow-motion destruction of the current civilization involves a mental and moral high-wire walk that can fatigue even an exercise enthusiast who meditates faithfully and adheres to a rigorous low-carb diet.

"Deacon was supposed to use a burner phone to call the big guy's burner," Regis says, referring to Boschvark, "but he didn't call."

"When was this supposed to happen?" Galen Vector asks.

"This morning. No later than noon."

"Call him about what?"

"About Sheriff Montrose."

"That prick. What about him?"

"Friday, Montrose said he wants his job back."

"You're jackin' me."

"I don't have the energy."

"The prick retired."

"Under pressure. He wants to change his mind."

"He can't."

"No, he can't. But there were negotiations on Saturday."

"Negotiations? Shit. Montrose is an unreliable ally. You don't negotiate with weasels like him."

Regis agrees. "Can't trust him. He has sympathy for the Nochelobo crowd."

"He sold them out," Vector says, raising his voice, offended by the former sheriff's sudden attack of conscience. "If the shithead feels guilty, he wants to give the money back, then we soak it in gasoline and make him eat it and light his breath on fire, see if does he just become a human blowtorch or maybe his gut explodes."

Not for the first time, Regis finds it puzzling that a man who looks as frivolous as Galen Vector can be so ruthless. Holding a forefinger beside his lips to remind the crime boss that discretion is required in this world of eavesdroppers, Regis mutters, "Killing a sheriff is no small thing."

"Former sheriff. And never popular. He wasn't a people's sheriff."

"They elected him."

"Some did. Most didn't."

"You're saying it was fixed?"

"As sure as I know my name."

"Well, I didn't need to know that."

"Yeah, you did. I'm making a point here."

"What point?" Regis asks.

"Say a prick like Montrose dies in a house fire."

"So then?"

"You think a thousand assholes are gonna show up with flowers and teddy bears to lay in his front yard?"

"Hard to picture."

"Most are gonna say it should've happened years ago."

"Still, it's got to look like a heart attack or something, and Nash Deacon's got to be in the loop."

"You said Nash is dead."

"I said something happened to him, he might even be dead, but we don't know."

"If he was supposed to call the big guy by noon, but he hasn't called him yet, then he's stupid or dead, and he's not stupid."

"He's been stupid in the way men sometimes are, thinking with his little head instead of his big head."

"Yeah? Who's the bitch?"

"Nochelobo's squeeze."

"Are you shittin' me?"

"GPS says he went there four days last week, including Friday, when he never left."

"That Trans Am is too old for GPS."

"We planted a civilian unit in it."

This does not sit well with Vector. "You do that to me, you'll all be too dead to get your project built."

"We'd never do that to you."

"I'm gonna put my guys on my Escalade as soon as I get back to town, have them strip it down, see what they find."

"Nothing to find."

"Damn well better not be."

"By our definition, you're a partner, but Sheriff Deacon is an employee."

"Belden Bead was also a partner, huh?" Vector says.

"Funny you should mention him."

"Am I laughing here?"

"Belden just disappears, we don't know where, and eight months later Nash Deacon disappears. We don't believe in coincidences."

"You said Deacon is at her place."

"When he didn't call at noon today, we discovered the tracking unit had stopped working at three o'clock Saturday morning, thirty-three hours earlier. We don't know why. He was still there then. He had been there since Friday evening."

"But now he could be anywhere."

"Four o'clock this afternoon, we put a drone over her property, gave it a good lookover. No sign of the Trans Am. Nobody's seen it or Deacon since Friday."

"He could be anywhere," Vector insists.

"He's there. Even if he isn't there, it's the place you've got to start looking, and she's who you've got to talk to first, before we start searching the whole world over."

"I've got to talk to her, huh? Why not the sheriff's office?"

Regis says, "Most deputies are in our pocket, but not all."

"Work on that."

"We are."

"Work on it harder."

"You've always got a few Dudley Do-Rights."

"Frame them for something."

"One by one," Regis agrees. "The thing is, if for some reason Belden went to this bitch and if what happened to him is what's happened to Deacon, we need to find out if she knows anything true about Nochelobo's death. If she knows too much, we don't want the wrong deputies hearing what she says."

"Whether she knows everything or nothing, once we interrogate her, then we'll have to waste the slut."

"Whatever you feel is appropriate. It's for delicate work like this that we brought the Bead family—and you—into this project."

Just then the bats take flight by the hundreds, surely more than a thousand, erupting from whatever cave provides their shelter. Because of their numbers, the flutter and flapping of their tri-jointed wings and the thin squeaks they produce in order to navigate by echolocation compete with the roar of the river. These little horrors usually come out at sunset, and Regis is not expecting this late appearance of the swarm. He hunches down and clasps his hands over the top of his head, flashlight beam spearing up through nightmarish forms with squinched, whiskered faces and ravenous, fanged mouths. Bats never tangle in people's hair. That's an old wives' tale. Regis knows it's a stupid wives' tale. Nevertheless, he covers his head and hunches during the minute the swarm takes to fan away into the darkness, snatching insects and devouring them in flight, as swift as swallows on wings five times thinner than surgical gloves. In a city, Regis might see one bat every decade, or maybe never see one. In this uncivilized territory, where there are many churches but not one high-end theater playing classic films on a big screen, where every restaurant offers a hamburger but not one provides any sushi, where half the locals homeschool their moronic offspring and where even the public schools cling to outdated definitions of literacy and science, there are *swarms* of rabid bats. There are poisonous snakes in great variety and wolves and bears and mountain lions and countless other reasons why all the smart people long ago fled to hermetically sealed apartments in comfortable high-rise buildings, in the cities where Nature has been tamed and fenced in parks and kept presentable with daily grooming. Regis hates this place.

When he stands upright and lowers his hands, the beam of his light falls on his companion. Vector's face is as expressionless as that of a dead man whose features a talented mortician has smoothed so perfectly as to suggest this person passed through life without ever experiencing an emotion of any kind. Behind his sunglasses, his eyes might be sharp with contempt, but his voice remains flat when he says, "I'll take three guys with me. We'll wait until midnight, when she's almost sure to be sleeping. We'll grab her by surprise. If she knows what happened to Deacon—maybe even Belden—we'll break her down and get the truth. She won't be able to lie to us. She'll try, but she won't be able. Then my guys will want to use her. Me too. Subsequent to all that, a properly staged house fire might be the best way to erase evidence of what we do to her. If for some reason it doesn't seem as if a fire can be made to look accidental, then come morning, we'll take her body into the woods, drop it down a sinkhole into a cavern far off any trail, where either it'll never be found or it won't be discovered until nothing's left but yellowed bones filled with mold instead of marrow. How does that sound?"

"Okay," says Regis.

Vector says, "Okay?"

"Good," Regis amends. "That sounds good. Perfect."

"Whatever we learn, I share with you. But I never want to be second-guessed how maybe there was some other information I could have cut out of her."

"All right."

"What does that mean?"

"All right, yes, it's a deal, no second-guessing."

"I'll be in touch," Vector says.

They leave the bridge at different ends.

After the bats, Regis doesn't feel that he can handle another close encounter with a fifty-pound rat in the reeking confines of the sawmill. Instead of taking a shortcut through the building, he walks around the massive structure to his Lexus SUV.

Having read about bats to confirm that they won't tangle in human hair, he knows that their eyes can magnify starlight to such an extent that any night landscape glows as though with a radiant frost. Those individuals that have remained in the immediate area might be looking down from on high even now, watching him as he makes his way to the sanctuary of his vehicle.

Behind the wheel of the Lexus, he locks the doors and starts the engine but does not immediately drive away.

A melancholy quasi-philosophical mood settles over him. He wonders how he's gotten to this place in his life. The Montessori school, Pencey Preparatory School, Harvard: Regis considers his academic journey, lingering on selected memories as if they are worry beads that, fingered long enough, will inspire in him the conviction that he made the right decisions. He hopes to convince himself that his work with Boschvark is in the service of what is right and true, even noble. When peace of mind continues to elude him, he focuses instead on the billions of dollars in subsidies the company has been granted to build this huge project, the additional billions that will be shoveled out to cover the cost overruns, the percentage of those staggering sums that can be siphoned off without risking discovery, and how much of that fortune will be passed along to him in a form that's taxed at a low rate if it's taxed at all. This approach to an analysis of his career is much more satisfying than pondering what is right and true.

At last, he releases the hand brake and puts the SUV in gear. His nerves are soothed by this pause for meditation, though as he begins his drive into Kettleton, he's overcome by the irrational suspicion that the sawmill is collapsing behind him, and not just the mill, but also the night itself and the world as he has known it.

43

FACELESS MEN ARE COMING

In the dream, standing in her yard, Vida is armed with a cross-bow, firing quarrels at the moon to remind it to illuminate her way faithfully with its full sphere even when, for everyone else, it has waned into the thinnest Cheshire-cat smile. She cranks back the bowstring and locks it and loads another quarrel in the groove and aims high, to gently pock the lunar surface with a reminder of her enduring love and authority. When she triggers the weapon, however, the fired bolt travels far short of its target and proves to be a unique firework that produces not pinwheels or fountains of bright metallic salts, but instead casts across the sky hundreds of small moons in sizes ranging from that of an orange to that of a melon. Those shapes don't fade as other fireworks do. They descend in glowing splendor and bounce off the lawn, transforming into silver-gray wolves as they rebound and cara-cole. A moment of beauty and delight dissolves into high alarm, not because the wolves mean her any harm, but because some of those miniature moons transform not into wolves but into men without faces, those who conspired to kill José Nochelobo. They have come to kill her, too.

She rolls up from sleep and out of bed and onto her feet with the immediate wakefulness of a firefighter answering the firehouse bell. The dream was more than a dream; it was an alarm. Although she hasn't expected trouble until long after dawn on Monday, perhaps not until Tuesday or Wednesday, she has nonetheless slept in the clothes she needs for the long trek into the mountains. She switches on the lamp. Her hiking boots stand bedside. She sits to pull them on and lace them up.

The pistol she took from Nash Deacon is on the nightstand, as is the scabbard in which he'd sheathed it. She threads the scabbard onto her belt and holsters the pistol.

How many are coming she can't foresee. She is sure only that it isn't merely one or two. She can't say what will happen to her, only that she is mortal and the odds of survival are low, of triumph even lower. She is afraid; she would be a fool if she were not afraid, but she will not surrender to dread.

From the closet, she retrieves a waterproofed leather jacket with a fleece lining and slips her arms into its sleeves. Even at this time of year, the nights are likely to be chilly in the higher elevations. She's prepared a backpack lighter than those she carried into the woods the previous day, approximately fifteen pounds of gear including two days' worth of food; she shrugs into it and secures the straps. From a shelf, she takes down a pair of high-powered binoculars and hangs them around her neck.

The folded page of notepaper is in a pocket of her jeans where she tucked it before bed. She takes it out and opens it and reads the words that have long baffled her.

. . . *two moon sun spirit below the smoking river* . . .

She folds the paper and returns it to her pocket.

She switches off the lamp and makes her way to the back door with the aid of a flashlight and leaves the house that has been her home for twenty-three years and keys the deadbolt locks. The sun is hours from rising, and the moon is mid sky, cratered by impacts that perhaps foretell the fate of Earth.

She veers away from the multipurpose building in which the old Ford pickup is garaged and enters the forest at the west end of the meadow. Among the second rank of trees, she sits on a table of rock skirted by Polypodium, a fern that rises from licorice-scented rootstock. She watches and waits and wonders.

She thinks, *Have pity on those who love and are separated, on the lonely, on those who mourn, on those who fear, on all the little animals that live their lives as prey.*

44

MEN WHO CAST NO SHADOWS

In the first hour after midnight, discussing matters of grave import on their way from the town of Kettleton to the property where Sheriff Nash Deacon seems to have disappeared, Galen Vector rides shotgun while Frank Trott drives the big Ford F-150 pickup.

In the back seat of the extended cab, Monger and Rackman are silent, for it isn't their role to speak. They are the equivalent of golems, as slab-bodied and blunt-faced as men made of mud and imbued with soulless life, supernatural in their seeming indifference to the world, tasked with nothing more than enforcement of the crime family's interests and the taking of violent revenge.

"This chippy must be somethin'," Trott says.

"How do you mean?"

"Takes four men to handle her?"

"She's given us reason to think maybe so."

"She a witch or somethin'?"

"Why would you ask is she a witch?" Vector wonders.

"Iffen she ain't some kind of witch, how's she make grown men disappear?"

"Probably pretty much the same way we've done more than a time or two."

"She ain't got the muscle we got."

"Sometimes brains beat muscle."

Frank Trott is having none of that. "Not so I ever seen. Brains or not, she's just another skirt."

"Not just another."

"How's she special?"

"You've never seen her?"

"Not so I remember."

"You'd remember."

"How special could she be, bangin' Nochelobo's kind?"

"From what I can tell, theirs was a clean, true love."

"Heard such a thing talked about, but I ain't never stood witness to it."

"Don't make the mistake of thinking she's loose and dumb."

"So then she ain't a woman after all?"

"Frank, you're lucky some righteous lady hasn't put a knife in you as a matter of principle."

Beyond the town limits, the county road is deserted, a black ribbon unraveling through the moon-washed land. The lack of traffic at this hour isn't unusual, but something about the way the lonely highway rolls across the undulant valley floor, disappearing and reappearing, disquiets Galen Vector, though it never has before.

Frank Trott says, "How we supposed to break the bitch, find out what she done, what she knows?"

"Do whatever it takes."

"No limits?"

"None. Too much is at stake."

"Was just you and me, I'd say let's make good use of this chippy before we break her. But I never want to see the brothers Frankenstein with their pants dropped."

Behind them, Monger engages in a noisy clearing of his throat. He's not preparing to speak, and he hasn't taken offense, because that isn't in his nature regarding a matter like this. The noise he makes is just an issue of phlegm.

"Belden, now Nash," Trott says. "So is this chippy takin' out who she thinks had somethin' to do with Nochelobo gettin' dead?"

"That's what we need to find out. Her motive, what she knows."

"Why's she wait eight months 'tween Belden and Nash?"

"Maybe she worried popping them close together would draw too much suspicion to her. Or, hell, maybe this has nothing to do with Nochelobo."

After a silence, Trott says, "No matter how good she looks, she's some hard kind of woman."

"Or just a survivor, only defending herself and good at it."

"Whatever she is, shit like this could blow up the project."

"Won't happen. It's too sweet a deal to let anyone monkey-wrench it."

"Almost seems somebody already done it."

"What's that mean?"

"Think about them eight months," Trott says.

"What about them?"

"Not a damn thing been done up on the plateau."

"A lot has been done," Vector disagrees. "It's in permitting. They need sign-offs from a shitload of agencies. It's moving along."

"At this rate, by the time it's done, I'll be wearin' them adult diapers and won't know my own name."

"The fix is in. They just have to make it look like they've followed the rules. Actually, the longer it takes, the better."

"How you figure?"

"The money's been committed with full inflation protection and easy approvals of cost overruns, with no performance deadlines."

"I ain't never had no problem with performance," Trott says, "but it's them deadlines can make a marriage grim."

"How *is* Cora these days?"

"Fatter, meaner, peckin' her new hubby into an early grave. So even if no ground gets broken, you think a blue-collar guy like me has a year-end bonus comin'?"

"You'll be pleased. Payments are already flowing, just not as big and fast as they will be later on."

"So we just got to be good citizens and do our part."

"That's right."

"Break the chippy for what she knows, kill her, burn the house down with her in it. Growin' up, I never woulda thought."

"Thought what?" Vector asks.

"How one day I'd be paid so handsome just for havin' fun."

"It's a great country."

"For damn sure."

Vector's disquiet has grown, and still he doesn't know why he is so uneasy. The highway is without another vehicle, as though it leads from nowhere to nowhere. When the engine is shut off, maybe the world beyond the windows will vanish, and a void will take its place. When they open the doors, there won't be air to breathe.

"Jesus," he says.

Trott glances at him. "Jesus what?"

"Nothing. I just . . . just realized we're almost there. The turn-off to her place is on the right, maybe a mile or so ahead."

"Ain't it across from the church house where four was shot?"

"Directly opposite, yeah."

"You remember that crazy fortuneteller?"

"What fortuneteller?"

"For a while back in the day, she worked her racket outta that house 'fore they made it a church."

"I heard some talk about her."

"I went to see her once," Trott reveals.

"You believe in fortunetellers?"

"This is eighteen years ago. I was nineteen. Weren't as smart about things like I am now."

"What did she tell you? How far off the mark was she?"

"Weren't no mark to be off from. She couldn't see a mayfly's future iffen it was one day through its two days in this world."

"But what did she tell you?"

"Says she don't want no money. Just wants what I value least."

"So she's working some scam."

"Yeah. I tell her, shit, I value everythin' high, 'cause I had to kick so much ass to get it all."

"She had a comeback to that?" Vector asks.

"She tells me I need some tough love. I start tellin' her what kind of lovin' I like best . . . but then, I don't know, I didn't feel right talkin' trash at her that way."

"That doesn't sound like you."

"Lookin' back on it, I don't understand myself. Anyway, she says she sees how I don't put no value at all on my soul. She says this breaks a mother's heart."

"She knew your mother?"

"Shit no. You could break a ball of iron sooner than break that bitch's heart. I wish she'd died in childbirth and spared me ever knowin' her."

"So the fortuneteller . . . ?"

"She says even the devil hisself won't want such a pitiful thing as my soul. She says she can't touch it neither until first I do some work to polish it up and give it at least a little value."

"Your soul."

"My soul."

"I don't see what her scam is."

"Weren't no scam. She starts talkin' about souls, I know she's bug-shit crazy, can't be nothin' she can tell me about the future or anythin' else. So I'm out of there before she can pick my pocket."

Trott brakes the car. "Here it is." He turns right into the dirt lane that leads to Vida's house.

"Kill the headlights and stop here," Vector says. "We'll walk in so we don't wake her till we want to wake her."

Monger and Rackman are the last to disembark. When Galen Vector sees them exit into the moonlight, it seems the vehicle can't have contained them, as if their emergence from the confines of the truck is a stage magician's illusion. They are not Samoan, although they have that formidable quality. If, as the Bible says, there were giants on the Earth at one time, Monger and Rackman are compacted descendants of that long-lost race. They are half brothers, born of the same mother two years apart. They work in concert, quick and light on their feet for men their size, moving to the same cadence and with the same pitiless intent. With only their bare hands, they can do to a man what others in their line of work would need pliers, hammers, and crowbars to achieve.

The unpaved driveway curves uphill and out of sight, flanked by deep forest. The pale dirt takes the lunar radiance unto itself, but because the source is at its apex, the four men cast not even the faintest of moon shadows.

45

SHE IS BOTH PREY AND HUNTRESS

From her point of observation among the western trees, Vida watches the men appear in the southeast, where the driveway leaves the embrace of the forest and curves into the open meadow. Faceless shapes, they seem to rise out of the earth like revenants lacking eternal quarters in either Heaven or Hell, previously content to lie senseless in forgotten graves with the bodies that decomposed around them, now summoned by an incantation to a violent haunting.

She raises the binoculars and glasses the uninvited visitors. The moon favors them not at all, and even at magnification, they remain phantoms.

Two proceed to the back of the house and take up positions flanking that door. The other two ascend the front-porch steps, moving out of Vida's line of sight.

Evidently, the latter pair are equipped with a battery-powered automatic lockpick of the kind intended for the exclusive use of the police. The still night doesn't carry the sound of knocking on the door. No shouted command or announcement of a warrant disturbs the quiet before the men are inside and windows brighten.

The back door is opened from within, and a fan of light arcs across the two individuals waiting there, proving that they aren't risen spirits, but flesh and blood. They go inside.

The residence offers few hiding places for a grown woman, and the searchers quickly eliminate them all. They return to the night and stand as a quartet, staring toward the smaller building, as motionless as carved stone, like perverse interpretations of the four elements—earth, wind, fire, and water—with the power to unleash the fury of quake and storm.

Whoever these intruders might be, they aren't officers of the law, uniformed or otherwise. Most likely, they are here because they know more than the law does about where Nash Deacon went on Friday and have expected some communication from him that they have not received. She doesn't need to know their names, for she knows their intentions, which are unmistakably wicked.

For the time being, there is no place for Vida in any town or city, where the powerful who control the inquisitional state are listening and watching and prepared to execute their agenda without concern about using excessive force; they have arrived at the dire conviction that excess is a virtue. The uncle who raised her with respect for the natural world and with gratitude for its gifts, the robed seer whom she visited when she was ten, and her experiences in this primeval land have prepared her to recognize and embrace the truth that, in a crisis like this, only Nature offers her refuge and only in its design can she find present hope.

As the four men move toward the smaller building, Vida lowers the binoculars and retreats from the table of rock. Both prey and huntress, she quickly slips deeper among the trees, initially reluctant to employ her flashlight.

For more than two decades, she has walked everywhere that deer prepared the easiest route in their perpetual wandering. She knows this unmapped maze so well that, even at night, she has no need of a magic ball of string like the one by which Theseus was led through the Labyrinth under Crete and found his way out after killing the Minotaur. With moonlight sifting through the thatch of branches, she relies on the spatial memory that has accumulated in her muscles and bones and nerves as surely as in her mind: how and where the well-known land rises and descends and turns, how and where undergrowth crowds her or withers back, how and where the canopy of trees occludes the sky or opens to a blackness salted with stars. Vida reads the way with her body as much as with her eyes, and with intuition as well as with hard knowledge.

If those men want her with such urgency that they will come for her quietly on foot, after midnight and four at once, they will also follow her into the forest, not in this foiling darkness but at first light. The farther she leads them through what is a wilderness to them but a civilization of the lesser animals to her, the more vulnerable they will become and the better will be her chances of surviving them.

46

PUZZLEMENT

The building behind the residence holds nothing that greatly surprises Galen Vector, though it does present puzzles to be solved.

The first is in regard to the midnight-blue 1950 Ford pickup that is so well maintained it's clearly an object of pride for Vida. The woman is involved in Nash Deacon's disappearance and might be responsible as well for whatever happened to Belden Bead. There is good reason to think that both men are dead. By the evidence of her disheveled bed in an otherwise pin-neat house, Vida rose and fled as though she had somehow been warned that authorities—or in this case worse—would shortly arrive. The second parking stall is occupied by a backhoe, and there is no indication that she might have had a vehicle in addition to the '50 Ford. In fear of either the law or the vengeance of those outside the law, she should have gone on the run in the pickup, not on foot.

When Vector expresses his puzzlement, Frank Trott says, "Maybe Deacon ain't dead."

"What is he, then?"

"Maybe he thrown in with her, hot as you say she is, and they done run off together in his Trans Am."

"Doesn't compute. Nash is on the gravy train here—the power of being sheriff, Boschvark laying a wad of cash on him every week. He throws that away, what does he have?"

"Somethin' good to stick his johnson in."

"Nash is the kind to take what he wants, not the kind who goes whimpering after it like a puppy. He isn't with her, and she isn't in his car on her own, or we'd be able to track her."

Monger and Rackman have gravitated to a wall hung with tools, among which are an axe, a hatchet, a reciprocating saw, a chain saw, a power drill, and a circular saw. The two hulks stand in silent veneration that perhaps isn't inspired by a love of woodworking.

"Another thing," Vector says, stepping to the backhoe. "The dark concrete under this machine."

"Dampness. Just water," Trott says.

"No shit."

"She hosed it off outside, moved it in here, and it dripped a few hours."

"You're a regular detective."

Having no ear for sarcasm, Trott nods in self-satisfied agreement. "Well, I got experience with machines."

"She recently did some serious digging," Vector says. "We need to have a look around, see what project she undertook."

47

A NIGHT WATCH OF WOLVES

At all times, the forest is simultaneously dreamlike and real. In daylight, it is a wondrous exhibition of green architecture, as pleasing as anything in a sleeper's best illusions. At night, Vida has often thought of it as a shadowy stage where moonlight pools like mist in places and starlight drips and magical beings—sprites, fairies, elves—seem to hide everywhere behind masks of leaves and cone-laden boughs, waiting to step forward and perform in an amusing midsummer night's dream. Now, however, this realm has no qualities fit for a tale by a master of light fantasy, but is instead eerie, alien, as if another universe wheeled through Vida's, the particles of one seething through the empty spaces between the particles of the other, with no catastrophic collision, but leaving behind strange matter and unknowable presences.

The eeriness arises from her awareness of the kind of men with whom she'll have to contend in this vastness, her beloved wild-wood having become a battleground, changed as she had never imagined that it could be.

Without either urgency or tedium, one hour folds into another. Now guided by a Tac Light when needed, she ascends at a measured pace through timeless woods and arrives at a crest beyond which a shelf of flat, open ground reveals shallow beds of bunchberry.

Already at an elevation so cool that snakes are unlikely to be on the move, she unstraps her backpack to use it as a pillow. She lies down in the whorls of green leaves and tiny white flowers for what bedding the bunchberry might provide.

Vida intends to get two hours of rest and be awakened when the first light breaks over her. Her sense is that, with morning, she won't just be fleeing from her enemies. She will also be advancing toward revelations that will elevate José's death from accident to murder and martyrdom in the eyes of those who thus far remain blind to that truth.

Her dreamless sleep is like a tide on which she floats, gently rising and falling between the world and the world not. Sometimes, as the tide lifts her toward the world, perhaps she hears sighs and soft panting, seems to feel other sleepers shifting around her as they react to their dreams. Her eyelids are so heavy they cannot be raised. She chooses to believe that Lupo and the pack have bedded in the bunchberry to look after her as she lies helpless, a pleasant conviction as the tide carries her down into a swale of deeper sleep.

48

ETERNAL FAWN

The evening before Ogden dies peacefully in his bed, when Vida is eighteen and he is eighty-five, they linger over dinner while her uncle fascinates her with stories of the nomadic peoples that once traveled the plains and mountains of this state, hunting buffalo and exploring—Ute, Cheyenne, Arapaho, Apache, and Shoshone. He has much knowledge of them and admiration for them. They were as deceitful and violent as human beings are in all times and places, but they were also as courageous and noble and wise in numbers alike to those of other cultures, with rich traditions and codes by which they ordered their societies. He is sentimental, but his sentiment ranges from sweet nostalgia to melancholy. "They fade away," he says. "So do we. This country isn't what it was when I was a boy."

Growing up, Ogden knew many people of the Cheyenne, Apache, and Shoshone nations who still kept proper faith with their history and ancestors. Three-quarters of a century later, few know the truth of the past in all its cabled fibers—or care to know it. Some operate casinos and are as slick as the Vegas sharpies who partner with them. Others boil their culture into a syrupy reduction of color and noise and dance, robbing it of its complex meaning while purifying it for the pleasure of audiences. With every generation, the young define themselves less by the history out of which they were born, and pour themselves into the one mold that globalism demands. This is also true of recent generations of other cultures, of all races and ethnic groups. The ruling elite loudly champion diversity but use the powerful tools of technology to shape everyone into like-minded worker bees and mindless consumers, into an obedient oneness. Her uncle has lived long enough to see this, weary of it, and mourn.

Toward the end of the evening, on a lighter note, he recounts vivid, charming stories about a Cheyenne maiden named Eternal Fawn. In his opinion, the other name imposed on her by the bureaucratic state isn't worth speaking. In 1953, Eternal Fawn was a medicine woman dedicated to preserving the knowledge of ancient therapies, but also an artist of great promise, working in pencil and in oils to produce portraits, often of the living elders of her nation, each rendered in exquisite detail, with great care and respect.

"The portrait of you in the library," Vida says.

"Yes. A gift from her."

Only now, after raising Vida for more than thirteen years, he reveals it was Eternal Fawn who divined the existence of the placer mine and led him to it, who taught him, among so many other things, which mushrooms are edible and which poisonous, who saved him from despair when he came home from a war fought against a merciless and depraved enemy.

After they clear away the dinner plates and pour fresh glasses of wine, he tells her more about the artist. Too subtle to be felt, a draft floats golden waves of candlelight over her uncle's face, a lavage that appears to wash away effects of his well-lived years. Or perhaps it is his memories of Eternal Fawn that, for this interlude, restore to him an appearance of youth.

Vida is enchanted by her uncle's revelations. "You loved her."

"The more amazing thing is that she loved me, too. I've thought about that for more than sixty years, and I still don't know why she did or how she could."

"Now, Uncle, no one could be easier to love."

"That's sweet of you to say, but you didn't know me back in the day. When I came home from the war, most of the light had gone out of me. I was a house of empty rooms—and over two years, she furnished them."

With her uncle's first mention of Eternal Fawn, a mystery has been born and grows deeper with each memory he shares. Now Vida asks that it be solved. "Yet you never married. Why not?"

Spectral light sheets against the windows, followed by the first thunderclap, which begins as a hard crash and fades into a scrooping sound, as if the gates of Heaven are opening against the resistance of rust.

"Her family was proud of their heritage and deeply committed to Cheyenne ways, she no less than her parents and two brothers."

"No intermarriage?"

"Not to anyone with skin like mine. They called me a *wasicus*, which is a Lakota word some other indigenous people adopted."

"That's so . . ."

"So 1950s," he says.

"But love is love, no matter what."

"She loved them, too. Maybe not more than she loved me, but she had loved them longer. They conceived her in love, and she couldn't imagine life without them. But that was the choice they gave her."

"How could she imagine life without *you*?"

"Don't blame her. I never did. She was grace personified, and she gave me back a life that the war had taken from me."

Sharper lightning and harder thunder than before crack the shell of the promised storm. Across the slate roof, rushing rain sizzles like oil in a hot skillet.

How odd it seems to Vida that she never asked—and he never explained—why he's lived alone for so many decades, until a niece he had never seen needed a home. Could it really be that two years of the Cheyenne woman's love was so profound that it established in him peace and contentment for the duration of his life?

He says, "I think it matters you know about her and me, how it was and how it could have been, so . . ."

When her uncle doesn't continue, Vida says, "So?"

"So you'll keep in mind that we don't get a thousand chances in this life. When one of the best kind comes along, it's rarer than you might know at the time."

The candlelight reveals tears pooled but unshed in her uncle's eyes, and her feelings for him are so tender that she's loath to ask why he chose a life alone. Perhaps tomorrow or the day after, in a moment less emotional than this, she'll pose that question.

In the morning, he doesn't come to the kitchen for breakfast. Vida knocks on his door. When he fails to respond, she enters his room and finds he has moved on from this world during the night.

After Herbert Lagare has come in his mortuary van and collected the body and gone, Vida is inconsolable. As she circles through the small house obsessively, every item inspires memories, and though all of them are good, they don't assuage her grief.

Soon she realizes that, the previous day, her uncle must have sensed his death impending. That was why, after keeping the story of Eternal Fawn locked in his heart for so long, he finally spoke of her.

Vida goes to the library and reaches across the turntable and takes the framed portrait down from the wall. She sits with it in an armchair. In youth as in old age, her uncle's face was benevolence made flesh, as if kindness were the very substance of which he had been created; in her experience of him, appearance and reality were one and the same.

The pencil portrait is on a page from an art-paper tablet and supported with pressboard. Vida turns the frame over. On the back, she finds a message in the artist's elegant hand: *If I live to a hundred, I will never forget your face.* Under those words is the stylized fawn.

49

FIND HER, GRILL HER, KILL HER

The night air smells of raw earth. Four flashlight beams travel the site of the excavation, where the infill has been compacted. The tread patterns of the backhoe tires have not yet weathered away.

"What the holy hell am I lookin' at?" Frank Trott asks. "You tellin' me she done buried Nash Deacon *and* his Trans Am?"

"Come daylight," says Galen Vector, "we might find where Belden Bead has wasted away to nothing but hair and bones in his Plymouth Superbird Hemi."

In the backwash of beams, Trott's face marshals itself from astonishment to indignation, to something that might be admiration for the woman's boldly executed solution to an urgent problem.

In Vector's experience, the heavy facial features of Monger and Rackman are never configured in other than one of two arrangements. The first is a deadpan, cementitious aspect that conveys no emotion or attitude whatsoever, their dark eyes as depthless as ceramic discs. The second is a vague, dreamy smile reminiscent of those on certain carved-stone gods that wait to be worshipped in crumbling vine-entangled temples, deep in the jungles of the South Pacific. Of the two expressions, the second is more disturbing because it always seems unrelated to present circumstances, as if what amuses Monger and Rackman is nothing that has amusement value for other people. In this instance, as never before, the smiles are accompanied by brief spates of tittering that cause the fine hairs to prickle on the nape of Vector's neck.

Trott says, "So where is the bitch? Where'd she go? She ain't taken her pickup. Buried Deacon's Trans Am, for Chrissake. She got no wheels."

"We're dealing with a mountain girl. She went to hide in the mountains."

"Can't hide for long."

"Maybe longer than you think," Vector says.

"This ain't no Jamaica. Winter in a few months."

"She knows that."

"She gonna hibernate up there with the bears?"

"Maybe she means to go through the mountains and come out somewhere we can't guess. Maybe she has a plan."

"What plan? Can't be no plan. She's wanted for murder."

"She won't be wanted for anything," Vector disagrees. "We can't take a chance of her in a courtroom. What the hell Bead and Deacon were doing here, what she might have learned about José Nochelobo's death—none of that can come out in front of a jury."

"So we got to go after her?"

"Find her, grill her, kill her," Vector says.

"What about this here drive-in graveyard of hers?"

"We'll bury her here. Baby makes three. Then the county takes the land for unpaid taxes. Boschvark buys the land from the county and donates it to Conserve to Survive."

"To what?"

"It's this nonprofit he set up. Conserve to Survive—CTS. He buys up land and donates it to CTS so no one can ever build on it and pollute the environment."

"Why, he's a genuine saint, ain't he?"

"He gets a nice tax deduction and lots of good publicity. CTS will come in, tear down the buildings, post no trespassing signs, and let nature take it all back to herself."

"Damn convenient. Got himself little cemeteries everywhere, people can be disappeared into them."

Vector says, "Oh, I imagine there might be a few unmarked graves on other tracts of CTS land, but that's not the great man's primary purpose with the nonprofit. He's got bigger things on his mind."

"Such as."

"History and his place in it."

Shaking his head with admiration, Trott says, "When I was young, I thought myself pretty slick. I see now I exaggerated my potential. I ain't never got what it takes to be as slick as him."

"He sets a high standard for slickness," Vector agrees.

"Now what?"

"I call Duroc-Jersey to get us geared up. Call Sam Crockett to bring his dogs. While we wait for them, we catch a couple hours of sleep if we can, then be on Vida's trail at first light."

50

THE RIGHT HAND OF EVIL HARD AT WORK

In his Lexus, speeding to the house shared by the half brothers Monger and Rackman, Regis Duroc-Jersey, New World Technology vice president and facilitator of the Kettleton project, is exhausted and irritable and worried that his nose is going to start bleeding. Ever since he was ten, for the past twenty years, whenever he is under extreme stress, which is too often, he is sometimes subjected to a nosebleed that can last for as little as fifteen minutes or as long as two hours. When a lengthier affliction passes, the room around him is littered with so many bloody paper napkins—which are softer than paper towels, more absorbent than Kleenex—it appears as if he's a serial killer who, having fully cannibalized his victim, must now gather up the remaining evidence of his feast.

During the past eight months, the main cause of most of Regis's nosebleeds has been Galen Vector. Periodically, he has a nightmare in which Vector—in plaid pants and a garish coral-pink polo shirt, the lenses of his sunglasses as black as collapsed stars—attends him during a nosebleed and tries to staunch the flow by pinching Regis's nostrils in locking pliers, then in a monkey wrench, and finally between the fixed jaw and the movable jaw of an iron C-clamp. In this dream, Vector's pencil mustache extends across his upper lip and down to his chin, and he insists on being called Ming the Merciless, which was a character in the Flash Gordon movies that starred Buster Crabbe in the 1930s.

Ming. Funny how the subconscious works. Regis's older brother, Foster, is an information-technology entrepreneur with numerous patents related to cloud computing, their parents' favorite child by a wide margin, and a fan of old science-fiction movies. Foster has a particular fondness for the character of Ming, perhaps because Ming was as much of a power-mad jerk as Foster. Regis would like to apply a pair of locking pliers to a part of his brother's anatomy more intimate than his nose.

If the address that Vector provided is correct, Monger and Rackman live in a handsome two-story Victorian with two turrets and elaborate architectural moldings. In a fairy tale, someone's magical godmother would occupy such a lovely house, and the hulking half brothers would dwell under a bridge, amidst a litter of children's bones that have been picked clean.

Following Vector's instructions, Regis is to meet with Wendy, whom he called "their wife." Apparently, Monger and Rackman are experienced hikers who, when they are not beating up those whom Vector wishes to have beaten, enjoy venturing into the mountains to marvel at its beauty, no doubt singing "The Sound of Music" as they caper through fields and forests. Wendy will have prepared their fully stuffed backpacks, hiking boots, and desired clothing.

Their wife.

Regis doesn't imagine that marital arrangements between the Bigfoot brothers and Wendy have been legitimized by a minister or a justice of the peace, but he isn't one to judge others as regards such matters. However, he *is* quite curious about what kind of woman would cohabitate with them. He expects that, physically, Wendy will be the female equivalent of a longshoreman, as lusty as she is well muscled and boldly tattooed.

If he's wrong and she's a long-legged beauty of breathtaking proportions, he'll consider hanging himself. Or maybe just quit his job. Enough is enough. The fourteen months he's been in Kettleton have led him to question whether it makes sense to dedicate his life to the acquisition of hundreds of millions of dollars no matter what grueling effort is required, no matter what ignorant hicks and boors and vicious backwoods criminals he must associate with, no matter how often he is required to kiss the asses of corrupt bureaucrats and politicians. That he could even ask that question is terrifying. *Of course it's worth it.* Kettleton is such a tedious and depressing place that it has made him a little crazy, just unhinged enough to consider stumbling off the path to wealth and power, into the weeds where most people wander through life with such lack of purpose that they remain forever powerless. Not Regis Duroc-Jersey. Not ever.

When he rings the bell at the Monger-Rackman residence, Wendy, the unlikely *trois* of the unthinkable *ménage à trois*, opens the door in a state of breathless excitement. "Goodness gracious, here you are already, but that's okay, don't worry yourself about a thing, I just got it all collected, so come in, come in."

She is the furthest thing from a longshoreman, and though she is not the kind of beauty to appear on the covers of magazines that undertake to arouse young men, she is a delight to the eye—slender, with masses of curly auburn hair, flawless skin, a sprinkling of freckles, and limpid blue eyes. She's much better than beautiful; great beauties are often cool and unapproachable; Wendy is cute enough to be an anime character. Regis loves

Japanese anime because all the characters are cute. It's getting harder all the time to find cute in the real world. Having been awakened to perform the task at hand, Wendy is adorable in blue pajamas with pink bunnies all over them.

In Regis's view, she's too cute to be hauling around heavy backpacks, but she insists on carrying her share of gear and loading it into his SUV, and she proves to be stronger than she looks. As Regis closes the liftgate, Wendy says, "What's this about?"

"A little hike, a day or two."

"Put together on the spur of the moment, in the dead of night, it doesn't feel recreational. Spin me another story."

"I'm just doing what I'm told. I can't say what it's about."

"Can't or won't?"

"Does it matter?"

She crosses her arms on her chest, just like some anime girls do when they won't back down from a threat. "I'm a mother to those boys, and I'm determined to set them straight."

Baffled by that statement, he says, "Mother?"

"Oh, yes, I'm younger than they are, but they very much need a mom, even if just an honorary one. Our mother, rest her soul, was a mess, a slattern and an alley cat. They need guidance, those boys, and I mean to set them right."

"Slattern?"

"Look it up, Mr. Jersey."

"I know what it means. I've just never heard anyone use the word. The thing is, I was told . . ."

"You were told what?"

"You were their wife."

"Must've been that wicked Galen Vector told you that. The man's soul is as dark as his sunglasses. I am their half sister. I allow them to live here rent-free, and I cook for them. It is my life goal to lead them to the light."

"How's that working out?"

"No one likes a snarky man, Mr. Jersey. I know my brothers are lazy boys who like the easy money of the criminal life. However, I'm winning their hearts and minds. I'll pry them away from Galen Vector and get them on a righteous path. In only a year, I've enjoyed much success with them. They take baby steps. The poor dears can't be made clean overnight. At least they don't murder people anymore."

Even here in the darkness of the driveway, with only the moon and the stars and the wan outspill from the porch lamps, Wendy's eyes are a resplendent and inexplicable blue, as if lit from within. Regis has never met anyone with a stare as direct and searching as hers. He realizes he's stood in silence for more than a few seconds, and then he belatedly comprehends what she said. "How do you know they don't? Don't murder people anymore."

"I've turned them on their axes just far enough that they can lie to the world but not to me. They can't lie to me anymore than you can, Mr. Jersey."

He hears himself say, "Oh, I'm a very good liar, Wendy."

She smiles. "You see?"

Surprised by his admission, he is astonished by what issues from him next. "No, it isn't a recreational hike. It's a search. They're tracking someone. Pursuing her. A woman named Vida. She was the fiancée of José Nochelobo." He bites his tongue. He literally bites it to silence himself, though not hard enough to draw blood.

"My brothers did not kill Mr. Nochelobo."

His tongue frees itself from his teeth. "No."

"Do you know who did, Mr. Jersey?"

"Not his name. Just that he was a professional assassin and a foreign national who came here directly from jobs in Syria and the Ukraine." Alarmed to hear himself making these revelations, Regis says, "Thank you, pleased to meet you, have a nice day," and hurries away from her, alongside the SUV.

As Regis yanks open the driver's door, Wendy puts a hand on his shoulder, and he pivots toward her with no less fright than if she had been a disfigured mutant sociopath with a chain saw.

"When you see my brothers," she says, "remind them of their promise to me."

"All right, yes, I will."

"No murder."

"None," he agrees.

"No violence."

"Oh, well, there will probably be some violence. Vida isn't going to, you know, just give herself up. Your brothers might not kill her, but they'll make it possible for someone else to do it."

"You and the despicable Mr. Vector and his amoral associates are beyond my care. You will do what you will do. But not my poor brothers. They must take a baby step from no murder to no violence. They have promised me. Remind them of their promise."

Her eyes are the unique, iridescent blue of the wings of a Ulysses butterfly, a flock of which he'd once seen in Queensland, Australia, years earlier. In numbers, with their four-inch wingspan, they had flurried out of the shadows, so dazzling against the vivid green of the rainforest that they seemed unearthly. In witness of their aerial waltz, he'd stood transfixed, overcome by a sense of the world as being far more than he'd thought it was, by a sudden awareness of mysteries and fabulous possibilities of which he had previously been unaware. Now, looking into Wendy's eyes, as when he'd seen those butterflies dancing in sunlight, he feels both that the Earth is unearthly and that by his life choices he has lost the ability to perceive wonders that are unfolding around him in every hour of every day.

"Remind them of their promise," she repeats.

"I will, yes, I swear," Regis declares as he launches himself into the SUV and pulls the door shut.

The next thing he knows, he's two miles from Wendy's house, a mile from his next rendezvous, with no idea how he got there. He feels as if he's sloughing off some spell that was cast on him.

Before visiting Wendy, he'd been to Frank Trott's trailer, where Frank's gear had been readied by his son, Farnam, who was wired on something even at that hour. To express dissatisfaction with having been required to exert himself, Farnam repeatedly stuck out his tattooed tongue. Perhaps twenty years old, rail-thin, teeth yellowed, eyes bloodshot, with one eyebrow, having risen from a sofa littered with issues of the magazine *Heavy Metal*, he wore a T-shirt with the word STUD in bold letters.

After Trott's trailer, Regis had visited Galen Vector's house, where the crime boss's hiking clothes had been prepared for pickup by Candy Sass, formerly known as Berta Gussman, who had left Kettleton at eighteen to become a porn star and, following a strenuous seven-year career that ended with an extreme allergy to penicillin, had returned home as the main squeeze of the mountain mafioso. Candy was still a looker, even after servicing legions, and she knew it. From Vector's collection of weapons, she provided four AR-15s and sixteen extended magazines, providing enough firepower to contend with Vida if it turned out the fugitive was going into the mountains to take shelter with forty members of a crazed militia. "You won't need a backpack for Galen. He don't carry his own. The others will carry supplies for him." As Regis piled the gear and guns into the Lexus, Candy played with one rifle as perhaps she had done in a steamy sequence in one of her epics. Regis kept saying, "Hey, is that loaded? Are you sure? Are you sure that's not loaded?"

Now, he's three miles farther down the road, and his eyes are burning from lack of sleep, and his stomach is sour from too many caffeine tablets. He's already mostly forgotten Candy Sass and the anxiety she inspired regarding his lack of hand-sanitizing gel. But he's unable to forget the smallest thing about Wendy, anime goddess.

With dawn but forty minutes away, he is speeding toward the property where, according to Vector, Belden Bead and Nash Deacon are buried in their cars, their graves as unmarked as those of pharaohs in pyramids buried deep under the shifting sands of Egypt.

Having been Montessori molded, Pencey prepared, and fine-tuned at Harvard, Regis should have no capacity for superstition. He should be as free from fear of higher powers and spectral presences as he is unconcerned about black cats and broken mirrors. But he can't shake the feeling that cosmic justice is coming down on him, on all of them who are pushing the project in order to drain its funds into their pockets, that the corruption of his heart is known and that his time to repent is running out.

He's further unnerved when a disturbing Cheyenne word springs to mind—*Maheo*. He had encountered the word a few times during the extensive reading he'd done to familiarize himself with Kettleton County and its history, before coming to this butt-end of nowhere. The Cheyenne, a very spiritual people, believe in a supreme being, Maheo, "The Wise One Above."

They also believe in another god, one who lives in the earth. Regis isn't able to recall the name of the god who lives underfoot. This failure of memory suddenly seems significant. An underground god is surely of a darker nature than Maheo, more likely to extract vengeance for crimes against the Earth. *And if you don't even know your enemy's name, how can you hope to know when he's coming after you?*

As he slows down to turn onto Vida's driveway, Regis says aloud, "That's stupid, just plain nuts. What's wrong with me?" He answers his own question: "You're tired. That's all. You're worn out." He isn't entirely satisfied with that explanation and says, "Hell no. It's a lot more than that. Everything's coming apart. There are forces rising that aren't supposed to exist."

Making the turn onto the unpaved driveway, he issues a sharp rebuke: "Stop talking to yourself, dammit. You're scaring me." And so he doesn't say one word more as the stone house comes into view, bathed in starlight, the moon having descended below the towering peaks of the western mountains.

51

WHAT WAS AND WHAT CAN BE

In this deepest level of sleep, past and future are one with the present, and all of time is accessible. Vida sits in a rocking chair. She is ten years old. The night is dark and deep, although the moon is four times larger than it has ever been before, as dull as tarnished silver. José Nochelobo stands in the yard with another man, their backs to her, gazing at the celestial phenomenon. Strange as the moment is, Vida feels nonetheless safe, at peace. But then the seer in white robe and yellow sneakers appears in the other rocking chair, and the mood abruptly changes when she says, "Give me the thing you value most, and I will consider telling your future."

"Before, it was the thing I valued least," says Vida.

The seer shrugs. "Everything is more expensive than it once was."

A low thrumming rises in the distance, as if some machine with a powerful but muffled engine is approaching.

Vida ages eighteen years in an instant. "I can't give you what I value most. It's not mine to give, and I'd never sell it."

"That," says the seer, "is the answer I wanted. Before you is your past and future, standing under the moon. Be not so foolish as to cling to what was, rather than embrace what can be."

Although still muffled, the engine noise is closer, a deep and ominous sound that seems felt more than heard.

"What's that?" Vida rises from her chair. "What's coming?"

"Death," the seer says. "When you hear it elsewhere than in a dream, move fast. Do what is expected of a woman who runs with wolves."

The seer evaporates, and a porch post vanishes, and a section of railing with balusters disappears as Vida moves toward the steps, which dissolve behind her as she descends to the yard. The massive moon recedes, and as it dwindles, José turns toward her, fading away before their eyes can meet. The landscape rapidly darkens under the diminishing moon, and when she steps around the stranger to learn his identity, he covers his face with one hand. An eye rimmed with a hoarfrost of lunar light regards her through a gap between fingers. Moon, meadow, and man become smoke, and the smoke withers away in an instant, and there is nothing in the dream except Vida. She floats in a void, as though she's an untethered astronaut adrift in space, and then she closes her eyes against the horror of nothingness and continues sleeping where further dreams remain unborn.

52

THE DOG LOVER

In the dream, Sam Crockett's face is on fire, but the flames don't concern him because he is convinced that he is safe in the presence of the fortuneteller regardless of what happens. Besides, his dogs are with him in the woman's candlelit kitchen, and they have kept him sane and happy in the years since fire took his face. The seer says, "There are dogs, and soon one even better than dogs."

The phone rings, and he wakes into an absence of flames.

Sam doesn't mind being awakened hours before he would otherwise arise to the new day, because the call is a request for him to bring his three best dogs to assist in a search. He takes great pride in his dogs.

When he hangs up the phone and turns on the light, the three German shepherds sharing the king-size bed—Sherlock, Whimsey, and Marple—grumble and snuffle and yawn. Four other shepherds occupy their dog beds in the corners of the room.

None of the seven rises from its mattress when Sam goes into his closet to dress. They lift their heads and watch attentively.

These dogs never bark unless their master issues the command to do so, which is *Speak*.

When he returns to the bedroom, dressed for the chase, seven tails thump seven padded surfaces, because the gear he wears is a promise that some of them will soon be engaged in an exciting hunt.

"Let's go," says Sam.

As if sprung from their beds by some mechanism, claws clicking-scrabbling on the wood floor, the shepherds follow him out of the bedroom in a more or less orderly swarm.

Years earlier, the kitchen was extended to provide an area for the watering and feeding of dogs. Before retiring for the night, Sam had set out four clean bowls full of fresh water.

Some of the shepherds will drink before eating, some after they have eaten, and others only after they have eaten and toileted. Each has his or her own ways and preferences. Dogs can be trained to be civilized and dutiful, but they can't be coerced into repressing their unique personalities, as can many human beings who will remake themselves into automatons and enchain their own souls in the name of one ideology or another.

Sam Crockett likes a few people, despises a few, and isn't sure what he thinks about most of them—but he loves all dogs.

While he starts one cup brewing in the coffeemaker and begins filling bowls with morning food for his pack, the shepherds cruise the room, savoring the smells of yesterday or exploring the contents of the toy box, or parading around with tennis balls in their mouths to suggest that a play session might be agreeable to them.

After they have eaten, Sam opens the back door, and the seven venture into the last of the night to toilet in the fenced acre that serves as the backyard. After the hunt, when it's light, he will bag the results of the morning potty session. He keeps the property clean for them, bathes them frequently, brushes their teeth three times a week, and adheres to a schedule for trimming their claws—none of which feels like work to him.

They are his children. Because of his face, he isn't likely to marry. His family is the four-footed kind.

When the dogs return to the house, he puts halters rather than collars on Sherlock, Peter Whimsey, and Miss Marple. The four who will not be going on this job—Nero, Kinsey, Travis, and Doc—use their eyes to guilt-trip Sam, but they know that there is always another hunt and that their turn will come.

During his absence, they'll use the hinged pass-through in the back door. Although he locks the house, it isn't necessary. There is no alarm to set. Kettleton is no longer the low-crime town it used to be—maybe nowhere is—but no security system can be as effective at deterring burglars as can a pack of German shepherds trained to be intolerant of intruders.

He phones his neighbor, Jessie Berkel, one of those people he likes, and leaves a voice mail. If Sam doesn't return from the hunt in a timely manner, Jessie will stop by to feed, water, and clean up after those in the pack who are staying home.

In the garage, the three dogs leap through the open liftgate into the back of Sam's SUV, lie down, and curl up for transport, as they have been trained to do. He tells them how good they are, and their attitude says, *Yeah, we know.*

Sam has never been to the house at which the search party is being organized, but he knows where to find it. He hasn't been told what they're seeking, although he imagines that it's competitors operating without permission of the Bead family.

Over the past four years, since returning from war and raising his shepherds, he has conducted searches at the behest of Sheriff Montrose, also for law-enforcement agencies in neighboring counties, and even for federal bureaus. He's found lost children, old folks with dementia who have wandered off, and escaped prisoners—for which he's collected rewards in addition to charging an hourly rate. Thanks to the industry and prudence of his mother, Pauline, who died while Sam was in a military hospital overseas, he doesn't urgently need the money he earns with the dogs. However, without this work, he would have no purpose and no hope.

For Belden Bead and recently for Galen Vector, Sam has used his long-tailed detectives to sniff out competition from meth labs and marijuana farms concealed in the primeval wilderness. Once he and his dogs, along with Vector's people, locate a drug operation, the sheriff's department raids the place and makes arrests.

Sheriff Montrose is aware of this work Sam does. He approves because he believes the county will remain more peaceful if drug and human-trafficking offenses, which can't be eradicated, are at least organized by one crime family. Montrose dreads intrusion by bloody-minded Central American gangs, which have been sending thousands of foot soldiers across the open border; they have a history of violent turf wars and campaigns of vengeance without regard for collateral damage wrought upon the innocent. Most likely, the sheriff also gets a slice of the action from the Bead family's operations.

Sam despises Vector as he also despised Bead, but he works with these bad guys because the targets are worse guys. The dogs love the action, and it keeps them at the top of their game. Maybe the money comes from people with dirty hands, but he and his pack don't do anything illegal to earn it. He has also been advised—not bluntly, but with discretion—that a refusal to assist Vector is likely to result in the poisoning of one or all of his dogs.

The dogs are his family. They are his life. The dogs don't care that his face is a mass of burn scars beyond repair, that he has no hair or eyebrows, that his nose is misshapen and his ears are rags of crushed cartilage pinned to his head by long-hardened cicatrices. The dogs love him, and he loves them. When Galen Vector issues a summons, Sam will do what is wanted with resentment but without regret. To keep his dogs safe, he will swallow his pride and bend his knee, which he refused to do when he was in the hands of his enemies, thousands of miles from Kettleton.

This is a time in history when it's best to endure the current shitstorm and keep faith that it won't last. America's ruling class is riddled with bad and stupid people who despise the lower classes, get rich by dealing with the nation's enemies while impoverishing their fellow citizens, and send young men into battle for a purpose ill defined, with rules of engagement that ensure the war can't be won, leaving those who fight it humiliated. Until better and wiser people wrench the country off the road to ruin, Sam Crockett faces the future with hope and gratitude, reminding himself each morning and evening that his life is short and passes like a shadow.

Eighteen years earlier, the fortuneteller had said he would endure a period of much suffering and sorrow. How right she was. She'd also said beyond that valley of misery, he would find greater happiness than he'd known before. Maybe he would. At the moment, if life gets no better than it is, that will be good enough.

Pale-gray light shoals against the dragon spine of the eastern mountains as he turns right off the county road and heads uphill. The trees shouldering the unpaved driveway recede to the left and right, encircling a large meadow, toward the back of which stands a single-story building with lights in its windows.

For some reason, though there is neither a steeple nor stained glass, the house reminds him of a church. He takes that impression seriously. He thinks it possible that ceremonies of innocence, the humble routines and kind sharing of daily existence that give life meaning, when performed often and for long enough, can confer on a house a hallowed quality. He's known such homes; he has known their opposite, where human depravity has so soiled a structure that an aura of evil shadows every room even when all the lights are lit.

Kitted for the mountains, four dark figures wait on the porch and steps. The house door is wide open behind them, as if they are fresh from some obscene violation of the home's most sacred spaces. The tableau they present chills Sam. He intuits that this search is different from all others to which Galen Vector has summoned him.

Two SUVs are parked in the front yard. He angles his Lincoln Navigator to a stop beside them.

By the time he steps to the back of the vehicle, carrying the master leash, the four men have descended from the porch and joined him. Sam knows Vector well enough to despise him, Trott well enough to be disgusted by him, and the stone-faced brothers only enough to wonder what creature birthed and raised them.

Vector seldom goes on these searches, but he is fully outfitted for this one. He has a cocked-gun quality about him, as though some offense has enraged him and he is hell-bent on retribution. As Sam opens the liftgate and calls forth Sherlock and Whimsey and Marple, Vector says, "These your best dogs? I said to bring your best."

"You know them, what they can do," says Sam. "There aren't any better. What's the hunt about?"

The dogs leap from the SUV and stand at attention. Panting with excitement, they look at the gathered men, the meadow, the house.

The master leash ends in a stainless-steel ring to which three subsidiary leashes are linked by rings of their own. As Sam crouches to attach the first of the three to the harness that Sherlock wears, Vector says, "The woman who lives here alone—she's gone missing."

"A missing person case? That's for the sheriff."

"Not this time."

"Why not?"

"Better you don't know."

Having finished the third of three connections, Sam rises to his full height. "Better for who?"

"Better for you."

"I don't think so."

"I'm not paying you to think."

Although the sun has not yet appeared, a tide of morning light breaks over the eastern mountains, transforming the scattered clouds from white to coral pink.

Sam looks at each of the four men, color coming into their dark faces and borrowed light into their eyes. He's not in their club. To them, he's a tool, nothing more. He's always known that. Previously, he has thought he's such a valuable tool—he and the dogs—that there's no risk they will, for whatever reason, dispose of him.

Each has an AR-15 slung over one shoulder, but that's nothing new. Every time they go in search of a rumored meth lab or a weed farm, though they intend only to spot it for the sheriff, there is always a chance that the competitors they mean to have evicted will see them and respond. And the deeper they go into these mountains, the more likely they are to encounter cougars, not to mention bears so large and fierce that a can of spray repellant, which provides a sense of safety in a public campground, seems woefully inadequate out there.

Frank Trott takes it upon himself to explain the stakes. "Who the bitch is and what all she done don't make no difference to you. But she maybe knows somethin' makes a damn big difference to Mr. Terrence Boschvark. Even a freakin' recluse like you gotta know that name."

The dogs are whining softly, eager to begin.

Sam says, "She 'maybe knows something.' What if she does? What happens then?"

"Ain't nobody can't be bought," Trott says. "No matter how righteous Vida thinks she is, there's a price she'll take, most 'specially if the cost for *not* takin' it scares the piss outta her."

"And if this Vida says she doesn't know anything? Will you believe her? How can you be sure she's telling the truth?"

Taking off his sunglasses, revealing eyes the color of brandy, Galen Vector says, "Sam, I like to think of you as a friend of the family. In a time of trouble, a friend of the family wants to help any way he can. He doesn't want to engage in a damn debate. Those dogs know how it is. Those fine dogs are ready to run. You need to be no less ready than they are. There's no other way you can be. The war that chewed you up and spit you out and the war here and now—they're the same, just this one's not conducted with as much noise. We find her, there'll be a fat reward on top of your hourly charge, say fifty thousand."

Sam's been told he's expendable if he isn't buyable. Because he isn't done with life yet and he has an obligation to his dogs, he buckles. "Well now, that makes all the difference." Although he has no choice, he feels as if a small light inside of him has gone out. It's not the first to have been extinguished, but maybe there aren't a lot more of them still glowing.

Trott produces a pair of women's panties. "Found these pretties in her launder basket. I suspect them hounds of yours gonna take her scent. For damn sure, I ain't smelled nothin' so good in years."

Monger and Rackman make a chortling noise like a sound they heard in a zoo and imitate as though it's a natural human reaction.

The dogs are not affronted by being offered the woman's panties instead of a blouse or a scarf, and though Sam is offended on their behalf, he doesn't give voice to his irritation. The dogs possess more dignity than these four men. Sam knows that to be true, even though Vector and his companions don't, and knowing it is enough for him to accept the insult in silence. The dogs know it, too.

Ears pricked and bodies tensed, Sherlock and Whimsey and Marple gaze up at Sam expectantly. They have the scent. They know the task. When they launch, one will occasionally be distracted to the length of its leash by a false or more interesting scent, but never three at the same time; the other two will draw the stray back onto the true trail, and their feverish enthusiasm will encourage one another into a heroic search effort.

At times during the hunt, Sam will be hard-pressed to keep pace with the dogs and will rein them in, much to their consternation. He can't be burdened with a backpack and remain in adequate control of the shepherds. Vector's crew carry water for the animals and their master, as well as for themselves and Vector. Sam has only Ziploc bags filled with chunks of jerky, distributed among his many pockets, to serve as encouragements and rewards for the dogs.

As the crown of the sun rises above the eastern crests, color spreads across the sky. Darkness retreats from meadow into forest.

With the end loop around his wrist and the master leash wound twice through the palm of his hand, Sam rewards the dogs with the word they desire. "Find."

They're off. The woman's scent is everywhere, and initially the shepherds reel in concert back and forth across the yard, even into the taller grass of the meadow. Their sense of smell is thousands of times greater than Sam's, nuanced beyond human comprehension. From all the spoor laid down since the last rain, they soon finesse that which is most recent, and Sam is running with them toward the trees behind the house, toward the foothills and the mountains beyond.

The dogs neither bark nor howl, lest they alert the quarry that an urgent pursuit is underway. With restraint that's hard-learned for such ebullient and expressive creatures, they limit themselves to soft whines and whimpers of excitement, panting and snuffling as they lead Sam and the others to a break in the forest undergrowth and onto a twisting trail that deer pioneered and have maintained perhaps for centuries.

In the cool, crisp air, songbirds wake and warble. Ribbons of low mist spool among the trees, beading ferns, silvering moss, while the undergrowth rustles with life unseen. Thick columns of darkness stand everywhere, seeming to possess true substance, though as the sun ascends through the morning, most of the shadows will melt away.

Sam has always been comfortable in unpeopled woods, where there is no one to see him for the first time and gape at his ravaged face and press him with foolish questions. On this occasion, however, the forest seems fateful, as though one of the shadows will shape itself into a cloaked and spectral form, stepping forward to settle the debt it had meant to collect in Afghanistan.

53

THE HUNT BEGINS

No wolves are present when Vida wakes. Perhaps there were never any resting in the soft green bedding nature provided, although she thought she had sensed them around her when she'd briefly drifted out of the depths of sleep and into the shallows.

From the broad shelf on which she'd passed the night, grass-land rises for maybe a hundred yards, broken by low stone for-mations like toppled monuments, leading to a renewal of the forest. This broad swath of open land is prime hunting ground for raptors, and even as the sun ascends into its fullness, what might be a red-tailed hawk appears in the distance, while a larger ferruginous hawk kites overhead in a widening gyre.

After her ablutions, after stretching exercises to get limber for what the day will require, Vida sits with a view of the forest below the shelf where she slept. She makes a breakfast of two PowerBars and a bottle of water.

What if she *is* destined to be a defender of the natural world, as José Nochelobo was in his way? What if, as the fortuneteller implied, Vida's life is somehow a reflection of the mythical life of the Roman deity Diana, goddess of the moon and of all the creatures that hunt or are hunted? What does that mean? What does it entail? For one thing, she will be hunted by those who believe the natural world exists only to fatten their wallets or serve their ideology, or to provide an excuse for them to rule others in the name of ecological virtue, and she will be justified in hunting them as they hunt her. A day of violence lies before her, whether she wants it or not, and she doesn't want it.

Although she dreads what is coming, she has prepared for it. She might end up sprawled dead among blue wildflowers, although she won't be the only corpse in that meadow. She has Nash Deacon's gun, but rather than use it, she prefers to dispose of it in the wilds where it will never be found, never be associated with her. If she must kill those who are intent on killing her, if there is no law enforcement on which she can rely, she must not use guns that can be proved to have been in her possession.

At all costs, when this is finished, she must resume life in her uncle's house from which they have harried her. The only future Vida desires is the past—the eighty acres, the small stone house, the books, the quiet, the patient processing of the placer mine gemstones, the visitation of wolves, the memories.

Dog voices. Not the howls of wolves. Sharp and eager. Quickly silenced.

Vida springs to her feet.

The search dogs are well disciplined. Although they must be hugely excited, she hears no sound from the pack after that brief spate of triumphant barking, which suggests they're no more than two hundred yards below, screened from her by the ranks of conifers. She hasn't expected dogs. But at the sound of them, she realizes they were inevitable.

She needs to move faster than she has intended; however, all things considered, the hounds are a positive development. Left to their own skills and instinct, the hunters are likely to lose track of her, requiring that she leave spoor so obvious that the men might suspect they are being lured into a trap, which they are. No matter how meager the signs of her passage might be, the dogs are certain to find them, know them, and never be distracted or misled.

She folds the wrappers of the PowerBars, inserts them in the empty water bottle, crushes the flimsy plastic, screws on the cap, and stows the condensed trash in a zippered pocket of her jacket.

She shrugs into her backpack, secures the strap at her waist, and stands listening. The dogs make no sound that she can hear, but they are still coming. She can feel them yearning toward her. They want her, but not to harm her, only to keep the promise they have made to whoever is their master. Dogs keep their promises, though the promises that people, in turn, make to them are less reliably fulfilled.

She turns away from her unseen pursuers and hurries up the grassy meadow toward the tree line.

54

A MAN IN NEED OF FIXING

After having brought all the gear to the searchers and after seeing them off with Sam Crockett and his hounds, Regis Duroc-Jersey is expected to remain at Vida's house until Galen Vector returns with the confirmation that they have left her naked corpse for the delectation of whatever carrion eaters might strip the flesh from her skeleton and break her bones to taste her marrow, in some remote ravine where the time-bleached remains will never be found.

When Regis took the job with Terrence Boschvark, he didn't expect to become an accessory to murder. If he didn't expect it, he must have at least intuited the possibility. The first time that he found himself at risk of the crime regarding José Nochelobo, Regis wasn't surprised. Now here he is again. There's the motivation of great wealth, of course, as well as the expectations of his parents and the competition with his brother, Foster. But he could spend years analyzing influences, seeking the hinge moment when he swung into the dark side, yet arrive at no enlightenment. The heart is deceitful above all things. Rare is the man who knows the full truth of his own heart, and Regis is aware that he doesn't possess that insight.

He spends some time in Vida's library, reading the spines of the novels on the shelves. He is impressed by the wide spectrum of literature that interests the woman, especially since she never went to college. How then did she know what books were worth her time? Or perhaps none of these books are of the right kind. He ought to know if they are or aren't. But he doesn't. Here are entire collections of authors whose names are new to him. For the first time, he allows himself to wonder if Harvard failed him.

An approaching vehicle rackets through the morning. When he steps onto the porch, an SUV pulls to a stop and parks beside his Lexus. It's a down-market brand he doesn't recognize.

Wendy gets out of the driver's door. Explosion of curly auburn hair. Flawless skin. Huge, limpid blue eyes. The pajamas with pink bunnies are gone. She's wearing black boots and black jeans and a blue blouse with black epaulets. She looks more than ever like a character from Japanese anime.

Regis is enchanted and frightened in equal measure, which is a weird feeling, but he understands it.

She understands it, too. She comes to him and stands before him and says, "I realized something after you left my place."

He doesn't dare speak, for he is again under her spell. He fears what revelations he'll make.

"I have long known that I have an important mission," she says.

He can't control his tongue. "You *look* like a person with a mission. You look like an anime heroine."

"I thought my mission was to save my brothers from themselves, but it might not be given to me to accomplish that. I've worked so hard on them. I've convinced myself that they can no longer lie to me. But my conviction might be self-delusion. After all, they're off on this woman hunt with the wicked Galen Vector. But you . . ."

"Me?"

"You." She smiled.

"Me what?"

"For sure, you can't lie."

"Nonsense. I'm a tremendous liar. I've spent my life lying about everything to everyone."

"Not to me. When you're speaking to me, you mean to lie, but when you open your mouth, all the truth spills out of you no matter how much you want to conceal it. That's what happened at my place. Several times. It just happened again now."

He shrugged. "Believe what you want."

"I'll believe what I know. I've been waiting eighteen years for you to show up."

"Eighteen years ago," he says, "I would have been twelve."

"I would have been ten."

"You didn't even know I existed eighteen years ago."

"I didn't know it was you. I just knew it was someone who could never lie to me and that together we would accomplish great things."

"What does that mean—'accomplish great things'?"

"I don't know. It's what the fortuneteller said. I guess we'll find out."

"What fortuneteller?"

"She operated out of a house less than a mile from here. I paid her with a five-pound block of cheese. Free cheese from the federal government."

"Cheese?"

"It was symbolic."

"Of what?"

"Of what I valued least, which was what my mother valued most."

"Your mother valued cheese above all things?"

"She valued what was free, what she could get for nothing. Momma was addicted to the dole and to defrauding the system as much as she was addicted to her cigarettes, booze, pot, jalapeño potato chips, chocolate-peanut-butter ice cream, and sleazy men, among other things."

"Why's a ten-year-old girl going to a fortuneteller?"

"Looking for a way out."

"A way out of what?"

"Out of a dead-end life. The seer told me to start my own business."

"The seer?"

"The fortuneteller."

"She told you to start your own business at ten?"

"I took up housecleaning. I'm a demon cleaner."

"At ten."

"Even before that. I like clean. I can't stand filth. In six months, I had four clients, four houses. When I was twelve, I added seamstress work."

"What about school?"

"School is school. I liked it. But work is better. Sixteen, I got a beautician license. Twenty, I opened my own salon with four employees. It's the most popular in the county. I like being busy."

"How does a girl of ten realize she's in a dead-end life?"

Wendy cocks her head and regards him with amusement or pity; he can't tell which. "How does a guy of thirty *not* realize he's in a dead-end life."

"Me? Hey, I'm going somewhere."

"Backward at high speed."

"I'm already rich."

"You'll never be rich enough."

"By any standard, I'm a success."

"Not by the standard that matters most."

"Yeah? What standard would that be?"

"Happiness. You think you're happy?"

"Absolutely."

"Then you don't know what happiness is. You're in a perpetual state of desperation. It's always in the back of your mind."

"What is?"

"That when Terrence Boschvark goes to prison, so will you."

"He's too rich and clever to go to prison. When he has to move outside the law to get something done, he insulates himself with so many layers of deniability that nothing can be proved."

"And you admire that?"

"Maybe I don't admire it. But I respect it."

"That's even worse than admiring it. I've got my work cut out for me."

"What work?"

"Fixing you."

"You're not gonna fix me."

"I don't mean like neutering a dog."

"Goddamn right you don't."

"Don't you go blaspheming. I guess I lost my brothers to the devil, but I'm not gonna lose you."

55

IN THE COMPANY OF MONSTERS

The dogs are on the scent, respectful of the restraining leash, although Sam can barely keep up with them. Sherlock, Whimsey, and Marple keen and pant and growl, but don't bark. Their excitement is transmitted to Sam as he hitches and staggers up the deer path with a desperate hold on his team. He is as much a member of the pack as he is the master of it, propelled by the thrill of the hunt. Vector and Trott labor after him; accustomed to hiking at a more leisurely pace, both are wheezing, especially Trott with his backpack, and one or the other mutters curses when he has breath to spare. They erupt from the lower forest onto a broad sloping meadow, where the woman is nearing the top of the incline and making for the higher woods.

For a few hundred yards, the underbrush has been so sparse that Monger and Rackman have been charging through it, parallel to the beaten path that Sam follows. Effortlessly, they bear backpacks that contain bottled water and PowerBars but also enough ammunition to win a firefight against a battalion of enemies. Implacable, like robotic terminators in a movie, they have about them the aura of men who will do anything, who allow no restraints to be imposed on them. Sam doesn't entertain illusions about Monger and Rackman, and yet when they come out of the forest to his right and see their quarry and open fire, he's shocked. The AR-15s can be accurate at a significant range, but the woman, Vida, is at the limit of a sure hit, maybe beyond it. They fire bursts, depleting their extended magazines, hoping that volume will bring luck that distance might deny them. From the last of the overhead branches, great flocks that have been perched in silence erupt into flight, dead brown needles spiraling down on the men and dogs.

As Monger and Rackman insert fresh magazines into their rifles and hook the empties to their utility belts to be reloaded later, Galen Vector, closely followed by Frank Trott, rushes into the open meadow. Vector is apoplectic. "Hold your fire, dammit! We want her alive. You know *we want her alive.*"

Monger and Rackman regard him with expressions as enigmatic as those of the carved-stone heads on Easter Island, as if to say they don't share his agenda and in fact find it incomprehensible.

Their silence and hard stares seem to surprise Vector, though in a moment his eyes narrow and his face becomes as pale as that of a cadaver on which a mortician hasn't yet applied the subtle color of a sleeper sleeping. "You work for me. When have you ever worked for anyone but me? You take orders from *me.*"

As Vida slips away among the trees, the brothers hulk up the meadow, ignoring Vector's question and his demand.

"I have issues to discuss with her," Vector calls after them. "For Belden, the Bead family."

The confidence with which Monger and Rackman disobey him suggests that whoever now employs them is so much higher up the ladder from Vector that they are guaranteed a rich future and immunity from the vengeance of the Bead crime family.

"Boschvark," says Vector. "He just wants her dead and buried deep. The pig-shit bastard doesn't care about family honor."

Sam has suspected they've been deceiving him, that they aren't interested in interrogating the woman to learn what she might know. Now their actions belie everything they said and implied. They have no intention of buying her off with Boschvark's money. This isn't a search. This is a hunt to the death. He doesn't know who she is, what she's done, what she knows. But his ignorance is an inadequate defense against the charge of being an accessory in a murder case.

Besides, there are the dogs to consider. What happens to them if he's arrested? Will they be impounded by authorities? Put down?

Vector and Trott are watching him like players at a high-stakes poker table, looking for a telltale that might reveal whether he's confident about his position or calculating a new strategy. Because he doesn't know the woman, these men will doubt that his sympathies could be with her; his survival depends on encouraging them in that doubt.

"Sam," Vector says, "Monger and Rackman think they've slipped their leash. Don't worry. They're mine. I've got them."

"You sure?"

"Nothing will happen to her. Except she's going to talk to me."

"They shot at her."

"They won't get another chance. She's safe. Those shithead brothers, those traitors, are dead. They just don't know it."

Sam doesn't believe him. If his disbelief is evident, he will be killed sooner than later.

"You've always been good to me," Sam says.

"Don't forget it."

"It's just my dogs."

"I love dogs," Vector says. "Your pack has done a lot of good work for me. Find the woman. I'll deal with Monger and Rackman."

"Find," Sam tells the dogs, and they are in the hunt again.

Vector stays close beside Sam as they ascend the meadow. "Don't hold the dogs back."

"I'm not holding them back."

"It'll be quicker to turn them loose and let them tree her."

"This isn't a raccoon hunt," Sam says. "They're not trained to tree anyone."

"She doesn't know that. They come at her fast, she'll panic, climb to keep from being bitten."

"Maybe she won't. Anyway, that's not how they're trained. They need the leash and commands to follow. Unleash them, they'll think the hunt is off. They won't go at her fast or at all," Sam insists, though his purpose now is to fail at this task without his dogs coming to harm and without taking a bullet in the head.

"All right, but don't hold them back."

To Vector and Boschvark and all the others, the woman matters because of something she knows, a secret that could bring them to ruin if exposed, whatever that might be. However, considering that she has remained free and alive with such powerful and unscrupulous people aligned against her suggests to Sam Crockett that the secret she's discovered is not the most important thing about her. There is something bigger at work here. Some quality or power she possesses that these men resent but also fear.

As they ascend toward the trees among which Vida disappeared, Sam is unaccountably reminded of an event from eighteen years in the past—the fortuneteller whom he paid with photographs of his father, photos that he no longer valued.

The table of many colors, the candle flames, the three figures of light pulsing on the wall, the woman's piercing stare . . .

"Will I be like him?"

"Your father?"

"Yeah."

"Like him in what way?"

"Will I betray people?"

"No. Not you. Never."

Although the meadow rises toward higher phalanxes of trees, somewhere ahead the land descends into the valley that is always just one hill away, the valley of the shadow of death.

56

BECOMING

Evergreens crowding one another, the air redolent of pines, the way mostly shadowed, morning light splintering through the boughs, the trail slippery with the dead needles of the trees, the brittle scales of fallen cones crumbling under her feet. In the wake of the gunfire, the only things Vida can hear are her labored breathing and the pounding of her heart. Although the forest mantles thousands of square miles of mountains and valleys, a curious claustrophobia closes around the moment, and the sounds she makes have a hollow quality, as if she is in a barrel or a metal-walled room, running from nowhere to nowhere on a treadmill.

She is fit, but sprinting uphill on a serpentine trail, even with just fifteen pounds on her back, will tax her into physical penury sooner than she dares to consider. At all costs, she must remain positive and focused. Four-legged trackers are fast on her spoor. Gunmen are even more intent on murder than she anticipated. In her frantic ascent, she breathes through her mouth; the piney fragrance is so strong that it isn't merely a scent, but also a pungent flavor—now medicinal, now janitorial—that cloys in her throat and seems to make breathing more difficult.

She worries about the dogs, about what they might be trained to do to her and how reliably they will adhere to their training, but she also worries *for* the dogs. Lupo is attuned to her in a way that she can't fully understand, that perhaps no one other than the long-ago fortuneteller could comprehend. If he becomes aware that Vida is in peril and if he arrives with his pack, what might happen when dogs and wolves meet? They are of the same genus but not the same species, the former domesticated and the latter wild. When she was but ten years old, she had been told that she was the protector of Nature and all its creatures. For years, that grand lifework seemed far beyond the talents of a young woman of the mountains, a placer-mine prospector and bookworm with a taste for isolation just short of hermitism. However, day by day since José's death, hour by hour since Nash Deacon first arrived on her doorstep, Vida has awakened to a deeper truth about herself, to the possibility of a daunting and yet thrilling mission that ongoing events appear to confirm, a destiny alike to what the seer foresaw eighteen years earlier. If there is any chance that such a solemn yet magical responsibility has been settled on her, she must never allow dogs and wolves to clash or to suffer at the hands of the vicious men who pursue her.

She thinks, *Have pity on those who love and are separated, on the lonely, on those who mourn, on those who fear, on all the little animals that live their lives as prey, but pity as well the animals that must kill to survive in this fallen world.*

Vida has no similar obligation to pity and protect *all* human beings, only those who are innocent as animals are innocent, those who are humble as little children are humble, those who are kind. She doesn't believe that any of the men on her trail are innocent or humble or kind, but if one such exists among them, she trusts that she will recognize him—and be able to spare him.

If she has a magical purpose, she doesn't have magical powers with which to fulfill it. The steepening incline and a stretch of trail providing uncertain footing force her to slow from a run to a quick walk. Her breath is hot, and she has broken into a sweat. Her abdominal muscles flutter. Her calves ache.

As her effort declines, she can hear more than her hammering heart and ragged exhalations. The new sound is at first a clatter that seems distant, unnervingly like a machine gun.

However, distance is an auditory illusion, and within seconds she realizes the noise originates nearby and overhead. Not a clatter of metal against metal. A deeper throbbing. The *whump-whump-whump* of flogged air, the underlying howl of a turbine engine. A helicopter. Something bigger than a sheriff's department chopper. A gunship? No. They couldn't have dragged the military into this. Perhaps a rescue helicopter. County law enforcement might have one of those.

Although the day is windless, the trees begin to shiver about thirty yards ahead of her and fifty yards to her right, pine boughs billowing, branches creaking. The disturbance proceeds toward her, passes perhaps twenty yards in front of her, and moves away to the left.

Puzzled by this development, Vida halts, trying to imagine their intention. The forest is so dense that the layered branches overhead allow only flinders of sky to be seen. So little light reaches the ground that the undergrowth is minimal in this area—deciduous ferns, wiry grasses, Corsican sandwort, pale colonies of fungus; the lowest branches of evergreens are often barren witchy-looking configurations. No airborne surveillance is able to provide meaningful assistance to the search party on the ground.

Surely even infrared scanning will fail to detect a heat signature here beneath the interlaced and many-storied boughs.

This is not the same sound as in the dream when she was sitting on the porch with the fortuneteller, not mysterious but distinct and easily identified. Yet it portends nothing good.

A change in the pitch of the engine noise alerts her that the chopper is executing a turn, coming back, as though quartering this area to confirm the pilot's suspicion. Or to take a second reading with some technology she can't name.

As the racket of the aircraft swells louder, Vida taps into a reserve of energy that for the moment had seemed not to exist. She springs forward, off the winding trail, taking as direct a path as the terrain and sparse brush allow. She avoids even the narrowest blades of sunlight that stab through gaps in the trees, as if they must be surveillance beams that can carry gigabytes of data to the searchers in the helo.

Although her life passes like a shadow, as do all lives, though she is but a moving shadow hurriedly navigating an architecture of stilled shadows, she feels that she is gaining substance moment by moment, becoming someone more formidable than she's been heretofore. She is exhilarated. Dogs are in pursuit of her and vicious men with rifles are taking aim and searchers in a helicopter are busy seeking, and Boschvark is scheming to kill her in some other fashion if this attempt should fail—yet she is enlivened and elated by the rising risk, currently prey but soon to become a huntress. For years, she's been uncertain of what the white-robed fortuneteller meant; then, when she understood, there had been additional years during which she doubted the woman's strange, mystical prediction could be fulfilled. All doubt is gone. She might not survive, but for a time she'll serve as the protector of nature and all its creatures that the seer foresaw. She now wears the mantle of José Nochelobo. If she's able to complete his mission, even if she perishes in the process, her short life will have been worth living. She runs, runs, runs, and all the shadows of the forest conspire to conceal her, seem to run with her like spirit guardians born out of the trees and risen from the earth, in celebration of her Becoming.

The evergreens shake, dead needles rain, dislodged pine cones rattle down through the branches, pine cones and something else. The helicopter is directly overhead.

57

BREAD UPON THE WATERS

A break in the trees. A swath of sky revealed. A clatter fills the heavens, and a shadow floats across the land.

At first, Galen Vector is merely surprised that a helicopter has joined this operation, but as it approaches, his surprise swells into apprehension when he discovers that no effort has been made to conceal that the aircraft belongs to one of Terrence Boschvark's companies. The twin-engine executive chopper with high-set main and tail rotors, large enough to be configured for eight passengers, is emblazoned with the red-white-and-blue New World Technology logo.

Has Boschvark decided that killing Vida is so important, the need so urgent, he can no longer afford the delay that occurs when he works through surrogates to insulate himself from blame? What would drive him to take such a terrible risk? Maybe he thinks his political connections are so numerous and at such a high level that he is immune from not just prosecution but also accusation—and he might be right.

Perhaps he is confident that not only will he never be held to account for his crimes but also that he can set up his associates to take the fall for him. Set them up and take them out in engineered accidents or by arranging for murder to look like suicide. It's not paranoid to consider such cold methodology. Vector himself has done as much to others who have served him well but ceased to be useful.

As if their actions are choreographed, Monger and Rackman pause in their ascent and take identical objects from coat pockets and plug them into their left ears. Communication devices of some kind.

With whom are they communicating?

No sooner is Galen Vector troubled by that question than it's answered when the brothers tap their left ears and look up at the helo. Evidently they are receiving guidance from someone in the aircraft.

Which means they were expecting aerial support. No doubt about it now; they're no longer his hired muscle. This is *their* mission, not Vector's. They have been freed from his menagerie of psychopaths and promoted into the ranks that directly serve Boschvark.

Vector has been used to marshal the search party on short notice, call up Crockett and his dogs, and be the sacrificial goat if something goes wrong. But why? He can't always imagine how people like Boschvark think; their extreme wealth and power free them from most human concerns and furnish them with motivations that are as incomprehensible to Vector as those of aliens from another galaxy. They aren't as easy to understand as parasitical crime families like the one that has long fed on this county. Maybe Boschvark has lost faith in that family and in Vector because Belden Bead was bested by Vida and then Nash Deacon also proved not to have the right stuff. Men like Boschvark often act as if impatience is as much a virtue as ambition; they want what they want, and they want it now. Whatever his reasons,

Boschvark evidently wants Vida dead in half an hour or preferably in ten minutes, rather than later this afternoon.

Unlike the billionaire, Galen Vector relishes the process of vengeance, not just the fact of it. He wants Vida to know terror and pain, humiliation and despair. He wants to spend hours breaking her before he kills her, whereas Boschvark wants only to have someone put a bullet in her head and dispose of her corpse, thereby quickly eliminating the threat she poses and insuring against any further delay to his project. What infuriates Vector is that he was told he could deal with the bitch as he wished, to the satisfaction of his darkest desires—and now that promise has been broken.

The helicopter executes a turn, apparently with the intent of quartering the land ahead, now moving north to south. As it changes direction, its starboard flank comes into view. The large boarding door is open. A man sits on the threshold of the passenger cabin, legs dangling, tethered to prevent a fatal fall. He is holding what appears to be a cumbersome rifle featuring a short, fat barrel with a large bore that might be three inches in diameter.

Although no gunshot is audible, scores of small objects larger than buckshot burst from the muzzle, expelled at far less velocity than from a 12-gauge. They travel perhaps thirty or forty feet in a spreading pattern before dropping into the forest. The gun must be a low-pressure air rifle, similar to toys that fire tennis balls for dogs to chase or to facilitate a game of war among young boys. In this case, the shooter's ammunition is a mystery. He inserts into the breech a cartridge approximately the size of a can of Coca-Cola, and again a swarm issues from the device like hornets erupting in anger from a tormented nest.

There is something otherworldly about the moment that renders Vector as transfixed as if he were witnessing an apparition. The helo floats through the morning, and in Galen's curious bewitched state, he has ceased to hear its engine or its rotary wing, so that the craft seems as quiet as a hot-air balloon, weightless yet ominous. The tethered man, sporting a beard and long hair, looks like one who sang with Creedence Clearwater Revival a long time ago, or like someone who, in robes, once walked the shore of an ancient sea. *Cast your bread upon the waters, for after many days it will return to you.* He's heard those words before, though he can't recall where. The good we have done returns to us, and the bad. Karma. No. That's bullshit. Galen Vector doesn't believe in any of that, not in an earned fate. Yet as the helicopter floats and as the bearded man casts something other than bread, and as the inexplicable silence lacks even the sound of Vector's hard-pounding heart, he is afraid as he has never been before.

58

STICKY WIDGETS

In the downdraft from the chopper, debris cascades from the conifers. Dead needles, pine cones, what might have been intricately woven pieces of long-abandoned birds' nests fall on Vida—and then harder objects rap against her like wind-driven hail. For a moment, she thinks insects are swarming, wasps or flying beetles, and she swats them.

These aren't bugs, however, not living creatures, but inch-long capsules of some kind, as plump as fish-oil supplements, but with what appears to be a gray plastic or metal surface. They come to her not as a consequence of gravity, but as if with the intent of angry wasps or with the eager seeking of mosquitoes responding to the scent that announces a mammal with a feast of blood beneath its skin. Like nettles, they fix to her jacket and jeans. Although they lack the tiny hooks that make all catchweeds so difficult to pluck loose and though they are dry to the touch, they stick stubbornly to her clothes. She tries to brush them off, but they won't be shaken loose.

Whatever these widgets are, they must have been dispensed from the helicopter. When she pinches one between her fingers, it seems as solid as a bullet, but she feels a faint vibration. They're not inert. Compact technology of some kind. Possibly produced by one of Terrence Boschvark's companies. With what purpose, what function?

She is reminded of Reyes Nochelobo, who traveled from Miami to Kettleton to settle his brother's estate and who brought to her the brightly wrapped birthday gift that José hadn't lived to give her. Reyes is ten years older than José and is afflicted with atrial fibrillation. He is on three medications, including a blood thinner, in addition to which something called a "Medtronic cardiac loop recorder" has been surgically implanted in his chest, in the hollow between two ribs; this device monitors his heart 24/7 and transmits the data to Medtronic in Minneapolis, from which it is available to his cardiologist by computer or smartphone. As José described it and as Reyes confirmed, the loop recorder has a five-year battery, can essentially transmit a continuous EKG to Medtronic from anywhere in the country as well as from many locations beyond its borders—and is approximately the size of one of these techno nettles that are stuck to her gear and clothes.

Maybe these widgets are nothing more than tracking devices, which is bad enough, but she can't dismiss the possibility that some might have a different function. If so much data and telemetric capability can be packed into a cardiac loop recorder hardly bigger than a lozenge that soothes a sore throat, why couldn't an object of similar size contain the stuff of a low-velocity smart bullet? An explosive charge. Tiny detonator. Technology that needs no marksman but guides the round to a target by some weird biological magnetism.

No. The lethality of a bullet is a consequence of its velocity, penetrative force, and deformation within the target; it carries no explosives. These widgets aren't impacting her, just adhering to her. And they're too small to contain a deadly quantity of C-4 or the like.

Unless . . . If half the forty or more widgets sticking to her are smart bullets and even if each is capable of inflicting only a minor wound, she could still be disabled by the number of hits she takes and might even bleed out.

Science fiction. As Vida struggles to twist and pry widgets from her jacket, she's scaring herself with science fiction. Yes, all right, but it's become a science-fiction world—surveillance satellites, lasers, hypersonic nukes, virtual reality, designer babies, smartphones that have rapidly evolved into supercomputers, artificial intelligence. Technological advances have accelerated so rapidly that scientists and engineers, in their all-too-human hubris and greed, give little thought to the dark potential of even the brightest and shiniest of the new powers they harness, new toys they create, and new social theories they advance. All progress is said to be purely good, although history is replete with evidence this is not true. Those, like Vida, who have held fast to their common sense are increasingly concerned—in the grip of an uneasiness bordering on dread—that the escalating power of technology has grown beyond humanity's ability to accurately assess its impact and control it, that we are the reckless agents of our annihilation.

As the racket of the helicopter fades, she tears off four of the widgets and drops them on a low rock formation that is as flat as a table and pounds them with a stone, but the fifth sticks to her right thumb as insistently as it had clung to her jacket. She is not a person who's easily given to fear; however, her frustration grows into angry consternation when she isn't able to shake off or strip away the damn thing. Search dogs are coming, as well as men with rifles, while she is still a mile away from the carcass of the crashed airplane in which she has stowed what she needs to survive the impending confrontation.

She unstraps her backpack and shrugs it off. Ten or twelve widgets cling to it. Four are fixed to her baseball cap, which she flings away among the trees. Her heart knocking, breath quick and shallow, she takes off her jacket and casts it aside.

The chopper isn't coming back. Evidently, they know she's been tagged. Like a cardiologist calling up a patient's Medtronic data, the killers on her trail know everything they need to know about her, although their intention is to take a life rather than sustain one.

Four of the devices are fixed to her jeans. She draws the knife from the sheath on her left hip. Shaves the razor-sharp edge along one leg. Reaps a thin fuzz of denim. She scales a widget from the fabric, but now the thing clings to the knife. She holds the blade to the table rock and pounds the stubborn burr with a stone until it dimples and falls away like a techno tick. Soon she's dealt with the remaining three, plus one fixed to her left hiking shoe.

The woods behind her slope down through layered shadows, with little evidence that morning was born earlier and is now mature. A flock of yellow-breasted western tanagers wings through a shaft of light, the soft whistles of their flight calls like the musical conversation of elves in this Gothic forest. Farther below, in another narrow intrusion of sunlight, a figure more menacing than birds looms into sight, a big man laboring upward, not near enough to be an immediate threat, but confident of where he will find what he seeks, and then behind him appears another.

Vida steps out of sight and stands with her back against the trunk of a tree. She slices the blade of her knife across the widget that's fastened to her hand. Although sharp enough to score stone, the cutting edge leaves no mark on the tracking device, suggesting that the thin capsule is made of an alloy stronger than steel.

Taking a deep breath and holding it, she presses the blade to her thumb and forces it under the widget, attempting to dislodge the thing as she had scaled others from her jeans. Whatever force binds the object to her is disrupted with a hot flash of pain. Taking with it two layers of skin, the capsule drops to the ground as her thumb darkens with a sheen of blood that forms into a trickle and drizzles toward her wrist.

Without realizing what she's doing, she sheathes the knife and takes several steps from the tree and finds herself kneeling before a low shrub with deep-green leaves. Although she knows the names of many plants, this one is strange to her. She isn't any version of a knowledgeable homeopath when it comes to the offerings in Nature's pharmacy, yet she plucks a leaf from its stem and folds it around her abraded thumb and applies pressure with her left hand as if she has no doubt as to what the effect will be. Her hair is an issue; there are widgets in it, but she doesn't dare delay to deal with them here, as the posse closes on her. She finds herself on her feet and moving fast uphill, south-southeast, neither on a beaten trail nor seeking one, confident that she can't become lost. The makeshift bandage doesn't peel away from the abrasion; instead, some substance in the leaf seems to combine with her blood to quell the pain and then to form a coagulating plaster that quickly stops the bleeding.

Her arcane knowledge, previously unrecognized, is only the consequence of her Becoming. Although she is no pagan, in some way she can't understand, the power of a myth that's thousands of years old is flowering in her. The ancient Greeks spoke of Artemis, the goddess of the moon and the hunt, protector of women and of Nature, while the early Romans called her Diana. No such goddess has ever existed, and yet the *idea* of such a figure has power that time and the passage of civilizations cannot erase, a power that has come down through the centuries to the mother-less daughter of a police officer who was murdered when his child was only five. In this time of crisis, Nature and her imperiled crea-tures need a champion, and some mysterious entity has chosen Vida to resist the destroyers like Terrence Boschvark.

As she runs through the forest at a pace she has not achieved before, sprinting like a deer, never putting a foot wrong, with no weakness of muscle or bone, she is breathing no harder than if she were resting in a chair on her porch, and her heart is not laboring. She wonders if she might be losing her mind, but her new agility and stamina, along with her instinctive awareness of where she is in this wilderness and where she must go, seem to be evidence not of disorder but of stability, not of insanity but of a primal wisdom.

The men who are after her have such contempt for women that they expect to overtake her quickly, overpower her easily, destroy her with pleasure. Her intention has been to lead them deep into these mountains, along a circuitous route, frustrat-ing and confusing them until physical weariness and nervous exhaustion make them less alert, as vulnerable as they will ever be. Recent events necessitate a change of plans. She needs to reach the crashed airplane that she furnished as an armory and take down her enemies sooner than later.

Vida breaks out of the trees and reaches the sun-splashed crest of the ridge. Bright blue flowers of *Gentiana verna* blanket the fertile earth between the shapes of bedded stone.

Having put some distance between herself and her pursuers, she can afford to pause long enough to deal with the few widgets tangled in her hair, but a better idea occurs to her. If she keeps moving fast, there is an advantage to being tracked. She races north along the ridge, across treacherous rock formations, with the alacrity of a surefooted mountain sheep. After a few hundred yards, she turns due east, plunging along a slope into a new neighborhood of less dense forest, through maidenhair ferns and snowy wood rush, having no concern about cougars or snakes, and certainly not about wolves.

59

REMEMBERING MOTHER

Frank Trott, now engaged in the pursuit of Vida, is the son of Tatum Tyler Trott, an associate of the Bead crime family. Tatum was a nonbeliever so serious about his atheism that he brutally murdered a minister and his wife, used a reciprocating saw to cut them into manageable pieces, bundled each of the twelve grisly portions—legs, arms, heads, and torsos—in a segment of plastic tarp with a ten-pound plate from the weight stack for the bench press he hadn't used in years, sealed the tarps with epoxy, and dropped the packages into a nine-acre lake on his property in a mock baptismal ceremony. Tatum was a good manager of the Bead family's illegal gambling activities and a successful debt collector for them. However, all his energy in high school had gone into bullying other students and terrifying teachers and building a record as a legendary truant, so that he lacked the most rudimentary scientific knowledge. He was undone by ignorance and a tendency to miserliness. The epoxy that he purchased was an inferior brand that succumbed to the acidity of the water. Although the lake appeared placid, the inflow and outflow of the stream feeding it and the action of wind created currents that worked at the edges of the tarps and rolled the bundles this way and that on the lake bed. Even wrapped in plastic, the gruesome packages contained enough oxygen to assist decomposition, which produced foul gases, creating disassembling pressure within the tarps. Frank, eighteen years old at the time, had been fishing when a corrupted, somewhat greenish arm wallowed into sight, fingers curled and thumb raised as if soliciting a boat ride. Frank's first thought was that this must be his mother's arm, because she had supposedly run off with a traveling salesman. But that had been five years earlier, and this limb had not been rotting in the lake that long. He netted it, brought it aboard, and studied it for a while. One decaying finger still wore a ring that declared JESUS HEALS, like the one long worn by Abigail Costigan, wife of Reverend Wayne Costigan, both of whom had gone missing two months earlier.

Although Frank recently graduated from high school, he was very much his father's son, with little interest in education and less interest in honest work, but with a keen eye for opportunity. He wrapped the reeking arm in a beach towel and took it directly to Horace and Katherine Bead, who were parishioners of All Faiths Church of the Holy Nativity and who in fact had financed the building of it and the installation of the minister who preceded Wayne Costigan and the one who followed him. Everyone in Kettleton knew that Horace and Katherine loved their church and were devoted to God. Frank's father, Tatum, also knew the Beads' reputation as devout Christians, but when arrested he assumed his detailed and highly incriminating knowledge of the family's gambling operations would protect him from prosecution.

He was wrong.

The lake was dragged on a Monday, when all additional pieces of the Reverend and Mrs. Costigan were recovered, although nothing of Frank's mother, Enola, was found. Tatum was arraigned that same day. His trial commenced on Wednesday. He might have been pronounced guilty by Friday if he hadn't hanged himself in his jail cell in the early morning hours of Thursday. Although Tatum left no will, the grateful county government, impressed by young Frank's sense of civic duty and his refusal to be cowed by his violent father, passed a special statute conveying to the young man his father's land and other assets. On a stormy night a year later, when Enola returned, announced that she was moving in, and declared herself the rightful owner of the place, Frank did not make the same mistakes that Tatum had made. Along with a few twenty-pound plates from the remains of his dad's bench press, he stuffed his mom's corpse into a metal drum to which he had welded four wheels and a strong tow chain. With Enola packed and ready to go, he welded a lid to the barrel. Having hitched the wheeled casket to his F-150 pickup, he towed it not to the lake but instead overland to a portion of his property that had been a bog since time immemorial. On the brow of a hill, he detached the barrel from the truck. He pushed it over the brink and watched as it gathered speed in the light of the full moon. As if it were some hellish conveyance serving as an alternative to a boat on the river Styx, trundling damned souls from the freedom of life into eternal servitude, it rattled down the slope, launched off the bank below, and landed with a tremendous splash in the swampy muck, where it sank out of sight into such deep, viscous sludge that it might eventually come to rest among dinosaur bones.

Because of the things he has done and the things that have been done to him, Frank Trott has an intuitional awareness of when he is in deep shit and exactly how deep it is. When the chopper appears, when Monger and Rackman—Tweedledum and Tweedledee—insert what appear to be communication devices in their ears and make contact with someone aboard the aircraft, the nature of this operation proves not to be what he believed it was, and he thinks he is in shit above his ankles. Then a guy aboard the helo begins to disperse swarms of objects with what looks like a tennis-ball gun, and Frank recalculates the depth as somewhere around his knees.

Following the departure of the helicopter, Monger begins to consult a device with a screen—not a phone, something Frank has never seen before. Then Monger announces, "She's been tagged."

"Tagged?" Galen Vector says. "*Tagged?* Since when have we been playing tag? What do you mean—tagged?"

Monger's deadpan expression conveys less emotion than an iron skillet, but Rackman says, "The little lady has a real bad case of cootie bots."

Monger smiles. It's the first time Frank has seen either of the brothers manage a genuine smile, and it is as disturbing a sight as a severed, rotting arm floating in the family lake. Monger says, "Cootie bots calling out to us wherever she goes."

"Song of the cootie bots," Rackman says to Monger.

Monger says to Rackman, "Coo-coo-cootie."

For a moment, it seems as if the brothers might laugh, which will be another first and not good. Instinct tells Frank that if the brothers break into audible mirth, they will punctuate the laughter with gunfire, and there will be blood.

"What the hell's going on here?" Galen Vector demands.

Although Vector appears angry, even enraged, Frank senses something greater than anger in his boss's demeanor, an underlying wariness that suggests he understands that Boschvark's confidence in him has diminished and that his position might not be secure. Worse, the billionaire's bold poaching of Bead family enforcers—Monger and Rackman, who now seem to work for him—suggests that Boschvark's decided to terminate his arrangement with the Beads and proceed with his Kettleton project without their assistance.

Evidently, Sam Crockett has reached a similar conclusion. "If the woman has been tagged," he tells Vector, "if she can be tracked electronically, my dogs have done their part getting you this far. No point paying us when we're not needed."

"Screw that," Vector declares. "I'm supposed to believe in cootie bots? I believe in what I can see myself, not what a couple sellouts tell me to believe. The dogs still have the scent. I can see they have the scent, how they're straining at the leash. Get them on it. You answer to me. Everyone here answers to me whether they think so or not."

With his torched face, Crockett isn't easy to read, but Frank is sure the dog handler is furious that he was lied to about their intentions toward the woman and wants out of this. Crockett's also perceptive enough to know that Vector is incensed that Boschvark has hired away the brothers without approval, that he is not going to tolerate even the smallest additional threat to his authority. If Crockett tries to walk away, Vector will kill the dogs. Therefore, Crockett won't walk away, but his simmering resentment will add to the instability of the situation.

As they move upland in pursuit of the tagged woman, Frank realizes that the brothers have separated without drawing attention to the maneuver; one now leads the procession and the other is at the back of it. Although Frank and Vector are armed, having Monger behind them with an AR-15 does not inspire an intuitive conviction that the shit they're wading through is growing shallower.

How odd it is that Frank keeps thinking of Enola, his mother, in these circumstances, when he should be concentrating intently on the threats of the moment. She cheated on her husband. She abandoned her son when he was thirteen. She came back only to cheat her son out of his inheritance. She was deceitful and greedy. Nonetheless, as never before, Frank is troubled by how she looked when he stuffed her into the barrel, before he welded the lid on it, how she gazed up at him as if her death-blinded eyes could still see. He doesn't believe he needs to make amends for what he did to her; he doesn't believe *anything* done to make his life easier or more pleasant ever needs to be justified. Yet he feels something unfamiliar and kind of creepy that might be regret or remorse, one of those words that mean almost the same thing but not quite, words that he would look up in a dictionary to get a clearer sense of their meaning if he was the kind of person who had the time and inclination to look things up. To suppress this strange feeling, he summons memories of his ex-wife, Cora, who has remarried, and step by step a more useful emotion, anger, burns the regret or remorse out of his mind.

60

THREE FOR BREAKFAST

After checking the contents of Vida's refrigerator and pantry, Wendy whips up a breakfast of multiple treats that can feed six if unexpected guests arrive. In addition to being an enthusiastic housecleaner, seamstress, beautician, entrepreneur, and determined redeemer of the souls of men drowning in their iniquity, Wendy is also a fantastic cook. She moves about the kitchen with balletic grace, making every culinary task appear effortless. The air is intoxicating, redolent of bacon, of eggs cooking in butter. Onions. Melting cheese. Cinnamon rolls. More herbs and spices than Regis can name.

They are seated at the table when, in spite of her slender form, she proves to have the appetite of a logger at the end of a day of felling trees.

Although Regis eats more than usual, he can't match the gusto with which Wendy addresses her meal, because he's talking more than she is, in fact talking too much. As if he's in a confessional and Wendy is wearing a purple stole, he reveals in some detail all the criminal acts he has committed in his service to Terrence Boschvark.

She reacts less with words than with nods and little shakes of the head and a widening of the eyes, as well as gestures with fork and knife, but Regis feels that she understands the remorse and even anguish that have taken him so by surprise. She doesn't have the power to absolve him of his sins, but she clearly has sympathy for him and approves of the way he is unburdening himself.

Finished providing her with enough revelations to send him to prison for decades, he now launches into a recitation of his many ethical failures that, while not crimes, nevertheless weigh on him. When he looks at her, he can't hold his tongue. Several times, he tries to keep his head down, but he *has* to look at her because looking at her brings peace to his heart.

They have finished eating and are having yet another cup of coffee when he says, "What am I doing here? What's wrong with me? I should head up the mountain, do something to stop them from going after her. But I don't know what. I'm not a man of action. I ought to be. Every man ought to be. I want to become one. A man of action. I *will* become one, but right this moment I'm at a loss."

"Relax, sweetie," Wendy says. "She can take care of herself."

"There's one of her and four of them. Five if you count Sam Crockett with his dogs, though he's a good man."

"She'll do what she has to do. My deceitful brothers, Galen Vector, the disgusting Frank Trott, all of them so in love with wickedness—they will discover they haven't pursued a defenseless woman. They have pursued the fate they've earned, and they'll get it. I tried my best, and now they'll get what they deserve, what they have seemed for so long to *desire*."

Regis is unconvinced. "How can you be so sure she won't be harmed?"

"Look around you, sweetie. Look at her library, her workshop, the condition of her pantry. A well-ordered house reveals a well-ordered mind. Her enemies have disordered minds. It's no contest."

"I think it's a contest."

"It's no contest," Wendy insists. "She's taken the words of the fortuneteller seriously, and that will serve her well."

"The fortuneteller? You said that was eighteen years ago."

"Life passes like a shadow. Eighteen years is the same as an hour ago."

Anyone else who said such a thing would strike Regis as screwy. Coming from Wendy, however, the statement seems true and wise, though mystifying.

He says, "How do you know Vida went to the fortuneteller?"

"The seer set up shop across the county road from this place."

"That doesn't prove Vida visited her."

"I know in my bones. Didn't you say that Belden Bead and Nash Deacon came here to use and break her?"

"That's what everyone believes."

"And where are they now—Bead and Deacon?"

Regis looks toward the window that faces the broad meadow of interments.

"She was ready for them," Wendy says, "because of the seer."

"Fortunetellers are con artists."

"The night before last, the seer told me something that's already come true."

"I guess the night before last is eighteen years ago, since they're the same."

"This was in a dream. Now and then, not often, she comes to me in dreams. Two nights ago, she showed me your face. It was the first I'd seen you. Last night, when you came to get my brothers' hiking gear, I knew you were the one who would never lie to me and that we would do great things together."

Evidently, they had left the front door open. Before Regis can ask what great things Wendy imagines they will do, a huge mountain lion, white as snow, enters the kitchen.

61

HAVING BECOME

Inside the torqued and cracked shell of the airplane that came to violent rest in the pine trees, the blood of pilot and passenger is so old that it has no attraction for the wild animals that were once drawn to the smell of it. Perhaps the raccoon, which was here when she arrived, has climbed to this aerie because it's preparing to give birth to a litter of cubs in the days ahead; the height of this retreat and the fact that it is a human construct ensure that many predators will avoid the place.

The animal hasn't come here in search of food. Its kind eat frogs, shellfish, crayfish, worms, mice, insects, fruit, nuts, and vegetables. The most it might find here are insects and not many of those.

The sharp claws of a raccoon and its characteristic courage make it a formidable adversary in a fight, so much so that its kind keep their distance even from one another unless they are mother and cubs of the same family. The individual that shares the ruined plane with Vida exhibits no aggression, but sits with its forepaws crossed on its breast and observes her with curiosity, eyes glittering in its bandit mask.

The raccoon doesn't hiss at her or growl or twitter, as its kind do. It sits mostly in contented silence and occasionally purrs, as it watches while she cautiously barbers herself with the sharp combat knife. Vida's little ring-tailed companion reminds her of a photograph of a contemplative monk that she once saw in a magazine.

She is certain that if she took the animal into her lap and stroked its belly as if it were a house cat that had been in her company for years, it would not resist. It isn't fear but respect for the raccoon's dignity that prevents her from testing that belief.

Earlier, she sensed that she was Becoming. Now, because of the raccoon, she believes that she has Become. She is whatever the seer foresaw.

Your future will be full of strife and struggle, loss and grief, doubt and fear, and pain.

Your future will be full of peace and comfort, love and joy, hope and fortitude, solace and delight.

You'll be a champion of the natural world and all its beauty, because you will neither wish to dominate it nor confuse it with what is truly sacred.

More than twenty-eight years of life have brought her to this moment, this place, have brought her out of the past and at last to the future foreseen. She might have many years ahead of her or only a few minutes. She can be a champion of nature either by standing fast as a protector of it or being murdered as José Nochelobo was murdered and becoming a martyr who inspires others. Her fate is not her choice. Her only choice is to resist or run forever, and she will not run.

62

THE KILL COUNT THEORY

In a most agreeable fever of anticipation, Rackman leads the way through the high forest, consulting the screen of the tracking device, which is strapped to his right wrist so that he can keep both hands on the AR-15. The moment will soon be at hand, the power and the glory that make life worthwhile.

Vector and Trott would rape the woman if they had their way, but Rackman has no interest in sexual assault, and he knows that his brother is likewise averse to forcing himself on a woman. Instead, Rackman and Monger are thrilled by the prospect of terminating her. This desire isn't a perversion of the sex drive. That would be an unfounded allegation. The brothers have no patience with unfounded allegations. They would be no less aroused if their target was a man or an infant whose gender was unknown to them. If you want sex, you pay for it, just as you pay for food and drink and TV streaming services. Eat too much, and you're a glutton; drink too much, and you're a drunk; if you must have sex every day or even more often, you're a satyr, a degenerate. That's what the brothers believe, and they have too much pride to wear any of those labels. To take a woman by force risks imprisonment; to claim to love her and marry her is worse than prison as far as the brothers are concerned. Both rape and the profession of true love exaggerate the importance of sex and diminish what is immeasurably more fulfilling—which is murder. Anyone can have sex; it's a cheap thrill. However, most people aren't capable of killing another human being. Taking a life is supposed to be left to God or governments, and both have kill counts to be envied, which is the first clue as to how much fun it is. An orgasm is a petty matter of a minute or less, with little risk other than a curable disease, but when you blow open someone's head with a high-power round or carve someone's guts out with a knife, *you know you've done something big.* You have set yourself apart from the ruck of humanity. Often the brothers can't remember a woman's face just a day after they paid for sex with her, but they long remember the faces of those they murder, which remain vivid in their deeply satisfying dreams. In dreams, those who have been murdered die over and over; Rackman and Monger can experience the terror and agony of their victims not as a petty matter of a minute or less, but repeatedly throughout the night, hour after hour. The surest measure of a happy life is a high kill count.

In the case of Vida, Rackman's only regret is that he might have to kill her without seeing her face at the moment of death. Boschvark, now more directly their boss than when he employed them through the Bead mob, has developed a superstitious dread of the woman. The brothers don't know the details, but the billionaire has supposedly declared, *That freaking Gorgon, if she can be killed, I want her head on my aegis.* Whatever that means. Boschvark is said to prefer that she's shot on sight, at the distance that fate presents her, and time is of the essence.

The four blinking tech-tick locators clustered on the tracking screen bring Rackman and the assassination squad to the mangled airplane suspended twenty feet above the ground, in the embrace of two crash-damaged trees. Neither Rackman nor his brother reads a newspaper or watches television news, which at best provide readers and viewers with lukewarm thrills of reported death and destruction, when daily life offers a much richer brew of the same. Nevertheless, Rackman heard of the plane crash back in the day when it happened, and he is only momentarily surprised by the suspended wreckage.

The signals are corroborated by the skinned bark of one pine and small freshly broken branches that indicate the route by which Vida ascended to this unlikely hideout. Even as the word *hideout* passes through his mind, he realizes that the aircraft is not primarily a place of concealment. It's instead a shooter's platform, an ambuscade. As the point man, he is the primary target. He can't see the woman. She's well concealed, but she's up there, finger on a trigger.

As Rackman sidles toward the cover of a nearby tree, he opens fire on the quarry's roost, emptying the rifle's magazine in three-round bursts. The skin of the aircraft is thin; the high-velocity rounds puncture it with hard barks of tortured metal. There's no need to conserve ammunition. Among them, the four members of this hit squad have enough ammo to kill the woman at least three hundred times.

63

AZRAEL OR RHADAMANTHUS

Three hundred pounds of muscle. A mouthful of stilettoes. Claws that can strike to the bone. She's white with pale-yellow eyes, but she isn't an apparition. Ears pricked forward, nostrils flared, she seeks sounds and scents for which a ghost has no need in order to conduct a haunting. She stands in the doorway, observing the kitchen and its two occupants, not with what seems like predatory intent, but with solemn curiosity.

Primitive instinct tells Regis to rise and brandish his chair before him. Civilized intuition argues that such a move would be a challenge to the big cat and instigate an attack rather than prevent one. He sits up straight, hands gripping the arms of his chair, ready to thrust to his feet.

He takes his eyes off the cougar only to scan the table for a weapon—where there's nothing more useful than a fork—and to glance at Wendy. Her reaction to the cat is as surprising as the arrival of the beast itself, for she appears relaxed and is smiling at their uninvited guest as if she purchased the feline in a pet store when it was just a cub and is proud of the magnificent adult that it has become.

Although he has not seen it until now, Regis has heard about the albino mountain lion that some locals insist predicts, by its appearance, an impending death.

"Azrael," he says.

The cat sits just inside the doorway, a change of posture that makes it seem bigger than when it was standing, because its proud head is lifted higher and its powerful chest revealed.

"Azrael, angel of death," Regis says, not because he believes such nonsense, but because the creature—by its size, color, and commanding stare—is so impressive that he understands how others might believe such a legend, especially the yokels who live in this benighted county.

"I wonder who started that silliness," Wendy says.

"Oh good, you don't believe it. I knew you wouldn't," he says, as if her dismissal of the superstition will cause the intruder to evaporate like a threat in a dream.

The cougar remains as solid as the refrigerator.

Some bacon is left on a serving plate. Maybe the lion will like the bacon. Or maybe the bacon will only whet its appetite.

"I've seen her a lot," Wendy says, "and her appearance has never been related to anyone's death, at least not any I knew of."

"How many is 'a lot'?"

"Oh, three or four times a year. The first was twenty-four years ago when I was six years old."

Something about that statement is peculiar, but the stress of the moment has rendered his thought process slower than his heart rate. Regis looks from Wendy to the cat to Wendy before he knows what sounded wrong and can shape his puzzlement into a sentence. "Twenty-four years ago? Do mountain lions live that long?"

"No. Maybe twelve to fifteen years in the wild."

"Then this must be the offspring of the albino cat you saw twenty-four years ago. Azrael Two."

"She's the same one," Wendy says with the quiet confidence of an anime girl who has scaled mountains and faced down dragons. "But she's not Azrael. She never was. And she's not just a cougar. She's here as Rhadamanthus."

The lion lifts its chin and assumes an even nobler look than the pose it took when first sitting this side of the doorway, as though confirming the name Wendy has attributed to it.

"Randa who?" Regis asks.

"Rhadamanthus," Wendy says, and she spells it. "A lesser known figure in Greek mythology."

The behavior of the mountain lion is so strange that Regis is beginning to feel, if not safe, at least not in immediate peril in its presence. That is the upside of this odd moment. The downside is that he's beginning to wonder if Wendy is in fact the wise and true and always reliable anime heroine that he wants her to be, or if she is instead so far down the river of eccentricity from him that they will never be in the same boat together.

"Lesser known figure," he says.

"He was a divine judge who lived—lives—in the underworld."

"Judge."

"It was said that Rhadamanthus judged souls when they were sent to him."

"And now he's a female albino cougar?"

"No, you silly. Be careful about mocking forces you don't understand. Anyway, what you see isn't a real cougar. The creature here before us is an avatar of Rhadamanthus."

"And you know this—how?"

"The fortuneteller enlightened me eighteen years ago, when I told her about the lion that people called Azrael."

"So when Rhadamanthus goes on vacation from the underworld, he takes the form of an albino mountain lion."

"Now you're getting even sillier," she says, and she pauses to eat a piece of cinnamon roll that remains on her plate. "He's not here on vacation."

"What's he here for?"

"The seer didn't say anything about that, but I figure he's collecting evidence for the trials ahead."

"What trials?"

"The trials of those souls sent to him in the underworld."

The cougar makes a solemn sound that might be interpreted as agreement with what Wendy said—if Regis was closer to being a citizen of Crazytown than he believes himself to be.

"Why would this Greek god—"

"Minor mythological figure."

"Why would he hang around Kettleton County of all places?"

"You've confessed your former ways, sweetie, and I assume you've given them up, but you surely noticed that Kettleton is steeped in corruption. The wicked are busy here."

"They're busy everywhere," Regis says.

"Of course they are." With one thumb, she indicates the cougar. "This isn't his only avatar. They're everywhere, too."

"Well, I haven't heard of anyone spotting an albino mountain lion in New York City. Or in Washington, DC, for that matter, where there ought to be legions of them."

Wendy sighs and shakes her head and looks at the big cat, and the cat sighs as well and shakes its head, a moment of mimicry that unsettles Regis.

"Don't you think each avatar," Wendy asks, "will be appropriate to the place where it gathers evidence? In New York, it might appear to be a junkie wandering the streets in a drug haze—or a pigeon flitting here and there. In Washington, a lobbyist perhaps, or a rat of one kind or another."

"You really believe this?"

"The world is a mysterious place, Regis, and the ways of the divine are even more mysterious."

"He's a minor figure. How mysterious can he be?"

"I'm not talking about the mysterious ways of Rhadamanthus, sweetie. I mean the mysterious ways of God with a capital G."

He looks at the cougar. He doesn't fear it nearly as much as when it first appeared. The cat cocks its head and regards Regis in such a way that his fear returns in full force.

"Three or four times a year? So you've seen her like maybe a hundred times? Has anyone else seen her so often?"

"Not anyone I'm aware of."

"So she's especially drawn to you. Why is she drawn to you?"

"I don't know that she's drawn to me."

"She's definitely drawn to you."

Wendy shrugs.

The cougar's tail, which lies across the kitchen threshold, swishes back and forth, thumping against the jamb, as if she's a golden retriever.

The massive lion so white as to seem radiant, the petite woman to whom a lie can't be told, dead men deep under the front yard and riding their cars to Hell, a seer of the future, ancient myths with strange new meaning, madmen born from the current culture . . . Regis feels that the universe as he knew it has recently intersected with a universe based on magic rather than science, that anything can happen, and he does not like it; he does not like it at all, except for one thing, one thing that he likes very much.

As the avatar of Rhadamanthus rises to her feet and strides out of the kitchen, Regis says, "Not just the lion."

"Not just the lion—what?" Wendy asks.

"Not just the lion is drawn to you."

"Well," she says with a smile, "aren't you a smooth one?"

64

WITHOUT A MOON OR WOLVES

Once Rackman starts shooting at the fuselage of the plane, the usually phlegmatic Monger becomes excited by the sound of gunfire, almost as inflamed as he gets in more intimate confrontations that involve knives and bludgeons and bare-handed strangulations. He hurries forward from the back of the procession, where he should remain to discourage Vector and Trott from doing something stupid, but when potential violence becomes manifest violence, he is quite capable of being stupid in his own right.

Of Monger and Rackman, the latter has a greater capacity for something like wisdom and for an approximation of self-control, which they both recognize. Indeed, they share a joke to the effect that, as to their relationship, Rackman is the brother and Monger the half brother. They both get off on violence, but Rackman is a connoisseur and Monger an eager enthusiast. They also recognize that on some occasions Monger's reckless bloodlust ensures a kill when Rackman's more carefully considered viciousness might have allowed the target to escape. They admire and respect each other for their different strengths.

And they are equally bewildered that their tedious half sister, Wendy, is committed to their redemption, with no desire to engage in a little satisfying violence of her own. She is a useful Christian, providing them with a home at no cost, cooking their

meals, and doing their laundry. This is for the most part a convenient arrangement, but her faith in their potential for righteous-
ness is annoying. If they are able one day to conceive of a lethal
accident that no one can prove to have been murder, thereby
inheriting Wendy's house and estate without arousing suspicion,
they will surprise her with their true contempt. However, considering their reputation, escaping blame for offing their sister is less
likely than getting away with other murders, because those who
hire them as hitmen are powerful people with a vital interest in
ensuring that Rackman and Monger escape arrest and indictment.

So in the current case, Monger can only pretend that it's
not this Vida person cowering in the aircraft, that it's his sister.
As he joins Rackman and opens fire, he has sufficient imag-
ination to see the bullets tearing through Wendy's body and
shattering her skull.

By the time Monger empties the magazine of his AR-15,
Rackman has reloaded and is ready to blast away again. In the
brief moment of silence between barrages, the echoes of gunfire
having quickly faded away through the muffling trees, an unexpected and bizarre event occurs. Monger happens to be looking
at his brother when it appears that a long metal bolt erupts from
the side of his thick neck, as if he is the Frankenstein monster in
a disguise that is suddenly coming undone.

Rackman stumbles sideways into a tree and turns his head
toward Monger. He's walleyed, and an eruption of snot hangs
from his nose. He opens his mouth as if to ask what just happened, spews blood, and collapses. Dead.

In the aircraft lie four locks of hair that Vida cut off with the wickedly sharp combat knife. Attached to the hair are four tech ticks transmitting the location where the barbering occurred.

She stands in shadows slightly uphill and far to the west of the gathered posse, sheltered on three sides by a stone formation. The raccoon, which she chased from the plane before she departed, has gone its own way.

Although she is perhaps a hundred and twenty or thirty yards from her target, the crossbow has a powerful scope, a maximum-distance range of almost four hundred yards, and no less accuracy than a rifle.

My heart is ready.

The moment she has fired at one gunman, she uses the built-in crank to winch the bowstring into place. She is so well practiced at this, she can perform the task almost as fast as if she manually cocked the weapon with a foot in the stirrup.

The quiver attached to her belt contains high-quality carbon quarrels, and she loads one in the barrel.

With a 150-pound draw, the crossbow delivers the quarrel—the bolt—at devastating velocity.

Although there is recoil with which to deal, there is no sound of a shot, thus robbing the other men in the posse of the ability to gauge her position with any accuracy.

❦

From where Galen Vector stands, just for an instant it looks as though Rackman has thrown down his rifle and dropped to his knees in prayer. Then the hulk falls forward on his face, and it's impossible to believe that such an arrogant man, who's able to commit extreme violence without a twinge of conscience, would prostrate himself before anyone or anything. Rackman is dead, as though felled by a curse murmured by a voodoo priest a thousand miles away.

Monger turns from the corpse, his brow furrowed with confusion, his mouth open in disbelief, as if he's forgotten where he is and doesn't know how he got here. A horn sprouts from his forehead, just above the bridge of his nose, and the center of his face appears to fold inward as if there's a void behind it.

※

In defense of my life, of whom shall I be afraid?

Though I walk through the valley of the shadow of death, I will fear no evil.

Following José Nochelobo's death and the informative visit from the mortician's daughter, Anna Lagare, Vida acquired the crossbow and a large number of quarrels in a neighboring state, where neither a permit nor an ID was required for the purchase. When this grisly business is finished, when these hateful men are no longer a threat, she can dispose of the weapon in such a way that no one can trace it to her.

When the crossbow is cocked, she quickly places another quarrel in the barrel, making sure to align the vane with the channel, and then nocks it in place.

One of the pursuers pivots in an arc, indiscriminately firing his AR-15, spooked into returning fire even with no target on which to draw a bead.

My life passes like a shadow. Yet a little while, and all will be consummated.

She brings the shooter close in the crosshairs of the scope and gently squeezes the trigger. With a *pop!* the quarrel flies.

❧

Although Frank Trott has ginned up anger toward his ex-wife to distract himself, nevertheless he keeps thinking of his dead mother gazing up at him from within the barrel before he welded it shut and dropped her in the bog all those years ago. As Monger fires at the airplane and Rackman reloads, Frank realizes it's the fact of Nash Deacon and Belden Bead buried in their cars—their barrels—that's causing him to obsess on the image of his mother. Strong men, hard men, yet killed and packed in their barrels and rolled into their graves *by a woman*. Neither regret nor remorse is troubling him, after all. He is loath to admit that it's fear, for he's not a fearful man, but indeed it's fear of cosmic retribution that has a grip on him. Then Rackman takes a hit.

❧

Rackman goes down hard, and Monger goes down harder, but Galen Vector is surprised that anything could rattle Frank Trott so much that he would crack and start shooting at bogeys, phantoms, nothing at all, but that's just what happens. When the rifle is out of ammo, Trott starts shouting challenges to Vida while he ejects the spent magazine and jams in a fresh one, screaming his fury at the top of his voice. In those old World War II movies set on islands in the Pacific, the hero always becomes exasperated that his platoon is being pinned down; in an act of courage few mortals can match, he charges up the hill toward the machine-gun emplacement, issuing a cry of outrage, heedless of danger, and takes out the two enemy soldiers hunkered behind a triple-thick wall of sandbags. This is exactly like that, except Frank is turning in a circle instead of charging up a hill, not in a valorous act born out of bravery, but in pure animal terror. Unlike the hero in a movie, Frank is deleted in a flamboyance of blood when a crossbow bolt apparently enters his open mouth and exits the back of his neck.

Sam Crockett has wisely fallen flat to the ground and pulled his dogs close to him. But Vector thinks it's even wiser to admit that the woman they've come to kill is no powder puff, and run for it.

❧

Sherlock, Whimsey, and Marple don't shy from action or trouble. The dogs are lying in hart's-tongue ferns, pressing against Sam as he has commanded, but they're still ready for the hunt. Aware of the tumult among the members of the posse but uncertain of the cause, alert to the gunfire but willing to entertain the possibility that the sound is celebratory rather than evidence of a serious threat, they swish their tails through the leathery fronds of the ferns, panting and shivering with repressed excitement.

For Sam Crockett, it's Afghanistan writ small. He can handle this. Pressed to the ground, he feels and hears his heart measuring the danger, pulse elevated but not racing, clocking under eighty beats per minute. He's never suffered from post-traumatic stress syndrome, largely thanks to the company of dogs, to the sense of family and the love they give him. He can handle this.

When Rackman is cut down, Sam is surprised. When Monger is dispatched, astonishment gives way to understanding. Back in the day, in one of the more remote regions of the Hindu Kush, high on those treacherous slopes, a Pashtun villager had chosen to forsake the common AK-47 for a crossbow. He came from a set-tlement without running water and with an open-pit community latrine, yet from some sympathetic foreign-aid group, he acquired the finest available compound crossbow, a powerful scope made in Switzerland, and a seemingly infinite supply of quarrels with four-sided points. His silent killing had a chilling psychological effect on the men with whom Sam served—but in time they put an end to him.

Immediately when Frank Trott is taken out, Galen Vector decides to split. Obviously, he knows nothing about the strategy of retreat that is most likely to ensure survival. He turns away from the scene with the evident intent to retrace, as fast as possible, the path they followed here. A man's broad back offers an enticing target. And though even an experienced bowman might take ten seconds to cock the weapon and nock the quarrel and take aim, no one is fleet enough to outrun a projectile with a range of a fifth of a mile and the power to punch through plate armor. Judging by the way Vector falls between one step and another, without a cry, and lies as motionless as the stratified rock of which the mountain under them is formed, Sam concludes that the quarrel cored his heart.

He knows little of the woman slated to be murdered, only that the Bead family and Terrence Boschvark want her dead; that whatever she might be, she is not one of them; that whoever she is, she is extraordinary. If she knows her enemies so well that she is at all times prepared to deal with them so decisively, even when they are as amoral and vicious as the crew that now lies scattered across this killing ground, then she must know—or at least possess the capacity to consider the possibility—that Sam poses no threat to her.

He dares to rise from the ferns, and at his command the dogs get to their feet as well. Sherlock, Whimsey, and Marple no longer wag their tails. Their excitement has subsided to tense caution and keen interest. They raise their heads, nostrils flared, drawing from the air a scent too subtle for Sam to detect—the ripeness of warm blood, a sinister smell woven through the odors of the forest mast and the piney fragrance of the evergreens. The aroma doesn't excite them; each dog in turn meets its master's eyes, and every gaze is solemn, as is required even by the deaths of men like these.

After a minute or so, movement to the west draws his attention. Carrying the crossbow but not holding it at the ready, the woman approaches through a distribution of light and shadow as entrancing and mysterious as the chiaroscuro in any work by Rembrandt. Even outfitted in hiking gear and on this broken ground, she moves with consummate grace, as if the land is being reshaped by some higher power to facilitate her progress.

As a boy, Sam had numerous enthusiasms. Trains, their lore and history. UFOs. The United States Marines, their triumphs and their sacrifices. Who built the pyramids and how. The myths of the ancient Greeks and Romans. As Vida strides toward him, he recalls a picture in a book that fascinated him when he was twelve—an Art Deco image of the goddess Diana on the hunt with bow and arrow—and he thinks this scene before him should be unfolding in the haunting light of the full moon, with attendant wolves accompanying her, as in the painting.

When she arrives, the dogs whimper with delight and wag their tails. They want to go to her, and Sam gives them enough leash to do as they wish.

The woman puts down the crossbow and drops to one knee. The dogs nuzzle her hands, and she strokes their faces.

When Vida gets to her feet, Sam indicates the four dead men. "I'm not a friend of theirs. They deceived me to get me here. I don't mean you any harm."

"I know," she says. "I saw you in a dream. I was sitting on my porch with a fortuneteller. The moon was four times its usual size, enormous. You and the man I would have married, if he'd lived, were standing in the yard, looking up at it."

She stops within arm's reach of him, and he is self-conscious about his face to a degree that he has not been in a long time.

"What's your name?" she asks.

"Sam. Sam Crockett."

"I'm Vida."

"Who was the man you would have married?"

"José Nochelobo. Did you know him?"

"Not personally. He was the high school principal. The football coach."

"And more than that. They killed him for being more than that."

"They said he died in a fall or something."

"They say a lot of things."

Sam surveys the four dead men. "So this is vengeance."

"No. I didn't seek this. They did. I want justice, not revenge."

"But it's done."

"Not nearly."

The dogs sit at attention, watching her, rapt.

A stillness has settled through the trees. The forest was familiar to him a moment ago. Now it feels like a strange place, almost unreal.

"Where did it happen?" she inquires.

He doesn't need to ask what she means. "Afghanistan. Saves me having to buy a costume every Halloween."

"Don't say such things. You served your country at great cost. That's noble. It's a noble face."

He does not respond. People say such things because they think they should.

As if she can read the thoughts that live behind his eyes, she says, "I'm not blowing smoke. I never do. When I see you, I see kindness."

After an awkward silence during which an apt reply eludes him, he reaches for something—anything—to say. "Feels weird."

"What does?"

"Standing here with four dead men. We should go. Somewhere."

"I didn't want to kill them, but I'm not sorry I did. The sight of them doesn't bother me. They're finished bothering me."

So he says, "A fortuneteller? White robe, yellow sneakers?"

"Yes."

"Then not only in your dream."

She studies him a moment before she says, "How old were you when you went to her?"

"Thirteen. My dad had left us. She reassured me that my mother could get past the betrayal and be happy again."

"What did the seer tell you about yourself?"

"To expect great suffering and sorrow."

"Afghanistan. What else?"

"That later there would be dogs in my life and 'new heights of happiness.'"

"And are you happy?"

"I won't say it's the heights. But it's good. I love the dogs. They need me. It's good to be needed. I'm grateful to wake up each morning. What did she tell *you*?"

"That I would be a champion of the natural world."

He frowns, though she might not realize it's a frown in a face reconfigured by fire. "What does that mean?"

"I guess part of what it means is getting justice for José and stopping Terrence Boschvark's project."

Indicating the dead men, he asks, "Isn't this justice enough?"

"No."

But for their voices, the quiet in the forest seems to have gotten heavier, like the hush after a deep snow when the wind has stopped and neither the birds nor other creatures have ventured forth into the cold.

He says, "What did the seer tell you in the dream? You're sitting there on the porch. The moon is four times its usual size."

"She told me, 'Be not so foolish as to cling to what was, rather than embrace what can be.'"

"That lady was nothing if not enigmatic. Any idea what she meant?"

Vida locks eyes with him. In her stare there seems to be an answer to his question. But she says only, "I need help to stop Boschvark."

If she isn't the most beautiful woman he's ever seen, he can't remember who was. Whatever he thinks he sees in her eyes cannot be what is really there. Even before his face was disfigured, he would not have been able to charm someone like this, and certainly he can never be with her now that he's become what he is. This isn't Paris, and he doesn't live under an opera house, but he entertains no illusions about his romantic prospects. He has everything he needs. Wanting something beyond his grasp, failing to achieve it, he might risk what happiness he now has.

He says, "Boschvark is worth like a hundred billion. I make my living with a pack of search dogs."

"It doesn't take money to stop him. It takes truth. Truth, courage, hope. *That's* what the seer meant."

"You think all this with her was—what?—supernatural?"

"So do you, even if you can't quite acknowledge it."

"Maybe. But then . . . What fortunetellers usually do is they string words together such that you can make what they say mean whatever you want."

Vida smiles and shakes her head and once more drops to her knees among the dogs, which lavish her with affection. "You and your pack here—who do you search for?"

"Escaped prisoners, people operating meth labs so deep in the mountains they think no one can track them, lost children, people with Alzheimer's who wander away from home, anyone who needs to be found."

She says, "Important work."

He shrugs. "The dogs do the work."

"You must know the county well, these mountains."

"I don't belong anywhere but here. The people have changed some, but the mountains never have."

"Not yet." She looks up from the dogs. "You know the Smoking River, where it is?"

"That's not an official name. It's a place along the Little Bear River, three hundred yards from end to end, where geothermal vents introduce enough heat into the water to make steam rise from it. About as remote as any place gets. A long time ago, it was a sacred spot to some Native Americans in these parts. Most have no knowledge of it, left it behind with memories of so much else."

"Two moon," she says. "Sun spirit."

"I know them."

"Them?"

"They use only their Cheyenne names. Sun Spirit is the wife of Two Moon. They've chosen a life of hermitage. They live just south of where the river smokes."

When Vida gets to her feet, the three dogs are seized by a new excitement expressed in whimpers of pleasurable anticipation, as if some purpose that has gripped the woman is one they can endorse.

"How far to this place south of the smoking river?"

"From here, if you have the stamina to stay on the move until nightfall, then start out at first light, you could be there by ten o'clock tomorrow morning, noon at the latest."

"That's way beyond the woods I'm familiar with. I'll hire you to get me there."

"Get there why?"

"I don't know."

"You don't know."

"But they will."

"Two Moon and Sun Spirit?"

"Yeah. Somehow, I'm sure they know something I need to know. Get me to them."

THREE

THE FUTURE IN
THE PAST

65

WHAT THE DEAD CAN PROVIDE

Monger and Rackman each died in the instant the quarrel found its target. Their hearts stopped and their blood pressure dropped at once to zero over zero, so that their wounds produced little blood. Relieving them of their supplies isn't wet work, but two people are required to shift and roll such large men to wrestle their backpacks from them.

Belden Bead had perished from an accidentally self-inflicted gunshot. Nash Deacon succumbed to mushroom poisoning as if Vida's life were an Agatha Christie novel. In the first case, she wasn't to any degree complicit, and the second was an almost genteel homicide. However, the sight of neck and head wounds inflicted by the quarrels attests to an escalation of violence that she regrets but for which she has no remorse—and to which, in the interest of survival, she might have to resort again. At least men like these, by their evil, ensure the absolution of those forced to kill them.

The brothers are carrying a lot of ammunition; Vida and Sam have no use for it. When the ammo is discarded, the backpacks will be bearable. The bottled water, protein bars, and dry dog food are sufficient to support them until they get to Two Moon and Sun Spirit, if the three German shepherds drink spring water where it exists.

"What do we do with the bodies?" Sam asks.

"We don't do anything."

"Seems we should."

"No time for it."

"But this isn't the deep wilderness."

"So?"

"Later today, maybe tomorrow, hikers could come along."

"These four won't be here then."

"What—they've got an appointment?"

"With a hole in the ground."

"Who puts them in it?"

"I figure one of them is carrying a traditional GPS locator. Boschvark will have insisted on that. His people are monitoring the signal. The search party stops moving, and goons come to see why. They'll disappear the bodies."

Sam understands. "Big money at stake. Can't let anyone wonder what they were doing here. Can the crossbow be linked to you?"

"No. Even if they had enough evidence to convict me ten times over, they don't want me in a courtroom with what I know."

"You can take them down?"

"I'm going to try."

"Boschvark?"

"Yes."

"His project."

"I hope."

As Vida and Sam strip unneeded items out of the backpacks, the dogs relax. Trained to be discreet once the subject of the search is found, they shy from the dead and settle on the ground.

Sherlock and Whimsey each lies with his chin on a paw, while Marple rests her chin on Sherlock's back.

After a silence, Vida says, "Once you get me where I need to go, take your dogs home."

"Why would I do that?"

"Why wouldn't you?"

"If these people had killed you, then they would've killed me. And my dogs."

"Maybe. I guess that would have been up to you."

"They wouldn't ever trust me to stay silent. And I wouldn't have."

"Just taking me to see Two Moon and Sun Spirit, you've done enough. Maybe already too much, from Boschvark's point of view."

"Then I have nothing to lose by hanging with you."

"There's always something to lose. In the future we're hurtling toward, there will be no bottom, no down-as-far-as-I-can-go. There will always be some place lower, darker, more terrible."

Sam gets to his feet, slips his arms through the pack straps, shrugs the weight onto his back. "Even if I wanted to chicken out—"

"You wouldn't be chickening out."

"Even if I wanted to, I couldn't."

"Principles can cost you everything, and maybe for nothing."

"It's more pride than principles. If I went yellow on you, my dogs would know."

"Your dogs."

"For a long time, no one's opinion has mattered half as much as what my dogs think of me. Maybe that sounds crazy to you."

"Sounds dead-solid sane," she says.

More than her beauty or the courage she displayed when dealing with four armed killers or her grace under pressure, those few words endear her to him. He wants her as a friend. His mirror has assured him that nothing greater than friendship is possible, but friendship is a kind of love and a priceless blessing.

❦

Little Bear River, where steam billows from the water, cannot be reached in the direction they have been headed. With the three dogs, they retrace their steps to where Vida was swarmed by tech ticks. Before heading west, she retrieves her leather jacket, uses her knife to scrape the widgets off, and puts on the coat.

From the small backpack she shed earlier, she extracts the cardboard tube containing the pencil portrait of her uncle and secures it in a side pocket of the larger backpack that she now carries. Whatever she might be called on to endure, she is more likely to get through it if Ogden is with her.

The crossbow is a burden, but one she must bear. She might need it. Even if there is no adversary against whom she'll have to defend herself, the instrument is emblematic of her fate, a symbol of her mission, an attribute of her soul. She carries it uncocked, with no quarrel in the groove.

The leash of each German shepherd is connected to the master leash. Although the dogs lead as if drawn by a scent to which they have been sensitized, that isn't the case. They have no spoor to follow. Sam Crockett chooses the route. Although he instructs the dogs with an occasional word, with a tug of the leash, he seems to influence the pack also by psychic means of which perhaps even he isn't fully aware. They negotiate the wilderness via trails smoothed by all the elements and by the many creatures of the forest and the fields, making way up and down the least precipitous slopes, by flat ridgetops and flatter vales wherever possible, as if Nature herself guides them in a metaphysical alliance.

The trails are often wide enough for Vida to proceed in step with Sam. Whether she is at his side or following, she glances back from time to time with the expectation that they are being pursued. If the forest and the journey are as mystical as they seem, not only bright spirits have come into these woods but also those with dark intentions.

66

A PHONE CALL

Whether the visitor was Azrael, angel of death, or an avatar of Rhadamanthus, judge of souls in the underworld, or nothing more than an albino mountain lion in a mellow and curious mood, Regis wants his mug of black coffee to be spiked with the strongest spirits in Vida's modest collection of alcoholic beverages. Having gone without sleep the previous night, he needs a steady input of caffeine. In addition, now that he has revealed so much to Wendy, is preparing to betray Boschvark in order to win this radiant woman's approval, and has been visited by a four-legged omen of death, he also requires a courage-boosting double shot of whisky.

Wendy pours the Scotch into the coffee and brings the mug to him, where he sits at the kitchen table, and he says, "I know you probably disapprove."

"No, not at all," she says with evident sincerity. "Morally, you've come such a long way in a short time. For what lies ahead, it's understandable you'd want a bit of confidence from a bottle. When we've been together long enough, I'll be all the fortification you'll need."

Regis wants to get up and take her in his arms and kiss her with all the passion he can muster, which is more passion than anyone would think when judging by the look of him. However, his stress level is so high that he's afraid he might have one of his Vesuvian nosebleeds. He dreads the thought of their first kiss being ruined by a volcanic eruption of blood.

His burner phone rings. Only Boschvark has the number.

Grimacing, he retrieves the phone from an inner pocket of his sport coat.

Wendy says, "What's wrong?"

"It's him. I have to answer it. Answering it is required."

"So answer it," she says.

"This won't be anything good."

"You won't know until you answer it."

"It's never anything good."

"Then don't answer it."

"He probably knows what I've told you."

"How could he know?"

"He knows everything."

"Ask him the name of the judge of souls in the underworld."

"Why would I ask him that?"

"To prove to yourself that he doesn't know everything."

"God help me," Regis says, and he takes the call.

Terrence Boschvark's manner of speech is as ingratiating and full of false earnestness as that of any third-rate lounge singer coddling his audience, although even at his most oleaginous he is unable to fully repress a sinister undertone. "May I ask to whom I am speaking?"

"This is Edgar Allan Poe," says Regis. "May I ask who's calling?"

"Good morning, Mr. Poe. This is H. G. Wells," Boschvark replies.

Although when properly purchased and activated, burner phones can't be traced to their owners, though the risk of conversations being tapped and recorded is virtually nil, the billionaire insists that every call begin with this charade and then be conducted in an absurd improvisational code.

As required, Regis replies, "I much enjoyed your novel *The War of the Worlds*," though it annoys him that the real Edgar Allan Poe died forty-nine years before that story of a Martian invasion was published.

"Are you alone?" Boschvark asks.

"Yes, I'm alone," Regis lies. He glances guiltily at Wendy, but she smiles to assure him that this is a justifiable untruth.

"Are you where I think you are?"

"I'm where you wanted me to be."

"I never doubted you were. Your reliability is of great comfort to me. You saw them off?"

"I saw them off."

"And none of them has returned?"

"None of them."

"I don't mind saying I'm greatly concerned. You know how much the well-being of my associates matters to me. Something's very wrong. They have come to a prolonged stop."

Both Vector and Rackman are carrying GPS trackers.

"A stop?" Regis asks.

"A full stop. Most concerning. Zero movement. The bird isn't moving, either."

"The bird?"

"The lovely bird. The bird is carrying four eggs."

"Eggs?"

"The kind of eggs that sing. Am I not making myself clear? The bird with four eggs isn't moving."

Regis decides that the eggs are four of the sticky tracking devices that they intended to drop on Vida when they located her. He also decides that Terrence Boschvark, in spite of all his wealth and power and animal cunning, is in some ways an idiot. "I understand now."

Boschvark says, "We're about to send a swarm of bees out there to scout the situation. Gather some pollen, so to speak."

"Bees," Regis says, and he wonders about his own capacity for idiocy when he at once translates the word to *drones*.

"We have underestimated the songbird before," Boschvark says.

Regis thinks, *"Songbird" equals Vida.*

"What if we underestimated the bird again?" Boschvark worries. "Maybe what we have here is less a songbird than a bird of prey. Maybe our bird laid the four eggs and flew away, while the hawks are still there but, you know, all of them with broken wings."

In frustration, Regis dares to say, "Can we stop with the birds and eggs, and just talk straight?"

"No. The thing is—maybe the bird is coming back to the nest. If so, you need to be ready to cage her."

"All those hawks have broken wings, and I'm supposed to cage the songbird that broke them? I'm grateful for the job you've given me, everything you've done for me, but bird caging isn't in my skill set."

"My apologies for being so blunt, Mr. Poe, but your skill set is whatever I say it is. Considering how agreeable our relationship has always been and the fatherly affection I feel for you, I hope you will hold no animus against me for reminding you of the breadth of your responsibilities."

If Regis is going to change his wicked ways for Wendy (which he is), if he's going to terminate his long association with Boschvark (which he must), if he is going to be required to testify against his employer (which seems inevitable), he must never forget that he knows too much. His life won't be worth spit the moment that the billionaire has any doubt about his loyalty. Given Boschvark's deep and mutually beneficial ties to the shadow state, elements within the FBI and the CIA and the ISA and the NSA and the EPA and the National Endowment for the Arts (for starters) will engage in a bidding war for the right to contract a hit on Regis and win the undying gratitude of the man who is at the moment posing as H. G. Wells.

Consequently, Regis says, "No animus. In fact, Mr. Wells, I'm grateful that you have clarified my thinking in such a graceful but impactful way. If the songbird does return to its nest, you can count on me to cage it harder than any bird has ever been caged."

"I'm delighted to hear that."

"I'm pleased that you're delighted."

"Now I'll order those bees to launch from their hive," says Boschvark, and he terminates the call.

Wendy says, "I assume you just lied to him."

"Sorry you had to hear it. But, yeah, the only bird I'm ever going to cage is him, when eventually I testify in court."

If this were a séance, no spirit would be needed to levitate the table. The power of Wendy's smile alone would do the job.

Regis drinks the remainder of his spiked coffee in two long swallows and rises from his chair. "The boss is sending drones to see what's happened to the search party."

"Sounds like what happened is what should have happened."

"Considering the fleet of drones he controls, the skies around here will soon be busy. Better leave before his people ID your SUV."

Getting to her feet, she says, "Meet me at my place."

"I'm going with you now. I don't dare take my Lexus. It's a company car, and they can track it wherever it goes."

Her SUV is of a humble make that Regis can't identify, but it isn't as poky as it appears to be. By the time Wendy speeds out to the county road and turns toward Kettleton, no drone has yet snarled into sight.

"I might have to hide out for a while," he says.

"Seems as if my wicked brothers won't be coming home."

"Seems so. I'm sorry."

"Oh, like I said, I'm done with those bad boys. They exhausted my grief for them a long while ago. You'll be safe at my place until all this is settled."

"Thank you."

"You'll have your own bedroom. I hope that doesn't disappoint."

"I wouldn't expect it to be any other way."

"Separate rooms won't be a permanent arrangement," she says, and Regis could glide forever on the promise of her smile.

67

DOGS AND DRONES

Noble and incapable of deceit, the dogs lead with enthusiasm, as if the names Two Moon and Sun Spirit, whom they met but twice, mean as much to them as any words in their vocabulary, as if they have made this long trek countless times in their dreams and know the way as surely as they know anything. They are Sam's firmest friends, always ready to welcome and defend, true kin to the dog that was the first of all animals to attend the babe in the manger millennia ago, what every human would be if humans were all humane. Since he was a boy, dogs have taught him how to be a good man, how to give without expecting to receive, how to live with joy in the moment, how to be stoic in suffering. Now, Sherlock and Whimsey and Marple weave among pines and hemlocks that stand like Druids of old, through mountains silent in primeval sleep. They follow ridgelines where sunlight transforms the straw-colored portion of their coats into shining gold. They descend into wooded valleys where lingering fog conceals all but their black backs and renders them as ambulant shadows in the thick mist. Sam is overcome by the strange conviction that, in the context of this journey, the dogs are something more than dogs. They are also known as Alsatians, but no breed name is sufficient to define them. They seem both to be his dogs and not his, gentle beasts born of myth.

The woman with him, Vida, is the force that changes the forest by her passage through it. Her presence awakens Sam to an awareness that these mountains he thought he knew intimately are in fact full of mysteries previously unsuspected and perhaps forever beyond his grasp. Some ineffable quality about her convinces him that she is more than he knows or can ever understand, and mile by mile, he's brought to the realization that there are depths and dimensions to himself of which he's not previously been aware. Since Afghanistan, he's thought of himself as nothing more than a creature born to live, hope, struggle—and die. He's seen no special meaning to his presence in the world, but this woman has somehow conjured in him a sense that he has a destiny worth pursuing and fulfilling.

Eventually the quiet of the forest is disturbed by a sound other than those made by Sam, Vida, and the dogs. The waspy buzz of common quad-rotor drones issues from multiple directions, swelling and fading and swelling, sometimes passing directly overhead. The search for Vida has resumed. Boschvark possesses an impressive squadron, more than needed to survey the Grand Plateau on which his project will be developed. During the hike, Vida suggested that the billionaire appears no less paranoid than he is ruthless; if a large swath of the mountains is being monitored this heavily, Boschvark is indeed a demon for surveillance.

Because Sam's attention is focused on avoiding the infalls of sunshine where he and Vida might be revealed to a drone hovering over a gap in the forest canopy, he is alerted to a new threat only when his three dogs abruptly halt. Out of shadows and into a shaft of light comes a wolf of daunting size and power. An inner radiance seems to shine forth from its gray eyes.

"Lupo," Vida says. "Good Lupo."

When the wolf responds to the name by sweeping his tail back and forth, Sam realizes that he is a crossbreed, part wolf and part Alsatian. Perhaps that is why Sherlock, Whimsey, and Marple neither cower from him nor greet him as they would another dog, but regard him with what might be perplexity or wonder or both.

"Lupo and I are friends," Vida says. "He visits me with the entire pack he leads. I once gave them several quarts of sweet wild blackberries. They didn't forget."

Sam has more questions than the circumstances allow.

"I'll explain later," she says. "We have a lot of ground to cover before nightfall."

As she speaks, the rest of the pack—five full-blooded wolves, no half-breeds—appears behind their leader as if materializing from another dimension.

When Vida, Sam, and the dogs continue up the current slope, Lupo and the pack parallel them at a distance of about twenty feet, respecting the dogs' territory even though they are not likely to fear them.

"They're here for more than a visit," Vida says, as if she and the wolves can mind meld. "I think they intend to accompany us all the way." She hesitates. Then: "Maybe somehow . . . I called them."

"Called them?" Sam says. "How?"

"I have no idea."

By the time they reach the point where the trees give way to an ascending stretch of open grassland, it is apparent that a drone is patrolling the perimeter of the meadow, which is an oval as long as a football field but not as wide. The vehicle is circling less than six feet above the ground, clearly peering into the trees, perhaps with both traditional cameras and a special unit that searches for heat signatures in the infrared spectrum.

"We'll have to backtrack and find another way," Sam advises.

Vida says, "Unless . . ."

As she speaks, Lupo and the five turn toward her, heads raised, ears pricked, eyes bright in the forest gloom. Abruptly, as one, they pivot from Vida, lope out of the trees, race into the meadow.

"In a room or the back of a van somewhere," she says, "there's someone sitting in front of a screen, monitoring the feed from this drone's cameras."

"So?"

"He might be trained in surveillance, but he's getting bored. And he's human, which means he has a weakness for spectacle."

The pack runs toward the drone, passes under it, and arcs toward the center of the meadow.

The drone turns from its sentinel circuit and moves toward the gamboling wolves. At play, they lope and twist, leap and tumble among one another, all the while leading the little aircraft away from Vida and toward the far end of the meadow.

"Come on, fast as you can," she says, and she breaks from cover.

Sam glances toward the capering pack as two wolves rise onto their hind feet, facing each other in a dance, forepaws combing the air between them, while the others chase on four feet, play biting one another's ears, licking, nuzzling, tumbling.

By the grace of such distraction, Vida leads the dogs and the dogs lead Sam across the meadow, out of the late-morning sunshine, into the piney shade, away into the wildwood. The roup of the drone fades, but the buzz of others rises from points across the compass, some distant and some nearer, as if a robot army from the future is encamped in the wilderness and preparing for war.

68

THE MEN WHO EVAPORATED

Regis Duroc-Jersey is confused, the poor dear, having taken the path of virtue out of his wretched life. He is fearful because when a close associate of Terrence Boschvark engages in free thinking and disagrees with his boss, that independence of mind is said to be disloyalty, which can lead to the destruction of one's reputation and financial ruination. Regis fears for his life as well because he's been a liaison between Boschvark and the Bead crime family, and the latter perhaps will think he knows too much to be allowed to go straight. Having never made it to bed the previous night, the sweet man—always a better soul than he believed he was—is exhausted. He needs to relax with a hot shower and sleep away the long afternoon.

Wendy prepares the bed in the guest room, provides towels in the adjacent bath, and sets out a decorative basket containing a variety of soaps and small bottles of emollient lotions. She draws the drapes shut not just in the guest room but also in strategic places throughout the house, ensuring that no snoopy neighbors or passing minions of Terrence Boschvark might catch a glimpse of Regis.

Not many years earlier, *minions* was a serious word; now, like a lot of other words, it's cartoonish. Wendy has thought a great deal about what is happening to her world. She believes the evolution of *minions*—and the degradation of language in general—is less because it is associated with characters in an animated-film franchise and more because most of the people in the leadership roles of every profession in this society are simpleminded and sound like cartoon characters every time they use the language—or as though they have stepped out of a bizarre world in a dystopian graphic novel. As a consequence, these cartoonish people are busy shaping a future world as unreal as Batman's Gotham or Mickey Mouse's hometown, a world that is therefore sure to fail.

With the windows draped against the prying eyes of minions, Wendy settles in the kitchen to plan and prepare a five-course dinner. She looks forward to a candlelit meal at a table set with beautiful linens and fine china and an array of silverware ranging from butter knives to coffee spoons. Although she appears to be as informal as a character in a TV sitcom about young moderns, she is at heart more suited to life at *Downton Abbey*, a traditionalist who places great value on order.

She expects visitors no later than three o'clock. At twenty minutes past two o'clock, a soft *bing-bong* issues from the through-house speakers of the music system, indicating that the gate to the backyard has opened. She is not surprised that they have entered her property from the alleyway rather than the street, because of course they will wish to be discreet.

She opens the door and steps onto the porch as they approach along the walkway that's flanked on both sides by red begonias. The one in the lead wears a gray suit, white shirt, and black tie; he's about five feet eight, so fresh-faced that he might be a Mormon youth come to share the promise of his church, except for a smile that curls into a smirk at the right corner of his mouth. Whatever knife he carries, it's sure to be sharp enough to gut a crocodile.

The second guy is very tall, as solid as a vault door, with a broad face as blank as that of a golem whose skull is full of mud.

Before the smaller of the two can announce himself or state his purpose, Wendy says, "You look like Galen Vector sent you," as if she is unaware that Vector is most likely dead along with the others in the hunting party that went after Vida.

"Who sent me doesn't matter," the suit replies. "What matters is the message I've been instructed to convey and the seriousness with which you receive it."

"So you're an attorney. Come in, and bring your notary public."

"He's not a notary," says the lawyer.

Wendy smiles. "I didn't think he was."

She decides not to offer them either a beverage or cookies.

They sit at the kitchen table. Wendy doesn't expect to need a firearm, but she occupies the chair that has a pistol fitted in a spring clamp under the seat.

"I know that you love your half brothers," the attorney says. "You want the best for them, as do the people for whom they work."

"The Bead family," she says.

The smirk, which has seemed like a permanent feature of his face, vanishes in a solemn downturn of the lips. "I don't know who that is," he lies.

"If you say so. Now what have you been sent to tell me?"

"For their own good, your brothers need to evaporate."

"Evaporate?"

"Not just vanish but cease to exist, live under new names, in a place far from here, never to return, never to have contact with you or anyone they knew here."

Unspilled, tears fill Wendy's eyes, wrung from her less by the fate of her brothers than by her failure to guide them out of their degenerate existence. Life passes like a shadow, and it's necessary to do something useful with your years. "What have those boys done now? What on earth have they done that makes it necessary for them to evaporate?"

"If I revealed that, I'd be putting them at risk. And you're better off not knowing."

Whether the golem has the power to speak remains unrevealed when he only belches as if to confirm what the attorney says.

"If you want to be sure your brothers remain safe in their new lives," the lawyer continues, "you must cover for them when anyone asks where they've gone."

"What am I to say?"

"You say they went to start new lives in South America."

"Where in South America?"

"Peru, Brazil, Argentina, wherever. It doesn't matter. They aren't in South America. You have to sell it. Can you sell it?"

"Well, I don't know. I guess I can try."

"You have to do better than try. If by your behavior you create suspicion about what's happened to your brothers or if, God forbid, you report them missing . . ."

Wendy looks puzzled, as if she is not quick-minded enough to read the mortal truth that underlies the story he's telling. "What if?"

The lawyer looks sad, and the golem leans over the table to deliver a far different expression from that of his associate. The latter belches again, and the former says, "Then for your safety, you'll have to be given a new identity and moved to South America with your brothers."

"But you said they're not in South America."

"Exactly."

She holds her expression of puzzlement for a moment, while they sit in silence, and then pretends slow-dawning enlightenment. "Oh."

"Two associates of your brothers, Galen Vector and Frank Trott, have also gone to South America," the attorney says. "It's a chore having to relocate all these people. Please don't burden us with the need to move you into a new life."

"I won't," she says. "I like it here."

"You have two beauty shops, a lovely home, a nice life."

"I don't want to evaporate."

Satisfied, the two men get up from the table. The golem opens the back door.

As he's about to depart, the attorney turns to Wendy. "One more thing."

"I know," she says. "You were never here."

"How could we have been? We don't even exist."

Smirking, he closes the door softly behind him.

Wendy opens a cabinet drawer near the cooktop and removes a colorful apron and uses it to blot the tears from her eyes before tying it on.

She wishes she might have had one more chance to convert her brothers, but she can no longer deny that she would have failed again because, frankly, they were psychopaths.

She prides herself on her fierce determination, which arises from having a meaningful purpose and bottomless energy, two of many qualities in which her slatternly mother was deficient.

Wendy had failed to save her mother from a long fall toward early death, and now she had failed her brothers. After waiting eighteen years for Regis, the fulfillment of the seer's prediction, she must not fail him. In the pursuit of his reformation, she will be decided, firm, inflexible, resolute. There are things about him worth loving, not least of all his inability to lie to her. She is putting it all on the line this time, and if she fails, she will be devastated. If she fails him, she does not know what she will do, does not know how she will cope, how she will find a reason to go on—except perhaps by opening a third beauty shop.

69

COME NIGHTFALL

Shortly before dusk fades to starlight, when the drones retreat and quiet settles across the mountains, Vida and Sam make camp on a gentle slope in open woods where spectral moonlight spares them from a blinding dark to which their eyes could never have adapted. They provide food and water for the dogs, and then sit with their backs to trees, eating PowerBars.

With the descent of darkness, the night insects remain silent. The great horned owls do not call to one another to establish their exclusive territories for the hunt ahead. The eerie, ululant cries of coyotes are not to be heard. If raccoons and opossums are foraging, they make less sound than mimes.

Vida knows—and surely Sam knows as well—that a mere human presence doesn't inspire such a profound hush as this among the creatures of the wilderness. It's as though the departure of the drones was followed by the arrival of some stalking ground-bound technology, robotic but stealthy, so alien that wild animals, though grown tolerant of humans, are reduced to alert stillness by this new and menacing intruder.

Strangely—or perhaps not—Vida and Sam are drawn to the same subject. Without suggesting the wisdom of whispering, they conduct their short and weary conversation *sotto voce*.

She says, "Do you sometimes wonder if our time is running out? Not just yours and mine. Everyone's."

"At some point," Sam says, "the machines won't need us, want us, or tolerate us."

"There is a poem about AI, by Richard Brautigan—"

"I know it. 'All Watched Over by Machines of Loving Grace.'"

She's surprised and pleased that he's familiar with the poem, but more important is what he thinks of it.

"The premise is bad science fiction," he says. "Machines might be graceful if by 'grace' we mean elegance and beauty in manner or motion. But they can never be loving."

Although she agrees, Vida says, "Some believe they can be."

"Even an ultimate artificial general intelligence, possessing all the knowledge of humanity, won't have a conscience or a soul. A *person* without a conscience is a sociopath. Sociopaths are incapable of love."

"A cure for cancer, solutions to intractable problems—an AGI might solve them all."

"Maybe. But sociopaths incapable of love are quite capable of extreme cruelty. In fact, they seem compelled to commit it."

After a silence, Vida says, "Maybe Boschvark's project here is a small threat in the scheme of things."

"Did your José think it was a small thing?"

"No. He said that many of our current crop of self-styled elites think they're gods. He said we've got to prove to them they aren't gods whenever we can."

"So let's finish the job he started." Sam's voice trails away, and he slurs the last word, and his head sags forward in sleep.

The dogs lie in a pile for comfort and a sense of security. Exhausted, they should be fast asleep, but they repeatedly lift their heads to survey the woods, as if some quality of the night reminds them that Death is in the world.

Later, when Vida wakes with her back still against a tree, the three dogs have succumbed; they're softly snoring. The great horned owls have found their voices, and insects sing. Also present are the wolves, sleeping in harmony with the Alsatians. Lupo raises his head to stare at her, his eyes full of the moon. Trusting the instinct of Nature's own, she allows sleep to take her once more.

70

AMBROSIA

Warm light strops the sharp edges of the amber cut-glass cups that hold the many candles, and the silverware sparkles as if each knife and fork and spoon were an instrument of supernatural power borrowed from a wizard's portmanteau. Pools of light pulsate on the dining room ceiling, and luminous waves wash up the walls, as though Regis and Wendy are in a glass vessel submerged in a golden sea.

No less marvelous than the ambiance, the food is the best he has ever eaten, pleasing to both the eye and the palate from the crab cake in blue cornmeal, through soup and salad and entrée, to the mandarin-orange crème brûlée. In Greek mythology, the food of the gods is ambrosia, but Regis doesn't believe that even the gods of old had eaten as well as this.

He lacks education in classical music, but the pieces Wendy has chosen to accompany dinner are neither loud nor too soft, of great beauty and yet perfect background to their conversation, although he finds her voice to be the most pleasing music of all.

He expects to talk of urgent matters—how to escape the wrath of Boschvark and the Bead family, how to stay out of the clutches of the politicians and authorities, how to protect his wealth from people and agencies well practiced at stealing. She will have none of that. She says that she can deal with those threats tomorrow.

"My brothers never learned a thing from me, but I listened to everything they said and learned all the wicked ways to thwart the law. I know to whom you can go to subtly change your appearance, to launder your money, to obtain new ID that can never be proved false. Using all that dirty knowledge to help you will be a clean thing." So instead, she speaks of herself in ways that reveal the essence of her, how she became who she is. Soon he's likewise revealing more of himself than he ever has to anyone else.

They are in living room armchairs, by the fireplace, enjoying coffee spiked with Baileys Irish Cream, when she says, "There's one thing you must understand if this is to work."

Here in the firelight, her eyes are bluer than the bluest sky and deeper. Although it will sound corny to tell her such a thing about her eyes, he decides to tell her anyway, but he finds himself saying she looks like the greatest anime heroine who ever slayed a dragon. He has told her that earlier, so now he is babbling.

"That's the one thing you've got to understand, Regis."

"What is? What one thing? Tell me."

"Although you set out to be a bad man, you wouldn't have been able to sustain that even if I hadn't come along. At heart, you're sweet and good. But you must understand that I'm not a cartoon."

"Cartoon? No, no, no. I never said that. I said you're like an anime heroine, which means you're wonderfully cute and smart and brave. Anime isn't cartoons. Anime is art. Anime is—"

"Animation."

"Well, yes, but—"

"It's a bad idea to marry a fantasy instead of the real woman."

In recent years, on those occasions when he has found himself breathless, it's been because of some megalomaniacal scheme

Terrence Boschvark has sworn to undertake and into which he has drawn Regis. This is quite different from that. "Are you saying you'd marry me?"

"For heaven's sake, Regis, I'd first have to be asked."

"Oh. Right. Of course. I'm sorry. So then—"

"Now isn't the time to ask."

"It isn't? When? When will it be time to ask?"

"When we're pretty sure you aren't going to be murdered. If I married you and the Beads or someone contracted a vengeance hit on you, I'd have to open a third beauty shop to keep from going crazy. The only place worth opening another one in this county is over in Dossburg, and I don't like that place. It's a tawdry little town."

71

SLEEPLESS IN MONTECITO

To sleep or not to sleep. That is the question. Boschvark has spent over two hundred million dollars funding studies on a wide range of health issues, including multiple attempts to determine where the lines between excess sleep, ideal sleep time, and sleep deprivation should be drawn and how each category affects a person's longevity. Every study has produced different recommendations, which infuriates Boschvark each time he receives the latest one. Even now, working out in the home gym of his estate in Montecito, California, though he hasn't received results of a new sleep study in more than a year, he *simmers* with anger as he thinks about the unreliable nature of scientists when they aren't paid extravagantly to form a consensus on an issue. If the research subject involves something that will affect a public policy he champions, he can get a hundred studies from universities and highly respected organizations that say the same thing with identical certitude. However, paying for a consensus on the issue of sleep would do him no good, because this is about his personal health, thus requiring accurate data supported by unassailable facts.

Terrence Boschvark intends to live for three hundred years if not forever. If the Singularity—the melding of man and machine—doesn't occur within the next few years, there will instead be a monumental discovery in molecular biology that swiftly leads to human immortality, and if there isn't such a discovery in molecular biology, then the breakthrough will come in genetic engineering. He is fifty-two years old, and when he thinks about the current average lifespan of a male, he gets so angry that he could strangle someone, anyone, if that would make him feel better, although of course it wouldn't, at least not enough better to make it worth all the bother that would follow the strangulation.

Every day, Boschvark takes 182 pills and capsules of vitamins, minerals, enzymes, and micronutrients that he believes will help him achieve life everlasting. *Except on infuriating nights like this when he suffers insomnia*, he sleeps in a custom hyperbaric chamber that supplies an environment rich in oxygen, thus facilitating brain health and ensuring that he's more clear-thinking than other people. Among additional procedures, every six months his blood is replaced with filtered blood from a group of younger men who submit to tests for diseases and whom he pays extravagantly for their donations.

In spite of all that, he still suffers from an allergy to wheat that greatly restricts his diet and puts him at risk of anaphylactic shock if he is accidentally served ordinary pasta when he has asked for rice noodles. A common sandwich would kill him. The damn wheat allergy causes him to fume with resentment every time he thinks of it, which is every time he sits down to a meal or wants a snack.

At the moment, he is not angry about his allergy or about the meager human lifespan. However, his vexation at his inability to sleep is exacerbated by a constant, abrading irritation that the four men in the search party are dead while Nochelobo's tart is alive and still poses a threat to the Grand Plateau project.

His workout isn't exhausting him enough to sleep; he gives it up. Boschvark has been on a high-protein diet and lifting weights all of his adult life, and his supremely oxygenated brain is housed in a body so muscled that he believes he could drag a stubborn horse anywhere he wanted to take it, although he has never tested that assumption. He dislikes horses because of an incident with a pony that his parents gave him for his birthday when he was eight, a humiliation about which he never speaks. Anyway, now that he has given up on both his workout and the possibility of sleep, what he needs is not a horse but his Gulfstream V jet.

He calls Tandor Shaft, a former Navy SEAL and one of three property managers who live on the estate. Tandor is assigned the four-o'clock-to-midnight shift and is ready to deal with anything from a malfunctioning toilet to an attack involving mercenaries hired by the biggest star on the Food Network. Boschvark has never met the Food Network personality, but the man once made an on-air joke about him and is therefore not to be trusted.

Now, he directs Tandor Shaft to wake Heath Granger and Shepherd Eagle, his full-time pilots, who are asleep in one of the estate's guesthouses. They must go to the private terminal at the airport in neighboring Santa Barbara and ready the jet. After taking a shower and receiving a fifteen-minute massage from his masseuse, who will also have to be awakened, Boschvark will be driven to the plane in the Mercedes limousine—the black one—by Tandor. Granger and Eagle will fly their employer to the accommodating airstrip on his nine-thousand-acre ranch that is four miles outside of Kettleton. He acquired the ranch—one of his nineteen homes—when his company was awarded the contract for the plateau project.

Since he learned that this Vida person escaped, he's endured an abrading irritation, which has matured into a bitter peevishness that makes it impossible for him to enjoy anything. He intends personally to direct the further search for and the inevitable capture of this impertinent woman.

72

TWO MOON, SUN SPIRIT

Although Sherlock, Whimsey, and Marple have been freed from their leashes so that they will feel equal to the six wolves, they remain obedient and close to Sam, currently ceding the affection of Vida to their wild brethren. Here on the long slope leading to the meadowy glen where Two Moon and Sun Spirit reside, the forest is dense, with such little undergrowth that they can proceed directly rather than on a wandering path shaped by generations of deer.

Accompanied by dogs and wolves, they pass through purple and midnight-blue shadows that are pierced by bolts of sunshine as narrow as the beams of penlights. Although Vida has never before been in this far reach of the wilderness, it feels familiar to her.

In the lead, Lupo looks back at her, and for a moment all is changed. The forest is centuries younger, the trees farther apart, and a more revelatory light pours down on them, not the light of the sun, but the ghostly light of a full and enormous moon. In spite of a sense of familiarity, she cannot ever have been in this long-ago place, for she had not yet been born, nor would Lupo and his pack have existed then. This is not a memory or a vision of a true past, but something stranger; it is almost a message of reassurance—from whom?—that although our lives pass like shadows, a continuity of experience shapes the world, and the world in all its glory would not be as magnificent as it is if even one of those lives had not passed through.

Lupo looks away from Vida, and the forest becomes as it had been before the curious change—the trees close-packed and gathered in deep gloom, sun streaming down in penlight beams, the moon once more on the far side of the planet.

When they come out of the woods and into the grassy glen, the house is as Sam described it; he's been here twice in his roaming with his dogs, although not when leading a search party. The place is modest. No more than eight or nine hundred square feet. Weathered cedar siding. Fronted by a deep loggia for shade in the summer. At one end, a fireplace chimney built of native stones. Sheet-copper roof greened by time.

Maybe three hundred yards beyond the house, legions of white spectral forms writhe skyward. The smoking river.

A second, smaller structure with its own chimney is a stable for two horses. Currently the stallion and mare are grazing in an adjacent pasture encircled by a split-rail fence; though they raise their heads and cock their ears, pausing in their eating to observe the dogs and wolves, they are not alarmed.

There is as well a deep stand-alone ice cellar that remains functional seven months of the year.

According to Sam, all structures were built by the residents with the help of others from the Cheyenne nation who did not choose to retreat from a world gone wrong but who supported Two Moon's and Sun Spirit's desire to do so. The building materials were brought to this remote site in pickups with all-wheel drive, which was the first time the raucousness of the modern world had penetrated this primeval realm though surely not the last.

The thirtysomething pair who live here tend gardens in these fields; the husband also hunts for game and otherwise forages the forest. Every six weeks, they make a three-day round-trip trek on horseback, into Kettleton, to purchase staples. Using a manual typewriter, she is a novelist of modest success, writing tales that some call "magical realism," but that she insists are "just the way things are."

Perhaps one of them happens to be looking out a window when Vida and Sam and their low-to-the-ground entourage emerge from the forest into the meadow. However, as Sun Spirit opens the front door and steps onto the loggia with Two Moon behind her, the rustic house and the grazing horses and the sun-washed glen seem to exist in a state of grace. Vida feels sure that, by a sense other than the common five, these people have known that visitors with a grave purpose are coming.

Sun Spirit goes to Sam, takes one of his hands in both of hers, and kisses his cheek. "Man of the hounds, woman of the wolves, each clothed in the same light."

Sam murmurs something Vida can't hear.

Dogs and wolves commingle around the woman, gazing up at her and moving with her as she comes to Vida. "Although I've never seen you before, why do I think I know you?"

"I wonder if you knew my fiancé—José Nochelobo."

The woman's hair is thick and black and glossy; it frames a face of chiseled features and matches the color of eyes that, in their seeing, seem always to be searching. "I've never heard that name before."

From her jacket, Vida retrieves the notepad paper that was given to her by Anna Lagare, the mortician's daughter. "This was found in the pocket of the shirt José was wearing the day that he was murdered."

"Murdered."

"Yes."

"I'm sorry for your loss."

"Thank you. I'm determined he won't have died for nothing."

Sun Spirit unfolds the paper and reads. "Two Moon. Sun Spirit. Below the smoking river."

Her husband joins her to read what, only yesterday, had been a cryptic message. He is tall and strong and has a face that might at times seem fierce, but his hand on his wife's shoulder rests with an unmistakable tenderness.

Vida says, "Someone must have given that to José before he addressed the crowd. Someone who thought maybe you could help him."

"Addressing a crowd? Was your fiancé a politician?"

"No. Quite the opposite. A teacher, a coach, a lover of nature. He was speaking against the Grand Plateau project."

"Project?"

"You don't know about it?"

"We seek to know as little of the world beyond this forest as possible. It is a world gone mad, and such madness as that can be infectious."

Although Vida's opinion of the world, in its present condition, is not as dark as theirs, she understands their viewpoint and must admit that their grim assessment might be right, her optimism wrong.

She indicates the note. "Do you recognize the handwriting?"

"I'm afraid I do not." Sun Spirit returns the slip of paper. "But come in the house. We'll have coffee. You can tell us about this project, and we might see why someone thought we could help your Mr. Nochelobo."

The wolves settle in the yard to sun themselves.

The dogs lie to one side of the front door, in the shade of the loggia.

Entering the house behind Sun Spirit, Vida takes only two steps before she halts in surprise. On the wall hangs an exquisite pencil portrait of a Cheyenne elder, rendered in such detail and with such power that it's apparent the artist captured not just how the old man looked but also the quality of his character and the condition of his heart. In the bottom right corner of the image, where the creator's signature should be, there is only a small, stylized image of a deer.

"Eternal Fawn," says Vida.

Sun Spirit turns, as surprised as her visitor. "You know her work?"

"I have one of her drawings."

"She never sold them."

"I didn't buy it. It was a gift to my uncle. My great-uncle. His portrait. In fact, I have it with me. How do you know her?"

"She was my grandmother."

73

BOSCHVARK FOREVER

Boschvark overcomes insomnia by escaping the Earth. Anger is usually the cause of his sleeplessness—exasperation with the idiocy of an employee, impatience with members of the media who report what they're told but do it incompetently, rage at tactics of competitors who skin him out of another hundred million dollars that should have been his, fury at the processes of nature resulting in less than an ideal human physiology that isn't just mortal but also allows for inconveniences such as headaches and hangnails and constipation. However, when ensconced in a jet, high above the planet, he is—if only for a few hours—able to feel disconnected from humanity, as though he's an entity unto himself, a glorious species of one, which is a status for which he's yearned all his life. And then he sleeps.

He is still sleeping when his Gulfstream V lands on his private paved airstrip at Rancho del Culebra Furioso, his nine-thousand-acre property in Kettleton County. He purchased this land in order to have a home within a half hour's drive of the Grand Plateau when work there finally begins. Currently he also raises llamas on the ranch for tax purposes. Eventually, using major defense contractors who can construct facilities with the greatest secrecy, he intends to install level-4 biological labs deep underground and staff them with dedicated scientists who will live here while they create new deadly pathogens and the vaccines to guard against the pandemics such microbes could cause. He has neither evil nor humanitarian motivations for funding this research; he is committed to it only because it's his belief that all multibillionaires have similar facilities and that, to preserve his lofty position in the social order, he must maintain parity with others of his kind.

Whenever Boschvark sleeps through a landing, as he does in this case because of exhaustion from chronic insomnia, Heath Granger and Shepherd Eagle, his pilots, are under orders not to wake him. The property manager and head housekeeper of Rancho del Culebra Furioso, Mr. and Mrs. Danvers, assist in the disembarkation of the sleeper and transport him to the primary bedroom in the main residence.

In spite of the comfort money can buy and the power over others that it provides, the sad truth is that even a multibillionaire has no guarantee of a smooth journey through life. For one thing, no amount of wealth can purchase good dreams. With a throttled scream, Boschvark wakes from a half-remembered nightmare in which he was so poor that he owned only three homes and flew commercial. He sits on the edge of the bed, sweating and trembling. When he discovers Mrs. Danvers has forgotten to leave a small plate of Belgian chocolate-covered mint patties on his nightstand, as is absolutely required, he is displeased. His displeasure quickly escalates into resentment, a bitter brooding over past failures of the housekeeper to serve him as diligently as she should. Now he is ready for the day.

After a scalding shower so hot that it has sensitized him to the many physical indignities the day will impress on him, he takes a late breakfast in the large conservatory at the north end of the house, among palms and ferns and orchids that aren't native to this territory. The food is excellent except for one detail. He is quite certain that the three mandarin orange segments arranged around a cherry atop the small serving of flan, which comes at the end of the meal, are not from a fresh fruit, but from a can. After finishing the flan, he sips his coffee and considers confronting Mrs. Danvers regarding her use of an inadequate choice of decorative citrus in violation of his standards. Instead, alert to the need to extinguish the Vida woman in a timely manner, he decides to tuck this culinary offense away in memory and let it fester for another occasion.

At the center of his office in this residence stands an immense black-granite-and-steel desk that some on the staff refer to as the "Darth Vader command center," though they are not aware that he has recordings of them making this amused reference. He isn't angered and calls no one to account for impertinence, because he likes the implications of their joke. Sitting in a black-leather steel-studded pneumatic office chair that looks as though it doubles as a personal aircraft for jaunts around the ranch, he uses the intercom to summon Mack Yataghan, the head of security for the Grand Plateau project.

Yataghan, a former CIA agent, has made a fortune sharing useful national secrets with Boschvark. To prove that his loyalty to his boss is forever and isn't as transient as that to his country, he has received an implanted molar containing a capsule of arsenic that can be detonated by remote control, though only by Boschvark. There is something psychologically wrong with Yataghan, but it's the kind of wrong that makes him just right for Boschvark's purposes. Anyway, even if the security chief were normal, he'd most likely still be holding this job. It always amazes

Boschvark what people will do for a salary of a mere two million a year.

Yataghan reports that, to eliminate all risk of a connection to New World Technology, the bodies of four members of the search party have been removed from the forest, wrapped in plastic, loaded in a truck, and driven to Mexico. They will be delivered to MS-13 to be thrown into a mass grave with the corpses of locals killed by the gang this week. They will be doused in gasoline and set afire and—when nothing remains but charred bones—will end up under eight feet of earth plowed over them and compacted by a bulldozer, after which the government will declare the site part of a national forest never to be developed out of respect for nature.

Because Boschvark has been unable to reach Regis Duroc-Jersey on the project manager's burner phone since their Poe-and-Wells conversation the previous day, Yataghan has been seeking the missing executive. Duroc-Jersey's company Lexus seems to have been abandoned at Vida's house. The man has not returned to his rental residence, where one of Yataghan's cohorts has been stationed to intercept and detain him. The security chief is of the opinion that Duroc-Jersey could be—but most likely is not—dead. More plausibly, the man is rattled by the wipeout of the search party; fearful that all the crimes committed in the interest of furthering the project will be exposed, he has probably gone on the lam.

With a few choice expletives, Boschvark expresses his contempt for the cowardly Duroc-Jersey. Vida's cunning, courage, and skill with a crossbow irritate him. The apparent duplicity of Crockett and his dogs peeves him. The incompetence of Vector, Trott, Rackman, and Monger angers him. He thumps his fists on his granite desk and demands that Yataghan find the hateful woman, Nochelobo's whore.

"We will," Yataghan assures him. "Meanwhile, just last night we found the other woman living in Texas under the name Susan Ivers."

Terrence Boschvark is a brilliant man who can pull the strings on an almost infinite number of puppets without tangling any, but for a moment he is flummoxed. "What other woman?"

"Anna Lagare. The mortician's daughter."

Boschvark sinks in his chair as though the weight of this new exasperation, atop his other angers, is a fearsome burden. "What kind of daughter disowns her father just because he wants to climb the ladder and improve his bank balance?"

"I hope never to have such a child," Yataghan agrees. "As we have long speculated, she did visit Vida before leaving Kettleton. She told her about the dart wound. Worse, she'd found a page from a notepad in the pocket of the shirt that Nochelobo was wearing that day. Someone had scribbled on it. 'Two moon sun spirit below the smoking river.' She gave it to Vida. That's what set the bitch on the warpath. She put the squeeze on Morgan Slyke for starters."

"And?" Boschvark demands.

"No reason to be concerned. Anna Lagare won't be talking to anyone about anything. She fell down the stairs and broke her neck. Fell down twice before she got it right."

"I wasn't asking about her. 'Two moon sun spirit below the smoking river'—what does it mean?"

"They're this Cheyenne couple who don't have the wilderness skills to live by the old ways, but they can't tolerate the new. Ten years ago, they rode off to live in harmony with the Earth, crazy shit like that. The place they settled is deep in the forest, near where the Little Bear River passes over geothermal vents and throws off steam. The Grand Plateau is between that place and Kettleton."

Alarmed, Boschvark gets up from his chair. "Two Moon. Sun Spirit. Why did they matter to Nochelobo? Why do they matter to Vida? Why do they matter to *anyone*?"

"We don't know. But maybe that's where Vida has gone—and maybe Sam Crockett with his dogs."

"How Cheyenne are they?" Boschvark asks.

Yataghan looks puzzled. "How Cheyenne?"

"How much do they believe in the old ways? How much do they know about the past? Are they at all committed to the Cheyenne nation or are they just Tontos? Can they be bought? Who can't be bought? Anyone can be bought. Do they want a casino?"

Boschvark hears himself and realizes he doesn't sound like Terrence Boschvark. He doesn't sound powerful and confident and righteously angry. He sounds like a pathetic striver who has only a billion dollars and is scared he'll lose it. He considers sitting down and speaking slowly, expressing himself in fewer words, but it's too late. Mack Yataghan has seen that his employer is alarmed, and to the likes of this man, alarm is the same as fear; fear is a weakness; the weak are to be despised, dominated, and exploited. In an instant, Yataghan has gone from being a reliable employee to a potential threat, because Boschvark has failed to mask his anxiety. It is not easy being the man who sits at the Darth Vader desk.

He only narrows his eyes because more dramatic gestures would be too much and confirm Yataghan's new opinion of him. Quietly, with no threat—a serenity that will worry Yataghan more than shouted accusations—Boschvark says, "I thought we knew every Native American living in Kettleton County, regardless of tribe, assessed each one, identified those who had no interest in the history of their people, and compromised those who expressed faith in their traditions."

"We did," Yataghan says. "There weren't that many of them."

"Not many," says Boschvark, "but two more than we thought. And two who may know the past, be proud of it, even want to defend it."

"I take full responsibility for the screwup," Yataghan says, which is what he'd say if he was still a faithful employee, which perhaps he is, though he can no longer be trusted. A time will come to deal with him. Right now there's a more urgent matter.

"What's it take for you to get there, to the place these two back-to-nature idiots are holed up? How soon?"

"Our people just wrung this out of Anna Lagare five hours ago. I was waiting until you woke and got started on your day. Where they live is an open glen. I can chopper there in half an hour."

"You and I," Boschvark declares. "You're a helo pilot. So just us. Ready to do whatever needs to be done."

Yataghan is astonished. "You're taking direct action yourself?"

"In this case, it's essential. We've got to reach Two Moon and Sun Spirit before Vida does. Everything might depend on it."

"Maybe. But I can put together a team. You being there—is it wise? I don't think it's wise."

If Boschvark narrows his eyes further, he'll be blind. "You might think I'm too finnicky to get my hands dirty instead of paying someone else to dirty theirs. But, see, you didn't know me in the early days, when I busted the balls of anyone who got in my way. I can still do it. I can bust them harder than anyone. Who's gonna finger me for anything I do? Nobody. Nobody ever has, and nobody ever will. Everyone's in my pocket. Let's go."

74

TO THE GRAND PLATEAU

The three dogs are off leash, responding to voice commands when Sam finds it necessary to speak them away from distractions, which isn't often. They seem psychic, as though channeling the desired destination from the humans who follow in their wake.

Close behind the dogs, Two Moon carries a collapsible shovel. Having left his backpack at the house because this hike will return them to the glen by nightfall, Sam totes a mattock. They aren't on their way to a placer mine; however, what they might dig up could have more value than all the gemstones Vida has unearthed since her uncle taught her how to find sapphires and chrysoberyls and other small treasures.

Hiking behind the men, the women talk of Eternal Fawn and Ogden, both gone and yet as present as anyone in this procession. Sun Spirit learned of her grandmother's first love only when Eternal Fawn was two days from death, having outlived her husband, Jim White Cloud, whom she loved but to whom she had never revealed that she obeyed her parents and broke off a relationship with a Wasicus whom she'd loved even more.

"She said she suffered no regrets," says Sun Spirit, "although I'm sure I saw a honeyed sorrow in her eyes, a sweet and mournful wondering about what might have been. My grandfather Jim was a good man but closed on himself like night-blooming jasmine in daylight. I suspect your uncle Ogden opened his heart more easily than did my grandfather."

"Wide open," Vida confirms, "at all times."

"For understandable but nevertheless wrong reasons," Sun Spirit says, "my great-grandparents stood stubbornly against the truest of true love." Her smile is a charming arc of irony. "And yet, if they had not forbid her to marry your uncle, I would not exist."

The wolves follow the women, their expressions solemn and their stares brightened by animal eyeshine, surveying the forest as if on guard for a threat they sense but cannot yet see.

75

WHISPER MODE

High above the land, in a rotary-wing aircraft nearly as quiet as a hot-air balloon, Boschvark and Yataghan drift through the early afternoon like sleepers in a dream about being reincarnated as eagles.

Terrence Boschvark loves more than money. He is also passionate about the extravagances that money can buy. The smallest of his many houses encompasses twenty-four thousand square feet of living space, while the largest is three times that size. His car collection, numbering two hundred and nineteen vehicles, includes seven Rolls-Royce classics, including three that once belonged to British kings and queens. He owns four billion dollars' worth of abstract expressionist paintings so meaningless and ugly that, displayed in one gallery, they would render connoisseurs of such art suicidal with delight. He collects exotic wristwatches ranging in price from fifty thousand dollars to half a million, as if with each purchase he is buying not just a timekeeping instrument but time itself, more years of life and perhaps even life eternal.

Each of Boschvark's residential properties includes a limited-production four-seat helicopter with the latest Blue Edge technology and state-of-the-art engine muffling, either on site or in a hangar nearby. Powered by a bearingless engine, the Blue Edge main rotor has five double-swept blades, each with three Blue Pulse flaps in its trailing edge that are automatically activated as many as forty times per second. This all but eliminates blade-vortex interaction that produces the *thwop-thwop-thwop* noise when a rotor blade impacts the wake vortex created by the blade in front of it.

With a portfolio of fourteen residences, Boschvark therefore owns fourteen expensive rotorcraft capable of traveling in what is called "whisper mode." Although this stealthy progress through the sky, especially at night, makes him feel superior to humankind and appeals to his inner child, or to whatever corroded version of a child still finds harbor in him, the fleet is not the extravagance it might appear to be. In addition to transportation, these helos double as security ordnance.

Having been secretly customized by a team of retrofitters, each craft is a gunship with a .50-caliber machine gun fed by a drum belt with a six-hundred-round capacity. An airborne weapon of such power is of no use when the need arises to deal with a curious trespasser or burglars or a team of kidnappers; his experienced security staff can deal with those annoyances using conventional means. However, because Boschvark is well connected with the shadow state and with those in charge of the Federal Reserve System, he is aware of the turmoil that will ensue if a catastrophic financial crisis occurs or is engineered. Society will collapse; violence will escalate wildly. Even people as well placed as Boschvark will be endangered if only for a few weeks, until the ruling class can effect the conversion from the current semi-fascist system to pure, glorious, rewarding fascism. His weaponized stealth rotorcraft, along with numerous other precautions, allow him to sleep at night—except on those occasions when people and events have struck in him a fierce anger that fosters insomnia more effectively than five pots of coffee.

At the moment, in spite of everything that's gone wrong, his dissatisfaction is mere peevishness, a simmering irritation, which is because he has taken matters into his own hands and will shortly eliminate the bitch Vida and everyone whom she has drawn into her crusade against the Grand Plateau project. He is taking direct action, which he has occasionally done before, always with great success. It's good to get out of the office, out of the boardroom, and into the field when it most matters.

With Yataghan in the pilot's seat, the rotorcraft floats twenty feet above the trees, angles down as the land slopes, and hovers over a glen where two horses graze in a section of a meadow that's enclosed by a split-rail fence.

Yataghan puts the helo down facing the house and kills the engine. The rotor blades silently slice the air one last time before falling still.

"What a dump," says Boschvark.

Both men carry pistols in shoulder holsters, concealed by sport coats. Those who have moved this far from civilization must distrust people so much that they will greet any visitor with hostility, but they are not likely to open fire without provocation. Mack Yataghan is an earnest and soft-looking individual who might be a bewildered choirmaster late for choir practice and looking for his church, but few would be perceptive enough to see in him a man who could set fire to an orphanage to clear a property and facilitate its sale to his boss for the construction of a thirty-story building of luxury condominiums. As for Boschvark, from his twenties he has modeled his appearance and relaxed way of moving after the all-time most beloved host of a TV show for children, Mr. Rogers; his viciousness, whether in matters personal or in business, always comes as a surprise to those who haven't already been put through the grinder by him.

By the time Boschvark and Yataghan step onto the loggia, no one has come out of the house to see why a helicopter has landed in the yard. Yataghan knocks on the door, waits, then knocks again, but no one responds. Boschvark tries the door, and it's not locked, and the two of them go inside, calling hello, asking if anyone is at home.

The house is larger than the average middle-class Manhattan apartment, but not by much. They need less than a minute to confirm that no one is here.

Yataghan notices the two backpacks on the floor by the sofa in the living room. Stitched to the top-pocket flap of one is a patch with a name and phone number. The name is Sam Crockett. The second backpack bears no name, but when Boschvark inspects its contents, he finds a pair of leather gloves small enough to be appropriate for a woman's hands.

"Wherever they've gone," Yataghan says, "they'll be coming back for their gear."

Surveying the twigwork furniture and Navajo rug and woven wall hangings, Boschvark grimaces. "You know where they must have gone. We'd be making a mistake waiting here for them. We catch them on the plateau, we can still take them by surprise."

76

EVERYBODY DIES

Ranks of conifers soldier on through the centuries, down the slopes in a perpetual green march, to the Grand Plateau, where for whatever reason they have, with rare exception, failed to conquer the three thousand acres of flat territory. Beyond the plateau, when the land slopes down once more, trees rise in phalanxes, their roots wound so securely through the soil and rocks that they can withstand even the winds of winter that shriek through the pass with greater force than in any other season.

Hunting hawks glide on the spring thermals high above. Here below, the soft soil offers small creatures easy burrowing, and tall grass—brown from winter but fast greening—provides cover to them. For now, the plateau is full of busy life, a thriving ecosystem that needs no justification but that should be celebrated in vivid myths, as the upland meadows of southern England and the animals thereof were celebrated in *Watership Down* and as another landscape entirely was mythologized in *The Wind in the Willows*.

Considering José Nochelobo's determined efforts to preserve this place, how odd it is that Vida has never been here before. She has seen videos and photos and maps, but nothing has fully conveyed the drama and beauty of this immense tableland with forested peaks rising above it on three sides. She's unprepared for the effect the place has on her. Her heart beats faster. She feels lighter, not lightheaded but buoyant, as if she might ascend in the crystalline air. She puts her crossbow on the ground and hugs herself.

With Sam accompanying him, Two Moon moves south, pausing to study the ground in those places where the grass has not taken hold, looking for flat stones that would mean nothing to most people but that he can read.

Although this plateau is remote in more than one sense, the three dogs have evidently been here before, as their master sought the solace of no company but theirs. Sam probably has thrown a ball for them on the plateau or a Frisbee, for they chase one another and gambol as though celebrating memories of prior visits.

By contrast, the wolves hang back, remaining close together and alert, troubled by some quality of the plateau or maybe anticipating a sudden threat.

At the moment, no wind is blowing. The high tableland lies in an expectant stillness.

🦋

Blue Edge blades with Blue Pulse flaps quietly carve the air, floating Boschvark toward the site where tens of billions of dollars will soon begin to fall through the air and into his deep pockets. Better yet, this will be only one of several projects like it that will make him the richest man in history.

Perhaps it's inevitable that he should think of José Nochelobo at this time, in this place. Mack Yataghan had recorded the fool's speeches, and Boschvark had listened to them obsessively, until they were burned into his memory. Although Nochelobo is now nothing but cold ashes in a bronze urn, Terrence Boschvark hates him with a singular passion. His enduring resentment ripens into anger as the dead man's words play through his mind.

Huge amounts of cobalt are essential to this technology. Little children in the Congo and other poor countries are forced to dig for it in narrow passageways that collapse on them. Kids as young as four. Thousands of enslaved children are the right size needed in these crude mines, these hellholes. They die by the hundreds, and those who survive will have short lives because of the contaminants they've inhaled.

Boschvark has inarguable answers to Nochelobo's objections. He could have mounted the stage and debated the fool. But he is not a showboater like Nochelobo. He does not enjoy the spotlight and is a man of humility. He could have said that the children come from a culture where they will be enslaved whether they're sent to the mines or not. Because their work has value, they are better fed as long as they can work. If the injuries they sustain are minor enough to allow them to go back to work, they receive medical care in a country where there is otherwise no such care for the masses. Forced labor *improves* their lives. Yes, some die, but get real. *Everybody* dies. No one lives forever. What matters isn't the length of life but the quality of the life you live. Choke on that truth, José.

In all of history, has there ever been a man more infuriating than José Nochelobo, more certain of his virtue, more irrational in his aims?

Anger is not an adequate response to such a stupid and prideful man. The mere memory of him enrages Boschvark.

He despises the bleeding-heart tone that made Nochelobo's followers swoon. The beloved football coach preyed on his audience's gullibility. *Construction of wind farms in the ocean are killing whales in record numbers, whales and dolphins. Already, the massive blades of modern wind turbines kill millions of birds every year. By the time this technology is built out, entire species of birds will be slashed into extinction. These aren't picturesque old Dutch windmills, my friends.*

You want us to make them picturesque? Boschvark would have liked to ask the idiot. Do you realize what that would add to the cost of a project and how much it would diminish each turbine's output? Paving the ocean floor with enough concrete to support thousand-foot-tall windmills isn't likely to kill a significant number of whales. They'll adapt. Whales love concrete. They live happily surrounded by it at SeaWorld. Everything adapts when it must. If anything's killing whales, it's the wavelength of the sonar used to map faults in the ocean floor before construction, screwing with the whales' natural guidance system. But we won't be mapping forever. After a few years, at most a decade, we'll be done with that, and the whale population will recover. You can't totally transform the world's power-generation technology without a few stupid whales freaking out and throwing themselves onto a beach to give the tree-hugging crowd something else to feel guilty about.

Sam Crockett swings the mattock once, twice, three times, and then steps back to allow Two Moon to do some light work with the collapsible shovel.

Remaining at a respectful distance from the men and their solemn task, Vida realizes that she and Sun Spirit are holding hands, as might two sisters who are long accustomed to providing comfort and courage to each other.

The granddaughter of Eternal Fawn says, "It is sad to say that my people, not just Cheyennes, but those of all the ancient nations, have long forgotten or ceased to care about this place. They build casinos. They TikTok and tweet and lose themselves in the forests of YouTube. They learn only what Google allows them to know, and year by year the past becomes to them less than it really was. The past was real, I think more real than the present. These days, so many are educated into ignorance, entertained by shallow amusements that drain from them the very substance of themselves, until they seem to have become ghosts long, long before their deaths. I'm only thirty-four, but out there in the world that Two Moon and I have left, I feel like a cranky granddam who has lived a century and sees the newer generations living for nothing but oblivion. Only deep in the forest do I feel young and hopeful."

🍂

The helicopter is in whisper mode as it floats through the day, but Boschvark is filled with a noisy rage that is escalating toward an even noisier inner fury. Vector, Trott, Rackman, and Monger would not be dead if Nochelobo never existed. Belden Bead and Nash Deacon would not be dead. The project would have been underway if Nochelobo had not instigated litigation against it.

He regrets that Nochelobo is dead, but only because he'd like to kill the sonofabitch again, this time not with a nerve toxin delivered by an air-rifle dart but with his own hands.

He is unable to evict the voice of Nochelobo from his head. *To generate the power needed for this one country in an all-electric age and to do it with this primitive technology, we'll need to cover at least three hundred twenty thousand square miles with wind farms, which is four times the size of South Dakota or as vast as nearly all the states along the Eastern Seaboard.* Everywhere coast to coast will be uglified.

Boschvark would have replied: No, no, no. Not everywhere. Maybe half the country, but not everywhere. Besides, beauty is in the eye of the beholder. What about that, huh? What about all of us who think thousand-foot-tall wind turbines are beautiful?

Seething through Boschvark's memory, José Nochelobo's voice declares, *The low pulsation of the massive hundred-forty-foot blades will agitate every creature in nature, with consequences we can't know. Already, people living within a few miles of wind farms experience migraines, insomnia, a greater incidence of high blood pressure, and other health issues.*

Wimps! There were people who complained about the noise of the first trains, the first planes, rock and roll. They'll get used to it or they'll move, or we'll put them somewhere they aren't bothered by noise.

Dead to the world but alive in Boschvark's brain, Nochelobo says, *Because the resin blades regularly fail but are so hard they can't be ground up and recycled, we'll require thousands of new landfills to bury them and the millions of lithium and sodium-ion batteries that also can't be recycled.*

Propagandist! That objection deceitfully ignores the fact that building and operating big new landfills, manufacturing an infinite supply of batteries, and strip-mining the third world for the rare-earth minerals needed for all those batteries will create many jobs. Many, many, many jobs. And profits. Among Boschvark's investments are landfills, battery makers, and mining companies. He knows a lot about how many jobs will be created. He has projections that show enormous profits. All those new workers mean more taxes paid and therefore more subsidies for landfills, batteries, and strip mines. It's like the cycle of life. It's a beautiful thing. If Nochelobo weren't dead, if he were yammering to an audience, Boschvark might mount the stage and give him the what-for.

"Less than five minutes to the plateau," Yataghan announces.

After a brief and shallow excavation, Two Moon and Sam move about a hundred yards south from the first site and set to work once more.

The women follow, no longer hand in hand. Vida has retrieved her crossbow. Lupo and his wolves draw closer but remain wary, sniffing the air and surveying the plateau with what seems like suspicion.

Again Sun Spirit halts at a distance from the men, and Vida follows her lead. Tradition must be respected here, old ways that were meaningful to those who lived by them, sacred rituals. It's important for those of us who follow our ancestors to grant dignity to them, because our lives also pass like shadows; in yet a little while, all will be consummated, perhaps sooner than we expect.

"Long before Columbus," Sun Spirit says, "and for centuries after he came to these shores, many indigenous tribes—you now call them 'nations'—lived in this territory, came and went and returned, this tribe dominant and later that one, and later still another. They were not nobler or more peaceful than those who came after them in later centuries and from other continents, and if they were much closer to nature than we are, it is only because they had no choice, lacking the amenities of modern life."

Vida recalls the nations her uncle spoke of. "Cheyenne, Ute, Arapaho, Apache, Shoshone."

"Those and many others," Sun Spirit says. "They've been wildly romanticized. Although they sometimes lived in tolerance of one another, they more often oppressed one another, went to war with one another, enslaved and killed one another—*for they were human*. When we deny their nature, we also deny their humanity and minimize the complexity of their lives. Like human beings throughout history, they could not get rid of a feeling of the uncanny, of a sense that there is an unseen dimension to life and something that comes after. They all thought this place sacred, and it was the one piece of ground over which they never fought, for each nation had its own section of this tableland that served as a burial ground. That has been long forgotten by many—and now, judging by what you've told us, the truth is being concealed by those who covet the place. In those far times, they didn't call it the Grand Plateau. It was the Land of Spirits Waiting. Waiting to be called from this world to another."

The grass trembles as if with a presentiment of wind that has not yet come to sweep the day.

Vida says, "And your husband—he's looking for proof of graves that will stop Boschvark's project?"

"Not bones, if that's what you're thinking. No need to dig so deep that he disturbs the dead. The grave will be layered, with the bones at the bottom. Above them will be certain objects, depending on the nation to which the deceased belonged. In many cases, there will be items that were placed on the raw earth of the fresh grave, items carved from stone or made from fired clay that over time have weathered into the earth and are easy to uncover. That'll be proof enough to get a court's attention."

Considering the tortuous path Vida has traveled from grief and despair to this triumph, from José's death to impending fulfillment of the mission to which he had dedicated himself, she's astonished to be here. Although the wolves seem vigilant, the dogs continue to frolic, and she is in a mood to take her inspiration from the dogs. Her heart is ready, this time for healing and happiness.

❦

Better yet, if Boschvark could go back in time, he would choke the infant Nochelobo to death in his cradle and do it with enormous pleasure.

Even in death, his nemesis won't leave him in peace. It's like a haunting, Boschvark's skull being the house and José Nochelobo an unrelenting spirit. *The endless mining, the wanton destruction of vast ecosystems on land and sea, the volume of wasted materials— this is by far the dirtiest technology we could choose. Nuclear fission, fusion, hydroelectric are all clean. Even natural gas is cleaner and far less destructive than what's needed to harness enough wind.*

"For now," Boschvark growls, "the money is in the wind."

Puzzled, Yataghan says, "Excuse me?"

"When wind doesn't work, we'll be where the money goes next."

"If you say so."

Here comes Nochelobo again, spooking along the hallways of Boschvark's mind. *The energy infrastructure that's taken a hundred fifty years to establish can't be replaced with something else in just ten years. It'll take fifty years or longer. Spending trillions on a worthless quick fix will crash the economy.*

"Meanwhile," Boschvark says, "a lot of people with connections will get very rich. There's nothing wrong with being rich."

"Nothing at all," Yataghan agrees, keeping his focus on their flight path.

"And if you're smart, you can make a fortune in a financial crash."

"I don't think I'm that smart," Yataghan says.

It seems to Boschvark that a chill is imparted to the air in the helo as the ghostly Nochelobo continues his rant. *When we've printed trillions in new money to harness the wind, when then the dollar collapses, millions of people will be impoverished.*

"Not if they do what I intend to do with every billion I make from wind," Boschvark says.

Because he can't hear Nochelobo's side of the conversation, Yataghan says, "What do you mean? What do you intend to do?"

"What do I intend to do? What do I intend to do? Buy eleven tons of gold, of course. For starters."

"That's a lot of gold."

"At the current price."

"What do you mean?"

"As the price goes up, a billion will buy fewer tons. But I'll keep buying. You damn well better believe it. I'll keep buying if it comes to that. If the country goes down, I won't go with it."

"Hey, are you all right?" Yataghan asks. "What're you so angry about? Did I do something?"

"Not you. Why the hell would I be pissed at you? It's that stinking piece of shit Nochelobo."

"He's dead," Yataghan says.

"I know he's dead. But he'll never be dead enough to suit me."

Boschvark's breathing is louder and more insistent than the sound of the five Blue Edge blades whirling overhead.

After a silence, Yataghan says, "Maybe it's a good thing I don't have that kind of money. What would I do with eleven tons of gold anyway?"

"Put it in a private vault, of course."

"I don't have a private vault."

"Better get several. Here, there, everywhere."

Out beyond the last of the treetops, the Grand Plateau comes into view.

Lupo and his pack race past Vida and Sun Spirit. The dogs break off their play to greet their wild cousins, but the wolves encourage the Alsatians to run west toward where the tableland meets a lower slope and the trees rise to provide cover.

In the south, Two Moon and Sam look up from their labors and toward the women. Something about their posture alerts Vida, and she turns to the north.

At first glance, as the rotorcraft approaches, it seems unreal because it glides through the air with so little sound that she can detect no sound at all.

Then she hears a muffled pulse or feels it more than hears it. She is reminded of the dream in which she and the fortuneteller are sitting on her porch at night, the moon four times its normal size, José in the yard with a man who covers his face with one hand. In the dream this sound arises. *What's that? What's coming?* she asks. The seer says, *Death. When you hear it elsewhere than in a dream, move fast. Do what is expected of a woman who runs with the wolves.*

❦

Even if Vida hadn't stuck her nose in where it didn't belong, even if she hadn't inconvenienced him by killing everyone sent to kill her, even if she had never discovered that the Grand Plateau was a sacred Native American burial ground that would eliminate it as a site for a wind farm, Terrence Boschvark would hate her. She was José Nochelobo's lover, which is reason enough to *loathe* the bitch. The sight of her standing defiantly down there in the tall grass with the Cheyenne woman *infuriates* him so much that he breaks into a sweat and feels his pulse pounding in his temples.

The .50-caliber machine gun can be operated either by the pilot or by whoever occupies the front passenger seat. Boschvark leans forward and presses a button to the right of the horizon indicator and below the altimeter. A panel drops out of the way, and a gun control extrudes. A targeting display appears on the windshield of the advanced glass cockpit, but he isn't going for the kill right away. He opens fire. Even though the weapon is a recoilless rifle, and imparts no vibration to the helo, sound clatters through the aircraft as if they're taking fire rather than laying it down.

"What the hell!" Yataghan exclaims.

Although he's enraged, Boschvark replies in his Mr. Rogers voice. "Relax. There's no one to see us being bad boys."

"I know, I know. That's not what I mean. Give me a chance to align with them. You're wasting ammunition."

"Now, now, Mack, I'm not wasting anything. I want to scare the crackers out of them first. I want them to run like rats, make them sorry for what they've done to me. *Then* I'll blast the shit out of them."

"Well, okay," Yataghan says, "if that's your plan. But remember six hundred rounds can spit out quicker than you think with that baby."

The moment ought to be a waking nightmare, but for Vida it has a dreamlike quality that is sublime instead of sinister, as if she has stepped out of the troubled world where she was born and into a magical realm. The forested mountains shelve high and higher to the east of her, as mysterious as a deep greenwood where creatures never named conduct lives unknowable, looming over what seems to be a slowly moving plateau as flat as the flight deck of a carrier ferrying souls from one existence to another. Wolves and dogs racing as if in harmonious celebration through tall grass from which erupt birds in song, the granddaughter of Eternal Fawn raising her right hand to scribe on the air a sign that might be meant to protect them from evil, the quiet rotorcraft racing toward her yet seeming to drift like a bubble aloft on a breeze as gentle as an infant's breath—all that and other wondrous strange details infuse the day with grandeur and beauty that fill her with reverence.

My heart is ready.

A sudden noise. Bullets stitch the flatland, but the mortal stutter doesn't shatter the mood. The flow of time has moderated until all action seems to be taking place in deep water, and even machine-gun fire fails to accelerate it. As the helo passes over her, she takes a quarrel from the quiver on her belt and turns toward the south in time to see Sam and Two Moon pitch forward into the grass, wounded or dead; if just wounded, then as good as dead with medical help so far away.

She reminds herself that what can be seen is temporary, but what cannot be seen is eternal. Repressing grief that would thwart her aim, bridling her anger, she winches the bowstring into place and slips a quarrel into the groove, her hands without a tremor.

My life passes like a shadow. Yet a little while, and all will be consummated.

Over the bodies of the fallen men, the helo executes a sweeping turn and heads north toward the women. Although without a weapon, Sun Spirit stands with Vida, faces the oncoming death machine, and does not sprint for cover. There is strength in solidarity, but also in suffering and in struggle and in hope.

❦

Boschvark lays down a pattern of fire closer to the women than he did on the first pass, and yet they stand unflinching as the helo approaches, as though fearless, as if they embrace the prospect of martyrdom. But they are only rats, and they should run like rats, like the vermin they are, infecting the world with their diseased thinking.

"She's got a crossbow," Yataghan declares with enough alarm to suggest he actually believes that such a primitive weapon poses a threat to them when they're cosseted in this magnificent rotorcraft.

"We're not defenseless like Vector, Trott, and the others. She doesn't have a forest to hide in this time. She's *right there*. A .50-caliber burst from crotch to face will cut her in two like a paper doll."

Just speaking the bitch's fate in those terms both excites Boschvark and winds the watch spring of his rage even tighter, so that he no longer cares if he can make them run like frightened rats, only that he can slaughter and be done with them.

The engine cowling is directly above the cockpit. The turbine mounted therein, heretofore muffled by sound-reduction technology that is almost miraculous, proves less reliable than a real miracle, erupting in a clatter and shriek of tortured metal and three hard pneumonic coughs of a machine in need of oxygen.

Yataghan says, "Well, damn."

☙

Some successful shots with a crossbow can fairly be attributed to skill alone. Some owe more to luck. Some can be accounted as the result of skill and luck in rare combination. In this case, however, skill and luck seem to have been assisted by a mysterious power deserving of a humble thank-you, and Vida speaks those two words.

The turbine air intakes are on the sides of the engine cowling. The exhaust portal is at the front, where escaping hot gases drive the many blades of the engine on their exit from the system; this round opening looks to be fourteen or sixteen inches in diameter. The carbon quarrel scores a hit on that maw, penetrating far enough to distort and crack a few of the turbine blades. Shrapnel from the quarrel and the ruined blades turn the cowling into a rattlebox, instantly doing further damage.

The engine dies. The five Blue Edge blades of the rotary wing stutter to a stop. The helo arcs eastward, away from Vida and Sun Spirit. It confirms the truth of gravity, impacting hard, tumbling across this Land of Spirits Waiting in a cacophonous mangling, until it crashes into the first trees at the foot of the ascending slope.

The hush that was interrupted by Boschvark's ill-considered assault returns to the plateau, but it endures mere seconds before shouting men disturb it. Vida and Sun Spirit pivot in surprise as Sam and Two Moon come running toward them, obviously not wounded. They had dropped to the ground to make more diffi-cult targets of themselves.

The four stare at one another in astonishment until gladness shapes their faces and makes music of their voices. Sun Spirit and Two Moon embrace. After the briefest hesitation, so do Vida and Sam. If he seems uncertain about his place in her affections, she gives him no reason to doubt that she will heed the advice the seer gave her in a recent dream: *Be not so foolish as to cling to what was, rather than embrace what can be.* In his scarred face, his eyes are beautiful and full of light. She kisses him.

The dogs and wolves come running from the woods to which they had retreated, as if in happy confirmation of the wisdom of the kiss, and Vida is overcome by joy she never expected to know again.

🐝

In the ruins of the helicopter, Terrence Boschvark wonders how long it will take for a dedicated team of the finest specialists to mend him. He doesn't care about the cost; he can afford whatever the doctors wish to charge, even make each of them a billionaire if he must. He assumes, for it's not in his character to fail to assume, that eternal life through the grace of high technology is still his destiny once he gets past this bump in the road. He's lightheaded, and his vision repeatedly blurs, and he's confused about how he got here and where "here" is, but he is in no pain, which surely means that his injuries are minor. The cockpit is torn and battered, and the air reeks of spilled fuel, but he's still belted in his seat, which is reassuring.

Not so reassuring is the fact that Mack Yataghan is also belted in his seat but is headless. In the crash, one of the double-swept rotor blades carved through a section of the cabin, and now Mack's head is in his lap, gazing up at his sheered neck.

Boschvark tries to move, but he can't even wiggle a finger. He can speak, however, and he mutters curses when the wolves appear at the portion of the cabin where a door and part of the fuselage were ripped away. He's not afraid. He's *angry* that they might complicate the work of rescuers who will arrive soon with sirens blaring.

When Nochelobo's whore appears behind the wolves and peers in at him, his anger burns into rage. "Die," he says, "die, damn you," as if he can kill by command. And then a funny thing happens.

Vida and the wolves fade away as if they are not real. As they disappear, darkness settles around the wreckage, and in mere seconds the pale, pocked moon rises as if time has accelerated. It is a full lunar sphere so immense that it seems to be descending on the Earth in an inevitable cataclysm. Before he is able to decide whether to be fearful or furious, a figure emerges from the night and stands silhouetted in the immense moon. An albino mountain lion. As white as a ghost but not immaterial. The idiot locals call it Azrael. He never would have imagined that an animal would one day speak to him or that it would issue an invitation. Although the cougar's face is fierce, its voice is matter-of-fact when it says, "Come with me." Everything goes black.

"They're both dead," Vida reports when she returns from the wreckage. "The chopper will be emitting a GPS signal, so someone will be coming sooner or later."

"It's best for all of us," Sam says, "if no one ever knows we were here, at least not at the time when this happened."

As the wolves lead the dogs and the dogs lead the people off the plateau and to the path by which they came here, Two Moon says, "Sun Spirit and I will ride our horses into Kettleton for staples the day after tomorrow. By then, everyone will be talking about the crash and Boschvark's death."

"We'll say we never knew about the project," Sun Spirit adds.

"Which we didn't," her husband says, "until you visited us. But when we hear about it, we can raise the issue of the burial ground."

"You'll make targets of yourselves," Vida warns.

Sun Spirit scribes the sign in the air that she previously made as though to ward off the helicopter. "If we can wake the remaining people of our nation from their long sleep, as well as those of some other tribes, there will be too many targets to allow them to turn the Land of Spirits Waiting into a three-thousand-acre bird-killing machine."

The fragrances of pines and forest mast replace the acrid scent of spilled aviation fuel, and green shadows welcome them down into the ancient, vulnerable, but enduring forest.

77

THE BOX

One month after the events on the plateau, Sam and Vida have enjoyed dinner together on seven occasions. This is the fourth time she has cooked for them at her house. Following dessert, she brings the brightly wrapped box to the table to be opened while they are having coffee.

She has intended to wait until her next birthday before opening this gift, and she has meant to attend it alone, lest the contents might wring too much emotion from her.

However, considering that the fortuneteller's advice has been worth heeding in all matters, Vida is prepared not to cling to what was, even though she will always treasure it, and to embrace what can be. Since she was orphaned at five, there have been just three men of the highest caliber in her life, and it seems right that she should in some ineffable way unite them here. In her uncle's house, where she welcomed José in his courting, with Sam's future and hers entwined, she opens the card attached to the gift.

She reads José's neat cursive aloud to Sam. They are the words that were painted on the seer's Volkswagen bus. "Look with kindness on those who suffer, who struggle against difficulties, who drink unceasingly the bitterness of this life." Under this, her first love has written, "As much as she did, you have the wisdom and the heart to show others out of the darkness and into light."

"I'll drink to that," Sam says, and raises his glass.

She cries, of course. The tears have been pent up a long time.

With some effort, she slides the shiny blue ribbon off the box without cutting it and avoids tearing the paper, for she intends to save them both.

Perhaps she should know what she will find inside, but she is surprised. A pair of bright-yellow sneakers.

78

SEEING

The house is larger now, as it needs to be not just to make room for Sam but also to accommodate his seven dogs. The expansion was paid for by the proceeds from the sale of his residence.

They work the placer mine together. She has taught him how to process the raw stones into beautiful gems.

He still offers a search service, although not to the likes of the Bead crime family. He has taught her how to work the dogs, which adore her, and always together they find lost children and wandering adults with Alzheimer's—and even an occasional escaped prisoner, for she fears no one or anything other than losing what she loves.

Lupo visits with and without his pack, but when Vida and Sam set out to pick wild blackberries, a full complement of wolves always accompanies them in expectation of their generosity.

They cut wildflowers to put on her uncle's grave and drape the headstone with holly on Christmas.

They give no thought to the buried Trans Am or the Plymouth Superbird Hemi with their eternal occupants. This is a world of many wonders and mysteries and miracles, but there are no ghosts.

From time to time, Vida is inspired to dress in a white T-shirt and white chinos and the yellow sneakers. She sits in one of the rocking chairs on the porch, sipping a mug of coffee. Although she has neither a decorated van bearing words of wisdom nor a banner with silver moons and stars, and though she doesn't ask for what a visitor values least, she never has to wait long before some-one—usually a local but now and then a total stranger—comes to sit with her. Each visitor has something she or he needs. Often, they don't know why they have come, but Vida always knows, for she has a way of seeing.

With deep woods all around, she feels safe here and at peace.

Most people regard the primeval forest as a threatening domain of wilderness trails that often lead bewildered hikers to their deaths, nests of poisonous snakes, dens of sharp-toothed predators—a realm where Nature is red of tooth and claw. To Vida, however, the forest is a place of solace and succor where she is welcome because she has knowledge of—and deep respect for—its ways. In her experience, it is civilization, riven by human arrogance and greed and envy, that is, at its worst, a forest of lost souls.

ABOUT THE AUTHOR

International bestselling author Dean Koontz was only a senior in college when he won an *Atlantic Monthly* fiction competition. He has never stopped writing since. Koontz is the author of *The Bad Weather Friend, After Death, The House at the End of the World, The Big Dark Sky*, and seventy-nine *New York Times* bestsellers, fourteen of which were #1: *One Door Away from Heaven, From the Corner of His Eye, Midnight, Cold Fire, The Bad Place, Hideaway, Dragon Tears, Intensity, Sole Survivor, The Husband, Odd Hours, Relentless, What the Night Knows*, and *77 Shadow Street*. Hailed by *Rolling Stone* as "America's most popular suspense novelist," his books have been published in thirty-eight languages and have sold over five hundred million copies worldwide. Born and raised in Pennsylvania, he now lives in Southern California with his wife, Gerda, their golden retriever, Elsa, and the enduring spirits of their goldens Trixie and Anna. For more information, visit his website at www.deankoontz.com.